FNG

By

John Heinz

Desert Ink
Publishers

Desert Ink
Publishers

Copyright ©2006 John D. Heinz Jr.

Published by Desert Ink Publishers, Green Valley, AZ

ISBN 10: 0-9790673-0-8
ISBN 13: 978-0-979

Printed in the United States of America.

Acknowledgements

I want to thank all those people who have helped me with this book, especially Shirley Sommerhalter, who believes in me and has from the start. She convinced me that I have the aptitude to be a writer and bought *On Writing*, by Stephen King, for me, and I was on my way.

Special thanks to Dr. Karen Shoenfeld-Smith of the VA's Psychiatric Division for her help with war's mental wounds; Mickey Foster, my friend and editor; Andy Davidson, my good friend, who helped and encouraged me in so many ways; my brother, Alan; Chris Morton; Christina Brown; Connie Podesta, the world-renowned motivational speaker, thrice-published author, and my brother Chuck's wife; David Watson, a fellow Vietnam combat veteran and fellow member of the Association of the 173d Airborne Brigade (Sept.), for his technical assistance; Gary Aden; Penny Porter, officer of the Southwestern Society of Authors; and last, but certainly not least, Suzy Baxter.

Contents

⸺PROLOGUE⸺

THE PLATOON WAS BEING ambushed.

He knew there were three bullets coming. The first took away a small piece of his shoulder about where a needle would be inserted to give him a shot. It tore off the skin and maybe a sixteenth of an inch of muscle. A profound sting told him that it wasn't serious. They'd said that you couldn't feel the serious ones right at first—too much trauma for the brain to handle.

The next and nearly simultaneous two bullets didn't hit him, although the second one tore off a piece of his fatigue shirt an inch above the hole made by the bullet that took away a chunk of his shoulder. The third one missed by five inches, but he heard it snap by. Only veins had been torn open—no arteries.

He'd known all three of the bullets were coming. As he dived into the sand behind the two-foot-high sand-and-bamboo berm that thinly separated terraced rice paddies, he wondered if he'd known because he had heard the noise of the three rounds exploding out of the machine gun … That must be it. No, that couldn't be the reason. Bullets travel faster than the speed of sound. He wondered how he could have known. Just in time, he had juked to his left and dived for the protection of the berm.

It was a good thing that he was here, he thought. He laughed out loud as he realized what an absurd thought that was. But the short laugh couldn't be heard above the noise of the instant battle.

The platoon was frantically firing in return, and grenades were exploding everywhere. Machine guns and assault rifles fired on full automatic. Grenade launchers chimed in with their eardrum-hurting thunks. Both sides were laying down as much fire as they could. The air was full of screaming metal.

He was still for a second as his body ended its slide from the momentum of its forward dive. Although his helmet was securely attached to his head by the chin strap, when the lip of the front edge hit the sand, it lowered to the bridge of his nose and cut into it. The sharp pain made his eyes water instantly.

Or were the tears that were blinding him caused by the sand in his eyes? He considered the fact that he was dangerously ignorant and inexperienced. How could he have forgotten to close his eyes when his face hit the ground?

He felt the back of his right hand wiping the sand and blood from his eyes and knew that he'd rubbed too hard because his eyes stung, but not as bad as his shoulder did. He blinked three times, and the sand came into focus four inches beneath his face as blood dripped into it from the tip of his nose, the plasma vanishing into the hot sand as the red cells coagulated and gelled, already darkening from their initial bright red.

Sand. Each grain was different, he noticed. He'd never really looked at sand up close before. And the grains were not just different shapes and sizes but different colors. Vietnam sand wasn't simply muddy gray-tan. Besides the grays and blacks, there were greens and browns and blues and opaque-clears and reds and pinks and yellows and rusts. There was a whole world of shapes and colors in the sand. Little rocks are what they were. Why had he never noticed sand before?

He had to concentrate, but there was no use looking at anything else but the sand. You can't see metal moving that fast anyway.

He felt it again! Or did he hear it? What was it? It was a signal. He knew that much about it as he rolled to his left again, over, over, over, three times. He knew that it was important to get away from that particular space. Someone who saw him dive there intended to kill him, he knew. He could feel it! He could feel the enemy's rage. And fear. Yes. They were afraid too.

This time he knew to close his eyes as the berm where he had been hiding jolted and then began disintegrating from the force of the machine gun bullets hitting it from the other side. He turned his face away as the tiny sand missiles tore into his face and hands and his ripped right shoulder, which was stinging even more now. But it was not because of the sand flying into it, he knew. The nerve endings, so suddenly exposed to the air and torn into shredded pieces, were awakening to tell him that he'd been hurt by something moving so fast that it had momentarily deadened many of the little sensors and damaged his body enough that it needed to be attended to.

Don't think about the pain! he thought. *Think about what's important! What should I do to stay alive a little longer?*

Clutching the wound with his left hand helped the pain a little. Not so much air could get to the nerve endings so violently assaulted. Shredded nerves don't like being exposed to air. Water's better. Blood's best. Just get it out of the air by putting it back together. *No, lidocaine is best,* he remembered. Deaden it, and then sew it up. That's what it wanted.

Slow down! God, please slow things down! Give me time to think of what to do! Shouldn't I be doing something right now? Maybe not. Just hang on. Hang on. I'm a medic, not infantry.

Infantry. Infant. Young soldiers don't question their superiors. They do what they are told.

Don't no one get hurt!

Don't no one get hurt!

"Medic up!"

Oh, shit.

Little clouds of gray-white smoke assaulted his lungs and nose.

Don't cough! Don't cough!

They'll know where I am!

Getting the Purple Heart had been so important before. It was a badge of courage and honor. His father was sorry that he hadn't gotten one. His uncle Don had three. Uncle Don had been a paratrooper with the 101st Airborne in Europe and had jumped on D-day. He was a quiet man, but they said he wasn't that way when he was a kid. He had paratrooper tattoos on both arms that he'd gotten in England.

He had always hoped that he could get the Purple Heart. Now he wondered why. Why had he wanted that so much? He couldn't think of a reason.

He considered the lies that were such an important part of growing up. Santa Claus had been a lie he'd found out when he was six years old. Then the Easter Bunny and the Tooth Fairy. Everyone was created equal. How much more of what he'd been taught was lies?

Why had grown men told him that war was so cool, such an adventure, so much fun? This was nothing like he'd thought it would be! It wasn't just scary. It was awful. It wasn't right. To him, it wasn't. Could he be that much different than he thought he'd be? Than *they* were? Was he a coward? Were any of the other guys here having fun?

He knew he was safe now. He knew but not just because the noise had stopped. As he pushed his helmet off his nose and looked over the top of the berm, he could hear the enemy running in the jungle.

Green. So many shades of green that they hurt his eyes. So many that they made up their own color spectrum. Brilliants to dulls, lights to darks, shiny-wet.

It was over for now, and the sudden rain sounded like BBs on his helmet. The only other sound was the running in the jungle, which was getting fainter. *Good.*

"Medic up!" This shout was the weaker voice of a frightened trooper who was not being much of a man right now. The thin shout was an octave too high. Too excited. Not cool. He knew that the guy wished that he sounded manlier at this important time to be a man. This was an important time to be a man.

It's OK to get up now, he thought. *I hope it's something I've been trained for. I hope I don't shake too much. It's important that I don't shake too much. It's all over now. I shouldn't shake too much.*

Don't get emotionally involved, he told himself, repeating what they'd taught him in medic school. Think of an injured body as if it's a machine that has to be fixed before it stops working for good. Work fast but sure. Stop the bleeding and keep 'em breathing. That's the first thing.

I just hope I don't shake too much, he thought again as he ran. It was over. He could be cool. He could be cool now.

Three months of medic school didn't seem as long now as it had seemed during those hot, summer-dozing days in San Antonio, waiting for the cool evening beer and laughter, his airborne wings displayed proudly on his chest. There hadn't been many paratroopers in medic school. He was beginning to understand why. Medics had to have an IQ of at least 125. He wondered how smart wanting to be here had been.

Weapon in one hand and aid bag in the other, he ran in the direction of the calls and the moaning—loud moaning, almost screaming but for its deeply concentrated, painful urgency. The wounded soldier was terrified, but he could be forgiven. He didn't have to be such a man right now. The paratrooper evidently didn't remember the tremendous pride and invincibility instilled in him in airborne school and AIT. He couldn't be blamed for that right now.

This was his first day in the field. How many grains of sand would he notice before it was finished? A twelve-month tour stretched incomprehensibly before him. Like the mystery of the universe's unendingness, the time ahead was unthinkable.

He'd make it. He'd get through it. He knew it. He'd dodged those bullets back there, hadn't he?

And God had a purpose for him in this life. God would see that he made it. He knew that God had a plan for him. He wouldn't die in Vietnam. He knew he wouldn't.

He wished it was twelve months from now.

He wondered if the frightened boy lying on his back trying to breathe through a hole in his chest had had confidence in his destiny. It didn't look like it. Maybe that's why he got shot. Maybe it was his own fault. He didn't trust in God. In his destiny. Uncle Don had said that, when he'd been shot, he'd zigged when he should have zagged.

"Hang on, Murphy! Hang on! You're going to be OK! You're going to be OK!" he said, as much to himself as to the wounded paratrooper with MURPHY on his name tag.

He wondered if Murphy was calling for his mother because he didn't want to hurt her, didn't want her to be upset by his death.

A sucking chest wound! I can do this! he thought, as his training took over and he took a knee beside his patient. He sat the patient up and felt for the exit wound on his back, just like in the film on sucking chest wounds in that hot classroom at Ft. Sam Houston. There it was! Yep, the bullet had gone right through. He could do this. He was trained for it.

He laid the patient back down and unbuttoned his fatigue shirt. With each frantic breath, bright pink bubbles came up through the dark-ringed hole and then sucked back into the wound. Murphy's eyes turned to glass, and all motion stopped; the hole didn't suck and blow pink bubbles anymore.

Hadn't they said that people's eyes rolled up when they died? Maybe he hadn't been paying enough attention on that day.

Dwight Johnson was a paratrooper and a medic in the 173d Airborne Brigade. He was a grown man. He'd be nineteen the day after tomorrow, if his luck held.

–CHAPTER ONE–

WELCOME TO VIETNAM

June 1965

SOMEWHERE ABOVE THE HIGH overcast, the sun shined hot and strong but here, forty miles north-northeast of Saigon, a June fog gripped the jungle, and it looked like a shady spring dawn. Except for the senses that pictures can't illuminate, stench and heat, it appeared to be a pleasant summer morning. But, like an electric blanket over an old, damp mattress, the jungle shimmered and glowed, birthing and killing spores, mold, insects, leaches, reptiles, and mammals. Thousands of years were cast again into the morning heat.

The helicopter's wiper blades licked at light drizzle. Visibility was ten miles with patchy fog on the ground. The Hewey pilots looked for the red smoke that the infantry radioman said he was now popping. There, at two o'clock and three miles out, it rose straight up through the fog. There was no wind.

Dwight Johnson had cotton mouth. He tried to swallow, but nothing happened. There was nothing to swallow but dryness. His breath was labored, even at two thousand feet, as if he were sitting in a steam room; however, bolting for the door would do no good.

He had joined the army straight out of high school, then basic training at Ft. Polk, Louisiana, parachute school at Ft. Benning, Georgia, and then, after failing his eye test for admission to warrant officer/helicopter flight training, he opted for medic school at Ft. Sam Houston in San Antonio. This was followed by six months of advanced on-the-job training in the ER at Ft. Polk and then twenty-eight miserable days on a recommissioned World War II troopship to Vietnam.

He was a grown man now. He could walk into a bar and buy a drink—at least in Louisiana. He'd be nineteen in three days, and although he got his share of attention from the ladies, he still saw a teenager in the mirror when he shaved.

Eight paratroopers filled the Hewey's cargo bay, along with their duffel bags and weapons. The helicopter's crew took up the remaining space, two pilots and two door gunners.

Four of the new troops faced front and four rear, sitting in webbed seats in the cargo bay behind the pilots. Fatigue shirts were already patched with sweat, the morning salt tablets depositing themselves in white streaks on the green cloth.

Wind buffeted everyone but the pilots, sleeves and pant legs flapping like a hundred little green birds' wings. Pilots and gunners talked to each other over intercomed flight helmets. The paratroopers could shout in each other's ears but had stopped the effort soon after takeoff, thirty minutes ago.

The two door gunners sat behind the paratroopers on each side, facing outward in spaces made for this purpose but which looked like an aircraft designer's afterthought. Each gunner held an M60 machine gun, which hung from a web belt attached to the roof.

The original floor gun mounts had long since been removed, along with the attached ammo canisters used to feed the belted ammo. Now the gunners were able to swing the guns from a sitting position, instead of having to stand and pivot behind them. Besides the added mobility and firing capability, the gunners could stay sitting on top of the two flak vest backs sewn to the seats, affording some protection from bullets or shrapnel coming through the thin aluminum skin of the aircraft from beneath and behind them.

An empty C ration can was taped beneath the ammo belt feed slot on the machine gun, replacing the prior belt guide, which had been a part of the old gun-mounted ammo canister. The ammo belt now fed from a metal ammo box welded to the floor beside the gunner, completing the retrofit. Army grunt ingenuity and innovation again triumphed over accepted military engineering genius.

Dwight didn't dare move his hands from their grip on his rifle for fear that the others would see the puddles of sweat from his palms. By their positions and expressions, he was sure they were doing the same.

Nose now lowered, the helicopter seemed to be dropping almost straight down. The troops gasped collectively as their stomachs rose up, as in a rapidly descending elevator. Quickly now, skimming the treetops, the pilots and gunners leaned forward in their seats, looking for muzzle flashes that would tell them they're being shot at. Dwight jumped as the right door gunner fired a fifteen-round burst into a spot in the dense jungle whizzing by twenty feet below, swinging the gun as the helicopter made a quick S-turn left, then right, the gunner's lips constantly moving into the boom mike pressed against them.

Three brass shell casings skittered across the floor, and the trooper across from Dwight picked one up and then dropped it immediately. *Green-ass should know better than to pick up hot brass,* Dwight thought. A quick smile passed over his lips as he remembered the old Mark Twain snippet in which a man picked up a hot horseshoe from the floor of a blacksmith's shop and immediately dropped it. The blacksmith said, "Burnt ya, did it?" And the man answered, "Nope. It just don't take me all that long to inspect a horseshoe."

Dead ahead the red smoke column was now only a hundred yards away and at least two hundred feet high. The pilot reared the chopper back to bleed off airspeed, its tail down at a severe angle, the two big rotor blades whipping the fog and smoke and clearing it away in violent red swirls. The Hewey strained to a brief hover before the overloaded chopper dropped into the muddy clearing with a thud, like a watermelon falling to a grocery store floor.

"Everyone out! Let's go! Go! Go! Go!" the door gunners screamed at the paratroopers.

The pilot's attention was directed straight ahead; he was looking at the paratrooper who had signaled them in, waiting for his outstretched, closed hands to open, turn palms up, and show the upward motion that would tell them that they were clear to take off. The air was now pink as the rotor blades dispersed the smoke into a rainy gray-rose haze.

Despite his excitement and anticipation, Dwight couldn't help but appreciate what a pretty welcome this was, the swirling, flowerlike, billowy pinkness a dynamic bouquet for him.

As the eight new troops jumped the two feet to the mud with their weapons in one hand, pulling their duffel bags off behind them with the other, two large gray plastic bags were thrown onto the cargo bay floor, each carried by two sweating grunts wearing flak vests and no shirts. The heaviest bag made a distinct thud as the skull of the body inside hit the aluminum deck, easily heard above the sounds of the whirring rotor blades and whine of the big turbine engine.

Suddenly the air filled with sand, twigs, pieces of cardboard C ration boxes, and other blowing debris as the rotor blades pitched to a downward angle to lift the chopper. Light now, it jerked off the ground and, with its nose down, built up airspeed while still in the clearing and then banked away to the left as it jerked upward to closely clear the twenty-foot-high treetops.

The chopper then became only a distinct *whop-whop-whop* sound, as it disappeared like a dream into the gloom. The red

else is trying to crawl under their helmet, and that's when you have to go to work! You'll get the medals all right, unless you go home in one of those bags first.

"But the good news is that you get tons of respect, even when the shit ain't in the fan. None of those guys back there in the LZ would have been laughing at you if they'd known you were a doc. Even the officers want to be your buddy out here, and many of them will want you to call 'em by their first names—no shit. 'Cause if they get hit, they want you to not just know who they are; they want you to *care* about 'em. You can see right through those turkeys. You'll see what I mean."

"Who's Charlie?"

"Shit, Doc! How green can you be? Ain't you heard nothin' about this shit goin' on over here? Vietcong, VC. Victor Charlie."

"Oh."

I wonder how long it's going to take for me to get rid of this FNG status. Shit, I thought that by being a medic, I'd be relatively safe. At least safer than the infantry.

"Hey, Cargo?"

"Yeah, Doc."

"Does Charlie shoot at medics on purpose? My dad said that in World War II, the Germans let the medics come out on the battlefield to help the wounded and didn't shoot at 'em; both sides did it."

"Oh man, Doc! Have you got some learning to do! We're going to have to make up a whole new name for you, instead of FNG: FGAD. Fucking Green Ass Doc! If Charlie can shoot you before anyone else, he will. He wants to bring down the officer, radioman, and medic above everyone else. Any one of those three going down can stop the whole platoon. Shit, Doc. When you get back to the world, go find your recruiting sergeant and kill him!

"And, by the way, lose that 'my dad' shit. We don't mention our families here. Family don't mean nothin' here, OK?"

"I guess I have a lot to learn, huh, Cargo?"

"You're not going to believe it, Doc. Just pay attention to what your guys tell you. I mean a *lot* of attention. Your life depends on it. So does theirs, come to think of it.

"OK, Doc, this is Charlie Company's Headquarters. Lay your gear up against these sandbags"—he motioned to the three-foot-high wall of sandbags surrounding the HQ tent—"and go on in and give a clerk your orders. I'm in First Battalion too. Bravo Company, second platoon. My squad's tent is about ten tents that way and over to the right three tents." He motioned back in the direction from which they'd come.

"My MOS is one-eleven, so we'll be seeing each other."

Dwight knew that one-eleven is the Military Occupational Specialty signifier for infantry. When troops met and talked, they invariably asked each other for their respective MOSs. He didn't know what most of the administrative and other noncombat MOSs were, like cooks, the different types of clerks and other administrative personnel, intelligence, and so forth, but virtually everyone knew that infantry is one-eleven and medic is nine-eleven.

Sabinski continued, "Rumor is that the battalion's staging an operation in a couple of days. We know this because they don't let us go into town for a few days before we stage so we won't leak info to the whores. The idiots don't seem to understand that Charlie knows when something is up the same way we do. Military Intelligence is the ultimate oxymoron.

"Come find me if you need anything, especially in the first week or so. Remember, the only stupid question is the unasked one. And don't worry about being an FNG. Believe me, Doc, no one messes with the medics, and everyone wants to help you shorten the learning curve as much as possible."

"OK, Cargo ... and thanks for your help. By the way, why do they call you Cargo?"

"I can't jump a T-10. I'm too big. Fact is, I'm the biggest guy in the whole Army Airborne. My first jump at Benning, I came down like a rock, so from then on I jump a modified light cargo canopy.

"Also, I can hump a lot more equipment than your average grunt, so I jump two Sally bags instead of one. I only have to release one; then it releases the second one when it hits the end of the line, same way that a static line opens your backpack and pulls the parachute out when you jump. Since I'm a machine gunner, I hump a bunch more ammo than the other gunners do, plus fifteen M79 rounds."

Dwight remembered that an M79 is a grenade launcher that looks like a short, single-barreled shotgun. It loads from the breach, like a double-barreled shotgun, except the barrel is about two inches in diameter, looking like a piece of three-inch pipe mounted on a rifle stock. The barrel is rifled so the round spins, for two reasons: accuracy, like a football or a bullet, and also the round won't arm until it spins a certain number of turns, after it has traveled about fifteen yards. That keeps it from exploding when dropped or hit by shrapnel or plowing through brush and debris on its way out. The round weighs about two pounds and looks like a .45-caliber bullet, but it's the size of a man's fist. He'd never seen an M79 except in photos.

Each infantry squad has an M79 man and sometimes two, as well as two machine gunners, an RTO or radio telephone operator called a radioman, and an NCO. Two of the infantry guys also crew for the M60 guys, carrying ammo and feeding the machine gun. Everyone carries a hundred-round belt of M60 ammo for the machine gunners except for the medic, who carries an aid bag; the RTO, who carries a radio; and sometimes the officer, if he's a standard-issue second lieutenant and there-fore thinks he's special and shouldn't have to carry any extra weight.

Medics usually cover a forty- to fifty-man platoon, made up of four ten- to fifteen-man squads. A company is usually made up of four platoons plus support people. A battalion is usually four companies; a regiment, four battalions; and so on.

The problem is that none of this is ever really the case, unless it happens by accident. Squads are either smaller, usually because of attrition, or bigger because the job, armament, and so on, require it. If the action is expected to get really heavy, there'll be two medics, which is always a bad sign to the troops. And many times, the platoon leader will be an NCO rather than an officer. Sometimes a battalion will have as many as eight companies, and so it goes, on up the line. Nothing regarding the shapes and sizes of units is ever quite as it should be.

All this is called TO&E for Table of Operation & Equipment. The entire U.S. Army runs on this, and since it's never as it should be, words have been invented to describe the results of military organizational efforts, such as SNAFU (situation normal, all fucked up) and FUBAR (fucked up beyond all recognition).

Dwight watched Cargo walking away. He appeared to be around six feet eight with a classic linebacker build and had a pigeon-toed, rolling, head-bowed gait that big, athletic men tend to have. If he looked from side to side, he shifted his eyes. His head didn't move much—economy of motion.

Dwight tried to figure out what it was that made the scene around him so unique. What was it that was so different than anything he'd seen before? Then it came to him. Everything was either green or gray. The ground was green and gray. The foliage was green or gray. The tents were green, as were the uniforms, sandbags, vehicles, tools, and boots. Even the vehicle tires and guns were either green or gray!

An ocean of tents stretched as far as he could see in every direction, and they all looked alike. They were about fifty feet by twenty feet with two poles holding them up in their centers. The tents were ten to fifteen feet apart. Angle iron stakes hammered into the sandy ground anchored the ropes. The tent sides were rolled up and tied, and each tent had identically stacked green sandbags around them, about three feet high, with three-foot-wide walkways in the middle of each long side and each end.

Most of the tents were primarily occupied by cots, foot-lockers, and gear—all green or gray. Each cot was covered with green mosquito netting held up by wood pole racks at each end. Many of the tents had a ten-foot square of green canvas at one end, stretched out to a couple of poles at the corners, about six feet high, where men were playing cards, talking, laughing, smoking, and just generally doing what soldiers do most of the time: waiting.

No one had seemed to notice him. He went into the head-quarters tent and walked up to a SFC who was working at a green field desk just inside the entrance, held out the manila envelope containing his orders, and said, "PFC Johnson reporting for duty, Sergeant."

There were two other men in the tent, seated in green wooden folding chairs at green field desks. Green wooden file cabinets and shelving lined the sides of the tent with spaces between for the breeze to blow through.

Dwight had become accustomed to people looking at his left breast when he walked into a room, where white airborne wings were embroidered on an olive drab patch, sewn on his fatigues over the left pocket. This was above a black patch sewn above the left pocket with u.s. army in gold. A white patch was sewn over the right pocket with johnson stenciled on it.

Although only an inch wide, the inward curled wings framing an open parachute stood out nicely on the uniform. This was the dominant point of pride on all paratroopers' uniforms, but no one in the room even looked up, except for the SFC that Dwight was thrusting his orders toward.

Dwight realized that airborne wings were no big deal here. Even the clerks were airborne in this outfit.

The sergeant's laugh was hearty, as he said, "What did you say, son?"

"Hey, guys, did you hear what just came out of this FNG's mouth? Holy shit! What was your last duty station, soldier, Hollywood?" The other two men looked up and laughed along with the NCO. "Let's see what you got there, kid."

The sergeant took the envelope and opened it, scanning with a practiced eye.

"Hey, great shit! First platoon's new doc's here! Just in time! They don't have to go out with that chicken-shit battalion doc again. Fantastic!" He stood up and extended his hand.

"Sorry about the ribbing, Doc. We get so many wet-nosed FNGs in here lately that it's hard to tell y'all apart. Welcome to Charlie Company. Hey, guys, say hello to Dwight Johnson."

The two other clerks, a PFC and a Spec Four, introduced themselves.

Dwight considered that Cargo Sabinski had been right: being a medic definitely had its advantages here—instant respect.

The sergeant said, "Bring me your fatigue shirts, and I'll have 173d patches and airborne tabs sewn on them and get 'em back to you in the morning." Looking at the four-leaf-clover patch on Dwight's left sleeve, he asked, "Where in Fourth Army were you?"

"Ft. Polk."

"Jesus! Did you go airborne to get out of there?" Training troops, especially in the extreme heat and cold of Louisiana, along with the primitive living conditions and impoverished and scant local society, made Ft. Polk one of the least desirable duty posts in the army.

"No, I was sent to the hospital there for OJT before coming over here."

"Well, I guess that makes sense. That place must be bustin' at the seams with trainees nowadays. Good OJT for a medic, I'll bet."

That's an understatement, Dwight thought. The military was gearing up for all-out war all over the country. Training facilities were stretched to their limits. On weekends the main street of the army town of Leesville was clogged with trainees out on pass, many for the first time in their two-month military careers. Prostitutes, gamblers, and loan sharks brazenly sought the boys-trying-to-be-men's $78 monthly pay. Bars, pawnshops, pool halls, and greasy spoons were the only businesses on the three-block-long main drag.

Dwight and his friend, Frank McMackin from Chicago, the funniest man Dwight had ever known, would routinely go to what they called the Saturday Night Fights together. The Barn, a giant red wooden building, aptly named with its high rafters, sawdust floor, and picnic-style tables, was a favorite place for basic trainees to congregate on their first night out. After six weeks or more of rigorous training, toughened bodies and the newfound thrill of esprit de corps, coupled with several pitchers of cold beer on the empty stomachs of kids who's parents had closely monitored their drinking only days before, made for some pretty exciting Saturday evenings at the Barn.

Dwight and Frank would get there just before dark, when there were still some booths open along the back or the side. The other side held a full-length bar, and the front was mostly large plate glass windows with bars on the inside because the owner had tired of replacing them twice per weekend. Most of the other booths would be occupied by other Ft. Polk permanent-party personnel out for an inexpensive night's entertainment.

Dwight and Frank would drink pitchers of beer and visit with these men while they all waited for the action to begin. Overweight waitresses circulated, carrying trays of beer pitchers, trying to smile under the weight of the beer and the anticipation of coming events.

The slick-sleeved basic trainees began filtering in groups of five to twenty—hot, thirsty, ready for action, and full of pride in themselves and their spiffy new uniforms. Differentiated from the trainees by their civilian clothes, the booth-dwellers ordered a reserve pitcher and waited for the inevitable.

Eventually, a drunk trainee would stand on his chair, raise his mug, and shout something like, "A Company, First Battalion!" And just as inevitably, some buzzed trooper at another table would shout, "A Company is a bunch of queers!"

Then the table of members of the proud A Company would look in the direction of the retort and shout something witty and profound like, "Oh yeah! Fuck *you*, cocksucker!"

"Who you calling cocksucker, you bunch of cornholing faggots!"

"*You*, motherfucker!" And the Saturday Night Fights would be on, McMackin laughing so hard that tears ran down his face and Dwight laughing at Frank as much as the brawling trainees. Sawdust, blood, and beer flew as high as the rafters, and barmaids scurried to get out of the way, clattering trays and plastic pitchers and mugs skipping from table to table to chair to sawdust floor.

Within a few minutes, the MPs arrived in force—at least five and usually more. The trainees who weren't taken away by the MPs would be thrown out, along with their torn uniforms, fat lips, and black eyes, and within forty-five minutes their replacements would be at it again.

The permanent-party troops in their civvies would be left alone. The management looked the other way as the booth-dwellers appropriated the full pitchers remaining after the room was emptied. After all, they were the ones who picked up fallen employees and hustled them to the safety of their booths. The whole evening usually cost under two dollars for beer and another two for tips for the barmaids.

McMackin was a pharmacist, and his duty life was pretty boring. He lived for Saturday nights.

Dwight refocused on the task at hand and said to the sergeant, "Yeah, between basic, advanced infantry school, and the fights and car wrecks off post, I learned a lot."

"Well, we're glad you're here, Johnson. Smitty will take you to your platoon and introduce you around. You need anything, don't hesitate to come see me, ya hear?"

"Thanks, Sarge. I won't."

"Call me Bill, Doc."

"Sure. Thanks, Bill."

Cargo Sabinski hadn't been exaggerating. Dwight was getting instant respect, but he knew that it wasn't respect for him, personally. It was for his medical knowledge and for what he was going to be expected to do under fire—especially for what would be expected of him to do under fire. *There's no free lunch*, he thought. He hadn't met any officers yet, though. He wondered if they would behave the same toward him. This was getting interesting. He smiled to himself as he toyed with the idea of asking Smitty to carry his duffel bag and weapon. Dwight shouldered the duffel and was grateful when Smitty took his rifle from him and said, "It's not far, Doc. Follow me." It was raining lightly but steadily now.

The troops had moved from the shelter tarps into the tents to avoid the rain. Some were lowering tent flaps. They were rigged so that they went out on the ropes, rather than straight down, enabling air to still flow through the tents yet keeping the rain from blowing in—another example of grunt ingenuity.

"Hey, Smitty?"

"Yeah, Doc."

"I think I need to get to the battalion aid station before I do much else. Who's the battalion surgeon? Do you know anything about him?"

"Not really. His name's Captain Copeland. Kind of a little baby-faced guy. The medics all like him, though—supposed to be good with the knife. He got a Dear John letter from his wife not ten days after we got in country and during our first operation. He apparently managed to put it out of his mind and save a lot of bacon. They say he flinches when anything goes off anywhere near him, but he gets the job done.

"His wife and kid, about fifteen months old or so, were with him on Okinawa when we shipped out. Beautiful bitch, she was. We were all kind of suspicious of her—too pretty, too big of a smile, if you know what I mean. None of us were surprised. Lots of the guys have gotten Dear John letters. I got one too.

"Why can't the bitches just wait until we get back? What's the big rush to fuck with our heads when we're in all this shit? A guy gets one of those letters before going on patrol or an operation and takes chances that he wouldn't normally take and don't pay attention to what's going on around him and endangers his buds. I mean shit, Doc; there ought'a be a Bitch School or something to teach the women how to fuck'n behave, don't ya think?"

Dwight decided not to answer. After all, he wasn't trained for this end of the medical spectrum. But he hoped that this attitude and problem with women wasn't typical in American combat outfits in Vietnam. If so, it could mean some real morale problems. He made a mental note to ask the other medics about it after he'd settled in to the routine and got rid of this damned FNG thing.

Smitty walked ahead, seemingly lost in thought. Smiling at himself, Dwight thought that the thoughtless bastard could have at least offered to carry his duffel bag!

Smitty turned to his right and entered a tent between sandbags and put the rifle on an empty cot that had a submachine gun lying in the middle of it but no other equipment around it.

"Just put your weapon anywhere, Doc. A few of the guys are out under the flap. Come on. I'll introduce you."

Three men about Dwight's age were sitting on ammo boxes outside, talking in the shelter of the tarp. It had been rigged so that the rain ran down to the far end into a trench and then down hill toward the road.

Smitty said, "Hey guys. Here's your new doc—Dwight Johnson."

They all looked at him with expressionless faces, and it wasn't one of those quickly-size-each-other-up situations that used to be what Dwight thought of as normal. No, this examination was at least a full two seconds longer, which was quite a long time, in such circumstances.

The black guy with RICHARDSON on his name tag finally smiled, stood up, and extended his hand. "Hey, Doc," he said. "I'm Jim Richardson. Everyone just calls me Rich. This is Don Pascone and Glen Bandy."

Bandy was tall and thin; Pascone, just the opposite—short and muscular. Both wore flak vests and no shirts. *This seems to be the uniform of the day here*, Dwight thought. Rich was about Dwight's height and build, with a medium chocolate complexion. He was a good-looking man with a nice smile and a distinctively shaped mouth that was almost heart-shaped; the middle of the top lip crested slightly downward, and the feature didn't disappear when he smiled, as one would expect. His teeth were as perfectly even as Dwight's, which had been helped along by braces in his youth. They shook hands all around.

What's the deal with these flak vests? Dwight thought. *Must be some kind of airborne combat trooper fashion statement or something. I'll have to admit, it does look kinda cool. Bad-ass paratrooper thing, maybe. Also, being open in the front and sleeveless, they've got to be cooler than this long-sleeved fatigue shirt.*

-CHAPTER TWO-

GG

AS DWIGHT WAS RELEASING Bandy's hand, he heard a series of ten or more close, strange-sounding explosions—kind of extremely loud thunks. The only explosions he'd ever heard before now had been in basic training, on grenade training day, when they got to throw a live hand grenade from a concrete pit with a nervous instructor standing close by, ready to kick a dropped grenade into a water trough in the front of the pit.

And then there were the phony demolitions in sandbagged rings that they were told not to get near on the infiltration course—that night when they had real machine guns firing bright red tracers just three feet over their heads as they low-crawled the course. The problem hadn't been the live fire, however; it was the possibility of drowning in the barbed-wire-covered pits.

The noise was coming from the north, the direction in which the Hewey had taken off. There was no particular order to these explosions, and they were in close succession. Only two or three seconds had ticked by since the start, but there had been twenty of these reports in that brief time.

Several of the paratroopers hollered, "Incoming!" as Dwight could see everyone in the process of movement, beginning dead runs. Richardson grabbed Dwight's arm on the way by, headed away from the tent, and yelled, "Stay with me, Doc!"

They ran to a sandbagged bunker, twenty feet away. It was two sandbags thick on the sides and three on the top, which was supported by the ubiquitous perforated steel planking that had been invented to make runways but was now used for everything from support girders for bunker roofs to walkways to the whore-houses in all the burgs and towns in Vietnam.

The bunker had a rectangular shape with one side three feet longer than the others, which turned again, as if it were going to make an outer square, but this wall ran just five feet or so. This was the entryway. In this shape, shrapnel or a bullet couldn't enter the door of the bunker without being absorbed by sand-bags.

The inside dimensions were about twenty feet square. There were spaces between sandbags on each side, about four and a half feet high and one sandbag high and wide. These were gun slits, to be used should the enemy get into the camp. There was a bunker for every two to three tents.

As the loud thunking reports continued, Dwight began hearing what he had figured out were incoming mortar rounds. Later, when trying to describe the sound to his family in a letter, he thought the best way to describe it was that it sounded like a flock of birds taking off, except that the Doppler effect of the round coming in made it sound as if the flock were coming toward him at two hundred miles an hour, and the increasingly compressed sound of the Doppler effect made it become both louder and more rapidly flapping.

Then, the explosions of the rounds when they landed were deafening. Of course, the closer the rounds landed, the louder they were. The really close ones sounded like the crack of light-ning only much louder, while the farther-away impacts made a boom, like in the movies but infinitely louder. No speaker system could ever duplicate the volume of this noise. The closer explo-sions, the ones that went *crack*, generated a white flash of light through the gun slits and doorway. The flashes of the farther-away rounds were orange. Pieces of metal flying through the air made at once a whining and whooshing noise, again louder than could ever be duplicated.

Rich was yelling in Dwight's ear, "When this stops, stay with me! We're going to the perimeter! Our station is that way!" He pointed north, the direction from which the rounds were coming.

"But first we gotta get our weapons! What were you issued?"

"An M14, but I don't have any ammo!"

"Then it's no good! They took 'em all when we got our M16s. Smythe left his grease gun for you, in case you'd want it!"

Just as Rich was finishing his sentence, a mortar round landed on the top of the bunker and sand came down all over them, but the roof held. There were between twenty and thirty men in the bunker, and no one said a word.

Dwight shouted, "That one didn't make any noise coming in!"

Rich shouted back, "You don't hear the ones coming down on top of you. Consider yourself special. Few men have heard an incoming mortar round and lived to tell about it!"

The barrage seemed to have stopped much more quickly than it had started. Suddenly there were no more sounds at all—no reports of the rounds leaving the tubes, no fluttering incoming sounds, no explosions. Dwight had never experienced such a profound silence.

"Let's go," Rich and several others said almost simultaneously.

After a momentary crush at the door, everyone ran to their tents to get weapons and ammo and then on to their positions on the perimeter.

"Don't get too excited," Rich yelled to Dwight, who was in a full gallop beside him. "It's daylight, and we're all in the base camp. They'd be fools to attack a whole brigade of pissed-off airborne troops. They're probably just fucking with us 'cause they know we're preparing for an operation."

Rich was now inside the tent; he bent over the cot that Smitty had indicated was Dwight's, picking up the rusty, mean-looking little submachine gun with a magazine about a foot long sticking down out of it next to where the barrel met the body of the gun. He simultaneously grabbed a medic's aid bag that was hanging on the mosquito net bracing at the end of the cot and handed them to Dwight.

"There're four more magazines in the aid bag! I'll show you how it works when we get there!"

"Here's something else Doc Smythe said to be sure to give you, if you wanted the gun!" He reached for something else hanging on the mosquito net brace and handed Dwight a black metal crucifix, about an inch long and sturdy-looking, on an equally sturdy-looking black metal chain. The Jesus was dark tan.

"Put it around your neck!"

Shit ... at this point, I'll just do what I'm told to do, but these guys'll need to know eventually that I'm no Jesus freak, I'm not superstitious, and I don't wear jewelry!

Rich hurried to his bunk, grabbed his M16 and a web belt with four ammo pouches and a canteen attached, quickly snapped the belt around his waist, put on his flak vest, which had been hanging on one of his mosquito net braces, and grabbed a belt of M60 ammo, which was in a loop hanging on another support post. He put the M60 ammo over his head, so that it was over one shoulder and hanging down on his other side, put on his helmet, and said, "Let's go!" Pascone and Bandy were doing the same things, including grabbing the M60 ammo. The four of them ran out the passageway together. Smitty had disappeared; he had gone to his own tent and station on the perimeter.

So now you know why everyone has a flak vest! You ignorant FNG!

Small arms and machine gun fire were opening up on the perimeter. He recognized the M60s and correctly supposed that the sharper, not-as-loud, cracking reports were the M16s. These were mostly being fired on semiautomatic. There was also the loud, distinct, *boom-boom-boom* sounds of at least twenty .50-caliber perimeter machine guns. He heard several other machine guns that he couldn't identify and wondered if they were enemy guns, but as long as Rich and the others weren't acting worried about them, he decided he wouldn't either.

God! I haven't been this fired up since football!

But then he heard more of those big thunking reports that he now knew were mortars! He flinched and instinctively started to veer off toward a bunker that they were passing. Behind him, he heard Bandy shout, "Keep going, Doc! Those are ours!"

The perimeter was mostly concertina wire on both sides of a pit full of more wire strung between short, sharpened iron stakes. Sandbagged machine gun pits were spaced about every fifty yards. There were sandbags stacked two high in a line between each gun pit. Behind these, there were shallow foxholes, each about a foot deep and six feet wide and four feet long, so that three or four men could lie down and fire over the sandbags. With cover from frontal fire via the sandbags and from mortars via the foxholes that they could scoot back into if they heard incoming mortar rounds, it was a good fighting position. However, it didn't seem like much cover to Dwight, especially considering the relative safety of the bunker that they'd been in.

Rich, in the lead, dropped into one of the foxholes, and Dwight went in beside him. Pasconc and Bandy jumped into the hole to their right. The others immediately started firing into the tree line, which was about fifty yards from the wire. Except for a few stumps, the area had been bulldozed to clear a line of fire.

Paratroopers were in varying degrees of firing their weapons, preparing to fire, running to the wire, and sliding into the holes, as if they were sliding into second base in a baseball game.

After a quick look into the tree line, Rich laid his M16's barrel against the sandbags in front of him and took the little submachine gun from Dwight's hand. He flipped open a little door on the front and side of it, exposing a large shiny cylinder that Dwight recognized as the bolt. There were two holes in it: one was half the circumference of the ink cartridge of a ballpoint pin, and the other was about the size of the end of his index finger and a quarter-inch deep.

Rich, holding the gun by its body with his left hand, put his right index finger in the larger hole, slid the bolt back, and let it go. It slammed forward, chambering a round and cocking the gun. Then, with an almost simultaneous motion, he thrust it back into Dwight's hands.

"Fire short bursts at the tree line! If you see any muzzle flashes, fire at 'em!" he said and began firing his M16 into the tree line.

With his left hand, Dwight pointed the gun toward the tree line, holding it by the base of the magazine, an inch behind where the barrel met the body; with his right hand holding on to the pistol grip, he jerked the trigger and released it. Instead of a burst, the gun made a loud pop, and that was it—one loud pop.

Dwight was instantly concerned but glad that this had happened in the relative safety of the base camp perimeter. The rusty old burp gun had obviously jammed on the first round. Even the relatively slow firing rate of an M14 would have let off three rounds with a trigger pull of that duration. Also, a medic needed nothing more than a .45-caliber pistol. He had been told that a pistol was what medics normally carried in combat. If the action got heavy enough for the medic to be involved, the enemy would be close enough for a pistol's range and effectiveness. Why would he need a machine gun? He suspected that the prior medic had been a John Wayne type. These thoughts passed through his mind in a matter of a few seconds, as thoughts tend to do in stressful situations.

He looked over at Rich, who had stopped firing and was looking over the stock of his weapon at him. Dwight could see only the upper half of Rich's head, but he could see by his eyes that he had a big grin on his face.

"Hold the trigger down a little longer," Rich shouted, his dipped upper lip, although stretched in an amused smile, still half concealing his left front tooth.

Dwight pointed the gun again and jerked the trigger back again, this time holding it.

Pop-pop-pop-pop. The little gun fired at about the rate that a running man's feet would hit the ground—just slow enough to almost be able to re-aim before the next round went off.

Dwight's opinion of the weapon changed immediately. Suddenly, this was the coolest gun he had ever fired. He fired again, this time nestling the wire stock tightly to his shoulder; he watched five rounds knock three-inch chunks of bark off of a tree fifty yards away, maintaining a pattern of about a foot square.

Again, he looked over at Rich, who was now laughing out loud. He looked to his other side and saw that Pascone and Bandy were both smiling at him.

Bandy said, "Damn! That's some pretty good shootin', Doc! Looks like you were born with that thing in your hand! Smythe would have been envious!"

He looked back at Rich, who shouted, "You look like you're getting your first piece of ass, my man! You should see the shit-eatin' grin on your face! When you run out of ammo, don't try to reload! I'll have to show you how to do it!"

Rich went back to firing into the tree line, and Dwight looked at the jungle in front of him. He saw no muzzle flashes and didn't think that anyone else did either. No one seemed overly excited, and there didn't seem to be anyone firing into any particular area.

He kept firing two- and three-round bursts, thoroughly enjoying himself and honing his skill at hitting where he was aiming and producing nice, tight patterns. After what seemed like a full minute, he ran out of ammo; he opened the aid bag, took out another magazine, quickly pushed the button on the side of the magazine receiver, pulled the spent clip out, and fluidly snapped the new one in. As he'd seen Rich do, he put his index finger in the hole to slide the bolt back.

"God damn it!" Dwight shouted, putting his finger in his mouth as quickly as possible and looking over at Rich, who looked back at him, shaking his head in amusement but also apparent disgust.

"Cease-fire!" "Cease-fire!" "Cease-fire!" was being shouted up and down the line. The noise of intense combat tapered off as the troopers got the word. Again, the silence was profound because of the juxtaposition of so much noise before it. Then shouts of "Platoon leaders, report!" could be heard up and down the line.

Dwight saw movement from the corner of his eye and looked back to his left. A big major was walking purposefully toward the wire, twenty yards to Dwight's left and twenty yards from the wire.

Rich said, "I told you not to reload, FNG-man."

"I forgot."

"Until you ain't no FNG no more, don't be forget'n shit, OK, Doc?"

"Sorry."

"It's OK … Better you learn to listen up this time than when the shit's real. You figured out what that crucifix is for yet?"

Dwight looked down at it dangling against the gun and realized that it was for cocking the weapon when it was hot. Rich smiled. "Airborne!" he shouted, and Dwight realized that many other troops were doing the same.

Son of a bitch! Dwight thought to himself. *When am I going to start catching on? Sabinski was right. My life and the lives of the men around me depend on me listening up and getting rid of this FNG thing. Damn it!*

"Airborne!" he shouted as best he could with his burned finger in his mouth.

Back in the tent, Dwight found that his duffel bag had been dumped out on his cot and a mosquito net had been put up on the braces. There was a note from Smitty stating that he'd taken Dwight's fatigue shirts to have 173d patches sewn on and that he'd brought and put up his mosquito net for him. He'd be back in the morning with the shirts.

He sat down on the cot, suddenly tired and hungry.

Rich said, "Things are slowed up a little 'cause of the mortar attack and all, Doc. They'll ring the chow bell soon. We're probably going on an operation in a day or two, so we need to bring you up to speed as soon as we can. Hand me your weapon."

Dwight handed over his now beloved grease gun.

"When you close this here dust cover, this pin sticks into this little hole in the bolt—that's the safety." He opened and closed the door that covered the top right and front half of the tube that made up the body of the gun. "This is a World War II weapon, but it's still used by Tankers and the ARVN love 'em because they're so light and small. Trouble is it fires a .45 round, the same as a .45 automatic pistol. So it don't have much range, only about fifty yards, so it's a shit weapon for infantry, but Smythe loved it and tried to smuggle it home in his hold baggage, but they caught him. If he hadn't been wounded and could have handled the details himself, I think he could have carried it off. He'd found it in the field; it wasn't issued to him. Look in your footlocker and hand me a box of shells, and I'll show you how to load the magazines."

Dwight opened the footlocker, pulled the top tray out, and saw several four-inch-square cardboard ammo boxes in the bottom. He took one out and opened it. It was full of fat little bullets that reminded him of bumblebees, not quite an inch long and as big around as a piece of chalkboard chalk. He handed the box to Rich, who had removed the full magazine and picked up the empty one where Dwight had put it on the cot.

Rich kept talking. "Smythe said it's a perfect medic gun onacconta it's light and small and you can sling it over your back when you're working. When the enemy's close enough that the doc's gotta be firing his weapon, you can raise a lot of hell with it. Sometimes, when he was trying to save ammo, Smythe'd fire it single shot. When the shit's in the fan and we're being resupplied, lots'a times they don't drop no .45 ammo, and when they do it's either boxes of loose rounds like this or in pistol clips, never in grease gun magazines. No one but you and a few tankers need 'em, and tankers never fire their weapons anyway. You docs don't got no time to be loadin' magazines in the field. Shit, you guys got just as much to do after the shit as during it.

"It don't have no selector switch on it, but it fires slow enough that you can fire one round at a time after you get used to it. Smythe would use that wire stock a lot too. I seen him hit a VC fifty yards away using it, firing single shot and aiming it like a rifle; it's sighted-in good.

"Smythe got it the third day we were here, down in the Delta. Some ARVN troops had run over an antitank mine in a jeep—killed all five of 'em. Smythe was in the back of a three-quarter-ton truck with several of the brigade medics on their way into Vung Tau to help out at a civilian hospital there. He said that he walked up to this MACV SFC who was supervising the cleanup and getting the jeep off the road and asked if he could help. The sarge told him nope; they were all dead. Smythe said he asked the guy if this happened very often, and this smart-ass says, "Nope … only once." Everybody's a fucking comedian over here.

"Anyway, Smythe was walking back to the truck and sees this gun lying in the grass. He picked it up and the rest, as they say, is history."

Dwight asked, "Why is it so rusty?"

"Well, for one thing it's old. They quit making these things when World War II ended, and this one was probably in use then. They're the least expensive and simplest machine gun ever made—just stamped tin, except for the barrel and bolt, which are the only machined parts in the gun. So it gets really hot, and when you fire it in the rain, it instantly rusts. Same thing happens with M60 barrels. The enemy tends to attack in the rain when we can't get air cover or supplies into the fight—levels the playing field for them a little, but we still kick the dogshit out of 'em. They don't play team sports as good as we do.

"The magazine holds thirty rounds. As you can see, it's easy to load at first because the spring in the magazine isn't very compressed yet." Rich was sliding the rounds into the magazine with easy rapidity. He handed it to Dwight and said, "Here. You do it."

Dwight started loading the magazine easily. After about fifteen rounds or so had gone in, he found it progressively more difficult to load the bullets. He had to push down hard on the last loaded round with the thumb of his left hand while pushing the bullet he was trying to get to slide in on top of it with his right thumb.

"OK, now let me show you something that Smythe discovered after he'd been thinking for a week that the magazines held only about twenty-three rounds."

Rich had pulled the wire stock off the gun and had put the gun down on the cot.

"See this little piece of wire sticking down here? It's a loader. Watch this shit."

He took the magazine from Dwight's perspiring hands and slid it up between the back two sections of the wire stock that made up the shoulder brace, laid the next round on the last round loaded into the magazine, and pushed the little piece of wire down on it, using his knee from below on the bottom of the magazine and his hand from above on the wire stock to press the bullet down. Bingo—it slipped right in. Within five seconds, he had loaded three more rounds.

"Wow! How cool is that!" Dwight said.

"Go ahead. You finish. You'll feel the bottom when the last one goes in—thirty, exactly."

While Dwight was getting the hang of it, Rich kept talking: "Smythe fell in love with that little sucker right away. Got a bunch of spare magazines from the tank guys, but they didn't tell him about the little loader thing. When he discovered it, he went back over there and told 'em that they'd forgotten to tell him about it. They said, 'No shit.' They all thought the magazines only held about twenty-three rounds too!"

The other squad members had been arriving while Dwight and Rich had been going over Dwight's new weapon. A couple of them had been looking on while the others were straightening up the tent and assessing damage. The closest mortar to their tent was the one that had hit the top of the bunker, without causing much damage to either the bunker or the tent, but there had obviously been a lot of flying metal, because the tent had many holes in it of various sizes, shapes, and degrees of jaggedness. None were over four inches long, and most were less than an inch. Sunlight dappled into the tent as if they were under a large shade tree.

Seeing Dwight looking around at the tent, a six-foot-tall trooper with a medium build and slight shoulders who had been watching Rich's instructions said, "Engineers will be by this afternoon to patch it up. Not much damage this time. Don't look like nothin's hurt inside. The round going off on top of the bunker caused all the damage to be above the equipment.

"I heard there's no dead and only a few wounded. Some dope over in Second Battalion shot his buddy in the back going into a perimeter position. Bullet went through above the right lung, so he's gonna be OK. I don't know when these idiots are going to learn not to chamber a round until they get to the perimeter, or at least not take their safety off. We been having way too much of that shit. I bet they bust that fucker bad."

Pascone said, "Yeah, that guy was really lucky that it went straight through. These M16s have such a small round and high muzzle velocity that the bullet will usually change directions when it hits a bone or even just cartilage. Did you see that gook that Bandy shot last week? The round went in his chest and came out his ass!"

Dwight was a little surprised that these men talked about killing people in the same way that he would talk about a hit on an opposing football player. He figured that his chagrin was just another part of being an FNG. He'd get used to this callousness with experience.

The tall guy put out his hand and said, "Hi. I'm John Rove. People call me Pensi because they think I'm a little too proud of being from Pennsylvania."

Dwight stood up and shook his hand. "Dwight Johnson. South Texas."

"Hi, Doc. Glad you're here."

"Good to be here. I hope I don't disappoint y'all. I'm already screwing up like a Russian jumpmaster."

"I'm sure you won't. Pascone tells me you did fine in the bunker and at the perimeter, said that you're a natural at firing that grease gun."

Dwight saw several of the men smiling at him. He blushed slightly and looked down at his boots.

"Yeah, but that's not all." Bandy said. "Doc can yell 'Airborne' at the same time he's suckin' on his finger!"

At this, everyone laughed, including Dwight. The others began introducing themselves, smiling. There was David "Simone" Martinez. Later, at lunch, Rich told Dwight that he'd soon learn why Martinez was called "Simone": every time Martinez saw or heard something that he liked, instead of saying something like, "Cool," he said, "See-moan!" Rich figured that it was a Spanish colloquialism of some kind indigenous to the El Paso area.

Then there was Terrance "T-man" O'Donald, who wished everyone would call him Terrance, which is precisely why they wouldn't. He hated "Terry," but he hated "T-man" even more.

Mike Simpson was from Tucson and had a pretty yellow '56 Buick convertible that he was substantially more proud of than his yellow-haired girlfriend, smiling from the front seat in the laminated photo he kept in his shirt pocket.

Jaime Ariza hailed from Bogota, Columbia. He'd dropped out of medical school at NYU to better learn English and was subsequently drafted. He had been sent to advanced infantry school and went airborne from there because, as he so eloquently put it, "Ju know, my freend, eef I got to go to fuckeen war, I want to got the best fighters there ees covereen me ass!"

Nigel Cartwright was from the UK and had also been drafted after dropping out of college and had gone airborne for many of the same reasons as Ariza had, but also because the males of his family had a great tradition of being in elite fighting forces. If anyone wanted to get a rise out of Cartwright real quick, they only had to say something derogatory about the queen.

Dwight would meet Staff Sergeant White, the squad leader and NCOIC, that evening, Pascone told him.

The ice was thoroughly broken now, and although there was still a long way to go, Dwight was fast becoming a part of the unit, which, he was to soon learn, was more of a family or a brotherhood than the military he had known heretofore. He would soon discover that when men depend on each other for their lives and those bonds are further defined by death and injury, a closeness develops that even identical twins would find indescribable. A kind of love for which there is no adequate description is formed and then nurtured by battle, rage, misery, hatred, and sacrifice. Dwight felt good. He was on his way to being a part of this tight-knit team.

Dwight, putting away clothing, gear, and ammo in his footlocker, said, "I'd better get over to the aid station and report in."

"Won't nobody be there, Doc. It's chow time."

As if on cue, a dinner bell began ringing. As in the cowboy movies, the bell was a triangular iron bar hanging from a chain. It was rung by banging another piece of iron bar against the sides of the triangle from the inside.

Pascone said, "Squeet," and they all started for the exit.

Dwight said, "Squeet?"

"Short for 'let's go eat,'" Rich answered. "Grab your mess kit and canteen cup."

"Oh." He'd just put his mess kit in his locker, and his canteen was on his web belt on the cot. He took both out of their covers, pulled the cup off of the bottom half of the canteen, and followed Rich out the door.

The squad walked together toward the ringing bell, talking and laughing easily now. Other squads were leaving their tents and doing the same.

Engineers were already repairing or putting up new tents, depending on the severity of damage. The air had turned cooler, the rain had stopped, and the sun was out, but more dark clouds were rolling in from the west. Others were building classic cumulus thunderheads to the north and south.

Pascone said, "Rains every day this time of year, Doc. You'll want to get several pairs of jungle boots and wear the driest ones when we're in base camp. You won't have any choice when we're out. Get lots of pairs of socks too."

Martinez said, "See-moan."

The mess hall was no mess hall at all but a tent where the food was prepared. The food was ladled from vats arranged on one side of the tent as the troops filed by, mess kits held out. Outside, there were wooden posts mounted in cement-filled holes with boards mounted about chest high where the men would stand to eat, facing each other; fifteen or so men stood on each side of each two-post unit, their mess kits and water-filled canteen cups on the board. Eating wasn't much of a social occasion, as the eating space was at a premium. Each trooper ate his food quickly and went back to what he had been doing before chow, leaving space for newly arriving troops to eat.

On the way back, after washing his mess kit by dipping it in a fifty-gallon drum of boiling, soapy water and then in another drum of somewhat clearer boiling water, Dwight asked Rich if he could get a little more time firing the grease gun. He figured that he would need to put at least a few hundred more rounds through the weapon to be completely comfortable with it.

"When you get back from the aid station," Rich said, "we'll go down to the perimeter for a little target practice so you can get real familiar with that little sucker. One of the things you're going to have to get used to is how hot it gets. You'll need to carry an extra canteen just to cool the gun. Get a bunch of that wide medical tape at the aid station and a bottle of that stuff they call Gentian Violet. I think it's a disinfectant or something, but the only thing Smythe used it for was to paint the tape after he put it on the gun. I think medical tape must be reflector tape! The first time he taped the grip, we made him take it off because you could see it two hundred yards away. I mean, he might as well have been wearing a school crossing vest or something. We use smudge pots to darken name tags, airborne wings, and the white border and wing on your 173d patch, just before we go out. Some of the white guys, especially guys as white as you, put it on their faces and arms too. We tried it on that medic tape, and it just wiped right off with the sweat from his hands. That Violet stuff does the trick, though. They must have sent all that shit back in Smythe's baggage. We couldn't find it.

"The tankers told him that a grease gun only costs the government $35 for each one. M16s cost over five hundred dollars! No shit. Oh, it also has a little oiler in the pistol grip, where you keep patches too, and the wire stock doubles as a cleaning rod! Whoever invented that gun was a fucking genius!

"There's a funny story about Smythe and that gun, but we don't spread it around too much, in case it gets into the wrong hands, so keep it under your hat. We were working with the First

ARVN Airborne Division when we first got in country, down in the Delta. The platoon was helping a bunch of MACV advisers train a battalion of ARVN troops. Those little ARVNs all carried cut-down M2 carbines, and they had a habit that we were trying to break them of, of firing them full auto all the time so they'd burn up all their ammo and then panic and run away.

"Anyway, we're working in rice paddies with tree line wind-breaks between them, and there's a platoon of these dorks ahead of us about fifty yards, just entering a tree line as we're leaving one, and a sniper opens up on 'em. Well, these dopes lay down in the fuckin' rice paddy instead of running on into the tree line and killing the fucker. Within a minute or so, they used up all their ammo, and they didn't even know where the fucking sniper was yet! So, in groups of twos and threes, as they ran out of ammo, they come running back toward us.

"We could hear the sniper throwing the bolt, cocking a fucking single-shot carbine and picking these guys off as they're running back to us. Course, we're all laying down fire to cover their retreat, but the sniper was using a small-caliber weapon and we couldn't find the muzzle flash. Anyway, this one gook gets about fifteen yards from us and goes down with a leg wound on this side of one of those little dike things between the rice paddies. The dike is about a foot and a half high, so he's got cover. Smyth jumps up and runs to the guy and gets a fucking Bronze Star with 'V' device for his bravery!

"Only thing is, that's when he first got the gun, and he hadn't discovered that tape trick to keep the grip cool enough to handle yet. That night, we were all sitting around smokin' dope, and he told us that he didn't run over there so much to help the guy as to put that fuckin' gun in the rice paddy water! No shit! We had tears running down our faces, we were laughing so hard! Doc Smythe gets a fucking medal for cooling off his weapon. No shit."

By this time, Rich and Dwight were in full chuckle, Dwight more amused at Rich's amusement and laughter than the content of the story. They entered the tent and put their mess gear away.

Dwight said, "How do I get to the aid station?"

"Go on back past Charlie Company HQ, and it'll be on your right about another thirty yards. If you get to Bravo's HQ, you've gone too far."

"OK. See ya, Rich, and thanks for everything."

"It don't mean nothin', Doc. Just be sure to bring back that tape and Violet shit. We'll go out to the perimeter and kill some trees. I've got some C-4 I want to play with too."

"C-4?"

"Plastic explosive. We use it to cook with, like Sterno, but most of us carry a half pound of it and some det cord. It won't explode without a blasting cap, so not to worry. We use it to blow up spider holes too, and it's a lot of fun to play with. I can take out a big tree with a chunk half the size of my fist. Believe it or not, but the brass encourages us to play with it so we can know how to use it and how much to use."

"Whatever you say. See y'all in a while."

As he started walking to the aid station, he thought, *Smoking dope? What kind of dope? Jesus, these guys kill people like it's nothing and then take narcotics to relax. Shit … They all seem like such good guys too. Oh well. I'll deal with it when I have to.*

The wind came up suddenly, blowing leaves, paper, twigs, and sand, stinging his hands and face and forcing him to lean into it while turning his face to the side and protecting it with the side of his weapon. It started raining, and the wind blowing it horizontally. Men were grabbing tent flaps and getting under cover. Dwight broke into a full run, holding down his fatigue cap with his right hand, and as he ducked into the Charlie Company HQ tent, he said, "Hey, Sarge … Smitty!"

"It's Bill, Doc."

"Bill. Thought I'd drop in to say hello. How you guys doing?"

Bill said, "Fuck you, Doc. You came in to borrow a poncho! I was born in the dark, but it wasn't yesterday!"

Smitty waved to him from his desk. They all laughed.

Smitty said, "How're you gettin' along, Doc?"

"Good, Smitty! You got kinda scarce a while ago—didn't say good-bye or nothin'!"

"Well, it just don't take me all that long to get tired of being in a bunker!"

They laughed again.

"Heard you developed a new paratrooper greeting for the brigade, Doc. You must be one of them natural-born leaders!"

"How's that?"

Smitty and Bill both put a finger in their mouths and said, "Airborne!"

Dwight laughed along with them. "Hey, guys, don't let that shit get all over the place, OK?"

Bill said, "Sorry, Doc, but it's already all over the brigade. We weren't even there, man. In fact, I got it from a guy from Second Battalion. He was telling the guys in the aid station about it. Smitty says that troops all over the brigade are greeting one another with it. You started a trend, Doc!"

Oh, fuck me! I've got a rep for being a dope at the aid station, and I haven't even met anyone there yet. So much for all that "respect" bullshit!

"Either one of you assholes got a poncho I can borrow?"

Bill said, "Sure, Doc. Take mine. I ain't going nowhere; it's hangin' by the door there."

"I'll be right back with it, Bill." He slipped the poncho over his head and stepped out into the rain. The wind had slacked enough so that the rain was now falling at a forty-five-degree angle. Puddles had formed and were getting deep. Trenches running downhill, away from the tents, were already swift streams.

He heard a rain-muffled shout behind him: "Don't worry 'bout it, Doc … I got another one."

Dwight could just make out Smitty's shout, which was weakened further by the pounding rain: "Double dare you to give the medics the Hot Grease Gun Airborne Salute when you go into the aid tent, Doc!"

Oh shit ... They've even got a name for it! I'm dog meat!

Then Dwight heard the distinctly muffled sound of "Airborne!" being shouted by the two clerks with forefingers in their mouths as he jogged toward the battalion aid station, high-stepping so that the puddled water wouldn't splash each foot in the air.

CHAPTER THREE

THE BATTALION AID STATION

HE SAW THE SIGN over the tent's doorway: FIRST BATTALION AID STATION—ENTER AT YOUR OWN RISK.

He jogged in without slowing, came to a sliding stop, and removed the poncho, looking around to evaluate the tent as quickly as possible.

Supplies and drugs lined the partially sandbagged sides in wooden shelves, which were protected from the rain by the tent flaps having been extended to shorter poles, three feet outside of the sandbags. There was an alcove in one corner, separated from the rest of the tent by a two-sided, waist-high cabinet that also served as a countertop. Above the cabinet was a sign that read PHARMACY. Two shelves reaching to the top of the tent were behind it, filled with bottles, jars, and other containers of drugs. Four cots on sawhorses were waist high in the middle of the tent, where three men stood over a trooper lying shirtless on a cot. One was suturing a laceration on the man's shoulder while the others looked on.

Dwight had learned from his encounter with the HQ clerks not to be too formal in his introduction.

"Hi. My name's Johnson. The new medic with C Company."

The three men glanced at each other, and all of them, including the patient on the cot, put their right index fingers in their mouths and said, "Airborne!" They all were laughing.

The man being sutured laid his head back down on the cot, and the suturer went back to work. The other two walked up to him, smiling, with their hands extended in greeting.

"John Copeland," a short, slight captain said. "Don't call me 'sir' or 'Captain' unless there are strangers around. This is Kent Powonka, NCOIC." He looked toward a big master sergeant about forty years old with graying hair. Captain Copeland didn't look much older than Dwight! Dwight recalled that NCOIC meant "noncommissioned officer in charge."

They shook hands, and Captain Copeland put his hand on Dwight's shoulder. "We hear you've had quite a first day!" They were both still smiling. "How's your finger?" Sergeant Powonka said.

Dwight held it up between them. "Not bad," he said. "I can hardly feel it."

Powonka said, "Doesn't look all that good to me, Johnson. Let's get it cleaned up; put some bacitracin on it and get it bandaged. You're not going to believe how things get infected here. Where's your aid bag?"

Shit! Not again. Can't I do anything right today?

"Sorry, Sergeant. I left it on my bunk."

"It's OK, Johnson. You've had quite a bit of excitement today. Bring it in the morning. We hold sick call at 0530 every morning but Sunday. All the medics are expected to participate. We've got to get you supplied up and try to get some training for you before we go out again, which looks like it's gonna be soon. You've got a lot to learn."

The doctor said, "We got your file and orders this morning. Looks like you got some pretty good OJT at Polk. Tell me about it."

"Well, sir …"

"John."

"Sorry, John, but I think that calling a captain by his first name is going to take me some time."

"I understand, Dwight, but respect in our profession comes from knowledge, accomplishment, work, and horse sense. You'll get used to it. Call me 'Doctor' if it'll make you more comfortable. Tell me about Ft. Polk."

Dwight recounted his experience as a medic thus far—that he'd pulled double shifts on Friday and Saturday nights, both to learn as much as possible and because he really loved the work, especially suturing, which there was plenty to do on those weekend nights. He told them about working weekdays in a dispensary in a basic training battalion, where he'd learned a lot about diagnosis and treatment, pharmacy, working with files, and organizing and running mass injections that all army troops were required to get during those first months of training.

He was introduced to Staff Sergeant Joe Blackburn, the medic who was finishing up and bandaging the trooper, who was now on his feet. He was then shown around, learning where everything was that he would to be working with.

Kent gave him four large pairs of bandage scissors and told him that he'd be using them more than any other tool at his disposal, except for hemostats. He was given a dozen of those and told to keep plenty of bandage scissors and hemostats in his breast pockets at all times.

Kent told him, "Those scissors will cut through boots, and you're not going to believe how often you'll be using them for that."

Dwight said, "Oh, while I'm thinking of it, I need a bottle of Gentian Violet and some wide adhesive tape."

John said, "Oh yeah, for your gun. Smythe went through gobs of it. Take a few bottles of acetone too. You'll need it to get the sticky adhesive off and clean the grip when you change the tape. The engineers have some new tape you might want to try; it's made for sealing ducting. They're using it for everything. Have you met Corporal Richardson yet?"

"Yeah, he taught me how to use the grease gun."

"Well, he's got a friend in supply. Ask him if he can get you a roll of that new ducting tape."

"Right."

After another hour of orientation, Dwight went back to his squad, dropping off Bill's poncho on the way. The rain had stopped. When he walked into the HQ tent, he decided to beat them to it. He put his left forefinger into his mouth and said, "Airborne!" His right one had a new tubular finger bandage covering his burn.

Bill and Smitty laughed and replied in kind.

Dwight, Rich, Pensi, and Pascone spent an hour on the perimeter, Dwight shooting the grease gun and they playing with C-4, blowing down trees, having a ball setting the charges, lighting fuses and yelling, "Fire in the hole!" and running to trenches on the perimeter for protection from the blasts and flying debris.

Late afternoon was uneventful except for the prevalence of the new airborne salute. Everyone was doing it, and, what was worse, everyone seemed to recognize him and know who he was now. He considered that fame was fine but notoriety was not his idea of fun.

Pensi said, "How's it feel to be famous, Doc? Your first day in the brigade and the whole U.S. Army Airborne has a new salute!"

The chow bell rang at 1700, and they started off to the mess area in twos and threes, Dwight toward the rear, talking with T-man and Simpson. He was clearly the low man on the totem pole, as he supposed that it should be. Even being the doc, he was the FNG, after all. He supposed that it would stay that way until a new FNG came in to take his place or until enough time and experience went by for this to no longer be so.

He couldn't believe it, but the beans and franks were actually delicious. He had never liked them before tonight. And scalloped potatoes! Yum. Standing up to eat wasn't so bad either. In fact, to his surprise, he rather liked it.

While Dwight was eating, a staff sergeant walked up and introduced himself. He said that his name was Barry White and that
he was the squad NCOIC, and he asked whether Dwight would
mind coming over to the LT's tent and talking to him and the
LT after chow. Dwight shook hands with him and told him that
he'd be there in a few minutes.

Dwight turned back to his food and asked Bandy where the
LT's tent was.

"I'll take you there, Doc. You about ready?"

"Yeah, one more minute." Dwight had gone back for
seconds.

When he'd finished, he coupled his mess gear and picked it
up from the table to wash and rinse on the way out of the mess
area.

They took a slight detour, two tents over from his route to
the mess area and two tents nearer to the mess area than their
squad tent. Bandy left Dwight at the LT's tent and said in a low
voice, "Watch your ass with this guy. He's insecure and has to get
up on his hind legs with FNGs. Just be cool."

-CHAPTER FOUR-

THE LT

DWIGHT WALKED INTO THE entryway and asked for Lieutenant Krouse. A tall, blond, good-looking man with a square jaw and a golden tan flashed a winning smile, took three steps up to Dwight, and said, "Hi, Johnson. I'm Tom Krouse. Call me LT. You getting settled in OK?"

Dwight felt the hair on his neck bristle as he shook the LT's hand. Something about the man just wasn't right. Smile too flashy? Tan too golden? Jaw too square?

I feel like backing up a few feet and barking at him!

The thought made Dwight smile. "Sergeant White said y'all wanted to see me, sir."

"Yeah. I figured that we'd need to meet sooner or later. I rather thought that you would come to see either me or White before you settled in. You know, just because the medic you're replacing slept in that tent doesn't necessarily mean that I want you to."

"Oh! Sorry, sir. I just assumed that I'd be sleeping there because that's where the company clerk brought me when I reported in and Smythe's aid bag and weapon were waiting there for me."

Several other junior officers were watching this exchange from chairs or their cots.

"Well, Johnson, it's customary in this man's army to report to your commanding officer when you initially arrive. That's me, in case you haven't figured that out yet. And as for that weapon, the M3 grease gun is a relic, and I don't run a museum here. This is a combat outfit, and we trust the army to issue us the best weapons for the mission at hand. When we're in a fight and being resupplied, you're not going to have time to be reloading those magazines, assuming that they drop any loose .45 ammo. You will be issued a .45-caliber semiautomatic pistol, and you will turn in that relic. Do we understand each other, Johnson?"

"Yes, sir."

"You're an FNG, son. The best thing you can do for yourself, your squad, your Company, the United States Army, and your country right now is to keep your eyes and ears open and your mouth shut. And don't *assume* anything, or you'll get yourself or someone else killed! This is serious shit out here, Johnson. Fuckups go home in body bags. Are we on the same page here, Johnson?"

"Yes, sir."

The LT took two steps over to the blackboard, picked up a piece of chalk from the chalk tray beneath it, thrust out his impressive chin, and wrote ASS/ U/ME in large block letters.

"When you *assume* something, Johnson, you make an *ass* out of *you* and *me!*"

Jesus Christ! I haven't seen anyone do that stupid little routine since Coach Michael did it in seventh-grade football practice!

"Yes, sir."

"I don't mean to be hard on you, Johnson, but this is serious business over here, and you've got to take it seriously. Staff Sergeant White will get you squared away."

Dwight followed the LT's eyes to see that White was standing behind him. He looked back toward the LT and saw that the other officers were all too obviously not looking at them, saying nothing and appearing to have stopped their conversations in mid-sentence.

Dwight came to attention and saluted, and the LT saluted him back but without coming to attention in return and turned back toward the other officers.

"As you were," the LT said.

Johnson followed White out the door, and they walked side by side for twenty feet before White said, "He's a chicken-shit som-bitch, Doc, but he's got enough balls when the chips are down. He won't ask his men to do anything he won't do, and he leads from the front—not afraid to expose his ass to fire. None of us like him much but we respect him, at least so far. The other officers don't like him very much either, so various versions of that little tirade back there will be all around the battalion by morning. I'll tell the men the correct version when the time is right.

"The only real problem we can see with him is that he's the jealous type. He didn't like Smythe because Smythe was smarter and braver than him. Smythe would be up doing his job when everyone else was trying to crawl under their helmets, so he's got it in for the grease gun too. I guess he thinks that the gun had something to do with Smythe's bravery; I don't know. Anyway, welcome aboard. Let me know if there's anything I can do for you. The LT was right about one thing, though. Be on constant alert. You're going to learn a lot in the next several days, and it's important that you pay attention, OK?"

"Sure, Sarge."

"Don't worry, Doc. Just get through your first combat or two, and everyone will be a little more relaxed with you, even the LT. Everyone's waiting to see what you're made of, and the medic is an especially crucial position, so don't disappoint us."

"OK, Sarge. I'll do my best. Thanks."

They were at the tent. White turned back toward his tent and walked away purposefully. Dwight could tell that White was embarrassed, and he counted that as a good thing. It looked as though White was a stand-up guy. He hoped so. He sure didn't like the way he felt about the LT, though. Dwight sat outside with the others and talked for a couple of hours, until it got dark. He decided not to talk about the meeting with the LT, and, thankfully, no one asked about it. They were all tired, and they hit the rack early. It had been a big day, in anyone's book.

As he was getting into bed, Bandy said, "We've got a place down in the supply dump where we go at night usually, but we're all too tired tonight. We go there to get loose and relax. Kinda like our own little EM club. We'll show you tomorrow night."

-CHAPTER FIVE-

HERO

DWIGHT AWAKENED TO A beautiful morning. He looked at his watch. It was seven o'clock. He stretched languorously. He pushed his left leg out a little farther, then his right arm, then his left arm, then his right leg, and then all his limbs at once, bowing his back and turning his head from side to side; then he relaxed everything and brought his arms back to his sides. *Life is good,* he thought. *But why do I feel so sore?*

He was safely under his mosquito net: olive drab respite. The sun was up, and the morning air was cool and pleasant. He relaxed and lay there, looking up through a hole in the tent that was at least three feet square. He smiled and turned over to his right side and dozed off again. He was a child in his mother's arms, four years old. They loved each other so much. He was safe. He floated a little, secure in the feeling that he was loved. Warmth was his domain. In the background, he heard Les Paul playing the guitar and Mary Ford softly singing "How High the Moon."

"Wait a minute!" He rolled onto his back.

The hole! A ragged hole! There were others too! The tent was in shreds! The grease gun was on his chest! Instinctively, he felt for his genitals. Sweat jumped from every pore as he threw himself off the cot, further tearing an already torn mosquito net. He stood beside his cot and looked around. Bandy, Simone, and Nigel were standing in the entryway looking at him, five feet away.

"What's up, Doc?" Nigel said, exposing and extending his upper front teeth, imitating Bugs Bunny.

Bandy simply said, "Sir," as if he were seriously greeting a high-ranking officer.

"Simone!" Martinez said.

"Morning, hero," Pascone said from behind him.

Dwight looked around, more thoroughly now. The tent was in shreds but only the top half. He must have looked ridiculous, he realized. He was wearing only boxer shorts, dog tags, and the big black crucifix hanging by its hefty black chain from around his neck. He had slept with GG, and the gun was in his left hand. He opened its dust cover and pulled the bolt back enough to see that the weapon was clear. There was no round in the chamber, but he could see that the weapon had been fired since he'd cleaned it after practice on the perimeter yesterday.

GG? Wait, where'd that come from? I slept with my weapon, and I'm calling her "GG." Her? I'm calling it "her"? I haven't fired her since I cleaned her yesterday. How'd that residue get in the receiver? What the hell is going on here!?

"Where's Rich?" he said.

Pascone said, "Dust-off took him out; don't you remember? You wanted to go with him! He'll be OK. Might have a concussion, but he looked OK. His pupils constricted when you shined a flashlight in his eyes."

Dwight rubbed his eyes. He recalled that "dust-off" was the code name for helicopter medical evacuation.

Pascone walked over and put his hand on Dwight's shoulder. "He's gonna be OK, Doc. Don't worry about it. He woke up and was talking when the chopper took off. Don't you remember? You were exhausted by then; he'll probably be back this afternoon."

I must look pretty screwed up. Everyone's looking at me like I'm standing here with a hard-on or something. I gotta get my shit together.

Dwight made an effort to look self-assured.

"Don, I need to talk to you for a minute."

Pascone looked at the others and followed Dwight out of the tent. They stood between the tent and the bunker, Dwight still holding GG in his left hand.

"How'd you know my name is Don, Doc? That's never been mentioned before."

"I don't know, Don, but that's not important right now. What happened last night?"

"What the fuck're you talking about, Doc?"

"I must have slept through it, whatever it was."

"Are you fuckin' serious, Doc? Come on, man. Don't jack me off! Fuck you, man! What're you doin'?"

"I slept through it, man! I was in my bunk the whole time! I slept through it!"

"Oh, shit, Doc. Let's take a walk." The other guys were watching them from just inside the tent.

The whole base camp was in chaos. They stepped around debris as they walked. Most of the tents were in tatters. Sandbags were knocked over. One side of a bunker was completely gone, pools of semi-dried blood turned brown inside of it.

"What happened, Don?"

Pascone took Dwight's elbow and led him to two folding chairs, sitting beside overturned sandbags that had once guarded a demolished tent.

"You're really fucked up, Doc. Something must have happened to your head last night. Be still for a minute, and let me look you over."

Pascone got up and went around behind Dwight and began looking through his hair with his fingers, looking for any sign that a small piece of shrapnel could have entered his head without causing an easily visible wound.

"I don't see anything, Doc. How do you feel? Does your head hurt any?"

"No, my head's fine. I'm a little sore, Don, but nothing serious. What the fuck happened?"

"Shit, Doc! You must be kiddin' me!"

"I'm not bullshittin', Don! What the fuck happened?"

"We were hit bad last night, Doc. Sappers got in the camp, a bunch of 'em. They were all over the compound, throwing satchel charges and grenades into tents and then into the bunkers when guys ran there for cover. There were at least twenty troops killed and over a hundred wounded."

Pascone rubbed his tired face with both hands.

"I slept through the whole thing, Don."

Pascone wiped his eyes on each sleeve. "There's something seriously wrong here, Doc. I don't know what it is, but don't you leave us, man. You ain't getting out of here that easy. Is that what you're doing, man? Going for a section eight?"

"No, Don! I'm not kidding! I don't remember anything but going to bed last night!"

"Doc! You killed a gook right in front of all of us, man! You saved all our asses and then ran off and saved the 173d Airborne's commanding fucking general's life, man! The general's aides walked you back here and tucked you in! And you're probably the only one in the brigade who went back to sleep! You're the talk of the town, Doc!

"Word is that the sappers came in through a tunnel that was here before we built the base camp. They'd been waiting 'til we were all here before attacking through it. The mortar attack was just to see how many troops came out to the wire. It was all a big setup.

"You came out of your bunk like a rocket when the first explosion went off, grabbed that gun of yours, and were on the way out the door in your underwear and bare feet, while the rest of us were still waking up! You caught a satchel charge in midair, kept running, and threw it up on top of the bunker, where it went off! Look up there, Doc."

Don pointed at the top of the bunker, thirty feet away. Open and tattered sandbags were hanging down from both sides of the front corner.

"That's what tore up the tent, man, but because you threw it up there, all the shit went over our heads. None of us have ever seen such quick thinking, Doc! It was like you'd practiced it or something!

"Then you put three rounds in the sapper's back, as he was running up the hill, about twenty yards from you; see that brown spot over there? That's his blood and what's left of his brains! We all saw everything, Doc! The sapper went down on his face, and you ran right by him, going God knows where!"

"Bullshit!"

"No, man! I'm serious as a fuckin' heart attack! But here's the totally unreal part. After you'd run by him, you juked to the right, just like a running back dodging a tackler, right when the sapper fired a burst from his AK-47 at your back. Then you spun around and put two more rounds in his fucking face! From fifteen yards away! Where'd you learn to shoot like that, man? And how'd you know the fucker was going to fire!? Everyone's talking about it, Doc, and that's not even the best part! At least if what we hear is true.

"You ran straight to brigade HQ, Doc! Two hundred yards away, and got there right when a sapper was getting there. They say you shot him in the back and then scooped up the satchel charge and stuffed it under the dead fucker and lay down on him, waiting for it to go off! Only it didn't, thank God. It would have killed you. And General Baxter and several of his staff saw the whole thing! The general's putting you in for the medal, man!"

"The medal?"

"The Medal of Honor!"

"No shit?"

"No shit! Then the general and a whole buncha brass walked you back here and put you to bed. You went straight to sleep, like it was no big deal! The general told us that anyone who wakes you is up for court-martial. You're the talk of the whole brigade, Doc—shit, probably the whole fuckin' army, by now! And how'd you know where brigade HQ is? How'd you know to go there?"

"Holy shit, Don. I gotta go see the doctor."

"No shit. Don't say nothin' to nobody but the doctor, Doc. This ain't good, man. Don't tell nobody, ya hear?"

"OK, Don. I won't."

"And stop that 'Don' shit, Doc. It's either 'Pascone' or 'Skipper.' The only person to ever call me Don is my mother."

"OK, Don, uh Pascone, sorry."

"I'm gonna tell Bandy and Rich about it. We'll talk it over, but there's no need for no one else to know, at least for now. Shit, man, you could end up in a loony bin instead of the fuckin' Rose Garden with the president hangin' the medal 'round your fuckin' neck!"

"OK, Don."

"Pascone!"

"Pascone."

"You sure you feel OK, Doc?"

"I feel as good as I've ever felt, Don. Never better, except for my feet."

He looked at the bottom of his feet. There were several scratches and abrasions but no cuts. They looked bruised and red.

"I can't understand why!" Pascone said. "You ran all over the camp in your bare feet!"

"Fuck, Don. I think I got a problem here."

"No shit, Sherlock. Go talk to Captain Copeland, but we want you back here with us. Don't you leave us, man!"

Dwight started for his bunk to get dressed. "OK, Don. I'll be back." He stopped and turned back to Pascone. "What happened to Rich?"

Pascone took two steps toward Dwight before he spoke, not wanting the others to hear. "One of the rounds you put through the gook's head ricocheted up and hit Rich in the forehead. By that time, it was going so slow that it didn't penetrate, but a .45's a big, heavy round, Doc. It knocked him out cold. He'll be OK, but you were real upset when you found out about it, when you got back with the general and his aides. He'll have some stitches, but we're pretty sure that's all—Purple Heart time."

Dwight went straight to his cot and began getting dressed.

The men were all looking at him and then at Pascone. "What's going on, Skipper?" Bandy said.

Pascone said, "I gotta talk to Bandy alone for a minute, guys. Sorry."

Pascone and Bandy walked over to the two chairs that Dwight and Pascone had been sitting in.

The other troopers looked at each other, over at Dwight, who was lacing up his boots, then back at each other, and finally over at Pascone and Bandy, who were sitting down in the chairs.

Jaime said, "Wha ta fuck ees thees sheet, man?"

Martinez said, "Seeemone."

Putting on his fatigue cap and picking up GG, Dwight started walking toward the aid station.

Pensi said, "I pity the poor LT that tries to take that gun away from him now."

Ariza said, "No sheet, man!"

Martinez said, "Seemooone!"

It was 0900 on a beautiful day. Sam the Sham and the Pharaohs were singing in his head, "Watch it now, watch it, watch it, watch it! Woolly bully, woolly bully, woolly bully."

"Hey, Doc!" Dwight heard someone shout. He realized he was walking by Charlie Company's HQ tent. Bill and Smitty came to the door of the tent.

Bill said, "Anyone get court-martialed for waking you up?" Bill and Smitty both laughed.

The last thing I want to do right now is spar with these fuckers.

"Don't believe everything you hear, guys."

Smitty said, "Modesty becomes you, Doc. I got a couple chicks for you to look up when you get to DC, man."

"I ain't goin' to DC, Smitty. This is all a bunch of overblown bullshit, guys—really."

Bill said, "Well, apparently Baxter don't think so, partner. The paperwork for the medal's already in the pipeline."

"It's all a bunch of bullshit. I gotta get over to see Captain Copeland. See you guys later."

Bill said, "Shit, Doc, you oughta just send for him! You been here one fucking day and night and already got the medal and invented a new airborne salute. At this rate, you'll be a bird colonel by nightfall!" Laughing, both Smitty and Bill put their right forefingers in their mouths and said, "Airborne!"

Dwight shook his head and began jogging toward the aid station.

Captain Copeland was sitting at his field desk talking to a trooper whose arm was in a sling. Kent, Joe, and two other medics were working on troopers who were lying on three of the four cots.

Kent yelled, "Tensh-hut!"

Everyone but the men on the cots came to attention. Dwight was visibly stunned as his mouth moved a little. Only a second passed, but it seemed much longer before Dwight regained his composure.

Dwight laughed and said, "Oh, bullshit! Come on! Get off it!"

Copeland said, "You have to say, 'As you were, men' before we can come off of attention, Dwight."

"Oh, bullshit!"

Copeland, Joe, and Kent walked up to him, laughing. Kent slapped him on the back and said, "Sorry, Dwight, but we couldn't help it. We've been waiting for you—heard you been putting in a little sack time."

Dwight said, "Sorry to disappoint you guys, but it's all a bunch of bullshit—really."

The captain said, "Well, if that's true, it's the best-documented and most well-distributed bullshit in the United States Army."

"Seriously, I just happened to be there, and things just happened. I really didn't have that much to do with it."

Kent said, "Right. Anything you say, pal. Where's your aid bag?"

"Oh shit, Kent. I have something really urgent I need to talk to John about, and I rushed over here as soon as I found out about it. I haven't even had any chow or shaved yet. Can it wait awhile? I really have to talk to the doctor right now."

"Sure, Dwight; I understand. It's OK, but if it's about Corporal Richardson, we heard from the Ninety-third Evac that he's all right and will be back soon."

"That's good news, but it's not what I need to talk about. John, can we talk privately?"

"Sure, Dwight; we're almost finished here. We're done with the seriously wounded, and they've been dust-offed to the Ninety-third Evac; let's go to my tent."

The doctor bunked in a tent like Dwight's, but there were only five other cots and there were stand-up lockers, chairs, and tables beside each one. John Copeland pulled up a chair across the field desk from the chair beside Dwight and motioned for Dwight to sit down. John had a concerned look on his face, like a father whose son had just asked for a private conversation, although the captain couldn't have been over twenty-five and looked more like twenty-one.

"There's something seriously wrong with me, John."

"Besides your balls being substantially larger than your brain, what's the matter, Dwight?"

"I swear, John. You're not going to believe this shit, but I don't remember a thing—nothing. As far as I'm concerned, I went to bed and woke up this morning to a bright, sunny sky!"

"Shit, Dwight. Are you serious?"

"I couldn't be more serious, Doctor. I saw all the damage and asked someone what happened; Pascone's his name. He took me aside and told me all about it."

The captain pushed his chair back, balancing it on its back legs, clasped his hands behind his head, and, looking into the space above his head, blew out a long breath of air through clenched teeth and pursed lips.

"Do you remember anything at all?"

"Nothing. I went to bed and woke up this morning—nothing in between."

"Amnesia usually happens with trauma. Does your head hurt anywhere?"

"No, I feel fine."

John got up from his chair and walked around the table. "Let's take a look." He looked Dwight's head over thoroughly, sifting through his hair, even though it was, at most, a sixteenth of an inch long; he also pressed around to find any tender spots. He looked behind and in his ears, at his neck and throat, in his nostrils and mouth, and at his eyes and eye sockets. "Just a minute. I'll be right back." He went out of the tent at a brisk pace and was back in thirty seconds.

The captain looked in Dwight's ears with a scope and then looked in his mouth and throat with it. He put a thermometer in his mouth and began taking his pulse. While Dwight waited the required three minutes, Copeland took a book down from his shelf and said, "You look bad."

Dwight cocked his head quizzically, thermometer under his tongue.

"Let's see," the captain said, thumbing through the book. "'Looks bad, feels good ... looks bad, feels good.' Here it is; you've got a chronic case of vagina!"

They both laughed out loud, Dwight catching the falling thermometer and putting it back in his mouth.

"Old joke, John."

"I know; I couldn't help myself."

They laughed again.

"No shit, John. What's going on?"

"I don't know, Dwight. I'm no shrink, but I'd say that you've had a serious psychological trauma and your brain has blocked the entire episode. Do you feel depressed, nervous, elated—anything unusual or maybe inappropriate for the circumstances?"

"No, except that I'm calm, but that'd be normal for me if I'd awakened on a nice morning after a good night's sleep. What should I do, John?"

"I'm not sure. For now, just go on back to your platoon and relax. You've pretty much got the world at your feet right now, so just take it easy the rest of the day. The pending operation has been suspended for the time being, so nothing should happen for the next few days. You're not supposed to know that yet, so don't say anything to anyone. I'm going to talk to a shrink friend of mine over at the Ninety-third Evac and see what he has to say. It could be that your brain will release this stuff when it thinks you can handle it. If that happens, I want you to come back here right away. I'll make sure whoever's here knows where to find me, OK?"

"Sure, Doctor. I wonder if it'd be OK with you if we could keep a lid on this for the time being. I don't see any reason for anyone to know about this who doesn't need to, OK?"

"Goes without saying, Dwight. Let's see if we can find out what's going on before we do anything else, but I don't think I can let you go on a mission until I'm sure you're OK."

"OK, John. Let's just see where it goes; hopefully everything'll just come back to me."

"Hopefully. I'm going to tell Joe and Kent about it, but they won't say anything to anyone. I want them to be sure to not put any pressure on you. OK?"

"Sure, John—whatever you say. I'm gone. See you later."

"I want to see you before you hit the rack tonight, OK?"

"Sure, John. I'll see you after chow then."

"See ya."

Dwight walked out into the bright sunlight.

Come to think of it, things are a little different. Ever since I woke up, I seem to be seeing better or more clearly or something. Colors are more distinct. The edges of things seem somehow sharper. What the hell could this be all about?

He started walking toward his tent.

I could eat a tire. I wonder what's for lunch?

GG had never left his hands.

New tents were going up everywhere. Troops were filling sandbags and unloading and loading trucks, and vehicles of every size and shape were moving between the tents and the makeshift roads that ran between the companies.

Unlike yesterday, the air was crisp and clean, and although it was hot, it was not uncomfortably so.

Also unlike yesterday, everyone noticed him now. The troops looked up and waved, some shouting, "Airborne!" but now not with their fingers in their mouths. Dwight waved back and smiled, but he was not comfortable with this newfound fame. He hoped it would blow over quickly, as the new airborne salute appeared to have done.

As he approached his tent, he noticed that the squad and some engineers were in the process of raising the new tent. All the men were obviously glad to see him and told him so: "Hey, Doc! How're ya feeling?" "Yo, Doc! What's happenin'?" "What's up, Doc?"

He slung GG on his back and helped Nigel pull a rope taught while Bandy and T-man tied it to an angle iron stake. Dwight looked at his cot and noticed that there was a new flak vest, and his shirts were neatly folded on top of it. Someone had put up a new mosquito net for him, raised the side, and neatly tucked the other three sides under his sleeping bag. His area was neatly squared away. He felt a surge of pride and affection in his chest for these men. They were *his* men, and he felt responsible for them.

Just as they were finishing up, the dinner bell rang. "Squeet" was said by several of them. They got their mess kits and canteen cups, but the walk to the mess tent was different now. They walked together, like a family going to church, talking and laughing. They knew that they now possessed what every combat trooper hopes for and dreams of but rarely achieves: they were a cohesive team, combat tested and confidently relaxed, ready for anything.

The least of them was now the first. The FNG was their leader. Deference to him by the men could be seen from both outside the squad and in. Dwight was like the alpha dog in a pack of coyotes: his countenance was just a little bit sharper, his eyes a little more watchful, his walk a little more certain, and his caring gaze over his troops a little more palpable.

The entire First Battalion filed through the mess area within thirty minutes, eating while standing, talking little, washing their mess gear, and leaving the area. Dwight was the only trooper carrying a weapon. GG was a part of him now, slung over the back of his flak vest while eating and in his hand when not.

As they began walking toward their tent, Dwight's quick but newly all-seeing gaze saw that most of the men in the mess area were looking at them—most in admiration and certainly a benign envy. Over in the officer's section, he spotted Lieutenant Krouse and several other officers looking at them. Krouse's uniform was heavily starched, ironed, and creased, his jungle boots were spit-shined, and his fatigue cap was blocked and starched. Dwight thought that he simply looked concerned and uncomfortable—not angry exactly but not happy either.

Dwight's gaze swept by the LT, and he hoped that he hadn't seen that Dwight had seen him looking, but Dwight took note of the fact that he was noticing *everything*. Whatever had happened to him last night, the good news was that he noticed things now that he hadn't before. He knew that this new, enhanced sense was going to be not only an asset to him in the field but also, much more importantly to him now, an asset to his men. It was his job to take care of them. A feeling of responsibility was steadily growing in him. The memory of his Labrador retriever's relaxed watchfulness sprang into his mind's eye.

I'll bet this is what she felt like with her new puppies. Shit, these guys aren't my puppies! What the hell is going on with my mind? I have to be sure to tell the doctor about this.

Dwight ducked into the tent. Rich jumped up from his cot, a bandage wrapped around his head. A quarter-sized spot of blood had seeped through, and Dwight could see that there was a knot on his head; however, his eyes were bright, and he was definitely happy to see Dwight.

"Hey, Audie Murphy, you ain't left for the States to sell war bonds yet?"

"Fuck you, Rich. How's your head?"

"Little headache but nothin' serious. You gave me sloppy seconds on that bullet, Doc. Seems like you could have put me out of my misery with a round that hadn't already gone through a fuckin' gook, man!"

"You should feel honored, asshole. Next time, keep your head down."

"Ain't gonna be no next time, Doc. Shit, from what I hear about your luck, I'm not going to let you get more than five feet away from me. Hey, I need to go to the latrine. Come on, Doc."

"Like I said, Rich, fuck you. You stay away from me, faggot."

"Be the best piece you ever got, sweetie!"

"Dream on, teenage queen!"

The men were all laughing. Dwight and Rich hugged each other. Dwight felt his eyes well up and had to turn away, as he said, "I gotta get over to the aid station and see if they've got any vaginal ointment for Rich. Someone put this pussy to bed. I'll be back in a while to take care of him."

"Eat me, Doc!"

"In your dreams, pussy-man."

He walked outside and wiped his eyes. GG had never left his hands.

John, Kent, and Joe were talking around a field desk when Dwight walked in. They all looked up.

Kent said, "Hey, Dwight. How're you feeling?"

"Great, except for the bottom of my feet!"

Joe said, "I'll bet! I think we should have a look before you leave."

"They're OK, Joe. Just sore."

Smiling, John said, "That's an order, Dwight. You got any news for me?"

"Well, kinda," Dwight said as he sat down and started removing his boots.

What do mean, 'kinda'?"

"Well, I don't quite know how to describe it. It's more emotion that anything else, I guess. But it's physical too."

Kent said, "Try to describe it to us, Dwight. No one here's going to laugh at you or think you're crazy. Just tell us everything you can about how you're feeling."

"Well, after talking to Captain Copeland this morning, I started thinking about it. First of all, when I woke up this morning, I thought of my weapon like it was a friend or my dog or something. I even had a name for her … it. I thought of her as 'GG.' And it's like I can't put her down, like she's a part of me. When she's not in my hand, I feel like an old man who's left his teeth out or something!"

Joe said, "That part's fairly normal, Dwight. Kent and I both saw that a lot in Korea. If you'll think about it, it's perfectly natural. You get through something life-threatening like that, and you feel that the gun's what got you through it. You're naturally going to be pretty attached to it. And popular psychology that a gun is a phallic symbol notwithstanding, combat veterans who've been in situations like yours tend to think of their weapon as a mate or a female, the same way pilots name their airplanes female names. Armor and artillery do the same thing with their guns and tanks."

John said, "What else?"

"Everything looks clearer and sharper than before, like I just got some new glasses or some shit! Like I have twenty-fifteen vision in both eyes! And, well, I just kinda seem to be more aware of everything around me. Like today at chow, I took a glance around, and I swear I saw everybody there! Individually! Shit, I even saw the pupils of their eyes from thirty yards away!

Kent said, "We've seen this before too. You've just been closer to death than most men will ever get. You have a heightened sense of awareness. Sorry to say this, but this part will probably wear off in a few days; it's something we'd all like to retain. Some keep it longer than others, but I don't know of anyone who's kept it forever. Your mind is telling you that life is short and that you should stop and smell the roses, so to speak. You're glad to be alive, so all your senses are more aware of themselves. You're essentially glad to be here. What else?"

"I feel a special closeness to my men. I was thinking on the way over here that I feel like a dog or cat with kittens or puppies, like they're my responsibility, that I'm here to protect them. And I can tell that they feel the same toward me, like they're depending on me. It's like we kinda know what each other's thinking. And also I know that they're all sort of looking up to me!"

The three of them looked at Dwight for a moment and then at each other; then they laughed.

Kent said, "We don't mean to laugh at you, Dwight, but shit, man! Today you"—he started ticking off points on his fingers— "caught a satchel charge in midair before anyone else could even put their feet on the ground and then threw it on top of a bunker; then you shot a gook and ran past him, dodged his bullets, and then killed him, saving your and your troops' lives. Then you ran off and saved the commanding fucking general's life and single-handedly killed two gooks there, running them down like dogs. Can you imagine what you must look like in your troops' eyes? They saw you put two rounds through a gook's head from twenty-five yards away with a submachine gun on full auto, and then you ran off and won the fucking Medal of Honor; then you went to sleep like you'd just got home from work at the factory or something! I wouldn't be surprised if they didn't drop to their fucking knees and make the sign of the cross when you walked up, for Christ's sake!

"As for knowing what each other's thinking, ask any married couple about it. You get close to someone, that kind of thing happens; it's mental telepathy and weird but normal and commonplace. Your first experience with it has just been accelerated, and that's probably why it seems so profound to you. This would have happened eventually anyway. You're going to get closer to those men than you could have ever imagined. Like I said, it was just greatly accelerated, that's all."

Joe said, "Do you remember anything yet?"

"No ... nothing."

"Well, like John told you this morning, come over here as soon as you do; your brain is keeping it from you for a reason. It may jump out at you suddenly and scare the shit out of you. John said that you've told a few of your troops about it. Is that so?"

"Yes. Pascone and Bandy, and I think they told Richardson about it."

John said, "Tell them about this conversation we had here. And tell them that if you get all weird and shit—like start screaming or hallucinating or anything—they should give you three of these pills and have you chew them up. Then, after you've calmed down, they should bring you here. Kent and Joe saw some of this in Korea. I'd never heard anything about it. It could be some kind of shell shock or something."

He handed Dwight a small pill bottle with six yellow tablets in it. The label read DIAZEPAM 5 MG.

Kent said, "To tell the truth, Dwight, my interest in your memory return is selfish. I want to know two things." Again, he ticked off points on his fingers. "How did you know to dodge to the side when that sapper fired at you and"—the next finger—"how'd you know to run to the general's tent, or even where it was? You'd just got here and hadn't known where *anything* was yet."

"I really have no idea, Kent. Truth is, I don't even believe any of this happened. What I can't figure out is why none of this shit scares me. Why aren't I scared?"

John said, "Well, part of it is probably because you don't know what happened or even that it happened at all, but what concerns me is that you aren't worried or upset. You just seem to be concerned, but why aren't you upset? You seem to be happy and even encouraged by the whole thing. I'm going to ask you a serious question, Johnson. And I want you to tell me the truth. Your life and the lives of your troops could depend on your truthfulness here, OK?"

Oh shit ... He called me Johnson. What could this be about?

"OK, Doctor."

"Do you have *any* history of psychosis or psychotic episodes?" The three of them were staring intently into Dwight's eyes.

"Shit no, Doctor Copeland! I mean, shit, I had a crush on my third-grade teacher, and I cried when I found out that she was getting married! But I don't think that's too bad!"

They laughed, except for Dwight; he was concerned.

John said, "If that's the best you can do, you're healthier than anyone else in this tent!"

Dwight breathed a sigh of relief. "OK. Well, I'm gonna get on back. The guys are waiting for me." He started putting his boots back on.

John said, "Right. OK, Dwight. You take care of yourself. See you at sick call in the morning."

"Right. See y'all in the morning."

Joe said, "Hold it, pardner. Let's see your feet."

Everything was OK—bruises and abrasions but no cuts.

John handed him two tubes of bacitracin ointment and said, "Put a light coat of this on those abrasions three times a day for the next three days. If you have any more pain than today or there's any more discoloration, talk to me. Also I want you to look for any red streaks running up the insides of your ankles or legs and any swelling in your legs or lumps or pain in your legs where they meet your balls, OK?"

The air was cooler, and the shadows were getting long. The greens were greener. The browns were browner. Everything was so *crisp.*

I think I'll just stay with the 'ignorance is bliss' bullshit, thank you, gentlemen. I feel great!

He put the pills in his pocket and broke into a dead run, headed to his squad tent.

I feel absolutely fantastic!

Dwight slowed up before he got to the tent and brought his breathing back to normal.

I don't want these guys to think I'm anxious to get back to them; I've got to maintain my cool.

He walked into the tent. Simpson said, "Hey, Doc. We been waitin' for ya."

"Sorry, guys. I've got to do medic stuff, and the doctor wants me to get a little training, so I'll be back and forth to the aid station pretty often."

Rich said, "Yeah, Smythe was there every morning for sick call, but he was with us on Okinawa, so he was pretty well trained up by the time we got here. You're the first FNG medic the whole company's had."

Nigel said, "We got some training for you tonight. We're going down to our own little EM club. Put on your fatigue shirt; it gets a little cool down there at night."

Dwight took off his flak vest and put on a shirt, noticing the new patch: a short, slanted red sword with a white wing coming up from it, like a flame, on a blue background with a white border. A blue tab was sewn above it with AIRBORNE in white letters. The patch and tab was about three inches tall by two inches wide—pretty but masculine also.

~CHAPTER SIX~

EVERYBODY MUST
GET STONED

THEY PICKED UP THEIR weapons and headed out. Dwight noticed that although T-man and Simpson had M60 machine guns strapped to their cots and Pensi had an M79 grenade launcher, they also had M16s, which they picked up. Nigel and Ariza picked up each side of a cooler, and they moved out down the hill.

The supply dump was enormous. There were hundreds of large aluminum boxes about ten feet square, called Connex boxes, some stacked on top of each other. These came into the brigade full, and others left the dump empty, every day. There were innumerable fifty-gallon drums; stacks of PSP, lumber, and canvas; boxes of C rations; and all manner of other supplies. There was a road behind this, and the ammo dump was on the other side and was heavily guarded. The supply dump was not.

The squad had built a shelter in the middle of the dump, in the area that held most of the lumber. The shelter was about fifteen feet square with a tarp the size of the ones strung at the ends of so many of the tents in the troop areas. There were canvas lawn chairs and a large field table with chairs around it; kerosene lanterns rimmed the entire area.

Dwight said, "How'd you guys manage this?"

Rich said, "White's best friend is the Supply NCOIC. White'll probably be here later, soon as he's done brownnosing the LT."

Simone said, "He got to do dat, man; eet's his fokeen job, man."

Rich said, "Yeah, he's one of us, Doc. He's a good guy."

Bandy and Pensi had separated from the rest of them, about twenty yards before they got to the shelter. They came in now, one carrying a case of Pabst Blue Ribbon beer and the other a case of Bireley's orange drink. Bandy opened the cooler. It was half full of ice. He started putting the beer and pop in it. Pascone and Nigel were lighting the lamps.

Rich sat in one of the chairs, motioned to one across from him, and said, "Sit down, Doc; take a load off."

Dwight sat down in the canvas chair and said, "Where'd you guys get all this shit? Especially the lawn chairs."

Rich said, "White snagged it all for us. He's got all kinds of connections, man."

Rich took a cigar box off of an upturned crate that served as a side table beside his chair. He opened it, took out a *Time* magazine, tore a page out of it, and laid it down on the box. Next, he removed a large plastic bag, opened it and poured about a quarter ounce of a greenish brown leafy substance onto the magazine page, and said, "They make these magazines out of super-thin paper, Doc, so they don't weigh much for delivering them by air to us. They make great cigarette papers." He was rolling the substance into the magazine page like a giant rolled cigar; he expertly ran a glue stick down the edge of the paper and sealed it.

Dwight said, "What is that?"

The biggest fuckin' joint you ever seen, huh, Doc? Weed's really cheap here—ten dollars a kilo."

"Joint?"

Rich said, "Oh shit, guys! I'm forgetting just how much of an FNG the doc is! We got us a cherry on our hands!"

Several of the men said, "No shit!" almost in unison.

Bandy said, "Bullshit! Doc, don't tell me you ain't never smoked weed before!"

"I don't take narcotics."

Rich said, "Doc, weed ain't no narcotic! It's just, well, weed. Marijuana. Reefer. Everybody but some of the older guys smokes it here, man. Booze can be dangerous, Doc. If something bad happens, the adrenaline will pop you out of a weed high. Booze can get you killed, man. Most of us drink orange pop and smoke weed. Sure, we'll have a few beers but nothing serious." He lit the joint, took several short drags, held his breath, and passed it to Bandy, who did the same and passed it on.

Dwight couldn't believe what he was seeing. Every one of them was taking a drag on it and passing it on!

It came around to Dwight; Pensi was holding it out for Dwight to take.

"No, thanks; I think I'll pass."

Rich said, "Oh, come on, Doc. It's not gonna hurt you. Look, we *all* wouldn't be smokin' it if it was a bad thing, would we? I mean, shit, man! Whaddya think … we're a buncha dope addicts? Take a hit, man; you'll like it. It ain't no big deal, Doc!"

Ariza said through clenched teeth, holding the smoke in his lungs, "Wha ju tink, Senior? Ju better'n us or somteenk?"

Pascone said, "Hey Ariza! Cut that shit out, man! He's just scared, man. Leave him alone!" Dwight didn't see Pascone wink at Ariza.

Bullshit! The one thing I don't want them to think is that I'm afraid! Shit … it can't be such a big deal … I mean, they're all doing it, and no one looks like they're going crazy or acting crazy or anything.

"OK, but what's going to happen? What's it feel like? I don't know what to expect."

Rich said, "Expect to get stoned, man! You gonna feel cool and like you ain't got no problems and like you just got about twenty pounds lighter; things'll look better and colors brighter."

Nigel said, "Just take a little hit, Doc. It ain't gonna hurt ya."

Dwight took a small drag and held it, as the others had done. Pensi was just now letting his drag out and taking a sip of orange drink.

Martinez said, "Seee-mooone!"

Simpson said, "The doc's cool, man!"

Dwight let out his breath, coughing a little. He smoked Lucky Strikes, so inhaling was no big deal to him. It appeared to him that the others were starting to act a little differently now. Rich was acting—well, how could he characterize it—cool. That's it, not that he wasn't cool before—cooler, he supposed. And, as Dwight looked around, the others were behaving the same, and they were having fun. Simpson had said something funny to Pascone, who was bent over laughing and staggering. A battery-operated radio came from somewhere and good mellow jazz was playing.

"I don't feel anything, Rich."

"I don't know what to tell you, mothafuckin' docta man! Maybe you ain't *took* a big enough *toke*!

T-man and Bandy doubled over laughing. "Took a toke!" T-man laughed.

Bandy assumed a mock boxing stance and threw a slow-motion roundhouse punch at T-man, who mimicked horror as Bandy's fist arrived as "the bird": middle finger extended. T-man, in return, slow-motion tackled Bandy waist high, and they both fell to the ground in gales of laughter.

Ariza said, "Took another toke, my docta freend!"

Pascone said, "Physician, heal thy*self*!"

More laughter.

Shit. Maybe I'm not susceptible to this shit. They're all sure having a good time. This is bullshit! I didn't take a big enough drag to do anything.

"Give me that thing." He motioned toward the joint, which was lying on the cigar box beside Rich. Rich handed it to him.

It had gone out and was less than half smoked. Dwight lit it with his Zippo, took in as much as he could fit in his lungs, and held it, mightily resisting coughing. After a few seconds, he couldn't keep the urge to cough away any longer and started coughing so violently that he had to stand up, staggering around the area. Pensi handed him an orange drink. They were all laughing.

"*See* mone!"

"All right, Doc!"

He started to take another drag. Rich stopped him by gently touching his arm. "That's enough for now, Doc."

"Shit, Rich. I don't feel *nothin*'!"

"Take it easy, my man; give it a chance. You don't wanna be fuckin' round with *this* shit, man. We don't want you goin' over the line your first time at bat. There's more where that came from. Relax and just let your mind wander where it wants to, Doc."

Dwight sat down in the lawn chair. The music was flowing out of the radio.

Hmm ... Man, that jazz is nice. That must be some kind of super-duper new radio out of Japan. Those little suckers are making some really nice audio equipment lately. Look at those lamps shimmer. The light is so softly coming to me. I can even see the beams coming out from the flame. Look how it's shimmering on the oil drums over there.

Dwight settled down into his chair, a warm relaxation spreading down through his body as he let out a contented sigh. He looked away from the lamp and slowly turned his eyes and head toward Rich, who was watching him.

A low, slow whistle escaped Dwight's lips. "Fuckin' A!" slowly came from his mouth, as if someone else were saying it.

Rich threw his head back in laughter. Dwight marveled at the structure of his perfectly arranged white teeth and the ridges in the roof of his mouth. He looked down at GG in his lap. He lifted her up and looked at her lovely symmetry—beautiful. What a work of art—mechanical genius. He released the magazine from the receiver and looked at the top bullet. He slowly slid the round out and held it at eye level. The soft light bounced off it into his eyes, making a little shimmering star where the copper jacketed bullet met the beautiful, shiny brass casing. Glorious, slow, soft jazz washed over him.

Then the radio announcer was softly telling him that he was listening to AFRS, Armed Forces Radio Service, in beautiful downtown Saigon.

A sudden, hard rain began beating on the tarp. Rich set a four-by-four beam, about seven feet tall, upright in the middle of it so the rain would run off. Several of the others were making a shallow trench around the shelter with entrenching tools locked at half angle—an easy job in the sandy soil. At the low side, they gouged a five-foot-long trench leading away from the shelter so that the water would run into it and downhill from there, keeping the water out of their area. Raindrops hissed as they hit the lamps. An animal screeched in the jungle fifty yards away where crickets and frogs put up a constant din.

Rich said, "I heard you came over on a troopship. We didn't have to go through that shit because they flew us in from Okinawa on C-130s. They say the ship broke down and had to be towed into Guam. That must have been a trip."

"Yeah, it was really bad. It started off bad and just got worse and worse. When we were boarding at the Oakland Army Terminal, we were really struggling because we were humping all our combat gear, our weapons, and our duffels. The navy guys were herding us like cattle in the ladder wells and screaming at us like we were a bunch of trainees, so someone finally cold-cocked one of them; the guy couldn't remember who did it when he woke up, so they wouldn't let anyone on deck until someone ratted on the guy, and of course no one would, so everyone got seasick; the stench and heat were unbearable. Then we hit a typhoon just six days out, and everyone got a lot sicker.

"Finally, we got to where we could keep food down, and the ship broke down; we were dead in the water for three days when a destroyer showed up and took five days towing us into Guam. That was twenty-six days into the trip."

Rich said, "Yeah, I heard you guys laid waste to the navy base there."

"Well, not exactly, but when you put a few hundred para-troopers ashore after an ordeal like that and give 'em all the beer they can drink, shit happens."

"What did you guys do?"

"Well, after we each had three or four beers, the navy showed up with about ten buses, which shuttled us to the EM Club. It was a giant facility and was only about half full of about a hundred or so sailors and around twenty or thirty marines. I can't believe that the navy brass didn't know what would happen next. Anyway, sure as shootin', some paratrooper informs the audience that marines are so stupid that they don't even know how to spell *corpse*. To their honor, thirty marines tried to take on over two hundred airborne troops, so the brawl didn't last long, but that's when the party really got cranked up. We threw the marines and navy out and told the employees that they could stick around and work for tips if they wanted to but we weren't paying for anything the rest of the night. The place had a flat roof, and it was a pleasant day, so guys started carting booze and beer up there, ready to make an extended Alamo out of it, if the navy got froggy.

"We had cut the wires on the phones so no one could call the shore patrol, so it took them about forty-five minutes to get the word and get there in force, but by that time it was way too late. A gaggle of our airborne officers showed up from the O-Club, but they were already half in the bag too, and they made a halfhearted attempt to get us out of the club and off the roof. Troops were yelling shit like, 'We'll be right there, sir!' and 'Give us fifteen more minutes and then hold your breath. We'll be right along, sir!'

"We could see them smiling but trying not to. We could tell that they were really kind of proud of us. This navy major—what do you call 'em? Lieutenant Commander, that's it. Anyway, this guy told us to get out in five minutes or he was going to send the shore patrol in to arrest us. Some guy yelled back, "What are you going to do, Major? Send us to Vietnam?" Of course, this brought the house down, and everyone then got really abusive with him, calling him a limp-wristed swabby and yelling stuff like, 'When you put on your combat gear, sir, do you blouse your loafers?' We told 'em to bring on the shore patrol; we were just getting warmed up on those marines.

There was a Filipino band, and they started packing up to leave; no way were we going to let that happen. They were told to unpack and keep playing and that they'd be paid well but they were going to play music until dawn, and they did."

"So what happened then?"

"Well, we realized that we had the navy by the balls, so we partied 'til the booze ran out around 0400; then we marched back to the ship in platoon formation with NCOs calling cadence, and we sang a couple of stanzas of 'Blood on the Risers.' We all had nasty hangovers, but we had tons of APCs on the ship and the ventilation system was working again, so everyone just sacked out. The officers were all hungover too, so there wasn't much trouble about it.

"We sailed that night, but the ship broke down again two days later, and we had to get towed into Midway. They didn't let us off the docks that time, but they gave us all the beer we wanted, so we had a good time. We were just thankful to be on dry land."

"Wow! Sounds like you guys made up for all the misery on the ship."

"Bullshit. If I have to go home on that sombitch, I'll renounce my citizenship and stay here! Shit, I can't believe how much I'm talking! Am I rambling?"

Rich said, "Naw, not really. It's your first time gettin' high. Just let it roll. Enjoy yourself. I enjoyed the story."

Dwight looked around and saw that several of the others had been listening too.

Bandy said, "Man, I wish I could have been there for that Guam gig! I'd give a month's pay to have experienced that."

Pascone said, "I know that ship must have been miserable, but you're in for some pretty serious misery here too; believe it, Doc."

Rich said, "Yeah, the French fucked around here 'til they got their asses kicked at Dien Bien Phu. Those frogs were so lazy; they hardly ever even went outside in the heat! They called this place Indochina. For us, it's Outdo-China!"

Bandy and Pascone thought this was so funny they were clutching their stomachs with laughter, which caused Rich and Dwight to erupt in gales of laughter too.

Bandy said, "Shit! We ain't sang 'Blood on the Risers' since we been here!"

Pascone started singing, and everyone else chimed in. To the melody of "Glory, Glory Hallelujah" they sang the quintessential paratroopers' drinking song:

He was just a rookie trooper, and he surely shook with fright

As he checked all his equipment and made sure his pack was tight.

He had to sit and listen to those awful engines roar,

"You ain't gonna jump no more!"

Gory, Gory what a helluva way to die,

Gory, Gory what a helluva way to die,

Gory, Gory what a helluva way to die,

He ain't gonna jump no more.

"Is everybody happy?" cried the sergeant looking up.

Our hero feebly answered, "Yes!" and then they stood him up.

He leaped into the blast, his static line unhooked.

He ain't gonna jump no more!

(Chorus)

He counted loud, he counted long, he waited for the shock.
He felt the wind, he felt the clouds, he felt the awful drop.
He jerked his cord, the silk spilled out and wrapped around his
legs.
He ain't gonna jump no more!
(Chorus)
The risers wrapped around his neck, connectors cracked his dome.
The lines were snarled and tied in knots around his skinny bones.
The canopy became his shroud, he hurtled to the ground.
He ain't gonna jump no more!
(Chorus)
Then they skipped to the last stanza and sang:
There was blood on the risers, there were brains upon the chute.
Intestines were a-dangling from his paratrooper's boots.
They picked him up still in his chute and poured him from his
boots.
He ain't gonna jump no more!

There was short laughter as they slapped each other on their backs, but the mood had turned somewhat solemn, as if in remembrance of fallen comrades. Dwight considered that this was probably why the old beer-drinking airborne song hadn't been sung since they had started losing friends in combat.

Then they separated into groups of twos or threes or settled into chairs and receded into conversation or their own thoughts. As Dwight's mind drifted, he thought about the trip to the base camp in the Hewey and started laughing out loud again, feeling just perfectly stoned.

Rich said, "What's so funny now?"

"I was just thinking about the helicopter crew on the trip here from Saigon. There were four newspaper correspondents interviewing us as we were fixin' to leave. This pinched-faced, thin-lipped bitch from the *New York Times* asked one of the door gunners how he could shoot women and children. He cocked his head to the side like he couldn't believe she was asking such a stupid question and said, 'You just don't lead 'em as far.' Even the other reporters laughed, but you could tell that she didn't get it—too funny."

Rich said, "Yep. You'll hear lots of gallows humor here; it's just part of the way we cope. You'll get into it. You'll see."

They settled back into their own thoughts again and listened to the music. Then Rich chuckled and said, "You're replacing one colorful fucking medic, you know?"

"How's that?"

"Has anyone told you about Smythe's visit to VC Mountain yet?"

"No. I haven't heard about it."

"Well, you know we landed at Vung Tau, down in the Delta, when we first got here. We were all wound up like an eight-day clock. No one had seen any action yet, and no one really knew if we were ever going to. We didn't know that Vung Tau was about as safe as you can get in Vietnam. We later found out that the VC send their troops there for R & R, so no one even needed to carry a weapon. It's still an unwritten rule between us and the VC not to fuck around in Vung Tau.

"After a week or so, Second Battalion came up here, and a couple days later we needed to set up communications with them, so the CO had a commo truck set up to broadcast to them. Only problem was that they had to get up high somewhere so the radios could get to them. The only option was to drive up to the top of the only mountain down there. They call it VC Mountain because it's a prime place for snipers because it's all jungle and the road up is a series of switchbacks all the way to the top, so you never know what's around the next hairpin corner.

"Anyway, they decide to send a squad in an APC with a .50 mounted on top to lead the commo truck—a little three-quarter-ton pickup-looking thing with a canvas cover over the back and another one covering the cab. The back has wooden bench seats running down both sides—perfect to mount an array of radios on. One commo guy drives and the other sits in back with the radios and covers the rear. They decided that they needed a medic to go along, in case anything happened, and they asked for volunteers. No one volunteered, so the CO says everybody will get a Bronze Star for going, so Smythe says he'll go because he wants to get a medal and he figured that this might be his only chance to get one."

"Little did he know!" Bandy said.

Rich said, "No shit! Anyway, Smythe had just got that grease gun the day before and was feeling like John Wayne, and he volunteered and was riding shotgun in the front seat of the truck. They start up the mountain, and the APC is a tracked vehicle, so it's making the curves easy. But that little underpowered and overloaded truck is struggling.

"The guy manning the machine gun on the APC is watching the jungle, and the vehicle don't have no rearview mirror, so it gets too far ahead of the commo truck. The three guys in the truck are getting really nervous by now and really pissed at the APC driver. I mean, they're losing sight of the APC for over a minute at a time, and they can't go any faster. Smythe is sitting there with his finger on the trigger, knowing he's about to be killed by a sniper who lets the APC go by and kills him without having to fear that .50, when they come around a hairpin in first gear with the back tires spinning and a monkey jumps and squeals in the bush."

Pensi had joined the group now, and they were beginning to laugh so hard that Rich was having trouble finishing the story. Finally he said, "Smythe cut loose with that grease gun, holding the trigger down for about fifteen rounds, and blew out both sections of the windshield and some of the canvas roof!"

Now everyone was in stitches, including Dwight. Rich continued, "Then the APC driver panics and drops the ramp, and the whole squad comes pouring out, locked and loaded; they all run down the mountain in the jungle to get to the truck as fast as they can, only to find Smythe and the two commo guys out of the truck and laughing so hard they could barely stand up! And the fucking monkey is *really* excited now and raising hell in a tree about twenty feet away!"

Dwight said, "He didn't hit him?"

"Shit no! He didn't know that you don't wag that gun around when you shoot it, and he didn't see the monkey at first, so he was just spraying the whole area."

Now Rich, Pensi, Bandy, and Dwight were all doubled over in laughter. Bandy was on his knees and fell over on his side, clutching his stomach, which served to redouble the others' mirth and cause everyone else to gather around, wondering what was so funny.

Ariza said, "Rich ees tellin de story about Smythe's Monkey Medal," and the others either joined in the chuckle or nodded their heads with a smile.

Dwight said, "What's the Monkey Medal?"

Rich said, "The next morning, the CO fell everyone out for an awards presentation. He'd had the engineers cut a big star with a wreath around it out of some sheet metal and hang it from a piece of American flag. It looked pretty impressive, really. We all stood at attention while the CO read the commendation about how Specialist Smythe had single-handedly taken VC Mountain and saved the entire battalion from a vicious and notorious VC monkey and that President Johnson had decided to have Smythe receive the medal in the field because the country couldn't spare him for even a day!"

Again, the laughter and remarks died down, and they settled back into their thoughts.

Rich said, "Time to go, Doc."

Dwight looked at his watch. Two hours had passed since the monkey story! It was barely drizzling as they sleepily trooped back up the hill to their tent.

Dwight's heightened state of awareness since the sapper attack made him open his eyes as a lantern's glow approached the squad tent. He glanced at his watch. It was 0400. He was in his sleeping bag, GG on his chest, in his hands.

Before the lantern entered the tent, Dwight could see that Sergeant White was carrying it; he held it at arm's length and high.

"Wake up, men!" he shouted. "Up and at 'em!"

Dwight was up on one elbow. The others were getting in the same position, signaling White that they were awake and ready to hear what he had to say.

"The operation is on!"

White began lighting the lanterns on each of the two tent poles as he spoke. The atmosphere was electric. Lights, lanterns, and movement punctuated the excitement that was spreading throughout the camp like dry brush igniting in a high wind. At once, Dwight felt the emotions of fear, dread, and excitement along with a silent prayer that was more of a thought than a string of words: *God, please don't let me fuck up!*

"We shove off at 0730. The officers are in their briefing right now. They'll brief the NCOs when they're done. Be in position in the staging area and ready to go at 0530. You'll be briefed by the company commander and then me and the LT. Chow is at 0430. Sorry, men, but this is a surprise to everyone but the brass. Apparently they decided to try to surprise Charlie. This is a big one! Both First and Second Battalions are in on it. Trucks to the airport and choppers from there. Full rock and roll, gentlemen. We'll be out a long time. Socks and underwear will be issued in the staging area.

"Doc Johnson, take your aid bag and get over to the aid station before you go to chow. You are to follow Rich's orders until I get back. I don't mean to belittle you, Doc, but this is all strange shit to you." Then he smiled and said, "FNG."

"No questions now. I ain't got no answers yet. Y'all know as much as I do."

See you guys at 0530!"

Lanterns were now lit all over the camp. Jeeps and other small vehicles were already moving. Dwight could hear the unmistakable sound of tanks, APCs, and other armored vehicles leaving the camp through the main gate.

Rich, Pascone, Bandy, and Dwight finished lacing their boots at the same time and stood up.

Rich said, "OK, Doc. I don't like this short notice shit, but we gotta make do. You feel OK?"

"Sure, I feel fine."

The others were standing up and joining them, standing around one of the tent poles, two and three deep. Rich and Bandy were both corporals, and they both were unconsciously taking on the persona and body language of professional soldiers in first-level command positions. There was no bullshit now; it was time for action.

Rich said, "Doc, we'll all try to keep an eye on you, but we got our own infantry shit goin' on. Try to keep up. Right now, I want you to pour two of your boxes of ammo into your ammo pouches. That should be all they can hold. If you have any more room, pour in as much of the third box as you can. Make sure your magazines are full and the gun oiler is topped off and you've got plenty of cleaning patches in the pistol grip. Then get on over to the aid station. When you're done there, get over to chow. We'll have your ruck and shit ready for you when you get back."

Dwight ammoed up and poured the third box, 200 rounds, into his aid bag and jogged to the aid station; his heart was pounding, but his head was clear. He could feel the pulse of the entire brigade. He felt as if he were high above it, looking down at the movement, seeing the coordination—the meshing of the gears as the big, complex war-making machine lurched into motion. The base camp was alive with a single purpose.

There was a fine mist in the air that he could feel on his face and see as blue-red halos around the lights. It was not fog—it was heavier than that—but not quite rain either. The ground was muddy and puddled in places, as it had been most of his short time in country. Unconsciously, he splashed joyfully through the puddles like a child. The atmosphere was palpable with both moisture and excitement.

Dwight slowed to a walk thirty yards from the aid station and wiped his face on his sleeve, GG's strap slapping his neck reassuringly. His aid bag was in his other hand and also hanging from his shoulder. Other medics were appearing in the mist-light of the lantern hanging on the entryway pole. As he walked in, he noticed that the cots and sawhorses had been moved outside to make room for the battalion medic briefing.

Medics were introducing themselves to him from all sides. There were only sixteen of them, but the impression was that it was a whole convention! The medics were talking in twos and threes, but they all noticed that he was walking in; they made a point of introducing themselves to him. He was the only one carrying a weapon.

-CHAPTER SEVEN-

WATER

THE BACKYARD WAS A wondrous place for an eight-year-old boy. The redwood fence that ran along behind all the houses in the neighborhood was easy to climb, and there were farms on the other side on this side of his street. This season, there were onions in the field, succulent and mild. He couldn't bring them home to his mother because she told him that to do so was stealing, but nothing was mentioned when he had onion breath every day that season.

World War II had been an eternity ago, but he was greatly influenced by it nonetheless. Eight years ago, the glory had ended. Daddy was off on another adventure now in a place called Korea. The boy hoped there would be a war for him when he grew up. Daddy was getting to fly almost every day and from an aircraft carrier too! How lucky could you get? Someday he'd be a fighter pilot as well, or maybe a doctor or a cowboy or a pro football player.

Mommy worked in her garden every day, and it was a beautiful thing to see. Corpus Christi's soil was rich, and the weather was good for growing. His mom grew anything she wanted to: banana trees, avocados, roses, geraniums, and all sorts of other fruits and flowers.

Dragonflies hovered and darted, flashing iridescent greens, blues, reds, and yellows as they ate mosquitoes on the fly.

The farmers had honeybees, and they were everywhere, busily doing their jobs and pollinating the plants and crops for the farmers. His mother had explained that they, unlike yellow jackets, were nice bees and did nothing but good things not only for their colonies and friend bees but also for us and the farmers.

The boy was a sponge for information, and it was so delightfully easy for him to acquire. Dad had bought him the *Book of Knowledge* encyclopedia three years ago, and he pored over its pages every day, some days more than others. He wouldn't understand until he was a grown man, but that purchase was the most important one of his life. Not only was it a font of information for him, but it had taught him to read before his friends could. He'd devoured all of the Hardy Boy mysteries before he was seven.

He wondered about bees.

Bees, like the boy, were born and then did what was expected of them. But they didn't have to go to school to learn what they would do when they grew up. They knew right away, and they just went right to doing their jobs. Or did they?

There were different types of bees. Some gathered, some attended the queen and hive, but only one was the queen. Maybe that was part of why they all worked together so well; they all had the same mother.

How much of what they did came to them by what his mom had explained was "instinct," and how much of it were they taught? the boy wondered. Did they watch the other bees and just do what they did? Surely that must be some of it. How much was taught, and how much was instinct?

He wondered how much of what he did and thought about had been taught to him and how much entailed following this thing called instinct that his mother had taught him about and that he'd looked up in the encyclopedia.

The bees worked together so well, and they never got into fights with each other. When his mom took him to the farmer's house to see the hives, it was easy to see that the bees loved each other; they touched each other all the time, sometimes just their antennae but sometimes other parts of their bodies too.

The boy searched the encyclopedia for days, learning about ants and other insects—then mammals. He couldn't find any who fought with their own kind in groups. Why did only people do this? His mother told him that it was usually because of money, religion, or land. Didn't bees, or any of the other animals, have money, religion, or land? No. Then why do we? She didn't know.

Daddy was off doing war again, but the boy knew that it was because his dad loved to fly; he didn't really want to kill people. But what about the people who did? How much of it was learned, and how much was instinct? he wondered.

There were some bees at the fountain every day. These bees were slow and lethargic. The boy could tell that they were lonely, even though there were many of them. They didn't touch each other like the bees in the hive did, unless they bumped into each other accidentally. They all seemed to have their minds on something else, and they were alone. They probed the droplets on the fountain and walked around as though they were sad. It was a sad thing for the boy as he watched this.

Many of the bees had tattered wings. One would eventually fall into the water, and the boy would save him. He would take him out and put him on the dry edge of the fountain again. But the bee had become stupid in its lethargy and would walk back to the water; it would act as if it was drinking and then fall in again.

It took him a few days, but the boy finally realized that living things go to water when they are in their final pain of death. The bees were in agony and wanted water. They were trying to redeem their ruined bodies with what they were made mostly of: water.

And then the boy understood that they were ending their agony by drowning themselves. They were ending their lives and suffering with the very thing that life is made mostly of: water.

Why, he asked his mother, did they have to suffer so much after spending their lives working so hard? It wasn't fair. His mother just pushed his head to her chest when he asked her why God was so mean.

Living things are alone and want water in their final agony. Death is lonely and thirsty.

The boy knew the answers weren't in the *Book of Knowledge*. He knew it was subjective. He, like everything else, would have to finally find out for himself. How lonely would it be? How painful would it be? How thirsty? Even for Jesus.

-CHAPTER EIGHT-

BATTLE

THE HEWEYS WERE FULLY loaded and cumbersome, lifting off of the iron PSP staging area at the Bien Hoa Air Base. There were around thirty in Dwight's flight, the first group off, maintaining close formation—the way they would be landing in the LZ.

The staging had gone without a hitch. This wasn't the first time the 173d had done this; they had the procedure down to a science. But it was the first time they had saddled up on such short notice, so particular care had been taken to allow for mistakes or omissions. Apparently there had been none.

The briefing had gone flawlessly. Each company was briefed by its commanding officer, usually a captain and then the first sergeant. They stood on a two-foot-high collapsible platform with a map taped to a three-by-six-foot blackboard. The area would be grasslands, woods, and jungle. They would be landing in high grass, and Charlie Company would double-time into the tree line to their right upon landing. Their initial job was to set up the perimeter and clear the area for the following units and then the light vehicles, light artillery, and supplies. The perimeter would then be maintained by follow-up units, and they would move out. Armor, APCs, and heavy artillery would arrive that evening and the next day by ground.

They would be landing in force into what they hoped was the teeth of a VC division that Intel had said was gathering there to stage an attack on the newly arrived First Infantry Division. The LZs could be hot, meaning that they could receive fire while landing.

They would be moving in a "sweep" operation with the First Battalion moving in a column up the middle. ARVN infantry would be covering the flanks, one brigade on each side. The plan was to hope that the VC brass would reconnoiter the advance and decide to hit the 173d in a flanking motion on each side of the column. It was expected that the ARVN would break and run, leaving the American flanks exposed. Normally, this would be a disaster for the brigade except that, in this case, it was expected and planned for. The column would be fortified on the flanks with mortars, extra machine guns, and recoilless rifles. What the VC wouldn't know was that a full brigade of Korean infantry was waiting in a nearby staging area to be choppered in and close the flanks on the VC from each side. The ROKs were good fighters and hated the smaller Vietnamese. Second Battalion would be in close reserve, prepared to reinforce the middle as the ROKs came in from the sides.

The success of the plan depended on the VC hitting the 173d's column in a flanking motion, thinking that they would be able to achieve victory in a conventional battle because the ARVN would retreat, leaving our flanks exposed. Then we would counterattack from both sides, effectively making two flanking motions, one on each side of our own. If the ARVN didn't run away from the battle, the plan would be ruined. In fact, Dwight thought, the front of the column will be weak because of all the fortification on the sides. A frontal attack could be disastrous because if the ARVN ran away, the front would be weakened as the brigade concentrated on covering the VC's flanking maneuver.

Dwight sat in the middle of the cargo bay of the Hewey, in onc of the seats facing forward. Four troops faced forward, and four faced the rear; gear littered the deck between them. Like the Hewey Dwight had arrived on, there were two door gunners, one on each side, facing out at the rear, and two pilots up front. The pilots had heavily armored seat backs and armor on their outsides. So when an LZ was hot, they would point the tail of the chopper toward the incoming fire.

They were at five thousand feet, above a cloud deck. Green and gray mountains were protruding up through the clouds in the distance, ahead and to their right. The combined engine, rotor, and wind noise was so loud that attempts at communication were impossible. The pilots and gunners communicated via headset intercoms.

GG's sling was over Dwight's left shoulder, the gun on his right side, but in his sitting position, she was in his lap on top of his aid bag, which was slung over his other shoulder.

Fatigue shirts and pant legs flapped violently in the wind. Strangely, the combined din provided what Dwight perceived as silence—a quiet time for random thoughts and feelings to pass through his consciousness. He was gladly surprised that he wasn't afraid. Time was passing in slow motion. His mother's face passed through his mind's eye and then the face of his little sister, Mary Beth, only three years old. Three younger brothers appeared: two in junior high and one in his first year of high school. He saw slow-motion memories of Sunday drives with the family.

He wondered why he didn't think of his girlfriend, Susan Susser. He couldn't even picture her face, probably because, as much as he tried to be, he wasn't in love with her. They had fumbled through sex together, that last week before he left for basic training. They both had learned from each other. She had showed him where she wanted to be touched and how to do it to bring her to orgasm, and he had taught her the same. She was so afraid of pregnancy that they had mostly done this with each other. Also, his penetration had hurt her, even after they'd done it several times. He smiled to himself as he realized that he was going into his first combat nursing a rock-hard erection, and then he realized that the troopers sitting across from him were looking at him smiling. Pascone winked.

These guys can't see my hard-on! No, they're amazed that I'm relaxed and smiling. They so obviously look up to me now, and I don't deserve it. At least I don't remember what I did to deserve it. God, please don't let me let them down.

Dwight noticed that the choppers were tightening up the formation and descending. His Hewey was in the middle rear of the formation. He had never seen so many helicopters at one time. White cloud was now swirling through the cargo bay, and the light dimmed to less than half its prior intensity as they quickly went through the thin cloud layer.

The gunners swung their machine guns forward on their web belts hanging from the roof and pointed at the receivers. Rich held his M16 out at arm's length, chambered a round, and put the safety on: the signal to lock and load. Dwight opened GG's dust cover and, using the black crucifix hanging outside his shirt, chambered a round and closed the dust cover, putting on the safety. Of course, the bolt was not yet hot, but he wanted to be sure to get in the habit. They broke out of the clouds at five hundred feet and dived to treetop level, skimming over the trees at a hundred miles an hour. Dwight tensed in his seat. He felt a twinge in his guts that felt like diarrhea; then it passed. He took a deep breath and let it out slowly, watching the jungle for muzzle flashes.

Suddenly they were over a clearing, all of the Heweys rearing back on their tails; they were bleeding off airspeed as rapidly as possible, straining to come to a low hover before setting down. The grass was at least four feet high but partially flattening down under each chopper from the powerful rotor blasts.

Dwight heard loud *tink-tink-tink-tink* sounds as he realized the Hewey was taking hits. A green tracer round came through the cargo bay. Both door gunners held their triggers down. Shell casings from the left door gunner's M60 poured into the cargo bay floor, rotor wash spinning them in all directions.

Holy shit! The LZ's hotter'n a firecracker! How'd they know we were coming!?

"Go! Go! Go! Go!" the door gunners yelled. They were now jumping off the skids, two feet to the ground. The long elephant grass was lying down from the air pressure of the big rotor blades; the tree line was fifty yards away, soaking up red-orange tracers from the door gunners of thirty Heweys. The amount of the enemy's green tracers had subsided significantly. Gunships— Heweys laden with forward-firing machine guns, rockets, and ammunition—were circling above the tree line, frantically firing at targets both seen and unseen.

Dwight's head cleared. He could see the situation clearly. There was probably a small contingent of enemy troops at every possible LZ in the area. After all, the mobilization had begun in Bien Hoa with the arrival of hundreds of helicopters yesterday. The enemy wasn't stupid.

He was twelve paces behind Rich and to his right twelve paces, so that one machine gun burst or mortar round would have less chance of getting them both. The grass was too thick to run in, but they were doing the best they could. GG's safety was off, and they were both ready. They were thirty yards from the tree line.

Something's wrong!

"Rich, get down ... now!" he screamed as he crouched and turned, spreading his hands out palms down to the men behind him.

"Down! Get *down!*"

Seeing them dive to the ground, he turned back to the tree line and dived, burying his face in the grass.

The tree line erupted with muzzle flashes as pieces of elephant grass snapped off over his head. He heard popping sounds as rounds broke the sound barrier as they passed over. Rich's M16 was on full auto in front of him. He heard the *tonk* of Pensi's

M79 twenty yards behind him as the big round whished over his head and exploded in the tree line, followed by another one not three seconds later.

Damn, Pensi reloads fast!

Dwight saw instantly that it hadn't been a second M79 round but that Rich had thrown a hand grenade and was preparing to toss another. Dwight pulled a grenade from its loop on his ruck strap and, holding the spoon down in the joint of his thumb and rising to his knees, threw it like a center fielder trying to throw a runner out at home, over Rich and into the tree line. Just then, a gunship opened up from above and behind them with both rockets and machine guns. The air was full of metal, all of it now going into the tree line; however, the rocket's explosions sent shrapnel back over their heads as Dwight buried his face in the grass again, and they all tried to get even lower to the ground than before. The gunship held its hover, twenty feet off the ground now and fifty yards behind them, hosing the tree line with its machine guns; its rockets were depleted now. Another gunship joined that one, and more rockets went into the tree line as a machine cannon on the second gunship joined in, its rounds screaming over the platoon and exploding in the trees.

Dwight looked back and to his left and could see the RTO's antenna above the grass, fifty yards back. The LT would be there, talking to the gunships. Dwight could see a man's head and shoulders running toward him; he could see that it was the LT.

Yep, the LT's got a pair of balls, all right. No one else is moving.

Strangely, Dwight could feel that it was relatively safe now. The immediate danger had passed. He stood up and ran toward the tree line, being sure to keep his distance from Rich, to his left.

"Let's go!" he shouted.

Dwight was beside Rich now, to his left twelve paces; Rich was up and running too. They broke out of the grass into the tree line, both holding their triggers down, putting as much lead in front of them as possible. They moved on into the trees and brush about ten feet as their eyes fought to adjust to the diminished light, diving and skidding forward into a prone position, looking and listening now. Quiet. Dwight could hear the squad coming in behind and to the sides. The loudest close-by noises were gasped breath as the troopers arrived; they also assumed a prone position. The sounds of battle were three hundred yards or more to their left side and three times further to the rear, on the other side of the LZ.

Dwight looked over at Rich, who smiled and gave him a thumbs-up sign. He smiled back.

The LT, with the RTO close behind, ran into the tree line, beside Rich; he went to the prone position and yelled, "Holy shit, Rich! I saw you guys get ambushed! Shit! They were laying for you, and there're no casualties! What the fuck!?"

"Doc knew they were there, LT. He yelled to get down just before they opened up!"

"What're you doing taking orders from a fucking FNG medic, Corporal?"

"If you'd seen what he did the other night, you'd obey him too, LT."

The LT looked over at Dwight. What could Dwight do? He shrugged.

What the hell did happen back there? How'd I know? I did, though. I knew! Well, whatever's going on, I'm not going to question it!

The LT stood up and quickly looked around. "First platoon! Spread out and set up the perimeter! White! Check the right flank and be sure the second platoon's over there!" He turned to the left. "Pascone! Check the left flank for the third platoon!"

Dwight rolled over, sat up, and removed GG's strap and then the aid bag. He pulled the magazine out, opened the aid bag, and put a fresh magazine in the weapon.

There are only nine rounds gone from that magazine, but it's best to be fully loaded. Wait a minute. How do I know I fired exactly nine

*rounds? I don't know how, but I know I fired nine rounds! I'd bet odds
on it. This is weird shit.*

A trooper that Dwight didn't recognize ran up to the LT from
his left. "Captain Thompson wants to see all platoon leaders, sir.
The perimeter appears to be secure, but have your men ready
for a counterattack."

The LT told the RTO to stay put and shouted loud enough
for the entire platoon to hear, "Everyone who has fired your
weapon, put in fresh magazines and be sure safeties are on! First
and fourth squads, recon the area one hundred meters into
the woods. There's a clearing up there; see if you can get to it.
Keep separation, and watch for snipers!" He trotted behind the
runner to the Charlie Company CP.

Dwight pulled the wire stock back on GG, pulled the light
magazine back out of the aid bag, and reloaded it using the
wire nipple loader on the extended stock. It took exactly nine
rounds.

*What the hell is going on here? I knew about the ambush just before
they opened up. I knew how many rounds I'd fired. I wasn't scared
because I knew what was going to happen! How in the hell could I have
known these things?*

The third flight of Heweys was arriving at the LZ and
disgorging paratroopers. More gunships were now circling the
area. There was some small-arms fire in the distance, but nothing
was happening nearby.

Dwight focused his attention to the immediate area. His eyes
were fully accustomed to the reduced light now. There were two
animal trails leading into the woods; one crossed directly in front
of Rich, who was also looking around. He was to Dwight's left,
twelve meters away. Dwight was lying in the other trail, which
ran straight into the darkened woods in front of him; the woods
were almost jungle but not quite so.

These were extremely deep woods, forming a solid canopy
above him but with enough space below the branches to allow

him to walk upright on the trail, so it wasn't really jungle. There were so many shades of green here. They were not like the shades of green that Dwight had noticed at the base camp; these were like art. They were like something he'd seen in impressionist paintings—shades blending into each other and yet distinct. Here a bright green, and there a dull but vibrant one. Here a green blending into another almost like shading. In another spot, there'd be a tremendous contrast of juxtaposed greens. By the trails, there was sparse brush supporting groups of bright red berries and red and pink flowers. Dwight watched the two patrols disappear into the brushy darkness thirty meters in front of him and down the trail past Rich.

Dwight could feel that one of the red flowers was dripping nectar on his neck, and he was aware that it ran from his neck down to his chest.

What? That's a lot of nectar—must have something to do with the gun and rocket fire into the plant life.

He rolled to his right and looked up at the flower, just as the next drop landed saltily on his lower lip. He tasted and saw it at the same time! The lower half of an arm and hand was hanging from a branch two feet above his head. The arm was gray-white with the red flower of its separation from its body hanging closest to Dwight's face; two small bones formed the flower's pistil. The next drop was preparing to separate from its source as Dwight moved his head to the side to avoid it, and he reflexively gagged, spitting the blood from his mouth. He then looked over at Rich, hoping that he hadn't noticed this. No such luck.

"Hey FNG-man! I forgot to tell you about what Charlie do when he meet up face-to-face with a gunship! Looks like that gook stuck around just a second too long. Probably another FNG, like you! Look, Doc. There's his head over there, and the rest of his body's over there!"

Dwight kept from vomiting, but it was close. He'd seen his share of carnage at Ft. Polk—the car wrecks and the trooper who'd been decapitated when a horse came through his car's windshield at eighty miles an hour—but he wasn't quite mentally prepared for this scene. The chipped beef on toast and powdered eggs he'd had for breakfast three hours ago had incubated to a texture and taste that made him swear that he'd never eat that again.

As he was wiping the blood off his neck and chest, he heard a loud shot—then another one. They sounded as if they had been only fifty feet away, but Dwight knew that the sound was amplified by the relative quiet. Then he heard the now familiar chatter of M16s on full automatic—then silence.

"Medic up! Medic up!" Dwight heard from the woods.

"Come on, Doc. I'll go with you," Rich said as he got to his feet. Dwight was on his feet, GG in one hand and his aid bag in the other. Rich followed close behind as they ran full speed up the trail. After about fifty yards, they were met by Ariza running toward them, who yelled as he was coming to a stop, "Simpson's hit! Come on, Doc!"

Dwight and Rich ran behind Ariza for another thirty yards. Simpson lay in the trail in a fetal position, blood darkly pooling around him. Three troopers helplessly hovered over him.

"He's gut shot, Doc!" Ariza said.

Dwight dropped the aid bag beside Simpson, slung GG on his back, and knelt beside the wounded paratrooper. His thigh touching Simpson's back, he put his hand on the trooper's upper arm.

"Roll over, Simpson. Let me see!"

"Nooooooo!" Simpson screamed. The agonized shriek was the loudest Dwight had ever heard come from a human being. Dwight doubted that a wounded gorilla could rival its magnitude. Then, after drawing a deep breath to power the next expression of unbelievable pain, Simpson wailed again.

"Straighten him out! Goddamn it, straighten him out!" Dwight shouted over the progressively louder din that had become the essence of the dying man.

"Simpson! Simpson! Let me see, man! Let me see! You've got to let me see, goddamn it!"

Rolling Simpson over on his back and straightening him out was easier than Dwight had thought that it should be. Dwight took a pair of bandage scissors from his top pocket and cut the shirt on a line between the two bullet holes, one on each side of Simpson's belly, two inches below his rib cage. He then saw why Simpson had been so easy to straighten out. Most of the stomach muscle that would have been employed to hold him in his protected position had been torn away. The large-caliber bullet had entered the left front side and then mushroomed and tore flesh, muscle, and intestine across the entire abdomen before exiting the trooper's right side. Two arteries were squirting blood with each pump of Simpson's rapidly beating heart. Dwight put the heels of each of his hands on the sources of the blood as, thankfully, Simpson lost consciousness.

"Is he dead, Doc?" Ariza asked.

"No, he's in more pain than his brain can handle; he'll be back. Here, Ariza. When I lift my hands off these bleeders, you put yours there. Push down hard. Ready? OK, *now!*" Dwight lifted his hands one by one as Ariza took his place from the other side of Simpson's body, pressing down harder than was necessary, Dwight knew, but what the hell? What's he going to hurt? Dwight considered this as he reached into his top left fatigue pocket, pulling out two hemostats. Then he opened the aid bag, removed a handful of four-by-four gauze bandages, stripped them from their sterile wrapping, and, with one swift motion, knocked the hemostats into the blood and dirt between Simpson's legs.

Come on, Dwight! This ain't your first rodeo! Get your shit together, boy!

Dwight wiped the bloody dirt off of the hemostats on his shirt and unclamped one with his right second finger and thumb in the scissorlike handles; he looked up at Ariza and said, "OK, when I say so, lift this hand off." Dwight picked up a stack of bandages, poised them over the wound, and said, "Now."

Ariza lifted his hand; the artery didn't pump immediately but let Dwight have just enough time to jam the four-by-fours into the wound just as Simpson woke up.

"Goddamn it! Hold him down! Hold him down!" The awful scream pierced the air again, sending several birds fluttering away from their homes once again. Dwight was aware of other troopers arriving on the scene, but he was too busy to wonder who they were or why they were there. Four men now had control of Simpson's writhing body.

Dwight put his face down to the wound, focused his eyes on where he knew the bleeder to be, and lifted the bandages off. As the artery pumped a squirt of blood onto his cheek, he grabbed the end of the artery with the hemostat, clamped it, and let the tool hang in the wound.

Over Simpson's screams, Dwight shouted, "OK, Jaime! Let's do it on the other one!" Poising the same bloody stack of bandages over the wound, he said, "Now!"

Again, Ariza lifted his hand, and before the artery could pump, Dwight pressed the bandages hard against it, focused his eyes, and then lifted the bandages. The artery opened and squirted, this time on Dwight's hand as he plunged the hemostat at it and closed the clamp. The artery pumped another dark crimson layer onto Dwight's hand.

"Damn it! I missed it!"

He unclamped, withdrew the tool, and shoved the now soaked bandages down on the wound again. Several drops of Dwight's sweat dripped onto his hand, diluting the blood and showing the white of his first two knuckles. He wiped his eyes on his sleeve.

"Jaime, I want you to take that other stack of bandages and shove them down here when I lift these, OK?"

"OK, Doc. I got it." They made the transfer as Simpson passed out again.

Come on, asshole. You're not gonna get a bunch more chances at this shit! OK, kid. The artery's sucked up into the muscle. You know where it is. Now just take your time and go up there and get it!

"OK, Jaime, I got it." Dwight covered Ariza's hand with his own as Jaime slipped his hand out of the grasp, keeping the pressure on the artery.

Dwight got down closer, focused his eyes, lifted the bandages, and let Simpson's still strong heart send a stream of his life's fluid onto his unblinking face. He pushed the clamp into the hole in the muscle, spread it a little, shoved it in hard this time, and closed the clamp; the ratcheting sound of the locking mechanism was loud next to his ear, his eyes inches from the wound. *Got it!* He released the hemostat, letting it hang from the wound, like the other one.

OK, what else we got here?

Dwight threw away the bottom four or five bandages of the bunch he was holding and, using the remaining ones, began dabbing blood from the wound, checking for venous bleeding. He saw four veins bleeding into the wound. These were slow trickles of blood coming from blood vessels that were coming back to the heart and therefore at low pressure—even lower now that Simpson had lost so much blood. Dwight closed these off using four more hemostats from his left shirt pocket and then snipped open a package of 4.0-gauge silk thread from the aid bag and tied off the veins by running a knot down the shafts of each hemostat.

Dwight then took two morphine syrettes from the aid bag and drained them into Simpson's arm, finishing just as Simpson woke up again, screaming.

Ariza was laughing in Simpson's face, tears rolling down his cheeks. "Simpson! Simpson! You're gonna be OK, man! Doc fixed it, man! You're going to be OK! You got morphine comin', man! Hold on! It's OK, man. You're gonna be OK!"

The morphine mercifully started having its effect as Dwight started an IV in Simpson's right arm while Rich held the bag.

He then hopped to Simpson's other side and started another one. Then he opened his canteen and rinsed the wound off. Simpson was quiet now, watching him from wide and slightly glazed pupils. "Thanks, Doc. I need water. I'm so thirsty."

Ariza opened his canteen, but Dwight held out his hand to stop him and said, "No. No water. His stomach and guts are ripped open. The IVs will hydrate him."

"Please, Doc. I gotta have some water! Please!"

"No, Mike. It'll hurt your body more than help. Also, it'll cause you more pain."

"I don't care! Please, give me some water, someone!"

Dwight had taken Simpson's canteen out of its holder and tossed it out of his reach.

Simpson said, "Damn you, Doc; you're cold, man."

"It's for your own good, Mike. Just hang in there. You don't need water like you think you do."

"Am I gonna make it, Doc?" The morphine was reaching its maximum effect now.

"You're gonna be OK, Mike. You had me a little concerned there for a few minutes, you big pussy." Simpson smiled as Dwight looked up for the first time since he'd knelt down, seemingly hours ago. The LT and half the platoon were looking on. Everyone, including Dwight, was smiling.

Dwight said, "What happened to the sniper?"

The LT said, "There's blood on the trail, so someone hit him, but he got away."

A trooper carrying a collapsed stretcher trotted up to the throng and said, "Dust-off's in the LZ waiting for us." He put the stretcher down beside Simpson, expanded it, and locked each end into place. Dwight stood aside as four troopers lifted Simpson onto it, Rich holding the rapidly running IV bags.

Dwight taped the two hanging hemostats closed so that they wouldn't open accidentally in the jostling to come and followed the stretcher bearers down the trail to the waiting helicopter. He shouted to the dust-off medic that he'd left the hemostats in rather than tie off the arteries in case they needed to be able to find them in surgery. He also instructed the medic to be sure to keep the wound wet.

"I know what I'm doing, man!" the dust-off medic shouted over the helicopter noise.

Smiling at Dwight and Rich, Simpson put his finger in his mouth and shouted, "Airborne!"

Dwight smiled and shouted back, "Fuck you, Mike," and he trotted away as the helicopter lifted off, being sure to close his eyes and mouth and hold on to his helmet.

Larger helicopters were now arriving with equipment and supplies. The machine was in motion.

So this is war, Dwight thought. He noted that when he was working on Simpson he had been almost devoid of emotion. He had felt nothing, either positive or negative; it had been a day at the office. No fear. No dread. But on the other hand, he *had* been challenged, interested, and excited. Looking back at the situation, he had thought of Simpson as more of a machine than a human being—a machine that had to be fixed before it was irrevocably broken. He was just doing a job. While he had been working, there had been no compassion or any other emotion toward Simpson, for that matter. He thought that he would need to talk to Doctor Copeland about this thing also. Was he already becoming jaded and moving toward inhumanity? He and Rich double-timed back to the platoon.

The day had become hot and humid, making each breath a labor. They were moving quickly now, and the extra weight they each carried made the march that much more difficult. The terrain remained the same: relatively flat, broad expanses of high grass punctuated by forest that wasn't quite thick enough to be called jungle. Dwight had seen terrain like this in Florida and Georgia.

They had stopped for a quick meal of C rations an hour ago and had covered around seven miles, Dwight figured. Surely the enemy knew exactly where they had landed, and their brass were obviously allowing the movement of the 173d and the ARVN troops on their flanks to be known. There was air cover in the form of single-engine spotter planes but no gunship helicopters. The 173d troops had been briefed as to what the formation was trying to do, but the ARVN brass and troops had not been. The ARVN officers were working under the assumption that they were responsible for the 173d's flanks.

There had been no enemy contact since the LZ, but they knew they were being watched. They knew that the enemy would choose if, where, and when to fight. It was hoped that the ARVN flanks would present a target too tempting to pass up.

Charlie Company was leading the phalanx with first and second platoons in line abreast and third and fourth platoons behind them. The remainder of the battalion was behind them, forming a column that was essentially two platoons wide, or roughly eighty troops, and four companies, or sixteen platoons (just under a thousand men) deep. Similar columns of ARVN troops were on each side.

It was hoped that the enemy couldn't see that the troops in the middle and rear of the 173d's column weren't carrying back-packs but instead were laden with ammo and weapons. Each of these squads had two M79s rather than the usual one and three M60s rather than two. Each man carried two 100-round belts of machine gun ammo and between four and eight M79 rounds, depending on their usual load capacity to do so.

They had stopped for rest and water, maintaining twelve paces of distance discipline. It was three o'clock, but the sun was high. They were in a broad expanse of grass, about a quarter mile across. Four hundred yards ahead, they would be entering another tree line. There were tree lines on both sides also that joined the trees ahead in a convergence that made a shallow horseshoe, ahead of the advancing columns. The horseshoe looked to be about seven hundred yards across at its widest point.

This is too obvious. They are in those trees, waiting for us. Shit! What the hell am I doing in the very front of this column? Damn, I'm scared. Shit, I'm scared! What the fuck are they doing, walking us into an obvious ambush? We're being sacrificed! The front of this column is going to be sacrificed!

Dwight saw that Rich was looking at him. "Don't look good, does it, Doc?"

"Shit, Rich. If they don't hit us here, they're not going to!"

"No shit! What's your sniffer telling you, Doc?"

"Nothing; I don't like it though, Rich. Looks like we're being led to slaughter."

Dwight looked around at the rest of the platoon and over at first platoon. Maybe it was his imagination, but everyone looked like he felt frightened. The troops either were zipping up their flak vests or had already done so.

Lieutenant Krouse and his radioman trotted up to him. The RTO had doubled the antenna over and hooked the tip to his flak vest to try to conceal his identity as much as possible. Dwight remembered that Cargo had told him that the VC tried to hit the platoon leader, radioman, and medic first.

The LT said, "Whaddya think, Doc?"

"Don't look good, LT, but I don't feel nothin' unusual."

"Well, Doc, you've got a reputation. Like it or not, everyone's got an eye on you. I don't mean to put any undue pressure on you or give you any more responsibility than you should have, but don't hesitate to sing out if you feel there's something I should know. Ya hear?"

"OK, LT. Where you gonna be?"

"Twenty-five paces behind Rich. I have to stay in the middle of the platoon so I can go where I'm most needed when things start happening, but I'll be within sight and earshot. Just be explicit if you do or say anything you want me to know about. Understand?"

"I got it, LT."

Dwight looked at the horseshoe-shaped tree line and felt his intestines contract, as they had before in the helicopter back at the LZ. His mouth was dry again, and he was sweating profusely. He wiped his eyes on his sleeve and looked over at the LT, who was doing the same. They looked at each other for a brief second and then back at the tree line. Word was being shouted up the line to move out; first and second platoons started walking. Dwight saw that the ARVN were dropping back thirty paces on each side and closing the gap between the two units so that the 173d was the point of the spear.

Dwight's pants and shirt were soaked with sweat. His breaths were shallow, and he could feel his heart pounding. There seemed to be more flies and insects buzzing around and landing on him than usual.

Calm down, kid. Don't hyperventilate. Calm down. Calm down.

He took a deep breath and blew it out through clenched teeth and extended lips, trying to establish a sensible rhythm to not just his breathing but his whole being. He felt out of sync with himself. He rotated his head around, trying to loosen and relax his neck muscles.

They were twenty yards from the tree line now. Fifteen. Ten. Five.

Nothing! I don't feel nothing! They're not here. No one's here!

They entered the tree line, hesitated a few seconds for their eyes to adjust to the light, and then kept moving. Dwight could feel the sighs of relief as they pushed on into the woods. He could feel the whole column relax a little. How could the VC have passed up such an opportunity?

They had to bunch up a little to get through the woods, but there was no danger, no large breach of order or separation. They were just a bit disorganized in the woods because the vegetation wouldn't allow them to maintain the formation that they had easily kept while in the open. The good news, of course, was that the trees and brush provided cover that they didn't have in the open. After two hundred yards, they started coming out into what looked to Dwight to be another grassy plain as large, if not larger, than the one they had just left.

Whew! Man, that situation had me going! This is a really big bunch of well-armed troops. The VC aren't stupid; I'll bet nothing happens this whole operation. They'd be fools to hit an operation of this size and caliber. After all, the 173d is the most elite unit in Vietnam, ARVN flanks or not!

Dwight looked to each side. The ARVN had come up to even with Charlie Company again, no doubt as relieved as the Americans. He looked back and saw that all of Charlie Company was out of the woods and advancing into the plain. The pace had picked up. He could feel the tension breaking as the entire column breathed a collective sigh of relief.

Holy shit! They're here! I can feel 'em! Hatred! That's what I feel. I can feel hatred! Their hatred for us! That's what this thing I have is all about—hatred. I can feel it when it reaches a certain pitch, just before they attack!

Dwight turned to his left rear and ran toward Lieutenant Krouse, yelling at the top of his lungs, "LT! They're in the trees back there ... on both sides! They're gonna hit us in the woods on both flanks and in the rear!"

Lieutenant Tom Krouse immediately knew the Doc was right. Instinct told him—not where the enemy was or that they were going to attack but that Dwight knew. The men within hearing distance could feel it also. Everyone had turned toward Dwight with looks of trepidation on their faces. Some with mouths open, others grim, they began looking back to the tree line.

"Dinks in the bush!" the LT yelled into the radio's handset. "They're going to hit the middle of the column on both flanks, in the woods and the rear flanks!"

Dwight was watching the tree line two hundred yards behind him. He felt the men of Charley Company's eyes on him. Everyone within a hundred yards was looking from him to the tree line and back at him again. There was no doubt in his mind.

He looked again at the LT, whose jaw was clenched and thrust forward, toward the tree line.

"We have to attack, LT!" Dwight heard himself shout.

Lieutenant Krouse yelled, "First platoon! Turn around! We're going back!" and then, with only a moment's hesitation, screamed as loud as he could, "Chaaarge!"

The platoon didn't have to be told again. The scent of battle was in the air now. Second platoon's LT was yelling for them to turn also. Eighty men were suddenly of a single mind.

Third and forth platoons, closest to the trees, were stopped and beginning to get the idea also. It reminded Dwight of a football team who had just intercepted a pass, and the team members were, in the blink of an eye, turning from defense to offense, doing whatever was necessary to take advantage of the situation—turning toward the opponent's goal line and blocking for their teammate, who was now turning the tables on the enemy.

The LT and RTO began running to the rear, which was quickly becoming the front. Rich and Bandy materialized beside Dwight. He glanced into their eyes; they knew he was right also. Suddenly, just like before, Dwight's mind cleared. The enemy was going to have to spring their ambush before they were ready. Dwight could feel the tension of the VC commanders. He could hear orders being shouted in Vietnamese! But the shouts were inside his head! Nonetheless, he could hear them. The order to attack was being given. His eyes were riveted on the tree line, especially to either side where he knew the VC was advancing. The woods were full of VC, running toward the ARVN flanks.

"Now," he said aloud. "They're going to hit us right now!" He saw third and fourth platoons fanning out and moving toward the trees. Bravo Company had been alerted, he knew. They had begun to emerge from the tree line, and Dwight could see them beginning to turn back into the woods and to their sides to set up a defensive formation. Lieutenant Krouse was running down the line, shouting orders and positioning troops.

At this moment, the woods exploded. Mortars, light artillery, heavy machine guns, light automatic weapons, and small-arms fire tore through the forest.

Dwight stood in awe. Just two football fields in front of him, the world was coming to an end for many human beings. The spectacle was like nothing he had ever even imagined. The woods were alive with explosions. Tracers, both red and green, laced the woods—streams of them, looking like two-foot-long neon bulbs streaking through the air. They blasted off from their sources as one tracer for every seven muzzle flashes of white light and then ricocheted in all directions as they struck the trees, like rapidly blossoming flowers gone mad; then they vanished as others took their places in bursts of bright red or green fire-flowers.

The explosions of artillery and grenades were white at their centers; these blossomed also but in only a millisecond. They cycled through the light spectrum in a vicious flash from white through blue to deep red, a puff of gray-white smoke echoing their prior existence. Pieces of metal sang in the air, their tones dictated by size and speed.

The gun and ordnance noises were incredibly loud and closely disjointed from their sources because light travels so much faster than sound; Dwight's brain was confused by the resultant lags. Large and small pieces of vegetation and soil sailed and twisted high into the air. A yellowish pall was already filtering the sun, and the first choking wafts of cordite entered his lungs.

Jesus God, please don't make me go in there! I can't do this! I'm not this type of person. I only went airborne to prove something to me and my family. I shouldn't be here. Oh, Jesus, please have someone get hurt out here so I can do my job here! I'm not infantry! I'm a fucking medic! I shouldn't have to go in there! I can't go in there!

Dwight heard a piece of closely screaming metal just as he felt a sharp sting on the outside of his right shoulder, just above the bicep. He realized that he had twisted to that side and gone to his knee, his right hand clutching the pain; blood was already seeping through his shirt and over his fingers.

"Doc! Doc! Doc!" Rich shouted as he ran up to him. "You hit bad, man?"

Dwight pulled down sharply on the three-inch tear in his shirt, ripping it past his bicep. It was a graze, open about an eighth of an inch deep and two inches long. It would need stitches, but the muscle didn't appear to be damaged.

Rich had been joined by Bandy and Ariza. Their eyes were saying the same things: *God, please don't let him be hurt bad!* And Dwight knew that the concern wasn't selfish. They were worried about *him.*

Sergeant White came running to the middle of the platoon. Dwight could barely hear him shouting above the noise, "First and second squads, follow me! Third and forth squads follow Sergeant Miller! Battalion wants us to hit their flanks! Bravo Company's holding their own in the woods! Let's go!

Noticing Dwight, White hesitated. "Doc! You OK?"

"Yeah, Sarge—just a scratch."

"OK! Let's go!

They double-timed toward the battle, their training automatically keeping them in formation; working as a team, they closed on the enemy. Dwight's peripheral vision told him that the ARVN units were already collapsing and they were running from the fight; the ones who had been on their flanks were running away in the direction the column had been heading, and others were following them as they ran out of the woods and away from the battle. Dwight could see movement in the trees; the VC were letting the ARVN run away without coming after them, even though they were easy targets. They wanted the Americans.

With a mid-stride shudder running throughout his entire being, Dwight felt himself change forever. Ghostlike, the paralyzing fear left his body, replaced by terrible, devilish rage. An animal had been born and unleashed, and he could feel his chest heave forward, his jaw clench, and his eyes flash to steel. The scene switched to slow motion, his body moving effortlessly and with the fluidity of a cheetah at full speed, going after the kill. His eyes showed him everything that they knew he should see; he shifted his head as necessary, catlike. Perfect coordination pulsed through his body, his heart keeping rhythm as the physical and mental metamorphosis became who he was.

Oh, God help me, I love it!

Dwight felt his body dodge to the right, then to the right again, and then back to the left. He could hear bullets snapping by as he entered the woods, his eyes adjusting immediately. Sergeant White and the others had gone to a knee. Seeing this, Dwight went down too. He felt GG jerk three times as he held her above his head and pointed forward. A shadow twenty feet ahead staggered backward three times with the impact of the bullets and fell to its back. Now the others in the two squads were firing. Dwight stood up, GG stuttering in his hands, "F-F-F-Fuc … k-k-k-k-king … b-b-b-b-b-bas … t-t-t-tards!"

"Airbooorne!" he screamed as he began running forward, Sergeant White and Rich to his right, Bandy on his left. A quick look to each side showed him both squads charging and firing.

They were thirty yards into the woods now. GG swung to his right, letting off three rounds. Dwight saw the base of a tree fifteen feet away throw an AK-47 rifle five feet in the air as a black pajama–clad figure sprang from a crouch into the air, landing on the back of his head, six feet behind. The figure jerked once as GG put two more rounds in his chest. Sergeant White glanced over at Dwight and then back forward as they saw paratroopers appear to their forward right side, shouting "Airborne!" and charging in line abreast.

Since the beginning of the battle, Dwight had been hearing the overbearing sound of a .50-caliber machine gun—a heavy machine gun that was mounted on armored vehicles and airplanes. Somewhat lighter versions were mounted in the wings

of fighter planes. A .50 is an extremely destructive weapon, as
had been demonstrated to him in basic training. He had seen a
single round knock a fifty-gallon oil drum full of water nearly in
half! Approximately thirty rounds had completely destroyed a
sandbagged bunker. This is an extremely advantageous weapon
for supporting ground troops. Dwight was glad to hear one so
close, as just the psychological value of such an awesome weapon
firing close in on the enemy troops was tremendous.

He figured that the 173d had somehow dropped a light
armored vehicle or an APC into the grassy plain area next to
the battle. How could they have been so mobile to be able to
do that? Wonders never ceased. What an outfit! Modern warfare
was truly amazing.

Dwight was certain that part of the reason for the enemy's
retreat was that .50 bearing down on them. The gun sounded
so close that it had to be here in the woods! *No way,* Dwight
thought. *They couldn't get an armored vehicle of any size or even a
small towed weapon in here!*

Sergeant White motioned the two squads to turn left. Two
platoons of Bravo Company and White's two squads now had
the enemy on the run. Dwight could see that the VC weren't
even trying to set up defensive positions. Here and there, enemy
troops were turning to fire or throw grenades but were being cut
down before they could do any damage, further emboldening
the screaming paratroopers' attack.

Dwight's hair instantly stood on end, and he felt a chill of
dread shoot through his body as he heard the chatter of an AK-
47 only a few feet to his left. How could he have missed a VC
soldier that close? He and GG turned in the direction of the
sound. Somehow he didn't fire, as he realized that Pensi had
slung his M79 on his back and picked up a dead VC's weapon;
the M79 wasn't of much use in these tight woods and may even
be counterproductive, as the rounds would have exploded in the
trees before reaching their intended objectives. But the moment
of consternation had allowed him a better view of the battle as

screaming, angry paratroopers charged past him, firing wildly at the enemy, both seen and unseen.

Dwight heard the .50 barking not ten feet beside him and saw two small trees fall twenty yards ahead as an enemy soldier trying to take cover behind one of them was blown apart—one arm, one shoulder, and part of his chest separating from the rest of his body in a pink mist of blood, muscle, lung, bone, and viscera.

Cargo Sabinski thundered past Dwight, unleashing another five-round burst from the big gun. It appeared to be an aircraft wing mount gun that had been modified by cutting the barrel down to about a foot long. An ammo can had been welded beneath the receiver group, and an eight-inch piece of steel tubing had been welded to the side of the heat disperser covering the barrel, as a front handle. This weapon, with ammo, had to weigh at least a hundred pounds, Dwight thought. Sabinski wore it with a sling over his left shoulder and the gun at his right side, as Dwight wore GG. For additional ammo, he wore a 100-round belt diagonally across each shoulder.

By this time, the battle had become a complete rout; the VC weren't even attempting to put up a fight. Dwight saw that running away from a bunch of pissed-off paratroopers is not a wise maneuver. Some VC were dropping their weapons and other equipment to lighten their load and hasten their retreat. They were being run down by the faster, bigger, better-equipped paratroopers.

"Cease-fire! Cease-fire!" was being shouted through the ranks, first by officers and then by noncoms. "Set up a defensive perimeter! Set up a defensive perimeter!" came next.

Dwight was stopped beside Sabinski; Rich, Pensi, Bandy, Simone, and Ariza were in front of them and to either side.

Sabinski let off another ten rounds from the big .50, and Dwight watched as another tree about twenty-five yards away, this one at least two feet in diameter, was blasted in half three feet above the ground. Majestically, the giant tree began crashing through the forest, limbs from it and the trees it was falling through snapping and popping as they dismembered. A cloud of dust and dirt rose into the newly opened roof of the now sunlit space of forest just ahead of them.

Dwight was riveted to Sabinski's diabolical grin as he took his left hand off the front handle of the .50, took the stub of a cigar out of his teeth, and let out a giant's yell at the destruction: "Airboorne!" Then, with the same hand still holding the cigar, he reached down and slapped Dwight on the back. "Hey, Doc. How ya *do*in'?" His Chicago accent was now very pronounced, especially on the *do* part, which was almost a *th* sound, the tongue nearly too far forward on his upper teeth.

Dwight stood in awe.

Jesus, this guy is big! He even dwarfs that fucking .50! This here's a one-man fucking wrecking crew! Holy shit!

A curl of blue-white smoke was rising from the stubby end of the big gun's barrel, like a cigarette sitting in a breezeless room's ashtray. Cargo Sabinski slowly pivoted the barrel to his face and, exaggeratingly pursing his lips, blew the smoke away. He then looked down at Dwight with his signature giant grin, threw his head back, and laughed the hearty laugh of the victorious.

Dwight heard laughter all around. Every paratrooper in sight was watching this interchange between two of the most observed men in the brigade. Dwight realized that he must look ridiculous, standing there looking up at this giant with his mouth hanging open. What could he do? He laughed too.

To say the mood was jubilant would be an understatement. Dwight had never felt such joy! And, hearing the chorus of "Airborne!" around him and throughout the woods, he could tell that the others felt the same. Even a bird colonel and two majors walking through the ranks were shouting, "Airborne!" with their jaws thrust out, teeth bared, and fists clenched; they punched the air with the hand not holding a weapon and inspected the carnage and their troops who had wrought it,

looking like victorious football coaches on the sidelines after a
big game.

"Medic up!"

Dwight looked for the shout. Thirty feet to his left and rear,
he could see two men bent over a trooper on the ground. Dwight
could hear others now taking up the cry in other areas of the
woods. He realized that there could have been previous pleas,
but the noise had been so loud and continuous that no one
could have heard them.

The man was lying on his back; a panicked look flashed in
his eyes as he struggled to breathe, pink foam coming from his
mouth and choking him. Dwight had slung GG on his back as
he'd trotted up to the man. Five troops stood up from their
positions around the wounded man. Dwight unslung his aid bag
and GG and laid them on the ground; reaching into his top left
pocket and removing a large pair of bandage scissors, he cut the
shirt open from bottom to top in five quick snips.

The man had a bullet hole in each side of his chest. The one
on the left had missed the heart by a good inch and a half; he
had a chance.

*OK, kid. You've been trained for this—classic sucking chest wounds.
Got to get this done before his lungs collapse.*

"OK, guys. Sit him up!"

Instead of acting on his orders, one of the troopers said what
they were all apparently thinking: "Do what?! He ain't going
nowhere, Doc!"

"Do what I tell ya, goddamn it!" Dwight shouted. Two troops
immediately knelt down and lifted the man to a sitting position
as he screamed in pain. A piece of yellow-white bone, a rib,
protruded from the hole in the trooper's right chest wound, as
he coughed pink foam in Dwight's face.

The big scissors swooped through the collar and down the
back of the shirt in five more snips, and the shirt fell away,
exposing the exit wounds.

"You!" Dwight said, pointing the scissors at the trooper across from him, "Hold the palm of your hands over each hole on that side." He moved aside and told the other man to do the same on his side of the patient.

"Just hold your hands on the holes so he can't suck any air in through them! Don't press too hard! He has to breathe!" The two troops let off pressure as the wounded man gasped, the pink foam immediately diminishing as he took a couple of life-sustaining breaths through his mouth instead of through the bullet holes, thanking Dwight with his eyes.

Dwight opened the aid bag, taking out four plastic packages, each about three inches by two inches, and snipped each one open and withdrew their contents, letting them fall to the ground.

"All right … lift this hand," Dwight said as he poised the plastic wrapper from one of the bandages over one of the exit wounds. He placed the wrapper on the hole and then put the bandage over it, letting the two-foot-long tails of the bandage fall.

"OK, put your hand back on it and hold it in place." The man did as he was told. Dwight then did the same with the other exit wound and told the men to lay the wounded trooper back on his back and to be sure the bandages stayed in place. The man screamed and passed out from pain as they did so, and Dwight quickly told his startled and confused helpers that the man hadn't died. He then went through the same process on the two entry wounds.

As he cut the bandage tails off and taped the bandages down, Dwight knew that he wasn't supposed to give the man any morphine. The rationale was that the patient may not fight as hard to keep breathing and would consequently let himself die. The man came to; he was breathing well but in horrible pain and began screaming again as he began shaking violently. Dwight knew the man was going into shock; horror was written in his eyes.

Fuck this! That's a bunch of bullshit! I'm giving him some morphine.

Dwight punctured the little toothpaste-like tube with the wire plunger that went down through the needle, pushed the needle into the trooper's trapezoid, and squeezed the morphine into the muscle.

"Oh, shit." The man said as the morphine began taking effect. "Thanks, Doc." He coughed again, but only a small amount of pink foam sprayed from his mouth. He reached up and wiped his nose and mouth on his sleeve.

As Dwight was writing the dose and time of the morphine injection on a piece of tape he'd put on the man's chest, a trooper ran up with a stretcher. Dwight had decided not to start an IV, in the interest of time. He knew that the sooner he could get him on a dust-off chopper and to the Ninety-third Evac and get his chest open, the better his chances were.

Someone said, "Doc, the other medics are all busy, and we got another one over here! Hurry!"

Dwight put the scissors back in his pocket, picked up his aid bag and GG, and stood up. At least twenty men had been watching, including the bird colonel and two majors. Dwight hurried behind the trooper leading him to another wounded man.

The man was unconscious, and a trickle of blood poured from his upper arm. Dwight cut through the shirt with the big scissors, exposing a bullet wound in the inside of the arm, three inches below his shoulder. He could see that the wound was pumping blood but only slightly.

Why isn't it spurting? If it's pumping, it should be spurting rather than this weak little pump.

Dwight rolled the man over to see if there were any other wounds and to look at the exit wound. It was centered on the back of the arm and slowly pumping also.

What's this all about? Why is he unconscious? This isn't a life-threatening wound.

"Oh, shit!" he said as he saw that the ground around the trooper was saturated with blood. The bullet had severed the brachial artery, the main artery of the arm.

Dwight put his hand where the arm met the chest and pressed hard, outward against the arm. The bleeding stopped. He then motioned to the nearest trooper and told him to take his hand's place with his own. He then opened his aid bag, pulled out a suture set, and tore it open, spilling tools out on the ground.

Come on, kid! You've got to relax! No time for screwing up now! Speed through cool. Speed through cool.

He opened a package of four-by-four gauze, picked up the scalpel handle and the little envelope that held a blade, tore it open, and attached the blade to the handle. He quickly stretched the man's arm out and cut down to where he knew the artery would be, just above the wound, and dabbed the incision with the four-by-fours. He picked up a hemostat from the ground and told the trooper holding the artery closed to let up a little. With the first weak pump of blood, he saw the artery and closed it with the hemostat.

OK, kid! If you can get some fluid in this guy quickly, you can save him. You can't put the IV here; the blood's going in the wrong direction. The brachial vein's going to be too hard to find and probably is collapsed anyway. You've got to do a cutdown on the femoral vein!

Shit! I've only seen photos of that procedure! I don't know how to do it! Damn! What do I do now? I don't have any choice. I've got to do it!

Dwight felt for the man's pulse in his neck. Maybe he'd be able to start an IV there. No, he couldn't feel it. No choice. He cut the man's pant leg near his crotch, dropped the scalpel on the man's groin, and ripped the pants open with his hands. He then cut a wide hole with the bandage scissors, exposing the crotch and upper thigh. He raised the leg up, bent it at the knee, and pushed it to the side, exposing the juncture of thigh and groin as openly as possible; he cut the man's underwear away.

He lay down on the ground on his elbows, his left hand pushing gently against the inner thigh, his face six inches from the man's groin. He carefully made a two-inch incision in the middle of the thigh, two inches below the groin, barely cutting into the muscle.

OK, kid … Here goes. It's going to be blue; look for anything blue.

He sliced in a little deeper and dabbed with the four-by-fours—nothing yet. Again—nothing yet. Again—deeper this time.

Dwight's hands and face were suddenly covered with blood! He couldn't see! He shoved his right hand into the man's groin to stop the flow and dabbed with the four-by-fours. The blood continued to flow. It reminded Dwight of opening the nozzle of a garden hose after turning the spigot off. The blood had come out hard at first, but now there was virtually no pressure!

Oh shit! This is a vein, you dumb shit! The blood's coming back to the heart! Not down from it!

Dwight moved his hand to the other side of the incision and pressed hard. He looked up at the man's gray-white face. He told a trooper to press hard where his hand was and moved up to the man's head and opened an eyelid.

"Nooooo!" he screamed.

He tore open the fatigue shirt and put his head to the man's heart.

Oh fuck! What have I done!? Oh no! No! No! I couldn't have fucked up this bad! No! This can't be happening!

He began CPR, hearing the man's ribs separate as he pushed down sharply with all his might, over and over.

Dwight settled back on his heels; the sounds of battle were distant now, on either side of where they had fought. He noticed the gold band on the man's left third finger. In his mind's eye, he could see a woman holding an infant son, sobbing. Four older men and women were trying to console her, but they were crying too.

As the scene continued in Dwight's head, he reached down and held the man's dog tags in his palm.

Abramowitz

Aaron

RA 18663582

O POS USA-R

JEWISH

Dwight was suspended in time, and he had to turn the clock back somehow. His mind frantically searched for a way he could have another chance at this. He wouldn't screw it up this time!

He threw his head back and screamed again: "Noooo!" There was no way out this time, no one he could put the blame on. There was nothing he could do to change the outcome of his stupidity; he had nowhere to turn. There was no use apologizing. It was over. It was the worst thing that could have happened to him. He had failed at the very thing he was in the army to do. It was his job, his responsibility. If only he had studied harder! If only he'd asked more questions! If only he'd worked harder at Ft. Polk. He should have known he'd eventually have to do a cutdown to the femoral vein over here!

He dropped the dog tags back on the man's chest, put his forehead down on them, and sobbed from deep in his heart, "I'm sorry! I'm sorry! I'm sorry. I'm sorry-y-y-y."

GG, slowly dislodged by the sobs, fell over Dwight's right shoulder onto Abramowitz's chest and shoulder, her barrel resting on the dead paratrooper's pallid throat.

Dwight felt hands on his shoulders as someone gently pulled him to his feet. Through his tears, he saw that it was the colonel he had seen earlier.

"Come on, son. That's enough for today," he said as he began walking Dwight slowly through the woods, his right arm around Dwight's shoulder. He was a good three inches taller than Dwight, maybe six feet two, and thin but in good shape, as all paratroopers must be. His hair was salt-and-pepper gray on the sides. He looked to be about Dwight's father's age, around forty, maybe a few years younger.

Neither the colonel nor the two majors said anything more; Dwight's sobbing quieted, but the tears kept flowing freely as he gasped for even breaths, trying to get control of himself.

He saw other medics working on wounded paratroopers. No one seemed to notice him and his escorting officers. Everyone had jobs to do—or were they avoiding his eye?

He saw Cargo Sabinski, Rich, Bandy, Pensi, and Ariza start back to their units.

As they approached brigade HQ, Dwight saw that five troopers were finishing putting up the brigade commander's personal utility tent—two poles and two distinct rooms but smaller than his squad tent. The protruding sides were made of netting material, to keep bugs out. From thirty feet away, Dwight could see that there were five wooden folding chairs and a field desk in the main area and three chairs and a table in the anteroom area.

The colonel told the two majors to wait there while he entered the tent and began talking to the general, who stood up as the colonel entered. They talked for a few minutes as Dwight and the majors waited.

A staff sergeant had followed them in, a clipboard in his hand. When the colonel and General Baxter had finished talking, he said to the general, "Sir, I've taken the liberty of instructing the company commanders to set up interlocking defensive perimeters. The ROKs are still mopping up. We're trying to get a body count before your meeting."

"Good, Sergeant. I'll be with you shortly; use your own discretion to interrupt me. Ring up Captain Copeland at the First Battalion aid station, and tell him that I need to see him right away."

"Yes, sir. Can I get you some coffee, sir?"

"Yes, please. And ask Private Johnson and the others if they'd like some too."

Dwight asked for black coffee and watched as the general was briefed on what he supposed were the details of the battle while the general's aide sent a runner for the coffee.

Just then, the general called for them to come in, and the sergeant followed with extra chairs.

When they were seated, General Baxter, looking at Dwight, said, "Well, Dwight, I hear you've had another interesting day. Do you remember all of what happened today, son?"

"Yes, sir, I think so. I made a pretty serious mistake resulting in the death of a trooper, sir."

"Yes, you did, but let me recount the day for you, just in case you may have overlooked some of it. You sensed an enemy ambush at the LZ and saved your squad and maybe the whole platoon. Then you saved PFC Simpson's life with cool and expert medic work. Then you sensed an enemy ambush again, this time maybe saving the entire First Battalion. Then, leading the flanking charge into the woods, among other things, you shot a hidden enemy soldier by firing a .45-caliber submachine gun over your head. Then you saved another soldier with a double sucking chest wound. *Then* you made what you call a mistake while trying to save another life.

"And now you, an FNG PFC, are sitting here in the august company of the finest fighting unit in the world's commanding officer and one of its battalion's commanding officers and his XO. In just a few short days, circumstances and an unexplainable psychic ability—whether a gift or a curse is for you to determine—have conspired to put you in a position of undeniable responsibility, a position so far out of the norm that I am literally at a loss as to what to do with you. Are you with me, son?"

"Yes, sir, I think so."

"There's an old story in Roman mythology where a king grants a trusted friend his wish that he can take the king's place for a day, with all its pleasures and privileges. The guy begins his day in a clean white toga with several beautiful maidens peeling grapes for him as he lies on a lounge, the promise of wonderful pleasures in their eyes.

"The man realizes that he's as close to heaven as he can get without dying, until he looks up and sees that there's a big sword hanging high over his chest, held there by a single horse hair. Well, of course he breaks out in a cold sweat, screams in terror, and jumps up. The king walks in the room and asks what the matter is.

"After the man tells him, the king explains to him that this is how his life is lived—that at any minute the consequences of his decisions could get him killed or worse and that there are men, even now, plotting his demise.

"Of course, the friend wants his old life back immediately and carries with him his newfound knowledge that there ain't no free lunch.

"Now how does this apply to me, you ask? Well, you have a lot of responsibility now too. But along with it, you have privileges and respect that no other enlisted man and most officers have."

The coffee arrived via a sweating, running PFC with no helmet and carrying no weapon. The aid—SONTAG on his name tag—took the steaming canteen cups from him and brought them to the three officers and Dwight.

Dwight said, "Thank you, Sergeant."

"It's my pleasure, Doc."

The general continued, "Now, I'm not going to blow any smoke up your skirt, Johnson. You fucked up today—no doubt about it. And you're going to have to live with it, and I can guarantee you that you'll never completely get over it. And no matter what you think about yourself right now and what you intend to do about your training, your decision-making processes, cool, or anything else, as long as you're in this business it'll happen again, over and over. But neither you, I, nor the other troops who depend on you can afford for you to get your dobber down right now.

"You're only nineteen years old, for Christ's sake! Three months of medic school and six months of OJT don't make you an accomplished surgeon. I realize that it doesn't do much good right now, but the fact is that you did the best you could, under the circumstances. Colonel Murcheson watched you work on both men, and everyone watching was amazed by and appreciative of what you did today."

"Yes, sir."

Captain Copeland double-timed up to the tent, took off his helmet, and walked into Sergeant Sontag's anteroom area.

General Baxter said, "Come on in, John. Can I get you some coffee?"

"No, sir, but thanks."

"Sit down, John. How much do you know about Johnson here's day today?"

"Well, sir, Johnson's an FNG. I haven't had much time to be sure he's up on SOP. I take full responsibility for what he did, and I'll be certain that it never happens again."

"Now, don't be so hard on the boy, John. Even you could have screwed that one up, especially under the circumstances."

Captain Copeland looked at Dwight and then at the general. Dwight looked down at his boots.

"I beg your pardon, Colonel, but I would have never given morphine to a man with a sucking chest wound, let alone a double one! That's pretty basic, sir."

"What are you talking about, Copeland?"

"The man died before we could get him in the helicopter, sir. Johnson shouldn't have given him morphine; it won't happen again, sir."

Dwight put his face in his hands, his elbows on his knees.

The colonel said, "I know nothing about that, John. I'm talking about another incident. Colonel Murcheson here watched Johnson try to place an IV in the big vein in a trooper's leg. He accidentally cut the vessel and then tried to block the blood flow from the wrong side of it, and the man bled to death."

"Sorry, General, but I haven't heard about that. All I know is that we got this kid in the aid station with a double sucking chest wound who Johnson had given morphine to, and we couldn't keep him alive because of it. The kid gave up and went to sleep. Quit breathing."

Dwight straightened up, put his head back, and looked up at the top of the tent, quickly wiping tears away with his sleeves.

The general said, "Well, Johnson, looks like you *have* had a bad day, indeed. You relied on your own judgment rather than army SOP on the first trooper and then did the right, and brave, thing on the second but made a mistake.

"Again, there's not much we can do about these things after the fact but learn from them. I doubt very much that there'll be another time that you go against SOP. And I suspect that you'll soon learn how to do the procedure that you tried to do but failed at."

Turning back to the doctor, the general said, "How do you feel about it, John?"

Captain Copeland paused as he looked at Dwight, who looked back down at his boots.

"You're at one of those crossroads, Dwight. You can either let these things get you down or you can choose to learn from them and move on; it's your call. Neither I nor the general, or anyone else for that matter, can help you here. But, as you think about it, try to understand that you're not a god; none of us are. You screwed up, and you're going to continue to screw up. All of us do—no exceptions You've got a lot of pressure on you, kid. You've got the choice to make, right now. No one can make it for you. Do you let it get to you, or do you learn from it and move on? Make the choice right now, Dwight; don't let it fester. What do you think?"

"I don't know, sir."

"Don't give me that shit, Dwight. We need you here. You're one of the most valuable people in this outfit, whether you like it or not. What's it gonna be, Dwight? Are you in, or are you going to mope around and feel sorry for yourself and let these mistakes get your goat?"

"I need to think, Captain."

"Again, we don't have the luxury out here to feel sorry for ourselves, Dwight. We don't have time for it, and neither do you. You have the ball, kid. Are you going to run with it or head for the locker room?"

"I'll manage, sir."

"Bullshit, Dwight! Either make the decision right now to leave it right here or tell me now that you can't. There's too much riding on your decision. You've got big responsibilities now, soldier—real big. All medics have big responsibilities, but you've already got a big reputation for a bunch of extracurricular bullshit in this outfit. A lot of people look up to you—look to you for leadership. I understand that you didn't ask for it to be this way, but that's the way it's turned out.

"Maybe I should send you to Saigon for psychiatric evaluation, but on what grounds would I do that? If you go into a blue funk on us, then I could do that, but you haven't done anything yet for me to think that you've become depressed. On the other hand, I can't send you into action again, knowing that these two incidents may have screwed you up and hindered your effectiveness.

"Or you can make the choice to get through it, but it has to be a conscious decision and you've got to stick to it. It has been my experience, and I'm sure the general will concur with this, that you should get back to work as soon as possible. Get back in the saddle, as they say. This is such a tried-and-true approach that it's proverbial. Get back on the horse that threw you as soon as you can, so you don't have time to think about it and let your fear overwhelm you.

"I don't mean to make light of this, Dwight. A lot has happened. But I have to know now, for the good of all those around you, do you choose to get through this, right now, or do you really need to think about it?"

Damn it. I can't leave my guys now. I have no choice. I can't do anything about the past. It's over. He's right. I have to move on. I've got a job to do, and the guys depend on me. I have no choice. I'll think about it all later.

"I'll get over it, sir."

"You have to get over it right now, Dwight. The general and I have to be able to trust that you will continue on like you have been doing. We have to make a judgment call here, and if we're wrong, it'll be a big mistake on our parts. Has this fucked you up, or are you going to learn from it and move on?"

"I'm going to learn from it and move on, sir."

"All right, Dwight. What do you think, General?"

"I think I want to know more about these psychic phenomena that've been going on, Johnson. Things have been happening so fast that no one has had a chance to talk to you about it, and more of it happened today. MACV's pretty curious about it too. I'm getting pressure from General Westmoreland's staff and MACV to brief them on you, and as soon as they learn what you did today, I'm going to have to have some answers for them. I've got business to attend to right now, Dwight, but I want to talk to you in detail. Go get that wound dressed, and be back here in forty-five minutes."

The general stood up, ending the conversation. The others stood, saluted, and walked outside. Dwight said to Captain Copeland, "John, can I talk to you for a minute?"

As they started walking, Dwight noticed that the air was cooler now and the shadows were getting long. The noise of combat was gone, replaced with the no-less-urgent sounds of preparing a defensive perimeter for the night and setting up camp. Shelter halves were being joined to make rows of olive drab pup tents, organized by platoons, and signs were already in place denoting platoons, companies, and battalions.

"I don't know what to say, John. I don't have any understanding of this thing. I just react to it. What do I tell him?"

"I don't know what to tell you, Dwight. Just answer his questions the best you can, I guess."

After a brief pause, the captain continued, "What's this about more happening today?"

"Well, let me think back a minute. I knew the VC were going to hit us when they did—I mean just before they did. And I knew their plan to let half of us get through the woods so they could cut us in two."

"How in the hell could you have known that, Dwight?"

"Got me, John; I just knew it, that's all."

"Then what happened?"

"I yelled out to the LT and then ran up to him and told him and then he kinda knew it too and passed it on to Brigade, and then I told him that we had to attack; he ran to the tree line to form up a counterattack while me and the squad kinda led the attack. It all happened in just a few seconds."

"Why would the platoon leader believe you, trust your judgment?"

"I don't know, maybe because of what's happened before."

"He just unquestioningly acted on your orders?"

"I guess. But I didn't really give any orders. I just told him what was going to happen. And then, when he didn't order an attack right away, I suggested to him that he do so."

"Well, this is some really strange shit, Dwight. Some guy in the aid station was spreading it around that you can dodge bullets and that you shot a VC, holding that gun above your head and not even being able to see the poor bastard—that you put three rounds square in his chest!"

They were approaching the aid station. A large tent had been erected, and there were several litters on sawhorses, wounded men on three of them. There were at least five large trunks full of medical supplies open on the ground, and the medics were finishing up superficial wounds and dispensing pain medication and antibiotics. The more seriously wounded and dead were either at the LZ awaiting dust-off or were already at the Ninety-third Evac Hospital.

Dwight replied, "Come to think of it, yeah; that did happen. I don't have any explanations, John; it's all as strange to me as it is to you."

"All right, Dwight; let's get that wound sewn up and get you going. You're scheduled to be center stage in less than an hour."

Ten minutes later, Dwight left the aid station and started walking in the direction he'd been told his company was. It had become nearly dark, and he became aware of why as it started raining heavily. He broke into a slow gallop, looking for signs. He stopped at what he figured was Bravo Company. Yes, he was at Bravo. Charlie Company was fifty feet that way, he was told, just outside the tree line.

The headquarters tent was up, and he ran inside.

Shouting over the rain pounding on the tent, Smitty said, "Hey, Doc, we heard you were at Brigade and have to get back there to hobnob with the general. Give me your shelter half. We had an extra one, and you're paired up with Richardson. They choppered in some sleeping bags, so it's not gonna be too bad tonight. Rich has extra C rats for you. See if you can grab a bite before you go. It's going to be really dark when you get back, so make sure you've got a flashlight. The LT told us to tell you to meet him here in twenty minutes; he's going with you to Brigade."

He put his hand on Dwight's shoulder, turning him toward the side of the tent and bending down so they could see under the tent flap; he pointed with his arm extended and said, "It's that one over there, next to that big tree. Drop the rest of your gear, and rest a few minutes. Keep an eye out for when the

LT gets here and then get back here. Welcome home!" He laughed.

"Thanks a lot!" Dwight laughed back.

Dwight took off his rucksack, unrolled his poncho, and put it over his head; he then picked up the ruck, put his helmet back on, and ran to the pup tent.

He lifted the flap and saw Rich reclined on a sleeping bag on the left side, his feet toward the front; braced up on one elbow, he was looking at him.

"Hey, Doc! Hear you been teaching General Baxter how to go about this shit, man!"

"Fuck you, Rich."

"Get your ass in here, and don't slam the door!" Rich said as he started opening a can for Dwight.

Dwight threw his helmet and GG on Rich's legs.

"Ouch!"

He took off the poncho, spread it out in his area, opened the sleeping bag on top of the poncho, and climbed into the tent. Kneeling, he then turned and buttoned the tent flaps together, took off his flak vest, and lay down on the sleeping bag, using the vest for a pillow.

"I don't know how long the trench is going to hold, Doc, but so far so good," Rich said, handing the can of beef stew and a plastic spoon to Dwight.

He was referring to the shallow trench that he'd scooped out with his entrenching tool around the tent for the water to run off in, rather than running into the tent. He had chosen a good spot under a tree. The rain came straight down from the tree, rather than hard from higher and slanting with the wind.

He lay on his back, his head raised on his flak vest, noticing that there was just enough light to see that the shelter halves were holding up well; he put two spoonfuls of beef stew in his mouth, barely chewing before he swallowed.

He had been through this twice before, both times in basic training. The tent would get soaked and water would eventually come through, but there would be no dripping. Water would run down the poles and down the canvas sides, but it would not drip—not great, but a hell of a lot better than being outside.

He looked at his watch: at least ten more minutes. He decided to wait for five minutes before he started watching for the LT going into the HQ tent.

The rain got heavier. He moved his poncho away from the tent pole nearest his head to stop the water from pooling on it.

"What're you going to tell 'em, Doc?"

"I don't know, Rich. I truly don't know what to say. I mean, how can I talk about something that I don't know about?"

"Just do the Abe Lincoln thing, Doc: honesty policy, my brotha." He smiled and rolled onto his back.

"Old Abe had some serious head problems too. He dealt with 'em with alcohol and drugs. You know about when they woke him up after he'd been on a ten-day binge and informed him about what he'd done while he was drunk; he stood up in amazement and said, 'I freed *who?*'"

"Oh, come on, Rich. I don't have time for that shit, man. What am I going to say?"

"Like I said, Doc; just tell 'em the truth. Wait for them to ask the questions, and then just answer them."

Rich rolled over to his side again, his head on his palm. "I'll be the general." In a pseudo-deep voice, Rich said, "Well, Private Johnson, you've had a great army career, so far. You've saved my ass; tried to give your life for mine; saved your squad's asses; killed a sapper after first dodging his bullets; been put in for the Medal of Honor; sensed an ambush in the LZ, saving your platoon's asses; got a Purple Heart; turned a badass ambush that could have been a victory for the VC into a rousing victory for the entire mothafuckin' brigade; and shot a VC out from behind a bush at twenty paces by holding your weapon up over your head. All this in just four days! Now what do you have to say for yourself, boy?"

Dwight sat up and pivoted around to the front of the tent, unbuttoned the top two buttons of the flap, and looked out toward the HQ tent.

"You're a lot a help, buddy."

"No, I'm serious, man. They'll lead the conversation, so just answer the fuckin' questions. You a hero, man! If you pull down your pants and shit on his desk, he'll probably bless it and have his aide-de-camp send some to President Johnson and the rest of it to his classmates at West-mothafuckin'-Point, man!"

"I don't know, Rich. I'm real nervous about it, man. I don't trust officers."

"Don't nobody trust officers, man; even officers don't trust officers. It's all politics up there in that rarefied air, Doc. So be careful, but don't worry about it. Just be short and to the point. Don't say nothin' you don't have to. Shit, man … maybe putting everything out on the table will help you to sort it out. That's why women talk so much, man; it helps 'em to sort things out."

Dwight said, "Here's the LT. I gotta go. See you later."

"Watch yourself around *him* too. He's OK for an officer, but he can be a sneaky little fucker too." Rich sat up, helped unbutton the tent flap, and handed Dwight GG and his flak vest.

Dwight put on the vest and then shook off the poncho and put it on; he took GG from Rich, put on his helmet, and stood up outside. It was raining hard—hard enough to already be washing the mud off of the poncho, he noticed as he trotted to the HQ tent.

Lieutenant Krouse had seen him coming and walked outside as he was arriving.

"How's the arm, Doc?"

"Sore but no big deal." Actually, it hurt like hell. The APCs helped but not much. He resisted rotating his arm to limber it up.

They started walking down the trail, which was now well defined. One company of both First and Second Battalion was camped in the woods. The rest of both battalions were in the open grass on either side and at the edges of the woods.

You know what this meeting is all about, Johnson?"

"Yes, sir; they want to know how it is that I sometimes know what's going to happen."

"How *do* you know, Johnson?"

"I don't know, LT."

"Come on, Johnson; at least tell me what you're going to say in there."

"I truly don't know, sir. I don't understand it, and I don't know what I'm going to say to them."

They passed the First Battalion HQ tent and were approaching the aid station. The rain was letting up a little. Their flashlight's red lenses offered just enough illumination to allow them to see the trail and the outlines of tents in the trees.

"I'll tell you, Johnson, when you came running back to me yelling that we were going to be attacked, I knew it too. It was like you passed the feeling on to me, or something. There was no doubt in my military mind."

"Yeah, I noticed that you didn't hesitate a second. That was a good thing too. We didn't have much time."

The LT stopped and turned to Dwight, shining the red light in his face. The rain pounded on Dwight's helmet. He hugged GG under the poncho, unconsciously fingering the safety/dust cover.

"Look, Johnson. I don't want you to lie, but I don't want these officers thinking that you were giving me orders. You understand what I'm talking about?"

"I think so, sir."

The LT turned back to the trail and began walking. When Dwight was even with him again, the LT said, "It won't look good for me, Johnson. This is my career. I want you to understand that."

"Well, sir, I intend to tell the truth. I don't think I was giving you orders, but the urgency of the situation dictated that I pass my knowledge on to you as quickly as possible."

"I know that, Johnson, and you know that, but I just want to be sure that *they* know that."

"Right, sir."

"You know, it wouldn't hurt any if you were to give me a little credit, Doc. I mean, I *did* take control of the situation and get the counterattack going. Maybe you could say something about that."

The tent sides were rolled down and sealed as well as possible, but it was obvious that there was a powerful lantern inside. The tent glowed in the darkness like a Halloween candle in a brown paper bag. A sign hung on a post by the trail, shining pink in the LT's light: HQ, 173D AIRBORNE BRIGADE.

There was a smaller tent to the left of the larger one, and it was lit up the same. Three silhouetted figures were hunched over a desk with a lantern on it.

The LT walked up to the large tent and opened the flap, and they both went inside.

-CHAPTER NINE-

DECISIONS

THERE WERE THE TWO battalion commanders, both full colonels, and their aides, both majors. Sergeant Sontag, General Baxter's assistant, was there, as was a sergeant major that Dwight had not seen before and Colonel MacMullin, General Baxter's aide-de-camp.

Lieutenant Krouse was introducing himself to the second battalion CO and Dwight was removing his poncho when the tent flap opened and three men walked in.

General Baxter, smiling as he arrived, beamed when he saw Dwight and, not even glancing at the other men, walked over to him with his hand extended. "Hi, Dwight. How's that arm feel?"

Dwight, unable to hide his embarrassment, felt his face and neck flush with color. "Fine, sir. Thanks for asking."

"Well, you're the last person in this outfit that I want anything to happen to. Have you ever considered the advantages of becoming a cook or"—the room's attention was on them, and everyone was laughing—"maybe a jeep driver?"

Dwight couldn't think of anything to say, so he just smiled. The general had his arm around him now, being careful not to touch his shoulder; the bandage was clearly visible because the sleeve was torn from the shoulder to the elbow, his PFC stripe hanging at an angle. Behaving more personally than he had at their prior meeting where he had been all business, the general was now obviously making a show of his affection for the young private.

"Gentlemen, I want to introduce you to the brigade's newest FNG medic, Sergeant Dwight Johnson."

Dwight's first response was to be embarrassed for the general. Such a memory lapse would normally be made only by a senile old man, and Dwight sincerely hoped that the general wasn't senile. Or maybe he hadn't heard right? They were all laughing and clapping. As realization began dawning on him, his mouth slowly opened and closed and then opened again, like a large fish's, soundless and unmoving except to breathe.

Dwight looked down at his PFC stripe and then looked away, but it was too late; they had seen his befuddled gestures and were laughing in earnest now.

The general slapped him on his good shoulder, "Don't tell me no one bothered to tell you that you'd been promoted to corporal, earlier. When was that, Munoz?" He was looking toward the sergeant major, who looked mock-quizzically at his clipboard.

"Sixteen hundred hours, sir."

Dwight's mouth began moving, but still no sound escaped; he was literally dumbstruck. This sight punctuated the mirth as the volume and intensity of the laughter went up another ten notches.

"Oh, yes ... my, how time flies!"

There was even more laughter now. General Baxter was himself now laughing so hard that he began coughing and had to put down his clipboard to cover his mouth and wipe the tears from his eyes; this had a multiplying effect on the other men, who then laughed all the harder also.

"Oh, and Munoz ..."

"Yes, sir?"

"When did you receive orders for Corporal Johnson to be promoted to buck sergeant?"

The sergeant major looked at the clipboard again, performed some calculations on his fingers, and said, "Sixteen oh five hours, sir."

This caused even more laughter as Dwight's blush deepened another shade.

"All new NCOs have some rough edges to be taken care of, Johnson, but you should have learned in parachute school that United States Army Airborne NCOs don't go around wearing bloody, torn-up fatigue shirts."

Then, looking at Sergeant Sontag, he said, "Sergeant, are you prepared to assist this young man in proper NCO etiquette and attire?"

"Yes, sir!"

Sontag picked up a fatigue shirt that had been lying folded on the table in front of him. He held it by the shoulder seams as it unfolded; Dwight's name, airborne wings, and new sergeant stripes and unit patch had been sewn on it.

General Baxter took it from him and handed it to Dwight, extending his hand. "Congratulations, Sergeant Johnson."

"Thank you, sir." Dwight took the shirt, rolled it up, and put it under his arm.

The general said, "Put it on, Sarge. We can't have you running around looking like a private!"

There was more laughter as Dwight took off his flak vest, put GG on the table, and changed shirts.

He was thinking clearer now and was beginning to see the reasoning that had brought this promotion about.

As if reading his mind, the general said, "You've given us no choice, Sergeant Johnson. We can't have a PFC running around giving orders, don't you see."

Dwight glanced at Lieutenant Krouse, who looked away as the general watched.

"Seriously, Sergeant Johnson." The general paused. "I accelerated this process for several reasons. Colonel MacMullin and I determined that we shouldn't wait until something else happened in the field to do this. For now, you will stay where you are and perform the duties of a field medic, but officially you will be my charge, attached to headquarters here with Sergeants Sontag and Munoz. You will, for the time being, remain under the direct command of Lieutenant Krouse and Colonel MacMullin, just as before.

"The United Stated Army's structure does not make accommodations for what is going on here. You obviously have a gift or a curse; whichever it is, we cannot ignore it. You are rather obviously able to see or understand things that none of the rest of us can, and you have shown the kind of courage and willingness to rise to the occasions put before you that American fighting men have, throughout history, become known for. So, while we can't give you free rein, we have no choice but to recognize your attributes and use them as best we can. To put it succinctly, we realize your value and your abilities, but the structure of the military impedes our ability to make special exceptions in rank, responsibility, and command structure. Do you follow me, Sergeant?"

"Yes, sir."

"Does anyone have any questions?"

Lieutenant Krouse said, "Exactly what authority will Johnson have, sir?"

"Well, Lieutenant, he is now an NCO, so he has the authority to make command decisions in the field and issue orders accordingly, not that he wasn't doing this before."

His rapt audience twittered, and it was obvious by their smiles and body language that they approved of these decisions.

The general continued, "But now he has the official capacity to do so. He is still under your direct command, but I strongly advise that you do as I heard that you did today: take what he has to say seriously, and understand that he isn't your average FNG grunt. Sergeant Johnson is henceforth an adviser to me, and that means that he is to you also. Are we in accord here, Lieutenant?"

"Yes, sir."

"And by the way, Krouse, what you did today did not go unnoticed. You exhibited not only courage and good command characteristics but good judgment in seeing Johnson's reasoning and insight and behaving accordingly. Organizing the defense and then leading the attack showed me good decision-making ability, leadership, and courage."

"Thank you, sir."

Reaching into his pocket, the general said, "And in accordance with these observations, Colonel MacMullin and I agree that you should wear these bars."

He opened a small blue jewelry box. The two silver bars of captain's insignia glistened in the bright light, against a blue felt background.

"As most of you know, Captain Bertonelly was wounded today, and although he'll be OK, he'll be going home. His leg is broken.

"Captain Krouse, you are herewith promoted to the position of company commander and the attendant rank of captain. You will maintain the position of platoon leader until your replacement arrives."

Now it was Lieutenant Krouse's turn to be speechless. His mouth hung open, just as Dwight's had. There was laughter and applause again as the general pinned the bars on Krouse's collar over his second lieutenant's patch and shook his hand.

"Thank you, sir."

Dwight was surprised that Krouse's eyes were glistening as he reached for Dwight's hand and even more surprised when they instinctively embraced, right hands still clasped.

Now the others cheered and clapped louder, approval in their eyes. Krouse and Johnson were by far the two youngest men in the room.

The men then congratulated the new captain and sergeant with enthusiastic handshakes and backslapping. As the momentum of the moment began to subside, the general said,

"Also, I have recommended both of you to receive the Silver Star for the valor you exhibited today."

Looking at his clipboard, he said, "Johnson, you can tell Corporals Bandy and Richardson and PFCs Simpson, Pascone, Ariza, Rove, Martinez, O'Donnell, and Cartwright that they will be getting Bronze Stars with 'V' device.

"If you see Cargo Sabinski, tell him he's getting one too; he should be accustomed to it by now."

Then he said, "OK, gentlemen, there's a lot to do yet."

He turned to Dwight and Krouse. "Captain Krouse, you are free to go. Sergeant Johnson, I would appreciate it if you would go to my tent and wait for me. Feel free to lie down on my bunk and rest; you've had a long day. I'll try not to detain you too long; I shouldn't be more than a half hour. The sergeant major will take you there."

"Yes, sir," they both said in unison.

The rain had stopped, the sky was clear, and the moon was full and dappling the forest floor with soft light as the breeze lightly moved the leaves above them.

In Dwight's head, Jerry Lee Lewis sang, "Goodness, gracious, great balls of fire!"

Dwight put out his hand to Krouse. "Captain ..."

Krouse took it and said, "Sergeant ..."

They both laughed as Krouse, not needing the red flashlight now, set off in a jog toward his company, his moon-shadow dancing down the trail beside him.

The sergeant major led Dwight to the general's tent, which was glowing with the diminishing light of a Coleman lantern, which was sitting on a field desk in the center of the room. The tent was sparse, for a general's quarters. There were two chairs in front of the small field desk, and one behind it. The tent had an entryway, but additionally there were two screened sides jutting out from the ten-foot-square main area, which contained the desk. A cot with mosquito netting fit into one, and a two-drawer file cabinet and two footlockers were in the other.

Sergeant Major Munoz, motioning to the cot, told Dwight to make himself comfortable and turned off the lantern.

Dwight's eyes quickly adjusted to the soft moonlight's glow as he listened to the drone of the officers' voices in the nearby HQ tent.

Dwight felt the cot jostle as the general sat down at the foot; he realized that he'd been asleep.

"Sorry, sir. I must have drifted off."

"I'm glad you did, Dwight. If anyone needs it, you do. It's been forty-five minutes since you left, so you've probably had an honest forty winks.

"I want to talk to you about this psychic ability that you apparently have. I want you to be as honest as you can be with me, Dwight. OK?"

"Yes, sir."

"To tell the truth, I have never believed in this sort of thing. I mean, sure, my wife and I have developed a certain mental hookup over the years. We know what the other is thinking sometimes or what the other is going to say, but I've always attributed that to simply knowing each other very well.

"Now, I've thought about this since the night that you apparently saved my life with it. I've talked to several people about it, including Captain Copeland and a psychiatrist at the Ninety-third Evac. No one seems to have much insight into it, either in basic knowledge or in knowledge of your particular situation. I wonder if you can shed some light on it for me, son?"

"I don't know if I can, sir. I can't really explain it. It just kind of happens."

"OK, Dwight, but humor me for a few minutes. I want to get it as straight in my mind as I can.

"Let's go back to the first time it happened. Has anything like this ever happened to you before the night of the sapper attack?"

"No, sir, not that I know of."

"Think hard now, Dwight. Have you ever known that something was going to happen before it actually did?"

"No, sir … never. I've already thought about that, and I can't recall anything like that ever happening before."

"On that night, you don't remember anything about the episode. Have you ever been told that something had happened to you that you didn't remember, before that night?"

"No, sir. That's a pretty serious thing. I would have remembered it."

"Do you ever get headaches or any other pain or symptoms that could even remotely be connected to this?"

"No, sir. I get headaches now and then, especially after I've had too much to drink, but nothing that a couple of APCs can't take care of."

A slight smile flickered across the general's face as he stood up and began to pace, hands clasped behind him as he looked at the ground.

"Have you had any memory lapses since that first incident?"

"No, sir. Not that I know of, sir. No one has said that anything has happened that I wasn't aware of. Everyone's been watching me pretty close, sir. I think I can be pretty sure of that, sir."

"Indeed they have, Dwight; indeed they have.

"When was the first time that you recall knowing that you were able to perceive a coming event like bullets coming at you or the enemy preparing to attack?"

"In the helicopter on the way into the LZ, sir."

"What happened?"

"A tracer round came through the cargo bay, sir. I jerked my head back just before it came through."

"Did you think, *Here comes a bullet?*"

"No, sir. It was like I just knew to get out of the way. I mean, I guess I sort of knew that a bullet was coming, but it didn't come to me in words or reasoning. The same thing happened today when we were charging the tree line; I dodged three times, and I heard a round snap by me each time."

"When was the next time you felt the enemy, after the tracer coming through the helicopter, I mean?"

"When we were approaching the tree line after we got out of the chopper; I knew we were going to be ambushed."

"How did it come to you then?"

"Well, let me think. I felt it first, like when you feel that someone is looking at you, only it was a knowledge … not just a guess. And it wasn't like someone was watching me. It was more like knowing that someone, or a bunch of someones, hated the whole platoon and intended to kill us.

"When the big attack was fixin' to happen, after we'd gotten through the tree line, that's when I understood that *that's* what I was feeling: hatred. I could feel the enemy's hatred for us."

"There's a story going around that you shot a VC today from a kneeling position, raising that gun of yours above your head and firing over a bush that you couldn't have seen him through. Did that really happen?"

"Yes, sir."

"How do you explain that, Dwight?"

"I don't know, sir. It really seemed more like GG knew."

"GG?"

"Yes, sir. That's what I call my gun—GG."

"Do you feel that your weapon is alive, Dwight? That it has a personality?"

"No, sir. I'm not *that* crazy, sir."

The general laughed and said, "You had me going there for a minute, soldier!"

"I can imagine, sir. This whole thing kind of has *me* going, sir.

"No … it's like I react before my brain registers what's going on. It's like I would have known the VC was there in a few more seconds, but this sixth sense, or whatever it is, acts for me before I have a chance to think. So it's like GG has a mind of her own when I'm in danger of being hurt by someone."

"Don't you think that's a bit dangerous, son … letting an instinct fire a weapon?"

"I know it sounds like it would be, sir, but at the time, there's just no question about it. I trust it completely."

"Do you feel infallible, Dwight? Tell me the truth, son. It's important."

"No, sir. But it's kind of like I know that this *instinct* is infallible. When I made those medical mistakes today, that wasn't anything to do with this instinct thing. That was my own flawed thinking. It's like I don't really do any thinking when I feel this thing happening; I just follow it, knowing that it's right."

"Do you think that distance has anything to do with it, like the farther away from something, the less you can perceive the signal?"

"I don't know, sir. I guess I just don't have enough experience with it yet to know about that."

"Do you think that this ability is getting any stronger or maybe any weaker? Has there been any perceptible change in your ability to feel these things?"

"No, sir, but like I said, I don't think that I've had enough experience with it to tell much about it yet."

"I'm going to suggest something, Dwight, but before I do, I want you to know that I understand probably a lot better than you do that there has been way too much responsibility heaped on you for your age and experience. Do you understand what I'm saying?"

"Yes, sir. I think so."

"But there's something that we have to look squarely in the face and deal with, Johnson. You effectively took command of the entire brigade today."

The general paused, not just to let this sink in but to see what Dwight would say.

"Well, sir …" Dwight paused for a minute. "Well, I guess I did, sir. I hadn't really thought about it that way, sir, but I guess that's just about what happened, sir."

"It was natural, Dwight; it just happened. And thank God, or whatever's responsible for your behavior, that it did. The enemy's plan was a good one. I had thought about it and had planned for the possibility of them hitting us when we got to the tree line. It never occurred to me that they would let us through and then try to cut us in half. They've never done anything like that before, but in retrospect it was a good plan. They would have cut our forces in half, achieved the all-important element of surprise, and taken our air support out of the equation by fighting us in the woods.

"Instead, we attacked *them* at their weakest, as they were in thin columns, setting up the ambush. If we hadn't had your knowledge and Captain Krouse hadn't acted on it as fast as he did, we would have been in one hell of a pickle."

"Yes, sir; I guess we would have."

"OK, Johnson. Here's what I want you to think about. As you are aware, it is my job to win battles and lose as few men as I can in doing so. I personally don't agree with the way that this war is being fought—body count rather than real estate being the objective—but I have no say in the matter. At any rate, I have to try to use my personal resources and the resources of my men as efficiently as possible in doing this. Do you follow me?"

"Yes, sir."

"I want you to think about something, and then I want to see you again tomorrow afternoon. I want you to think about how you can best help me to do my mission.

"Now, I know that you have loyalties and feelings for the men in your platoon; I understand that. But I want you to try to put yourself above the woods and look at the whole forest rather than the individual trees, if you get my meaning. The brigade is more important than the individuals in it or its units.

"Also, I'm going to ask that you don't talk to anyone about this; I don't want anyone to influence your thinking, including me. I've thought long and hard about it, and this is the best I can come up with. I want to know *your* thoughts—no one else's.

Do you see what I'm doing here, Johnson, what I'm trying to get across to you?"

"Yes, sir. I think so, sir."

"OK. Go get some sleep, Sergeant. I've talked to Copeland about this. See him after chow in the morning. I'm having a hot breakfast for all the men flown in at dawn. He's been instructed to give you plenty of time to think. You OK with this, son? Is your head clear? Do you feel all right?"

"Yes, sir. I feel fine, sir."

"Tell me the truth, Dwight; a lot is riding on it. It would be perfectly understandable if you're confused, upset, or nervous. Are you certain that you're OK and thinking straight?"

"Yes, sir. I guess I feel just pretty normal, sir."

"Good, Dwight; the only thing I ask is that you be honest with me, OK?"

"Yes, sir."

The general's face flared in the light of a wooden match that he'd struck on the desk as he raised the lantern's globe with his other hand.

"OK, Sarge; I'll see you tomorrow at sixteen hundred. Sleep well."

"Thank you, sir; you too."

Dwight picked up his gear and walked out into the moonlight. He put on his flak vest and helmet, slung GG on his back, took in a deep breath of crisp, dry air, and looked up at the stars as they twinkled down on him. He smiled, twinkling back at the universe, and set off jogging down the soft-moon trail.

Rich awakened as Dwight lifted the tent flap and lifted his upper body on one elbow as Dwight laid his poncho on the ground and unrolled the sleeping bag. "I don't believe what I'm seeing, man! Are those sergeant stripes on your sleeve?"

"Please … be just a little more respectful in the way you address an NCO, Corporal."

"OK. Fuck you, Sergeant!"

"That's more like it, Corporal."

"What the hell is going on, Dwight?"

Dwight recounted the story as he took off his boots and socks, leaving them outside to air out, and, removing his pants and shirt, climbed into the sleeping bag, again using his flak vest for a pillow.

Rich stopped Dwight's narration of the events to say, "I can't believe you sleep with that gun, man. What's the deal with that? It's like a teddy bear or something."

"I don't know, Rich; it's like I don't feel safe without her."

"Have you always been weird, or did this just happen since you got in country?"

Dwight had just got past the part where he was promoted to sergeant and why. He finished with Lieutenant Krouse being promoted and decided not to talk about his meeting with the general.

Rich said, "Oh, that's just great. Now we're gonna get some green-ass FNG lieutenant for a platoon leader who don't know shit from wild honey! Getting an FNG platoon leader is risky business, Doc; you never know what you're gonna get. Every single one of 'em has to start his career as a platoon leader, which means *we* have to train 'em while they're supposedly leading us! What a screwy system.

"If the army had any brains, they'd make 'em a grunt first and *then* make 'em officers, after they learned the craft. And it *is* a craft, man—just like being a plumber. No one would ever even suggest that you send a man to plumber school and then tell him to lead other plumbers while he learns the craft; it's crazy, man. More than that, it's fuckin' dangerous!"

"So what happened then?"

"What do you mean, 'What happened then'?"

"What do you mean, 'What do I mean'? I heard Krouse's voice in the HQ tent two hours ago! Where you been for two hours?"

"I took a nap."

"You took a nap?"

"That's right."

"Where the fuck did you take a nap?"

"On the general's cot."

"You took a nap on the fuckin' general's cot!"

"That's right."

"Does the general cuddle good; did you fellas go all the way?"

"Eat me, man."

"Sounds to me like that's already happened tonight, big fella!"

"The general told me to go and rest on his cot while he finished up the meeting with the battalion commanders."

"Why didn't he tell you to go back to your unit?"

"He wanted to talk to me."

"About what?"

"Oh, you know … this and that."

"Come on, Doc; what 'this and that' is you talking about?"

"Oh, man; he wanted to know how I know when something's going to happen."

"And?"

"I told him I didn't know, that I don't understand it myself."

"And it took you two hours to tell him that?"

"I told you, man. I slept most of the time."

"Bullshit, man; there's something you're not telling me. Why're you holding out on me, man; what is it, man? You can trust me; you know that. Come on; tell me what he said."

"It's really just a bunch of boring shit, man; he had a theory about it and wanted to talk about it, that's all."

"What was his theory?"

"He thinks it has something to do with quantum physics or some shit."

"No shit? Now that sounds interesting; tell me what he had to say."

"I didn't really understand it, man; it's all Greek to me."

"That's OK, man; I want to hear what he had to say. Just do the best you can; what the fuck did he say, man?"

"Shit, man. I don't know; he said that quantum physics really screwed Einstein up because it fucked with his theory of relativity in that quantum physics postulates that subatomic particles can't be observed or predicted because the mere act of observing them causes their actions to change radically and that things are ultimately just random acts and that therefore there is no order to the universe."

"Wait a minute! Wait *a minute!*" Rich sat up, his head pushing the side of the tent so hard that the pressure pulled two of the stakes up on his side.

"You got into a discussion of quantum fucking physics with the general?"

"Well, it wasn't really a discussion; I mean, he did all the talking."

"So, what does quantum physics have to do with you being able to tell when someone's going to try to kill you?"

"Well, the general thinks that Einstein's idea of time travel is a bunch of shit and that's where he went wrong and that he should have stayed out of quantum physics entirely and just quit while he was ahead with relativity."

"What the fuck you talkin' 'bout, man? What's all that bullshit have to do with mental telepathy?"

"Who said it has anything to do with mental telepathy, man?"

"You did, asshole!"

"No I didn't, man! The general just wanted to talk about it!"

Rich jumped him, and they rolled over twice with the impact; the tent wrapped around them, weapons, gear, and sleeping bags going in all directions as they grappled in the mud and grass.

Dwight wrestled as hard as he could, but his laughter made him too weak to gain the upper hand.

Rich soon had him facedown in the mud, sitting on him; Dwight's arm was in a hammerlock behind his back.

"Ouch! Ow! Goddamn it, Rich! You're breaking my fuckin' arm, man! I give! I give!"

"You best talk to me, asshole, or I'm gonna break yo muthafuckin' arm clean off!"

"OK! OK, man! I'll talk! I'll talk! Let go my fuckin' arm, man!"

"You promise, asshole?"

"I promise! I promise! Shit, man! Let go of my arm, man!"

Rich let go and stood up.

"Shit, Rich! You almost broke my arm, man!"

They both realized that men were gathered all around; others were running up. There were several red-lensed flashlights, some focused on Rich and Dwight and others illuminating the way as their owners approached to see what the ruckus was.

Luckily, beyond the drain trench of their tent site, there was mostly grass, so they were both wet but not very muddy.

"What the hell is going on here?!" Sergeant White shouted.

"Just a little wrestling match, Sarge," Dwight said, brushing wet grass off his underwear, body, and legs.

"Were you guys fighting, Rich?"

"No, Sergeant. Doc was thinking he could get the best of me, and I had to demonstrate to him that he couldn't."

Dwight said, "Bullshit, Sarge! I was laughing too hard at his weak-assed efforts to put up any resistance."

White said, "OK, assholes! Get this shit cleaned up, and get some sleep."

Then he shined his light around. "Everyone back in the rack! It's just a couple of idiots with nothing better to do, gettin' a little too familiar with each other! Go on!"

He turned back to Rich and Dwight, who were now standing next to each other, both in boxer shorts. "Anything I need to know about here, boys?"

"No, Sarge," they both said.

Dwight said, "Just goofing around, Sarge."

"OK, back in bed, you dopes. And no more of this shit; we all need to sleep. OK?"

"Sure, Sarge," they said. "Promise, Sarge."

Wordlessly, they put the tent back up, arranged their gear; toweled off with their fatigue shirts, and got into their sleeping bags.

Rich said, "Well?"

"Well, what?"

"Motherfucker, you don't think I'll fuck you up, you be wrong!"

"OK! OK! Take it easy, man."

"Tell me what happened, man."

"I can't."

"Whaddya mean, you can't?"

"The general told me to go lie on his cot while he finished up the meeting with the two colonels, and then he woke me up and told me that he wanted to talk about this shit that's been going on, but after we were done, he made me promise that I wouldn't tell anyone about what we talked about."

"Wait a minute! What was it that you talked about?"

"I can't tell you!"

"Why not?"

"Onaccounta he don't want no one to influence my decision."

"What decision?"

"Shit, man; I've told you too much already!"

"Bullshit, man! What kinda decision is it; he want to send you to the Pentagon or something?"

"No … nothing like that."

"Well then, what? He want to make you his aide?"

"I can't tell you, man!"

"Bullshit! That's it, ain't it?"

"No, man! I told you; I can't tell you!"

"That's it! You gonna be the general's water boy, huh?"

"No, man. I told you, Rich; I can't tell you."

"OK, man, but I just want you to be sure you think long and hard 'bout leaving us, man. We got a lot a history together in this short time, man; you think about that, and who your friends are, Doc."

Shit, this is exactly what the general was talking about; I've got to think about this with a clear head. But this friendship shit clouds it all up. Damn; now what do I do? How can I be objective in a situation like this? Rich is right; what about my friends? These guys depend on me; what am I going to do if something happens to one of them because I wasn't here to help?

"Rich?"

"Yeah, Doc."

"Don't say nothin' to the other guys; OK?"

"OK, Doc, but you know, we've all gotten kinda used to havin' you 'round, man. It's really going to be hard on all of us if you go away."

"Yeah; I know, man."

"Night, Doc."

"Night, Rich."

-CHAPTER TEN-

NEW BEGINNINGS

BEFORE DAWN, AS THE general had promised, four two-rotor Chinook helicopters full of hot food and cooks to prepare and serve it arrived, two in each clearing on either side of the woods. The morning, like the night before, was clear and crisp. The temperature had not gotten above seventy-five degrees during the night, and, if the humidity stayed low, the day might be a nice one.

There had been no enemy activity. There had been several night ambush patrols sent out at dusk, but there had been no contact. This was a good sign that the enemy was far away, licking its wounds and regrouping after a bitter defeat. Long-range recon patrols had been choppered out at dawn to look for them.

The ARVN troops had been re-formed on the flanks and seemed to show no shame for their rout at the VC's hands. They could be seen strutting around with their little, cut-down M2 carbines, acting victorious, as if they had had something to do with winning the battle.

The paratroopers scarfed down the meal of powdered eggs, ham, toast, SOS, and coffee and were told in their company formations afterward to stand down. The day would be spent resting and recuperating. Replacements for those killed or wounded would be flown in from the reserves held back at the base camp for this purpose.

Dwight reported to the aid station for sick call after chow. His shoulder was extremely sore now, and the slaps on the back in congratulations for his promotion were painful. However, after wincing at the first few, the word got out, and other well-wishers throughout the day were deferential to his wound.

Dwight was sensitive of the possibility of envy and anger for his being promoted to sergeant so quickly and without first wearing corporal's stripes, but he soon saw that his fears were unfounded. It seemed that everyone knew his worth and value to them and the outfit as a whole, and he saw no resentment at his good fortune and popularity.

Captain Copeland told him that he wasn't needed for sick call and to go get some rest, and Dwight could see that there was little to do. It was evident that the brigade was in good spirits and that few men, even if they'd had minor physical problems, wanted to spend any time at the aid station when they could be in the relaxed atmosphere of a stand-down with their buddies, rehashing the excitement of the victorious battle.

Dwight found himself wandering the perimeter, going from machine gun nest to machine gun nest, saying hello to the walking guards between them and trying to think.

He was well known throughout the brigade by now. The troops' names were prominently stenciled on their fatigue shirts, but most of these were partially covered by flak vests, so he had to resort to, "Hey! How're you doing, buddy" or "Fine, and you?" in response to their greetings. This was embarrassing, especially since he had always prided himself in being able to remember names and faces, but what could he do? He would just have to live with it and hope that people wouldn't think him stuck-up or self-centered.

He decided to quit the touring and found a tree near a machine gun nest, in the woods, with low branches that would be easy to climb. A breeze had come up, and the leaves were rustling; the long branches swayed and dappled the soft morning sunlight on the forest floor. He climbed the tree, being sure to have the attention of the guards, both walking and in the gun nest. He didn't want to be mistaken for a sniper.

He climbed about twenty feet up and noticed an ideal bough. A branch, six inches in diameter, went out parallel to the ground twenty feet and thinned to make up four branches, each two inches in diameter, forming a cradle. He could recline on two of the branches while the other two supported his arms and upper shoulders. He crawled out to the swaying bough and reclined as he had imagined: perfect. There were plenty of large leaves all around him, but his view was unobstructed. The big, grassy field where he and much of the battalion were camped stretched out before him. Another tree line was a thousand yards away, and he could see another large, grassy field beyond that. There was a small mountain range five miles further.

His added weight at the end of the sturdy branches made the bough sag and intensified its swinging back and fourth in the fifteen-knot breeze. He couldn't have found a better spot to think.

He tried to let his mind drift aimlessly, but it kept coming back to his men and especially his squad, men he knew he could depend on and who each had special talents and abilities, all of them valuable in a fight, all well trained and battle proven. Leaving these guys would not be easy.

Helicopters and spotter planes droned lazily in the sky, engines throttled back to preserve fuel in their observation missions. He could hear the indiscernible talk and easy laughter of the perimeter guards, the rustling of leaves, and the feel of the swaying of the bough in the wind. All combined to lull Dwight into an easy but aware slumber.

He was on the team bus, on the way home at night after winning their high school district title game; he had never experienced such jubilation. There were New Year's–style party hats, horns, confetti, streamers, and beer. It was 1963, and life was as good as it could get; he had never even imagined such happiness and joy. There were no superstars on the squad; the team had done it together, and they all knew that their talent, but especially their hard work and emphasis on teamwork, had paid off, just as Coach Singletary had convinced them that it would.

Dwight awakened, gently smiling, still relishing the memory in his half-awake state, the dream still partially real. Then it came to him! *That's it! That's it! I have it!*

He looked at his watch: 1400. He'd missed lunch, but he wasn't hungry. He clambered down the tree and set off in a trot for his company area. He had two hours to report to the general, but he was certain that he had the answer. He needed a pencil and paper.

Dwight arrived at Charlie Company HQ out of breath. "Hey, Smitty … Bill!" Without waiting for an answer, he said to the two surprised clerks, "Can I borrow a pad and a pencil?"

Smitty said, "Sure, Doc." Handing him his clipboard and a ballpoint pen, he said, "What's going on?"

"Oh, I just had an idea, and I need to get it down on paper; thanks!"

He turned the door and walked back to his tree a hundred yards away, thought punctuated by his furrowed brow and chewed pencil eraser.

This time, the guards were gathered together, obviously discussing the antics of the passionate FNG medic, who, although greatly appreciated, had become cause for many varied topics of discussion and query.

Dwight climbed back to his bough and began scribbling his thoughts.

He was finished by 1520 hours, and he relaxed in the swaying, rustling bough and tried to play devil's advocate, to blow holes in his ideas. He could find nothing negative of any major importance—little things, sure, but nothing that would derail the basic reasoning. The concept and planning seemed solid.

He thought, *How should I present this?*

Since he was a small child, he had observed his father's masterful command of the people who worked for him and his clients—and his family, come to think about it. Dwight had watched his father in social situations, and he knew that his dad always did things the same, even in dealing with Dwight and his brothers. He listened well and made suggestions that he knew people would accept and then moved on, leading his subjects down the path that he wanted them to go on but making it seem that they were arriving at conclusions together, with mutual reasoning.

He started for brigade headquarters feeling happy and confident. He remembered his dad's voice telling him on several occasions, "Carpe diem, son." Seize the moment.

There were ten or more field-grade officers sitting in wooden folding chairs in a semicircle around the general, who was holding court. As Dwight approached, he could hear laughter as the general joked with them. They were attempting to be at ease, but this is not the natural frame of mind of field-grade officers in the presence of a general officer whose brief word could either make or break their careers.

As Dwight approached, he was smiling and anticipating a stilted greeting. After all, there wasn't a man in the group below the rank of major, and he was violating their territory, so he made sure his entry was where the general could see him coming. His appointment was to be in five minutes, so he figured that the general would graciously welcome him and dismiss the officers.

Dwight froze in his tracks, mouth open in surprise, as the general came briskly to attention and shouted, "Tensh-hut!" A couple of the officers' heels literally came off the ground as they jumped to perfectly erect attention, two clipboards clattering to the ground in front of their surprised owners.

The general said, "We have a Medal of Honor recipient in our midst, gentlemen; the approval from the president came in this morning."

A short, muscular major, appearing to be over forty with graying hair, brought up his right hand in a crisp salute.

"Frank, you know there is no saluting in a combat zone," the general laughed.

"Oh, right; sorry, sir."

"It's OK, Frank; it's not often that we have this happen, is it gentlemen? Sadly, most men who get the medal do so posthumously."

Everyone remained at attention, knowing to do so until the general broke his own position.

Dwight was on the spot. If he said, "As you were, gentlemen," it would sound preposterous, him being an enlisted man and still a teenager and these men being field-grade officers and between the ages of thirty-five and sixty!

It suddenly dawned on Dwight that the general may have planned this encounter to see how he would handle it. He said, "Thank you, gentlemen; I really don't deserve this attention, either the medal or this display of respect. I just did my job, the same as everyone else here does."

The general laughed his big, hearty laugh and stepped up to Dwight, his hand extended in greeting, as the others relaxed and turned toward Dwight, smiles of approval on their faces. Their expressions and body language said, *This kid is all right.*

The general said, "You know, Sergeant? I don't know of any Medal of Honor winner who has not said the same thing, and I know that you honestly believe it, but it ain't necessarily so. If it were, everyone would have one."

More composed now, Dwight said, "Thank you, sir."

Dwight dreaded what he knew was now coming. Every one of these officers was going to shake his hand and slap him right on his sore and tender shoulder. He was more than surprised to find that, although they all exuberantly shook his hand, none of them touched his sore shoulder. This indicated to him that the general had told them what was going to happen. Most importantly, he could see that he had passed this examination; he had been accepted into an elite club of combat commanders.

He humbly basked in their appreciation and admiration, as each officer shook his hand and made brief comments: "We're all proud of you, son." "What's it feel like to be a bone fide hero, Sergeant?" "Take care of that arm, Sergeant; we need you to stay healthy." "Thanks, son; we all appreciate what you've done for the brigade and your country." "Anything I can do for you, Sergeant, you let me know, ya hear?"

As the officers departed in twos and threes, the general led Dwight to his tent, his hand on his good shoulder. A group of troops materialized and began folding chairs, picking up paper cups and ashtrays, and generally policing the area. Sergeant Major Munoz followed the general and Dwight into the tent.

They sat down around the general's desk, the general behind it and Dwight and Munoz at each front corner, forming the points of a triangle.

The day had turned out to be warm—ninety degrees or so—but not hot. A dry breeze cooled them gently as an orderly asked if they wanted anything to drink. The general asked for iced tea, and Dwight and Munoz followed suit.

The general said, "Well, Sergeant, were you able to come up with any ideas?"

"As you suggested, sir, I've thought about how I can best serve the brigade. Knowing what I do about its objectives and my abilities, I think I just may have a pretty good idea how you can best use me, sir."

The general and Sergeant Munoz exchanged glances, as the general cleared his throat. "Let's hear it, Dwight."

"Well, sir, I was thinking that you probably want to both test and maximize whatever this telepathy thing is, so I tried to think of how we could do both at the same time. To put myself in the best position to be the most effective, I tried to ask myself exactly what it is that we're trying to harness and use here."

Dwight paused. He couldn't say something like, "Are you with me?" That would sound condescending and put the general on the defensive and probably ruin his presentation. On the other hand, he needed to see if the general was in accord thus far.

The general said, "OK, Dwight. I agree with that. Please continue."

"That's just the problem, sir. We don't have enough experience with *it* yet to know exactly what *it* is. So, it seems to me that we should try to replicate the circumstances as best we can but also put me in a position to be able to react to *it* for the entire brigade—to try to keep the circumstances as much like they are now as we can but be in a position to respond and act for the brigade, rather than just a platoon, company, or battalion.

"We got lucky in the battle, sir; if Lieutenant, or rather, Captain Krouse hadn't been close to me and if he hadn't been close to Bravo Company and their commander hadn't been receptive to what he said, the brigade could easily have not responded to *it* in time and lost a lot of men, maybe even the battle."

Dwight paused again.

The general said, "Agreed; please continue."

"So, I propose that we set up an organizational entity expressly for this purpose so that you, rather than a junior-grade officer, can be directly in the primary analysis and decision-making position, and I can be in a position that is as much like it is now as possible, so that I'm getting and responding to the signals like I've been able to thus far.

"It could happen that, if I were in a relatively safe position— say, with you in the rear—I wouldn't be able to pick up the hatred that I think is the key to this thing. In other words, sir, if it ain't broke, don't fix it."

The general said, "Well now, that's something I hadn't considered; what kind of 'organizational entity' are you suggesting?"

"Maybe we could form a separate platoon, sir—a headquarters platoon, which would report directly to you and be directly under your command. You could then put us anywhere you thought we would be most effective, in both an analytical *and* combat role, connected by radio directly to you. I could remain in circumstances that afford me the ability to still pick up the enemy's emotions, with the people around me that this 'sixth sense' thing that I have is trying to protect."

Smiling, General Baxter said, "You think you're pretty slick, don't you, son?"

"I beg your pardon, sir?"

"I was born in the dark, but it wasn't yesterday, Sergeant. You've figured out a way to stay with your buddies *and* move into this new responsibility, haven't you, Sergeant?"

Dwight couldn't keep the blush from rising from his throat to his ears, blotching his face.

He stammered, "Well, sir, I ..."

The general and Sergeant Munoz both threw their heads back in a hearty laugh.

"You should see your face, Dwight! Ah, I envy you the natural honesty of youth!" He laughed.

"The thing is, it makes perfect sense! I like it! You're OK, kid!" He laughed again.

"And just how do you envision this new and 'separate' platoon of yours operating, big shot?"

Now Dwight had a chance to laugh along with them, as he walked around to the general's side, clipboard in hand. Munoz walked around to the general's other side while Dwight explained how he conceived of the new HQ platoon maneuvering in tandem with other platoons, companies, battalions, the brigade as a whole, and even other divisions, emphasizing teamwork, flexibility, and surprise.

For the next two hours, they discussed, made adjustments, talked strategy, and generally formulated a working plan of TO&E for the new unit. Munoz had to leave twice to change and redirect the general's other appointments and obligations, which had been planned for the remainder of the afternoon.

When they were finally finished, the general stood up, extended his hand to Dwight, and said, "I don't know if this thing is going to work or not, Sergeant, but if it doesn't, it won't be because we haven't given it our best efforts.

"I need to get this entire outfit back into garrison; talk to my superiors and, if they approve of it, to MACV and Westmoreland; and then get this show on the road.

"In the meantime, I want you to talk to the troopers we talked about and make certain that they are up to it. Any who aren't or are concerned for their safety in unorthodox maneuvering can go in peace and won't be thought ill of. Of course, they must be sworn to secrecy.

"You told me that you could trust them, but I want to emphasize that if this gets out before the necessary planning and groundwork have been laid, it could queer the whole deal. Do you understand me, Sergeant?"

"Yes, sir."

"Sergeant Munoz, the plans have changed; we're discontinuing the operation. We've been in this meeting for over three hours, and I've had to cancel or change some important appointments. I'm sure the entire officer corps and the NCOs are already buzzing about it, and that just may be a good thing.

"I want you to go ahead and confirm to them that something is up. Shit, they all know that this thing had to come to a head sooner or later, and plenty of people have seen us in here working on something; we have no choice but to make the best of it. The rumor mill is already lit up, so we may as well make the fire burn in the direction we want it to.

"Tell 'em that the 173d Airborne Brigade has just *started* kicking Charlie's ass! That's all they need to know, for now. That'll put the fire in their bellies!"

Dwight put on his flak vest and helmet, slung GG on his back, shook the general's and Munoz's hands, and started out for his platoon.

He heard music in his head again as Little Richard wailed, "Good golly, Miss Molly! You sure like to ball!"

Dwight was starving, and Rich had stowed three boxes of C rats in the tent for him. He had become adept at using the little P-38 can opener that all GIs learned to use in the field; he could now open a can three times as fast as he could in basic training. It took no more than ten seconds now, and he tore into a can of beef stew, greedily spooning the layer of yellow grease on top into his mouth.

Rich said, "There's talk all over the brigade, Doc. What's going on?"

Dwight answered, "What're you hearing?"

"That you and the general and that sergeant major of his were in a serious meeting for most of the afternoon; then there's a bunch of different stories. No one knows what's rumor and what's fact."

"What are the rumors?"

"Shit, Doc … everything from you being his right-hand man to going to teach at the War College! Come on, man; you got to tell me something!"

"We were discussing the Pythagorean theorem's use in battle tactics."

"You were discussing *what?*"

"You know … the square root of a right triangle equals the sum of the square of the other two sides."

Rich drew his fist back and said in mock fury, "Don't make me take you down again, cowboy!"

Dwight laughed. "OK! OK! The general told me I could tell you about it, but you have to keep it a secret."

"You know you can trust me, Doc."

"Yeah, Rich, I know, but this shit has gotten real serious; if it gets out before the general has the go-ahead, it could screw up the whole deal."

"Ok, Doc; cross my heart. Tell me!"

Sitting under the tree beside their tent, Dwight recounted everything that had happened, starting with the tree. Rich listened without interrupting except for exclamatory remarks like, "No shit!" or "Whoa!" or "In-fucking-credible!"

Everyone knew that Dwight was telling Rich what was up and to respect their privacy. There was electricity in the air, and they knew that something big was happening; it was all they could do to mind their own business until it was time to know what was going on.

As Dwight was finishing the story, Cargo Sabinski came sauntering up between tents, his big machine gun hanging on his side, its belted ammo clattering in its box against his thigh.

"Hey, Doc. How ya *do*in'?" he said with his Chicago accent magnified.

"Great, Cargo! How're *you do*in'? Dwight said, mimicking Cargo's accent.

They all laughed as Dwight said, "Cargo Sabinski, meet Rich Richardson."

Cargo said, "Yeah; I've seen you around, Rich. How're you *do*in'?"

Rich said, "Fine, Cargo. I've seen you around too—you and all the other two-story buildings."

They laughed and Cargo said, "The general sent word to my CO that you needed to talk to me, Doc. What gives?"

"Well, first of all, the general wanted me to tell you that you're getting the Bronze Star for your bravery in the battle."

"Thanks, Doc, but big fucking deal; I already got five of 'em!"

"Yeah, he said that you should be used to it by now."

"What do I get for turning Boomer here loose on that tree and lettin' a little sunlight into the fucking forest?" Cargo said, patting his gun.

They laughed as Dwight noticed that everyone within a hundred yards was watching their interchange. *Time to get to work*, he thought.

Dwight said, "Rich, why don't you gather up the squad, including White, and meet me and Cargo under that tree over there." He pointed in the direction of his tree. "It's the one I told you about. You'll see me and Cargo there."

"OK, Doc; see you in a minute."

Dwight and Cargo began walking to the tree, which was just inside the tree line, a hundred yards to the north, near the perimeter.

Cargo said, "What's going on, Doc?"

"First of all, Cargo, I've got to swear you to secrecy. No matter what your decision, you have to swear not to tell anyone about this until the general says it's OK."

"Don't worry, Doc. I'm all ears; what gives?"

"Let's wait for the other guys before I get specific, but I want to know how much you know about me and what's been going on, before I go any further."

"Well, Doc, you got an even bigger reputation than me in this outfit. Everyone knows that you got some kind of ESP thing goin' on and that because of that, you can dodge bullets—that you saved the general's life, saved your squad twice, and tipped off the brigade on the ambush that ended up us seriously kickin' Charlie's ass yesterday, among other things."

"Yeah, well, that's pretty much it, I guess. The general wants to maximize this talent I have or whatever it is. He wants to put it to work where it will do the most good, and he thought that you might be able to help out with that."

"Shit, Doc; I don't even know what *I'm* thinkin' most the time, much less what the fuckin' enemy's thinking!"

Dwight laughed. "I don't either, Cargo. It's more like I just *feel* something, and I *know* what's fixin' to happen. I think it has something to do with me being able to feel hatred or anger or something."

"Can you feel when our guys are pissed?"

"No; it has to be directed at me, or maybe I should say *us*."

"Shit, Doc! That's a pretty handy thing to have in a fuckin' war! I want to be as close to that shit as I can be; whatever's on your mind, I'm in!"

"Don't be too hasty, Cargo; wait 'til I've told you about it. The shit could get pretty deep."

"Shit, Doc; that's even better! I'm in!"

Dwight laughed as he and Cargo unslung their weapons and sat down in the cool grass under the tree. Like yesterday, the dry breeze was gusty at about fifteen knots, and the evening temperature had descended into the low eighties. The leaves of the tree were as big as saucers, greener and shinier on one side than the other, rustling together like pages in the wind, only a few feet above their heads.

Dwight felt his chest swell with pride and affection as he saw Rich and the others coming through the grassy field, fifty yards away. Bandy was gesturing with one hand, his M16 in the other, as he talked to Rich. Pascone and Pensi were also talking. Simone, T-man, Simpson, Ariza, Nigel, and White were either listening or engaged in private thoughts.

Dwight's only real concern was Sergeant White. How would he respond to Dwight suggesting that he relinquish command of the squad to form the nucleus of Dwight's new platoon? Dwight knew that he would have to be careful and humble, but after all, it wouldn't be the same squad. In fact, it wouldn't be a squad at all; it would be a new platoon with around thirty more men in it. Anyway, once White knew the whole story, he shouldn't be upset. But Dwight knew that to be successful in his presentation, he must be careful, with all of them.

Dwight and Cargo stood up as the others arrived, and Dwight introduced them to Cargo. Some knew Cargo better than others, as the greetings indicated.

Dwight said, "Everyone have a seat; this shouldn't take long."

Dwight stepped a few feet away as the men sat down in the grass under the tree, facing him. Sergeant White waited until the others were seated so that he could be sure to sit at the rear. He wasn't smiling, and there was a definite expression of consternation on his face.

"I'm sure you guys are curious about what's been going on with me and the general and ..." Good-naturedly, the men interrupted with, "Ya think?" "No shit, Sherlock!" "Whatever the fuck gave you that idea, Doc?" and "I didn't notice nothin'; did you guys notice anything?"

"All right, all right; you guys wanna know what's going on or not?" Dwight laughed.

The twittering calmed down, and Dwight said, "The general told me I could tell you guys what he's planning, but you have to promise me that you won't say anything to anybody about it until he says it's OK. So, before I continue, we all have to agree that what I tell you here today is top secret. You all have security clearances, so I just need to know that you understand and swear to that. We can talk among ourselves but to no one else—absolutely no one.

"Now, I know this sounds silly, but I have to read you a statement; each of you has to say that you swear to it, and each of you will be witness to each other's swearing. Does anyone have any questions so far?"

Sergeant White said, "Who put you in charge here, Doc? With all due respect, this is *my* squad, and you're the newest member of it. Why wasn't I told about this before and ordered to hold the squad meeting? It's nothing personal, but I'm not too comfortable being ordered around by an FNG medic!"

Dwight said, "I'm sorry, Sergeant. No one is usurping your authority, and this isn't about the squad; it's much bigger than that. I'm going to explain it to you, and then all of you can decide if you want to be a part of it. Are you OK with that, Sarge?"

"I don't know; let's hear what you've got to say."

Dwight looked down at his clipboard and read the top secret statement that they would have to agree to, stressing that failure to comply could result in courts-martial for treason and that the penalty could be as severe as death.

Dwight then looked at each one of them, calling them by name and rank and asking if they agreed, purposely leaving Sergeant White for last so that he would have adequate time to think about it.

"Sergeant White?"

"I swear."

Dwight told them about the general asking him for suggestions about using his abilities to the best advantage of the brigade and the resultant meeting and the proposed TO&E of the new headquarters platoon.

After he had finished, he asked if there were any questions.

Sergeant White said, "I don't have any problem with any of this, Doc, but I do have one question left out of the TO&E. No matter how special this separate platoon is, it has to conform to army rules and regulations. How can you be heading this thing up being a buck sergeant? Army regs require that a platoon leader be an officer."

"I don't know, Sergeant; there's a lot to be worked out yet. All I can tell you is that the general has decided to use me in a way that he believes will be best for the brigade, and that entails me heading up a specialized platoon.

"Anyone else?" He waited and looked for any concern. Everyone but White seemed to be in accord.

"OK. There are two more things to cover. I haven't been around long enough to be able to do this, so I'm going to ask you guys to come up with a list of men who you'd like to have with you when the shit's in the fan. We're going to need twenty to thirty more men. We won't need this list until after the deal's done, so it'll be a couple of days, but we do need it by the day after tomorrow though, at the latest.

"And lastly, if anyone is uncomfortable with this, we need to know today. This is completely voluntary, and as I told you, there will be quite a bit of additional training, including a HALO school that the LRRPs have had to go through also, so although dangerous, it's an established school here in country, down by Saigon. For you ego-trippers, we'll get Vietnamese Airborne Wings after the HALO training, just like the LRRPs wear. Speak now, gentlemen, or forever hold your peace."

Sergeant White said, "I need to think more about the command structure before I make a decision."

"OK, Sarge, but the general told me that I have to tell him by 1800 who's in and who's not. Whatever you decide, I have to know by 1730."

"OK, Doc. I'll get back to you."

"OK, gentlemen, that's all for now, but I can't overstress that this is top secret information. The general wanted for me to be sure that you all know that divulgence of anything discussed here today can result in court-martial for treason."

Later, when Dwight got to brigade HQ, Sergeant White was waiting there also.

As Dwight and Sergeant White looked at each other in an uncomfortable moment, Sergeant Munoz said, "The general is ready to see you, Sergeant Johnson."

"Thank you, Sergeant."

Dwight walked into the main area of the tent where the general was working at his desk. The general stood up and extended his hand in greeting. "How're you doing, Dwight; how's the arm?"

"Fine, sir."

In a lower voice, so White wouldn't be able to hear what he was saying, the general said, "There's a Sergeant White out there wanting to see me. Munoz tells me it's about the new platoon and that White is your squad leader."

"That's right, sir."

"What's going on, Dwight?"

"He wants to know more about the command structure, sir; he says that a platoon should be commanded by an officer. I think he's uncomfortable with me being so new and inexperienced and being put in charge of the new platoon, sir."

Dwight noticed that the general's face and neck colored as he shouted to Sergeant Munoz to tell Sergeant White to come in.

White walked into the tent and said, "Good afternoon, General. I wanted to talk to you about …"

"Hold on a minute, Sergeant! I wonder if you'd mind very much telling me who you are first."

"Oh! Sorry, General; I thought I heard Sergeant Munoz tell you who I am, sir."

The general said, "I realize that you probably know a lot more about military protocol than I do, Sergeant, but am I correct in believing that there is, oh, kind of a standard operating procedure when an enlisted man presents himself to an officer on official business, especially when that officer happens to be the commanding general of the entire outfit?"

White's face colored and he said, "Oh! Yes, sir, but I noticed that Sergeant Johnson didn't, sir, and I …"

The general was clearly angry now. His face went red as he leaned forward in his chair, the veins in his temples and forehead standing out.

Raising his voice, he said, "*You* are not Sergeant Johnson, soldier!"

"No, sir; I'm sorry, sir, but I …"

Raising his voice another octave, the general said, "Why don't we start by you coming to attention, Sergeant!"

Visibly shaken, Sergeant White came to attention.

His voice now back to a constrained, conversational timbre, the general said, "Now … maybe we can start all over again by you introducing yourself."

Sergeant White relaxed and extended his hand over the desk saying, "I'm Sergeant Barry White, sir, Johnson's squad leader."

The general came up out of his chair, slapping both hands on the top of the desk as he leaned forward in Sergeant White's face with such speed and force that both White and Dwight jumped. Luckily, Dwight's response was imperceptible to the other men, since he was seated, but Sergeant White recoiled back to attention, a string of saliva running down his chin.

Screaming now, the general said, "Did I say 'At ease,' Sergeant?"

"No, sir."

Even louder, the general said, "Then give me a hand salute and state who you are and your reason for being here, Sergeant, just like you were taught in basic training!"

White brought his right hand up in salute and said, "Staff Sergeant White … uh … ah … requests to speak to the general, sir."

The general stood up and stormed around the desk, leaned into the stricken sergeant's face from the side, and shouted, "Who the hell do you think you are, soldier? You know that you don't simply walk into a commanding general's office and strike up a conversation!"

"Sir, I …"

"Shut up, Sergeant!"

The general backed away, composed himself, and, smoothing his fatigue shirt with both hands, slowly walked back to his chair and sat down; he folded his hands on the desk in front of him and cleared his throat.

"Now, you'd better have a very good reason for this breach of military etiquette and protocol, Sergeant; what is it?"

"Sir, I wanted to talk to you about …"

"You wanted to *talk* to *me*?"

"Yes, sir, I …"

"You thought that I would be sitting here with nothing to do, waiting with bated breath to talk to a staff sergeant whom I've never even met, much less requested the honor of his conversation?"

White knew enough to stop talking this time. He looked pitiful, especially with foamy spittle on his chin and being unable to wipe it away as he was still at attention. His only concern now was for his career and his stripes.

"Do you have any idea what the United States Army would be like if NCOs or even field-grade officers could just walk into a general's office when they felt the urge, Sergeant? Are you familiar with the term 'chain of command' and why we have it, Sergeant?"

Again, White kept silent.

The general shouted, "Answer me, goddamn it!"

"Yes, sir, but Sergeant Johnson said that it was top secret, so I didn't know who else I could talk to and …"

"You did not *think*, Sergeant; if you had *thought*, you wouldn't be here right now!"

Turning to Dwight, the general said, "Did you fail to tell this man that you had been put in charge of the new platoon, Sergeant Johnson?"

"No, sir. I told him that you had put me in command of it, sir."

Turning back to White, the general said, "Now, then, am I to understand that you have questions about *my* authority, appropriateness, decorum, or ability to formulate a special platoon with Sergeant Johnson at its head, Sergeant White?"

"No, sir. I just didn't understand how a new buck sergeant could be put in charge of a platoon when …"

"So do you doubt my wisdom or my authority, Sergeant?"

"Neither, sir; I just …"

"It *has* to be one or the other, Sergeant; now which is it?"

"Neither, sir."

"So, would you agree, Sergeant, that it is highly probable that I may possess both the authority and the mental capability to make a decision regarding *my* brigade?"

"Yes, sir."

"I'll ask you again, Sergeant; why are you here?"

"I don't know, sir."

"Well, I've just spent ten minutes of my valuable time entertaining some staff sergeant whom I didn't ask to see so that I could get myself all wound up, only to find out that he doesn't even know why he's here! Turn the door, Sergeant, and if I don't see some improved thought processes by you in the very near future, you will lose those stripes. Am I making myself clear, Sergeant?"

"Yes, sir." White saluted, did an about-face, and left the room.

The general and Dwight's eyes met; then the general leaned back in his chair, locked his fingers behind his head, stretched, rotated his head around to release the tension in his neck muscles, and said, "An unpleasant circumstance, that, but necessary now and again."

He leaned toward Dwight, bracing himself on his elbows, and said, "You are moving into a command position, Dwight; it's being thrust upon you much sooner than you, and many of the officers and men, are ready for. War does that; war is where the rubber meets the road in the military, son. War brings out specifically needed talents and abilities in certain men, and, by the same token, others are soon recognized as not having the basic abilities needed of a commander, or even a private soldier.

"It just so happens that you have assets that your country needs. You have two things that are surely needed of soldiers in wartime. The ESP thing you don't have much to do with, but bravery, coolness under fire, and especially your ability to lead men and command their respect are the most valued attributes needed of military leaders.

"You are under a tremendous amount of pressure, and you're going to be under a lot more. You're going to have to learn fast, especially from your mistakes.

"You should have told Sergeant White, when the issue first came up, that not only had I put you in charge, but that he should tell *you* what his decision was. He instigated a power play with you, and he should have known better."

Dwight decided to not mention that he had in fact told White to get back to *him* regarding his concerns, but he decided against it, for fear of further increasing the general's negative impression White; there had been enough harm done.

The general continued, "But, when something like that happens, it is *your* job to bring him up short, right there and then, in front of the men, so that none of them are ever tempted to pull something like that themselves. It would have solidified your authority while putting the others under notice that you won't tolerate them questioning your authority.

"It is important for you to exhibit to those under you that when you have been given command and authority, you will not be hesitant to use it. If any quarter had been given that man and he'd been emboldened to doubt your authority in combat, it could have been disastrous. Do you understand what I'm trying to get across to you, Dwight?"

"Yes, sir."

"How did the meeting go?"

"Good, sir; everyone but White is aboard."

"Do they understand how important it is for this to remain secret until I say differently?"

"Yes, sir."

"Good. This incident with Sergeant White will be all over the brigade in a matter of minutes, so, as we should always do, we'll use it to our advantage. I turned the volume up high enough for those men out there …"

Dwight glanced outside and saw that there were at least twenty men outside, in various poses of trying to look busy while they strained to hear what was being said in the brigade HQ tent.

"… to hear that I was seriously angry. I want everyone in the brigade to know that they should be careful when dealing with you. Because of the fact that what we are doing is so highly

unusual, the men and officers need to know where you stand
… and quick.

"If I were to allow even a small breakdown in authority, it
could spell trouble down the road. I want you to try to soak all
this stuff up, Dwight—not just the obvious lessons but the impli-
cations also. Try to read between the lines. You've got a lot to
learn, about both command and tactics, and you've not much
time to learn it in."

"Yes, sir."

"OK. We're pulling out in the morning; we're cutting the
operation short and stating that the reason is the breakdown in
the ARNV discipline, resulting in their retreat, which exposed
our flanks. This will serve both to throw the enemy off the scent,
because we don't want them to know about this new unit or any
tactics we may be planning to employ with it, and to cause the
ARVN officers and MACV to step up their training and cohe-
siveness.

"When you get back to your squad, it'd be a good idea to talk
to Sergeant White and be sure that he understands that you
still support him and respect him as squad leader; don't burn
any bridges or make any enemies that you don't have to. You'll
never know when you may need him, and it's simply a wise way
to conduct your life.

"Have you decided who your four NCOs will be?"

"Yes, sir. Sabinski, Richardson, Bandy, and I had thought
White, but in lieu of him, I'd choose Pascone."

Raising his voice a little and turning toward the anteroom of
the tent, the general said, "Did you get that, Sergeant Major?"

"Yes, sir."

Turning back to Dwight, he said, "Sergeant White is out. If he
asks, tell him that I said so; he shouldn't be surprised."

"Yes, sir."

"I've talked to General Westmoreland at length about you
and our situation here. He is in complete agreement with what
we are doing, but he had a suggestion that I found intriguing.

He is going to set up a special, accelerated officer and NCO training program for you and a few of your men. Sergeant White was right; you'll have to be an officer to command a platoon, and your squad leaders will have to be NCOs.

"You all will be going to MACV headquarters in Saigon for two weeks of both classroom and field training and then seven more days of HALO school, coupled simultaneously with leadership training. MACV's best and brightest will be shepherding you.

"And, as General Westmoreland said, if you're on such a fast track, this would have soon been necessary anyway. It's just a lot smarter to get it done now. I need you here, but Westy agreed for us to do only small-unit actions and reconnaissance patrols until you're back and the new unit is combat ready and coordinated with the rest of the brigade. While you're gone, we will be training to that end.

"You've got the undivided attention of some really important people, Dwight. I want you to understand that you are going to be carefully observed the entire time you're away; don't let me down.

"If this is all OK with you, you'll be wearing a second lieutenant's bar by this time tomorrow, and you and four new buck sergeants will be winging your way to Saigon for the most intense training you've ever even imagined. Sergeant Munoz will have your orders, correct ID cards, and new fatigue shirts and Class 'A' uniforms with proper rank and insignia applied.

"Bring the men up to date, and have your NCOs ready to go and be at brigade HQ at 1400 tomorrow.

"You OK with all this, Lieutenant?"

"Holy shit, sir!"

The general smiled and, in mock indignation, said, "Watch your mouth, Lieutenant! You're now an officer and a gentleman, and I expect you to behave accordingly."

They laughed as Dwight stood up, came to attention, saluted, and said, "Will that be all, sir?"

The general stood, came to attention, saluted back, and, extending his hand, said, "That is all, Lieutenant. I'll see you tomorrow at 1400. Congratulations."

"Thank you, sir."

-CHAPTER ELEVEN-

OH, BABY

THE CARIBOU, A SMALL twin-turboprop cargo and troop-carrier plane designed for short field operation, was noisy and afforded Dwight a chance to think. The top cargo door was in the up/open position, allowing Dwight, Bandy, and Rich to lie on the inclined, lower door/ramp and look out into the partial vacuum and windless panorama behind the airplane.

Pascone, Sabinski, and the loadmaster were the only other passengers sitting in the webbed seating along each side of the cargo bay. The two pilots could be seen in the cockpit twenty feet in front, separated from the cargo bay by small, partial bulk-heads, on either side and behind them.

As they left the Bien Hoa Air Base airspace, Dwight was amazed by the number of bomb craters in the topography below. He could see that the craters were relatively new, as there was little vegetation growing in them. They all had water standing in them. In some places, the ground looked almost like a moon-scape. *They must be from B-52 strikes*, Dwight thought. Most of them looked to be at least fifteen feet deep. No matter how much vegetation eventually covered them, he knew they would be there forever. *Sad*, he thought. He wondered how long it would take the mental scars of the people to heal as the vision of Abramowitz's femoral vein emptying his life onto the muddy earth reentered his memory. He shook his head and tried to vanquish the memory and realized he'd never had such a vivid one before. He got up and walked back to sit down in the webbed seating, wiping perspiration from his face, although it was cool at five thousand feet.

Pascone came over from his seat on the other side of the airplane, sat down beside Dwight, put his hand on his shoulder, and shouted above the noise, "You OK, man? You look like you've seen a ghost!"

Dwight shouted back, "Yeah, Don. I'm just not used to hanging out the door of an airplane without a parachute on, that's all."

Pascone knew Dwight better than that but decided not to say anything more. He was concerned for his friend, but it was obvious that Dwight didn't want to talk about whatever it was that had troubled him so greatly.

Saigon was bustling and seemingly safe. Most of the servicemen they saw weren't carrying weapons, although Dwight and his men had kept theirs. Dwight had checked into the BOQ and the others into the EMQ on Tan Son Nhut Air Base; they reported to MACV, which was on the air base; changed into their dress khakis; and were told that they should report at 0830 in the morning. Paratroopers are very distinguishable from other army troops in dress uniform because, besides wearing airborne wings, they wear jump boots that are both bloused and spit-shined, so they stood out among the other army and air force men. They were free to go into town, the PX in Cho Lon, which was just outside the gate, or wherever they wanted—so long as they stayed in the Saigon area.

It was only 1530, so they decided to try for a decent meal downtown.

The rooftop bar in the Continental Hotel displayed a beautiful panorama of Saigon and beyond. The river was a mile to the east, and Highway 1 could be seen leaving the city to the north, past the stark concrete buildings of the University of Saigon on the outskirts.

Dwight had warned his men to watch themselves and how they behaved and that they were almost certainly being observed.

This situation was all new to Dwight, but the others had all been to Saigon several times on pass. The men were going to Tudo Street, where the action was, but Dwight thought it would be best for him to stay away from that part of town. He was more than conscious of the fact that he was being fast-tracked and that he must watch everything that he did and said. He thought that it would be OK for his men to go there and have fun, but he realized that he should start behaving like an officer and especially a combat commander.

As the others left, promising to be prompt at 0830 tomorrow and without hangovers, he moved to a small table by the railing, under an umbrella, and ordered a cognac and a black coffee.

As he was intent on making out various landmarks to the north, he didn't notice that someone was standing beside him. As he looked up to acknowledge the waiter bringing his drinks, he saw her. She was a tall, blond westerner. He quickly took in her fine-featured, square-jawed face and saw that she was wearing a low-cut black evening gown and black high heels.

She smiled, displaying fine, even teeth and full, red-lipsticked lips. A pearl necklace swung forward as she bent to sit down next to him, displaying full, high breasts.

She crinkled her nose cutely as she said, "Hi, Lieutenant. I've been watching you. My name's Beth. Beth McNay."

So, this is how I am being watched tonight! The general is a sly, old fox. I should have known he'd make this as pleasant as possible for me—he and his buddy, General Westmoreland. This is really a nice gesture! I wonder what they're expecting of me. I'll just play along and enjoy myself. Rank does have its privileges!

Smiling, he got up, pushing his chair back with the backs of his legs.

Taking her proffered hand, he said, "Hello, Beth; my, what a pleasant surprise. I have to say, I'm gaining a new appreciation for the army's training."

Beth, still displaying her glistening teeth but de-crinkling her nose, cocked her head to the side, like a dog trying to decipher his master's meaning; a single pearl swung from her pierced ear on a silver chain.

She said, "Sure, Lieutenant Johnson. I'd love to be part of your training."

He saw her eyes wander languidly from his name tag to lower on his body and then back to his face as she said, "What's your first name, Lieutenant? And please, sit back down."

"Oh, sorry; my name's Dwight," he said, as he sat down.

As if you don't know, beautiful. I bet you even know my service number!"

As she lowered herself to the chair beside him, she said, "So, how long have you been with the 173d?"

OK, I guess we have to make small talk about something. I'll go along with her.

"Only about a week or so; I've come to Saigon for some specialized training. I'll be here for a couple weeks."

Looking at his left shoulder, she said, "This is the first time I've seen the 173d patch close up. I'd always thought it was a white bird, but it's a red sword with a white wing on it. I like it."

Then, before he could respond, she said, "What kind of additional training?"

Oh, right. She's already trying to see if I'm going to divulge classified information! This is almost an insult. How stupid does she think I am?

"I'm sorry, Beth, but I can't tell you anything about it. It's classified."

Then, to change the subject, he said, "What are you doing in Vietnam?"

"Well, that's a coincidence, Lieutenant. My mission is classified too. I can tell you that I'm with the United States Government, but that's about all.

Dusk was settling on Saigon, and streetlights and the lights of the city were glowing in the gray light.

The waiter came and asked Beth if she wanted him to bring her drink to the table.

She looked from the waiter to Dwight and batted long eyelashes twice, her blue eyes glistening in the spark of the waiter's match as he lit the candle on the table.

Dwight, for the first time in his life, felt his heart literally skip a beat. *My God,* he thought, *but she is beautiful!*

Hold on, kid! She's just doing a job. Don't get yourself all riled up. Even if this was for real, when she finds out you're only nineteen, she's history anyway.

He said, "Sure, of course. Bring it over, please."

The waiter left, and Beth leaned toward Dwight and crossed her legs, flashing both stockinged thighs just enough for Dwight to be able to see that the stockings were held up by a black garter belt.

He looked back to her face and realized that he'd been caught.

OK, she wants to play games? I can do that.

"Sorry, but you have absolutely fabulous legs, and war is hell."

She crinkled her nose in that oh-so-cute way of hers, lips parted in a half-smile, eyes squinting with the crinkle; then she laughed out loud.

"You are very observant, Lieutenant! You must be in intelligence."

"Yes, ma'am. You guessed it."

"So, that's what the school you're here for is about? Intelligence?"

"Yes, ma'am."

"Please, call me Beth, Lieutenant. I guess I can tell you that I'm in intelligence too. What kind of intelligence are you in?"

"Please, call me Dwight, or sweetheart; either one is authorized."

They both laughed as the waiter brought her drinks and smiled knowingly as he put coffee and cognac down for her.

"OK, sweetheart. What branch of intelligence are you in?"

"Appendages."

"Appendages? You mean like American units attached to the Vietnamese?"

Dwight smiled and leaned forward and, lowering his voice conspiratorially and motioning with his fingers for her to come closer, said, "No, I've been sent to Vietnam to reconnoiter and report directly to the president on the state of tall, blond women's lower appendages … legs."

Beth withdrew in mock shock and threw her napkin at him.

She said, "And *you're* an officer and a gentleman?"

"I did say 'ma'am'!"

"So, what are you going to tell the president in your dispatch tonight, Lieutenant?"

"So far so good, Mr. President."

They both laughed, and she gently slapped the back of his hand. A six-piece band, dressed in black pants and shoes, white coats and shirts, and black bow ties, began playing "Stardust."

This is fun! I feel like we're in a '40s movie. I'll be Fred Astaire, and you be Ginger Rogers.

The waiter came and, offering them menus, asked if they were going to have dinner.

Batting her eyes again, once this time, and cocking her head, she smiled and said, "Hungry, Lieutenant?"

"Famished," he said, slowly batting his own eyes, knowing that the candles would showcase his blue eyes for her. He could see that the effort wasn't lost on her, as she lowered her eyes demurely.

They took the menus and opened them as she again raised her eyes to Dwight's. He was watching; his mouth was open a little, his face was relaxed, and his eyes were hooded just a bit. He smiled at her, and she crinkled her nose again as they both laughed.

Damn, I feel just too cool; she really knows what she's doing. I don't think I've ever felt better about myself. I wonder if she's been trained to do this. This woman is definitely making me feel like officer material!

They looked at the menu in silence as the band ended "Stardust" and segued into "Harbor Lights."

She folded her menu, laid it on the table, opened her purse, and took out a package of Winstons, reaching for Dwight's Zippo on top of his Lucky Strikes.

As her hand touched the lighter, Dwight moved his toward it, watching her face. She left her hand on the lighter, waiting for his hand to arrive, their eyes resting on each other's. Slowly he laid his fingers on the back of her hand.

"Please," he said. "Let me …"

"You may … ," she said, sensuously sliding her hand from beneath his as their eyes continued to embrace each other's. She licked her lips, again casting her eyes downward as she drew in a deep breath and squirmed slightly in her seat.

He lit her cigarette as she put her fingers on the back of his hand, guiding him to her. Her nails were perfectly done in a red that matched her lips, which pouted with the motion of the initial draw on the cigarette; two gold ring bracelets fell toward her left elbow as she pulled the Winston away from her mouth with her other hand.

Now it was his turn to look away. His breath was coming in short gasps, and he had to regain his composure.

Looking out over the now brightly lit city, he said, "Saigon is beautiful at night. You'd never think that there's a war going on."

Looking at GG, slung on the chair next to him, and then back at him, she said, "No, the VC leave it alone, for the most part. Most Americans don't carry a weapon here."

"Does it bother you that I carry mine?"

"No, not really. Actually, you don't see that many paratroopers in Saigon, so people know you're not from here, anyway."

The spell was momentarily broken, but Dwight could see that she didn't want it to be. Her eyes were almost pleading with him to resume their tête-à-tête. He stood and, putting out his hand to her, said, "Dance?"

Joy in her smile, she took his hand, stood, and said, "I'd love to!"

They walked under the colorful lights strung over the top of the dance floor and bandstand. The darkness outside was now complete, making the restaurant lights seem brighter and the predominantly white decor of the bar even whiter.

She moved against him, and their bodies began to flow into each other's as the band began playing "To Know Him Is to Love Him."

He heard her sigh as her gentle fingers on his neck pulled him closer, her thick, fine hair on his cheek, neck, and throat.

He tried to bow his back away from her so she wouldn't feel his erection, but she would have nothing of it. She slowly brushed it with her thigh, causing an even stronger reaction as he gasped. It was pointing downward at a painful angle as she gasped also and slowly moved her thigh from the side to the middle, gently sliding his penis toward his other leg so that it was free to stand at its natural upward angle. She pushed her belly to it, her mons against its base and his scrotum, her belly embracing its shaft.

They backed their heads away to look at each other. Her face was tan, but her skin was milky-clear; her red lips were parted, as were his. Slowly their bodies moved together as their lips touched, eyes closed, feeling each other—lightly, languidly, savoring the moment.

The band switched to a new song by Wilson Picket, "Mustang Sally," and he said, "Whatever you do, Beth, don't leave me now! If you back away, we'll never be allowed here again!"

The song was just slow enough for them to stay together, and they both laughed as she backed away just enough to give him relief but not enough that people would be able to see his masculinity straining against his pants.

She said, "How do you like the Astros this season, Tex?"

They both laughed as his passion receded to an acceptable level.

The waiter followed them to their table, order pad in hand. As they sat down, she smiled at the waiter and said, "I'll have the Chateaubriand, medium rare, with new potatoes, green beans, and iced tea with lemon, please."

The waiter looked at Dwight, who said, "I'll have exactly the same, please."

As the waiter left, she said, "Don't you think it's quite a coincidence that we were both drinking coffee and cognac and then we wanted the same thing to eat?"

Coolly, he reached for his cognac, saying, "I don't believe in coincidences," and he raised his snifter in a toast, as she followed suit.

Their glasses rang as he said, "Us."

She smiled and said, "Us."

Little did she know that he didn't even know what Chateaubriand was, and the main reason he'd ordered coffee and cognac was that his mom and dad often had ordered that at fine restaurants, but he'd realized that he did like it, after all.

The meal was wonderful, and Dwight wondered how the Continental Hotel could acquire such fine beef while the army couldn't. If fact, some of the C rations had been canned during the Korean War—not that he was complaining. He actually liked C rations.

As they were finishing their meals, the waiter asked if they were going to have dessert, and they both answered that they were not.

When the waiter had left to get the bill, she said, "Actually I am looking forward to dessert, but not here."

"Where would you like to have it?"

"Well, I've already made arrangements to have it served in my room."

Holy shit! This can't be in her job description!

"Sounds wonderful!"

"The check has been taken care of. Are you ready?"

"As you were aware when we were dancing, I was painfully ready then!" And then he said, "Thank you for the dinner and drinks. I owe you."

"I'm sure you'll think of some way to repay me, Lieutenant."

"Yes ma'am; I think I just may."

She stood up, took his hand, and said, "Come on, cowboy. I think you're fixin', as you say, to get your chance."

He slung GG on his back, and they took the elevator to her room.

The elevator was empty, and, as soon as the door closed, she put her arms around his neck, pressed against him, and slowly kissed his lips, drawing away slightly to lick his upper lip and then, slowly, the bottom of his upper teeth and then his tongue; as his tongue met hers, she urged his tongue into her mouth with hers. Then they both sighed as their lips held each other and then parted, fully and softly.

His manhood had risen against her, but this time she reached down and held his testicles for a second and then slid her gentle fingers and thumb up his shaft, giving it full turgidity as it responded with a mighty throb.

They both gasped as she gently squeezed him, eliciting another great throb as he involuntarily thrust himself stronger against her hand, causing a moan from them both.

Her room was directly across from the elevator, and her hand was shaking as she thrust the key into the lock.

Inside, she bolted the door, opened his pants, and caressed his buttocks and thighs as she slid his pants and boxer shorts down to the tops of his boots, his penis throbbing against her cheek.

He was taking GG off as she, now kneeling, put him in her mouth. She moaned as he gasped, again involuntarily thrusting slightly toward her.

"He said, "Wait! Stop! I can't hold it off! I can't stop it!"

She moaned and took him further into her mouth, holding the base of his shaft with one hand and pulling gently downward on his scrotum with the other, moving her tongue firmly under the bulging head.

He quivered violently as a loud groan escaped him. Unrestrained, he thrust forward as her hand on his shaft controlled him so that his thrust didn't hurt her as he came in shuddering spasms and she hungrily consumed his essence.

She then lay on the bed, bringing her knees up, high heels digging into the bedcover as she rotated her hips up to him in slow, rolling motions, begging him with her motion and her smoky-dark eyes, her black-lace panties glistening with moisture.

He knelt and, reaching under her buttocks, pulled her closer to the edge of the bed, and, sliding his hands from the top of her panties in back, he stroked her buttocks; his fingertips gently caressing the full length of the deep center of her cheeks, he pulled her panties off. She moaned and moved against his hands, arching her back as his fingertips brushed the bottoms of her labia, now swollen and deep purple with desire.

She reached down to the top of her femininity with both hands and pulled up on her swollen outer lips, exposing an engorged pink-purple clitoris beckoning for his tongue. He slowly licked from the bottom of her labia to her clitoris as her heels shook the bed, his hands now holding her buttocks. Answering the thrust of her hips toward him, he kept moving his tongue against her clitoris, focusing on it.

"Oh, my God!" she gasped. "Please don't stop!"

He moved his tongue harder, his chin pushing gently between her labia into her vagina as she thrust even harder, pushing him further into her and his tongue more firmly against her clitoris.

Her squeal started deep in her throat and then raised itself two octaves as it reached her mouth and nose. She shuddered violently as waves of orgasm took control of her body, her high heels ripping into the bedcovers: "Oh God! Oh! Oh! Oh! Oh! Stop! Stop! I can't take any more! Oh God, please stop!"

Wiping his face on his sleeve, he lay down on his back beside her, and she put her head on his chest, her leg over his. Aftershock shudders still consumed her as she moved her mons rhythmically against his leg and slid her hand under his shirt, running her fingers through the fur of his chest; she purred and cuddled against him.

Seeing him erect again, she languidly held his shaft and massaged the length of it, moving the skin from near the base up to the head.

She said, "I'm not through with you yet, Lieutenant."

She stood beside the bed and slowly undressed, pulling her dress over her head and unfastening her bra; she watched him watch her and giggled as he throbbed when her breasts became free, nipples taut, framed by large, plump areolas.

Leaving her high heels, garter belt, and black stockings on, she showcased her long legs for him, moving her eyes from his to his manhood as it throbbed again and back to his eyes.

She slowly untied his boots and took them off, along with his socks. Then his pants came off from around his ankles, and she bent over him and took him in her mouth again, this time stroking his shaft slowly with her lips and tongue, looking into his smoldering eyes as another groan escaped him.

She straddled him on one knee and the other high-heeled foot. Giving herself enough altitude to position him between her labia, she sat down suddenly; going to both knees, she swallowed his shaft far into herself, and they both moaned with the delicious pleasure of the penetration.

Now they took their time. He caressed her pouting nipples as they swung to him, gently squeezing them between thumbs and forefingers as she rocked on him; moving him within her while rubbing her clitoris against his furry pubic hair, she climaxed again.

Shuddering, she fell on him, her head on his chest, her nails biting into his shoulders from around behind them, but not hard enough to hurt him.

He said, "I want to get behind you."

"Yes," she said as she climbed off of him and knelt on the bed beside him, gathering a pillow under herself for her head and chest.

He knelt behind her and positioned his glistening manhood gently between her now even more swollen labia. She moved hard against him as he thrust into her; again they both moaned with pleasure, him holding her by her hips. With long, steady strokes, he watched his shaft, glistening and swelling even larger and harder as he approached orgasm.

She felt its growth, and she moaned and pushed herself up with her hands; she moved back against him with each of his thrusts as they gained in strength and frequency.

She squealed with her own orgasm as she felt him swell and harden even further for his.

He both groaned and shouted as the strongest orgasm he'd ever experienced consumed him. He didn't even consider that the entire hotel could probably hear him. The world was only theirs as he, all of his strength and being centered in his maleness, drove himself into her as far as possible, her orgasm convulsing around his shaft, further intensifying his and milking him with its spasms.

Still in intense pleasure and maintaining his erection, he began stroking again, this time bending over her; bracing himself on his left hand, he reached around her waist and began gently massaging her clitoris with the middle finger of his right hand.

"Oh, my God!" she squealed and bowed her back, causing even deeper penetration and further unhooding her clitoris for his gentle touch.

She reached her left hand to his, which he was using to brace himself, and pulled upward on his wrist, indicating that she wanted him to use his finger to touch the tingling orifice now so exposed to him.

Putting some of his weight on her for support, his finger gently entered her as she moaned in approved ecstasy, approaching yet another orgasm.

She whispered, "Please don't stop!" as they rhythmically moved together, a finger of each of his hands and his manhood moving to a single purpose.

Now it was her turn to have the strongest orgasm she had ever had. She screamed as she experienced what she had only half believed was possible before this: a whiteout. Nothing existed for her but her intense and all-encompassing pleasure—not even sight or color. It only lasted an instant but seemed to last a lifetime. Then the sensations became so intense that they were painful. She reached back and grabbed his wrist, pulling his finger out of her and then, just as quickly, with her other hand, took his hand away from her tortured clitoris.

She then lay down, pulling him out of her. Gasping for breath, she said, "Oh, honey. I'm so embarrassed! I don't know what happened! I just turned into an animal or something!"

"Beth, please don't be ashamed. You were being a woman— the most wonderful woman any man could ever even dream of! And I got to be a part of it. I'm not only honored, but I've never experienced anything like that either!

"I literally wouldn't trade it for anything, and I'll never forget even the smallest detail. Whatever it was that just happened, I'm damned sure it's nothing to be ashamed of. My only wish is that we can do it again ... soon!"

"Oh, Dwight. I've never done anything like this with a man, I promise! But that *is* the most exciting thing that's ever happened to me. Hold me, please."

He lay down beside her, and she put her head on his chest and her leg over his, her fingers again caressing his furry chest. Neither of them paid any attention to the now cooling fluids of their pleasure on the bed and on their genitals, bellies, and legs.

The air-conditioning was cool, so Dwight, not wanting to break their embrace, reached over and covered them with the bedspread.

She sighed and nestled into his body as they both fell asleep.

Beth stood talking to Dwight as he showered and shaved. They both nibbled the Danish and drank the coffee that room service had brought on the silver service cart she had wheeled into the large bathroom. She said, "Will we be seeing each other again?"

"Are you kidding? The best lover and most exciting woman in the universe wants to know if I ever want get together again?"

They both laughed and she said, "How can I get in touch with you?"

Dwight turned around from the mirrored basin where he was shaving, using her little pink lady's razor.

"You are kidding me, right?"

"No? Why would I be kidding you; what do you mean?"

"You *were* ordered to keep an eye on me, weren't you?"

"What the hell are you talking about, Dwight?"

"Come on, Beth. When you walked up to me last night, you said that you were watching me!"

"Well, I *was* watching you! I'd been watching you and how you handled your men. I was watching a good-looking, cute paratrooper officer in confident command of himself and his men.

"I was watching his men respond to him with respect bordering on adoration. Good grief, Dwight! Most of the women and some of the men in the bar were doing the same thing I was doing! Most of the officers here are pencil pushers—chairborne rangers. Maybe you don't know it, Lieutenant, but you stand out like a sore thumb at the Continental Hotel Bar, especially with four big, mean-looking paratroopers treating you like you're the Messiah or something. Who was that giant, by the way?"

"Wait a minute! Wait a minute! Are you telling me that you weren't sent to keep an eye on me?"

"Honey, if this weren't so amusing and you didn't look so perplexed standing there naked with shaving cream on half your face, holding a lady's razor, I think I'd be angry!" She laughed.

"We're in a war here, and you're a dashing, young airborne officer, and I've got a dangerous job too, and I just saw that I had to make my move and that tomorrow literally might not come for either of us, so I did something brash and out of character for me. I picked you up.

"You're the first man I've had since I last slept with my boyfriend in San Francisco five months ago. And I'm not ashamed to tell you that last night and this morning, I had the best loving I've ever even imagined!"

After a short pause, she continued, "Why would someone be watching you?"

Dwight said, "Oh, Jesus; this changes everything!"

"I hope it's for the better! I can't stand the thought of us not seeing each other again, soon."

"Like I told you last night, sweetie, I can't tell you anything about why I'm in Saigon except that it's for two weeks of specialized training. Who do *you* work for, then?"

"OK, Lieutenant, I'm going to tell you something, but you have to promise me that you won't tell anyone, not that it's any big deal … I mean, it *is* but just the little that I'm going to tell you isn't; I'm with the CIA."

"You're a spy?"

"That's all I can tell you, Dwight."

"Well, I guess it's OK for me to tell you that you can find me by calling MACV headquarters at the air base, but I'd rather that you didn't, at least not for a few days. It may be a breach of security for me to have told you that; I don't know. Do you have a phone number where I can reach you?"

"All I can give you is the phone number for the hotel, room 217. Here, I'll write the room number inside this hotel matchbook."

She picked up a pen from the dresser, wrote the number in the matchbook, picked up his pants from a chair, and put the matches in the left front pocket, telling him where to find them as she did so.

She said, "Do you think you'll be able to get away to be with me at any time during this training?"

"I honestly don't know, sweetie. I report in an hour and a half, and then I'm in their charge for two weeks. The training is going to be intense; I do know that much. I'll try to call you tonight. I'm in the BOQ at the air base for now. I don't know if I'll stay there or not. If I don't call you tonight, it'll only be because I can't, like if they have me out in the field, which is highly possible."

"Can I ask you if you were in that battle that everyone's been talking about?"

"Yes, I was in it. What did you hear about it?"

"Well, the buzz is that there's some hero medic there who has all kinds of balls and has ESP or something. They say he can even dodge bullets and won the Medal of Honor the second day he was with the brigade. I know how rumors get going, but much of it is true; I've read the intel. Do you know the guy? Have you ever talked to him?"

Dwight laughed, causing him to cut his chin. "Ouch! Yes, I've met him. How'd you hear about it?"

"Well, it's supposed to be top secret; they don't want the enemy to know about him, but they're dreaming. There's talk about it all over Vietnam *and* Washington. My job and security clearance make me privy to some of it, anyway. Is it true?"

"Well, I know what happened, but again, I can't tell you anything about it."

"What do you mean 'again'? Does this top secret training you're doing have anything to do with the medic?"

"I can't talk about either one of these things, Beth."

"They *are* connected. I know this because you said 'again.' You wouldn't have used that word if they weren't!"

Dwight had finished shaving and began dressing, a spot of blood coloring a piece of tissue paper on his chin.

Lacing his boots, he said, "I can't say anything more, Beth; please don't press it. I've already said too much. Please don't say anything about this discussion to *anyone*. It's very important to me that you don't. Promise?"

"Of course, honey; I promise. I would never do or say anything that could hurt you."

Dressed now, he stepped up to her and put his arms around her waist. She put her arms around his neck as they looked into each other's eyes for a long moment—she searching, he consoling.

She put her head on his chest and shoulder and kissed his throat as he pressed her to him, his hands on her back.

She said, "I understand that you can't tell me anything, Dwight, but my job gives me access to just about everything I want to know about. I'll know your mother's maiden name and virtually all there is to know about you by, oh, nine thirty."

Startled by the realization that she wasn't kidding, he held her at arm's length, trying not to look panicked, and said, "I want you to promise me something, Beth."

"Sure, honey … whatever you say."

"Please take me for what I really am. Please don't be judgmental. If you are really able to find out all these things about me, please don't; damn, I don't know what to say!"

"What's the matter, Dwight; what are you afraid of? Oh, honey …" She held him close, putting her head back on his chest. "I don't care what your background is. I know enough about this man I'm holding to know that he's a good man and that I want to be with him. I don't know if I'm allowed to say anything about love at this early date, and I certainly don't want to scare you off, but I know that I have strong feelings for you and that I don't want to be anywhere near any other man but you."

"OK, well, please just don't judge me. I *want* you to know all about me. I don't want to hold anything back from you. I mean, you'd find it all out eventually. I guess it's probably best that you find these things out from a third party, anyway. Just please try to stay in the mood you're in right now when you read about me. Try to remember who and what I really am, rather than the way things appear on paper."

Again, she backed away, looked into his eyes, and said, "Good grief, Lieutenant! What could it be about you that's making you so upset?"

"Well, I hope that you won't think ill of me, and I do think I know you well enough already to know that you won't. But let's just say that you're going to be a little surprised by what's in my dossier."

"Oh, I don't think so, Lieutenant. It's my job to see a lot of surprising things. Virtually everyone has skeletons in their closets. You'd be very surprised what's in important men's files; strong men do strong things. And anyway, you don't have enough miles on you to have all that thick of a file. I think you may be overestimating your ability to shock me, sir."

Dwight laughed. "Well, let's just say that I have no doubt that you're going to be entertained."

"I already have been, Lieutenant!"

They both laughed, and Dwight shook his head and said, "We'll see."

-CHAPTER TWELVE-

TRAINING

DWIGHT WAS FORTY-FIVE MINUTES early, so he had plenty of time to change into fresh fatigues, polish his brass, and touch up the spit shine on his boots.

His men were waiting for him in the main room of MACV headquarters, and Dwight was proud to see that they also were all standing tall in freshly cleaned and starched fatigues, polished brass, and spit-shined boots.

Cargo Sabinski said, "Yo, LT! Where have you been all night? We were worried about you; your wife Richie here made two trips to the BOQ during the night to see if you'd come home yet!"

"I stayed at the Continental."

Bandy said, "What happened, LT? No shit, we were worried about you. Staying gone all night like that isn't like you."

Rich said, "Come on, you idiots! Can't you see? It's written all over his face."

Cargo said, "What the fuck you talking about, Rich?"

"Can't you see it, Cargo? Look at that shit-eatin' grin on his face, that rosy complexion, that relaxed swagger. The man's in love; our new lieutenant got some major lovin' last night!"

Pascone said, "Shit; he's right! The LT's in love! Look at him!"

Dwight was trying unsuccessfully to put on a serious face, which served only to cause him to blush as his facial muscles, despite his attempts to maintain a passive expression, forced his eyes and the corners of his mouth to smile.

He said, "Bullshit, guys; I had too much to drink and decided to stay the night. Shit, it was really nice: a real bed, room service, the works!"

Rich said, "Yeah, right, Doc; excuse me … Lieutenant. You got room service and the *works*, all right; it's written all over your face, man. You can't bullshit a bullshitter! This is *me*, your old buddy, pardner! I been to two county fairs and a farmer's union picnic; you can't put anything over on *me*! You be smitten, my brotha!"

They were all laughing when a full colonel came into the waiting area from a door leading to the office area. He said, "Lieutenant Johnson?"

Thank God for small favors, Dwight thought as he said, "Yes, sir?"

The colonel was a few inches taller than Dwight, probably six feet four and two hundred pounds. He had broad shoulders and a barrel chest. He wore Masters Airborne wings; his khaki uniform was smartly tailored, and his boots were spit-shined. He looked to be forty-five to fifty, and the combat unit patch on his right shoulder was the Screaming Eagle of the 101st Airborne Division.

Dwight also noted that he had at least six rows of ribbons, including the Silver Star with two Oak Leaf clusters, the Purple Heart with two clusters, and the Bronze Star with three clusters. Army Airborne wings and a Combat Infantry Badge rounded out the ensemble on his left breast. He wore Vietnamese Airborne wings over his right pocket.

He said, "Hello, Lieutenant. I'm Colonel Wetzel, one of General Westmoreland's aides. I'll be coordinating your training," he said as they shook hands.

He turned to the other four men and said, "I'll be coordinating your men's training also."

Extending his hand to Cargo first, he introduced himself all around. When the formalities were finished, he said to Dwight's men, "Some of your training will be together and some will be separate and different from the lieutenant's.

"Let's go back to a conference room, and I'll give you a brief overview; then, after a thorough physical exam and lunch, the lieutenant and I will be spending the remainder of the day together, and you will be working with Sergeant Major Fromhurst. He is also an aide to General Westmoreland."

With only a few questions from the men, Colonel Wetzel explained what was going to happen for the next three weeks; the third week was for the HALO training along with small-unit assault tactics and additional leadership training.

He and Sergeant Major Fromhurst would be shepherding them through the various phases and also doing some of the actual training. They would also be accompanying them to and assisting them with the HALO training, the final day of which would involve a night jump in the Mekong Delta, and they would be required to form up, simulate a reconnaissance mission, and find their way to a pickup destination at least thirty kilometers away from the drop zone.

They would be training with Chinese-made AK-47s so that, when and if they got into a firefight, the enemy wouldn't be able to discern their exact location or number, as their weapons would sound exactly like the enemy's. Dwight would be allowed to keep his grease gun, as the enemy sometimes used a Chinese-made copy of it. The colonel said that anyone who could put three bullets in an unseen enemy soldier's chest at fifty meters with a short-barreled .45-caliber submachine gun could certainly keep it if desired, no matter what the TO&E called for.

Today, and the remainder of the week, would consist of basic leadership orientation and training. The following days would progress into advanced leadership training, small-unit tactics, reconnaissance patrolling, and information gathering, coupled with survival training.

The second week would involve intelligence-gathering techniques and field exercises. They would spend two days with the Twenty-fifth Infantry Division's intel units, participating and training on an actual upcoming operation, the specifics of which would remain unknown to them until the actual deployment, for top secret classification purposes. Some of the work would be in the classroom, but most would be in the field. They would be flown in and out of situational training locations by helicopter.

They would be spending most nights in the BOQ in a special suite of rooms with a common meeting area so that they could do homework and work on problems together. Their gear had already been moved to the suite, and they would be directed to it by whoever was at the BOQ service desk or, in his absence, the Officer of the Day.

The remainder of the new platoon had been manned, back at the 173d's base camp, and was also beginning training today. They would be joining them for the weeklong HALO school in two weeks.

According to the colonel, anyone challenging the enlisted men's right to be in officers' quarters should be respectfully informed that they are on special mission training that requires and authorizes them to be there. The same goes for the officers' mess or anywhere else on or off the base.

The colonel then gave each of them new ID cards and collected their old ones. They were exactly like the old green ones except that they had their new rank, were red, and hung on a black cord. None of them had ever seen a red military ID card before. The colonel informed them that it conferred special privileges on them and that it should be worn on the cord around their necks when they were on the base or anywhere else where officers or men would have opportunities to talk to them.

Everyone on the base should be aware that any personnel with a red ID should not be fraternized with, except for official or necessary business. Anyone who either did not know this or who otherwise tried to engage them in conversation should be respectfully informed that they are in top secret mission status and that they are instructed to not be in contact with unauthorized personnel.

The new IDs should be removed from the cords and kept in their wallets when off the base.

They were not to discuss any aspect of the training or even that they were part of the 173d Airborne's new unit. They would wear civilian clothing, provided for them and already in their quarters, when on leave on Sundays and, if asked, were to say that they worked for MACV on the air base.

They would be training twelve or more hours per day, and there would be homework every night except Sundays; they would have Sundays off. They would be expected to use their Sundays for rest and recuperation, and excessive alcohol consumption on Sundays would not be tolerated and not allowed at all on other days.

An air force flight surgeon and medics were waiting for them at the dispensary, where they would get a thorough flight physical. The chief surgeon was in possession of their medical files and shot records. They had all been prequalified by this doctor, who had read their files and found everything in order; barring anything untoward turning up in their physical examinations, they were cleared to begin their training beginning at 1300 hours, immediately after chow. The officers' mess desk sergeant would recognize them by their ID cards and direct them to their designated chow area.

For security purposes and the fact that their schedules would be different each day, they would be taking their meals in a special section of the officers' mess, segregated from everyone but their trainers. These would usually be working meals, where they would be participating in lectures and problems while eating.

Dwight called Beth's room from a bank of pay phones outside the officers' mess after supper, at six thirty.

Instead of Dwight hearing, "Hello" on the other end, Beth answered by saying, "So you're the hero medic!"

Dwight said, "What? How'd you know it was me?"

"I can't tell you that, Lieutenant … or Sergeant … or Corporal … or Major. What *is* your rank today, lover?"

"Oh, Jesus."

Oh! Excuse me! What is your rank today, Jesus?"

"Beth, I don't know if we should be talking like this. I don't know if this line is secure and …"

"I do."

"You do what?"

"I do know if this line is secure. I also know that you're talking from the fifth phone from the north end of the third bank of twelve phones outside the officers' mess at Tan Son Nhut Air Base and that you've spent the day with Colonel William "Billy" Wetzel, aide-de-camp to Westy and that you'll be going to HALO school in two weeks, where I will be assisting in your training."

"What!?"

"That's right, cowboy; you and I have a future together, whether you like it or not."

"What in the *hell* are you talking about?"

"I'm talking about the fact that I'm having a lot of fun right now, big stud. I know just about everything there is to know about you, and you know almost nothing about me, but that will change soon.

"We're going to spend the day together Sunday, and I'll tell you all about it then.

"By the way, you *were* being watched last night, so the people who need to know know all about our little tryst. They bugged my room after they saw us dancing together. We have no secrets, my darling, dear, brave, clairvoyant, whatever-rank-you-are-today."

Dwight said, "You're going to be instructing my platoon at the HALO school?"

"That's right, cowboy. You're *fixin'* to be as surprised about me as I was about you. For starters, I have over six hundred jumps. I taught HALO in its infancy at Benning in '62. I'm the only female to have completed the army's parachute training and am an army-designated master parachutist via both the 101st and 82nd Airborne Divisions and am the only female to have gone through jumpmaster school. But, most important as far as you're concerned, I invented and tested the Seven-T-U."

"Seven-T-U?"

"The hottest and most maneuverable canopy in the arsenal; rate of descent is twenty-one feet per second, so you and your men better be good at PLFs. It's the parachute you'll be using after qualifying with the Double-L, a slower falling and less maneuverable canopy."

"Holy crap; I'm not believing what I'm hearing!"

"As you were told this morning, Lieutenant, you have a lot to learn.

"I've got to go. Have fun, and please think of me when you're alone at night. I'll see you Sunday morning. Oh, and there are no longer any bugs in my room."

Dwight said, "I'm speechless!"

"I'll bet *that* doesn't happen very often! It sure didn't last night, studly. I've certainly never heard of a nineteen-year-old behaving in such a manner, but I can think of several million women who wish there were a few more of you!

"There'll be a jeep waiting for you in front of the BOQ at 0930 on Sunday morning. Don't try to argue with the driver; he'll be under strict orders to bring your pink ass straight to me!"

Dwight laughed, "I wouldn't even consider it. Duty, honor, and country, you know."

Dwight heard her moan a prayer—"God, please get Sunday here quickly!"—and the phone clicked dead.

He hung up and stood there in shock with his hand still on the handset, when he heard a voice behind him say, "Come on, Lieutenant! The rest of us would like to make a call too."

Dwight looked back and realized that lines had formed behind each phone.

He said, "Oh, sorry" as he stepped away from the bank of phones and began walking toward the BOQ.

On Sunday morning, Dwight dressed in the new clothes that had been procured for him: tan slacks, a navy-blue polo shirt, blue socks, and brown Weejun loafers. The jeep and driver were waiting in front of the BOQ.

Word of his affair with a senior CIA operative was out among the MACV intel people and, via the training staff, was common knowledge among his men. The ribbing had been merciless, and he wanted to get away from them almost as much as he wanted to be with Beth.

Apparently, the brass approved of their liaison. U.S. intelligence and the army were working together progressively more closely nowadays because of the combined clandestine and military nature of this war.

This particular endeavor was of keen interest to both organizations, as they hoped and were now planning for a both psychological and physical advantage over the enemy by melding Dwight's talents with the military and intelligence aspects of the U.S. forces, to both devise and enact strategy and demoralize the enemy's tactical capabilities.

They hoped that this would be the core of a new strategy to replace the one of pure force of numbers and technology that the enemy was currently having some degree of success thwarting with stealth and guerrilla tactics.

Dwight had been allowed to carry GG, even though he was wearing civvies.

During the twenty-minute ride to the Continental, he thought about the training of the past week and how much he and his men had learned. Although exciting, the training had been grueling. The physical aspects hadn't been so bad; after all, they were paratroopers in an all-airborne infantry outfit. There were no fighting forces in the world in any better physical condition.

However, neither he nor his men had been prepared for the scholarly aspects of the training and how much material and problem solving had to be learned, memorized, and regurgitated in both oral and written examinations.

He was particularly worried about Cargo Sabinski's seeming inability to absorb complex tactical planning and engagement problems. Either he wasn't mentally capable of it or he had relied on his brawn and force of power for so long that he had rendered himself incapable of thinking his way through problems, rather than simply bulldozing his way through his life as he had apparently done thus far.

Cargo was going to have to either rise to the occasion or they were going to have to bring someone else aboard, before they were so far along that the new man wouldn't be able to catch up. This was going to be a tough decision, but if Sabinski couldn't be relied on, for whatever reason, he'd have to go. Friendship couldn't be taken into account with something this important.

Dwight had had a talk with Cargo this morning and was amazed to find that the big guy didn't realize that he was failing the program. Dwight had told him that he was and that he had to start performing better or that he'd have to be replaced.

Cargo's response was one of surprise, and he promised to try to do more thinking and less bulldozing his way through things. He was upset and really wanted to be a squad leader in the new platoon, and he stated that, rather than go into town, he would spend the day studying and going back over key problems.

Dwight thought that maybe Beth would have some insight for him—some way to get Cargo on the ball and with the program.

The day was hot and the temperature was already in the low nineties, but the air was not too humid. It had rained every day of the past week, making some of their field problems inter-esting.

The men had taken to their new AK-47 rifles well and actually liked them quite a bit better than their M16s. The weapons were total opposites; the M16 was like a Ferrari and the AK-47 like a Double-A fuel dragster.

The M16 was finely machined and complex, which, too often, resulted in jamming problems, whereas the AK-47 was big, heavy, and low-tech; it utilized the old-fashioned gas system, which used the gas from the propellant to drive a piston that threw the bolt back, throwing the spent shell casing out. Then a spring pushed the gas piston back forward, chambering another round.

The World War II– and Korean War–era M1 Garrand used this system, as did its successor, the M14. The AK-47's piston and its tube were over the top of the barrel (where the M1 and M14's cylinder was beneath the barrel), making the weapon look more, to Dwight, like a plumber's tool than a rifle.

The M16 used a small, high-velocity .223-caliber (the diam-eter of a .22 rifle's barrel but with much more powder behind it) round that would tend to ricochet because of its extremely high velocity, even when hitting small branches and twigs; however, it had terrific range and accuracy. Also, the rounds were much lighter, so more ammo could be carried and loaded into the gun. And it didn't kick much, so it could be easily held on target while firing full automatic.

The AK-47's rounds were larger, 7.62 mm, so they plowed through underbrush effectively, giving the gun a big advantage over the M16 in the jungle. But the weapon kicked too hard to fire full automatic and keep on target, so it tended to "climb" on full auto. Firing single-shot was also advisable in order to keep from running out of ammo—not a good thing to do in a firefight.

But what the men liked best about the AK-47 was the fact that it was almost impossible to jam. They had actually put mud in the receiver, and the weapon would still work! The M16 would jam with a little dirty water in the receiver.

So the consensus among the men was that the AK-47 was the best weapon for jungle fighting, mainly because it wouldn't jam and the round would plow through the jungle on its way to the target. Also, an armor-piercing round could be utilized in the AK-47, whereas the M16's bullet was too small in diameter to put a tungsten steel core in it. The platoon would be supplied with all AP rounds, which would pierce body armor, the enemy's body, and then through the other side of the body armor!

Dwight's new polo shirt was already wet under his arms and in two spots on either side of his chest when he walked into the hotel lobby. Apparently, a tourist carrying a submachine wasn't a normal sight in the Continental Hotel's lobby, as most of its occupants turned to look.

He went straight to the elevator and to Beth's room and knocked. She opened the door wearing a red see-through negligee and matching high heels. Again, she wore the pretty, little, single-pearl earrings, hanging on quarter-inch-long silver chains. A strand of pearls hung around her neck. Her lipstick was the same color as the shoes and negligee, and her makeup was perfect. She was wearing Chanel No. 5, Dwight's favorite.

Smiling through pouting, slightly open lips, she shifted her weight to her right leg, bringing her left thigh slightly in front of the right, her left heel lifting off of the floor.

Dwight gasped as his eyes stopped wandering over her body for an instant as he couldn't help focusing on the dark promise of her pubic hair, showing deliciously through the two layers of red of the negligee and panties.

Beth giggled huskily as she reached out and gently touched his testicles with her fingertips and then ran them up his now stiff shaft, straightening it for him to its up-pointing, natural position. She then put her fingers and thumb around his penis, gently pulled him into the room, and began undressing him.

"Beth, I ..."

She put her right forefinger on his lips and said, "Shhhh; there'll plenty of time for talking later."

She pulled his pants and underwear down and took him in her mouth for just a few intense seconds. She then removed his loafers and socks and put him in her mouth again.

He unslung GG and twisted to put her on the blue, over-stuffed wingback chair by the door, but, as he was doing so, a shudder ran through his body. He flipped GG's dust cover up, releasing the safety, turned around sharply, and fired five rounds through the door.

They heard a body loudly crumple to the floor outside the door, as Dwight opened it.

The body of a hotel bellboy, wearing black pants and white shirt, lay against the opposite wall. There were two bullet holes in his forehead, one under his nose and two in his heart.

Beth screamed, "My God, Dwight; what have you done!? Are you out of your mind!?"

Blood was pooling from the body, running across the hall and onto Dwight's bare feet. Doors were opening, and men and women were coming out into the hall to see what was happening.

Unaware that he was wearing nothing but a navy-blue polo shirt, a smoking submachine gun, and a half erection, Dwight took two steps toward the body, picked up a large, brown, soft-sided briefcase, turned around, and ran through Beth's room, throwing the briefcase into the bathroom.

He then ran back, grasped Beth's wrist, and pulled her into the hall. He pivoted to his left and, dragging Beth along with him, ran twenty feet to the next room, whose occupants, a middle-aged Western man and woman, were standing outside the door, mouths open and staring in disbelief.

Dwight threw the two of them and Beth on the floor and lay on top of her as he screamed, "Everyone get down! Get down!"

Shrapnel ripped through the wall of Beth's room, as debris and gray-white and then black smoke sprang out of the open door. The explosion temporarily deafened them as Dwight got to his feet and ran to the window at the end of the hall, firing four rounds through it as he ran, each bullet hitting a corner, taking the entire window out of its frame and shattering it to the street below.

As he got to the window and looked down, he raised GG and emptied the remaining twenty-one rounds into a black Citroen pulling away from the curb in front of the hotel.

The car sped up, turned sharply left, and plowed into the broad stone steps of the Opera House, across the busy street, climbing halfway up the stairs before coming to rest in a smoking ruin of bullet holes and shattered glass.

A crowd had already started to gather as the left rear door opened and a bleeding body fell headfirst onto the steps and rolled down six feet to the sidewalk.

Dwight felt Beth's left hand on his arm and her right on his back as she looked over his left shoulder at the carnage in the street. People were beginning to look up at him as he realized that he and Beth must be quite a sight—him, standing there, framed by the brown stone of the handsome building's thigh-high window frame, naked except for a navy-blue polo shirt, and holding a smoking machine gun; Beth standing behind and beside him, strikingly beautiful in a red see-through negligee, legs and buttocks lifted and tightened by the unseen high heels.

He turned back and walked back down the hall to the room. Ten or more people were now in the hallway. Dwight noticed the hotel's concierge and several other uniformed or suited hotel staff.

He saw that his shoes and overnight bag had been blown into the hall. He stepped into the loafers to keep his feet from being cut up any more than they already had been by the shards of broken glass and tile from the demolished bathroom.

His canvas overnight bag was torn in several places and the zipper was jammed, so he put his thumbs into one of the larger holes and ripped it open, spilling most of its contents on the floor. Among his change of clothes and his shaving accessories were two of GG's full magazines.

He slipped the empty magazine out of GG and inserted a fresh one. He then tugged on the black chain around his neck, pulling the black crucifix out of his shirt, and inserted its base into the finger-hole cocking mechanism and chambered a round.

He then closed the dust cover, putting the safety on, and went inside the room and found his pants on the floor by the bed, which had been pushed against the wall by the blast. The pants had several holes in them but were serviceable. He put them on, thankful that the zipper still worked.

He said, "Beth, find a phone and call MACV and get someone from Special Ops over here. Then call your people and do the same. I'm going across the street and check the car out."

She had already put on a red T-shirt and was putting on a pair of jeans. She said, "I'm way ahead of you; watch yourself down there. Hang your ID around your neck before you leave the room. There are going to be a lot of people with guns down there, so make sure they know who you are. Act like you're in charge of the situation, and you *will* be; understand?"

"Yes, *ma'am*! I love a take-charge kind of woman."

"You were obviously right about the sapper. I just hope you were right about the car too."

"I was right; see you in a minute," he said as he took the red ID card out of his back pocket and hung it around his neck, put the remaining full ammo magazine in his back pocket, and went down the hall to the stairs. People wordlessly moved out of his way.

GG slung on his back, he walked out the front door of the hotel to the car across the street. Those who saw him coming moved out of his way. He elbowed his way through the others. A white-uniformed police officer and two QCs (Vietnamese Army MPs) fell in behind him. The red ID and his demeanor were having the desired effect; everyone was deferring to him.

He opened the right front door, pulled the body out on the steps, and went through its pockets. The man was Vietnamese, in his forties or fifties, and wearing a black business suit, white shirt, and thin black tie. His black hair was cut in a crew cut. He was wearing a brown leather shoulder holster, which held a small nine-millimeter pistol. There was nothing in his pockets. *Strange*, he thought.

He checked the two others—one in the right rear seat and the other who had fallen out and rolled down the steps—and they were exactly the same, including the pistol and identical shoulder holsters. The driver had a small black billfold with a few hundred piastres and a driver's license in it, which Dwight handed to the policeman.

There was a loaded AK-47 on the floor of the backseat. Blood, brains, and bone were blown all over the inside of the car; they had each died from head wounds.

All four bodies were now on the steps beside the car, where Dwight had pulled them out to check the contents of their pockets. He didn't really know what he was looking for, but he figured that it was an appropriate action, if for no other reason than to further establish his authority.

He was reminded of the old story of the young bull snorting and pawing the ground when a big stud bull was being taken off a truck to breed with the cows on the ranch. The other bulls had asked what he was thinking; the big stud could take him apart in seconds. The young bull had said to them that he didn't want to fight the new bull; he just wanted to be sure that the big stud knew that he was a *bull*!

At this thought, he couldn't help but smile to himself, and he noticed that the three policemen who were intently watching his every move smiled also.

"Holy smoke … I really *am* in charge here!"

A U.S. Army MP jeep squealed to a stop, and two MPs jumped out as the crowd separated to let them through.

The first MP to arrive in front of Dwight reached out and examined his red ID card; he released it, came to attention, and saluted. The other one, now standing beside the first, followed suit.

Dwight returned their salutes without coming to attention himself.

The first MP said, "What's going on, sir?"

Dwight, reading the MP's name tag, said," I can't tell you anything more than what you see here, Sergeant Morales. This situation is classified top secret. There'll be CIA and Special Ops people here in a few minutes to answer your questions."

"Did you kill these men, Lieutenant?"

"As I said Sergeant, I can't talk to you about it."

Beth had now materialized and stood a little to Dwight's left and a few inches in front of him, her body language and gray CIA ID card hanging from her neck helping her take command of the situation.

She said, "Sorry, Sergeant; neither I nor Lieutenant Johnson can tell you anything right now. There will be others here soon who will be authorized to talk to you."

Then she said, "Lieutenant, can I talk to you for a minute?"

He said, "Certainly, Agent McNay."

To the MPs, he said, "Excuse me, men," and he and Beth stepped ten feet away, to the end of the steps, near the ornate railing.

Beth said, "What did you find out, Dwight?"

"Nothing; that's what's so strange. None of them but the driver had any ID. No wallets—nothing. The driver had a little ID case wallet with nothing in it but a driver's license and a few hundred piastres. They are all dressed the same and have identical shoulder holsters and nine millimeters—weird."

She said, "Not as weird as you think; they are probably North Vietnamese operatives. The few times we've caught them with their pants down like this, the MO has been the same; they overplay their hand by having no ID and dressing like that—all the same."

Then, looking at the bodies and noticing that the entire crowd was watching them, she said, "Damn good thing too. This could have been just a little embarrassing, if they had not been so obviously North Vietnamese spies. I guess this 'top secret' stuff regarding you hasn't worked too well for us; the cat's out of the bag now, for sure. It's time to get you off the street, cowboy."

She then handed Dwight the empty magazine he'd left in the room and said, "I was told by headquarters to get out of the hotel and to not go back in. There'll be someone here soon to whisk us away."

Dwight said, "Where are we going?"

"I don't know for sure, but you've got to complete your current training before we start the HALO school, so I would think that we'll be going to MACV. I don't know where they'll put me, but there's not much doubt that we're both targets now. We'll just have to wait and see."

Two Americans in blue business suits and white shirts got out of a black Citroen and walked up to them as two jeeps arrived, each carrying two field-grade army officers in khaki uniforms. The six of them purposefully headed for Dwight and Beth.

The first to arrive were the two blue-suited men. Beth knew them and introduced them as CIA honchos. One was her direct supervisor, David Bergman.

As soon as they were introduced, Bergman said, "We have orders to get the two of you out of here, right now. Let's go."

The four army officers—a major, a lieutenant colonel, and two full colonels—stopped them. One of the bird colonels said, "Whoa … where are y'all going so fast? We need to talk to Lieutenant Johnson, here."

The colonel had a southern accent that sounded like Georgia to Dwight. He was short and powerful-looking and was the only one of the four wearing airborne wings and bloused boots. He wore the "Double-A" of the Eighty-second Airborne Division as a combat unit patch on his right shoulder, and they all wore .45 automatic pistols on their waists and MACV patches on their left shoulders.

The two CIA men showed the officers their IDs as Bergman said, "I'm sorry, Colonel, but we have orders to get him out of here as soon as possible."

Dwight, looking up to the roof of the two-story building across the other street from the hotel, jumped three feet to his side, clearing a line of fire and, flipping GG's safety off, fired five rounds from his waist.

Literally everyone in sight had been watching their conversation and, along with Beth and the six men, turned in the direction that Dwight had fired. A bolt-action rifle with a scope attached clattered to the sidewalk beneath the second-story roof of the building. A man was slumped over the parapet, blood from head wounds running down the side of the building.

Bergman shouted, "Let's go … now!"

He grabbed Dwight's arm, and they ran toward the black Citroen. Dwight and Beth were shoved into the backseat as the two CIA men got in the front and raced away. The army officers followed in their jeeps.

Pandemonium had broken out as the panicked crowd began running for whatever cover was closest to them.

Bergman, who was driving, said, "How the hell did you know that sniper was there, Johnson?"

"I don't know."

"I guess what we've been hearing about you is true, then."

Dwight said, "I guess; where are we going?"

"A villa just outside town to the west. It used to be the plantation house of a giant rubber plantation there. Its seclusion among the rubber trees makes it perfect for a CIA Operations Center. It's top secret, so I have to get rid of these army guys before I can head there."

He double-parked the car and, leaving the engine running and the door open, walked back to the first jeep that had come to a stop behind them. He carried a large handheld two-way radio that he'd picked up from the center console of the Citroen as he got out.

Dwight and Beth watched as he talked on the radio for a few seconds and then handed the radio to the airborne colonel.

The colonel listened for a few seconds, and then Dwight saw him mouth the words "Yes, sir" and hand the radio back to Bergman. The two jeeps did a U-turn as Bergman got back in the car, closed the door, and pulled away. He said, "Army three-star generals seem to have quite a bit of influence on colonels."

The other CIA man was now on the radio, telling someone that they were on the way in.

Bergman said, "Lieutenant, I have a question about that gun, unless that too is top secret."

"No, there's nothing classified about it; it's a standard-issue .45-caliber, M-3 grease gun."

Bergman said, "A .45 has an effective range of fifty yards. That shot was an easy hundred yards, and you hit him in the head to boot. How'd you do that?"

"Well, to tell you the truth, I wouldn't have been able to tell you at the time how I did it, but, in retrospect, I took windage and elevation into account and then fired five rounds rather than one. Also, his head and arms were the only things visible, so I had no choice but to hit him in the head."

"You mean to tell me that you did all this windage, elevation, and aim calculation in the millisecond between the time you jumped to the side and began firing?"

"Yep; but it's more like GG did it."

"GG?"

"The gun's name is GG."

"Oh, of course. Silly me ... I should have known that." Then he shook his head in amazement.

"Several people will be meeting us there, including Colonel Wetzel. Prepare yourselves for a major debriefing, boys and girls."

Dwight and Beth sat back in the seat, considering the recent events and how they would describe them. Beth smiled to herself as she considered how she would describe the fact that she was on her knees with Dwight in her mouth when he killed the sapper.

She looked over at Dwight, who was looking at her. The two CIA men wondered what on earth could be causing these two kids to be laughing so hard at such a serious time.

-CHAPTER THIRTEEN-

PARTY TIME

THE VILLA WAS ABSOLUTELY beautiful. Built in the French Colonial style of the turn of the century, it could be seen from the beginning of the driveway, a quarter of a mile away, in the middle of a giant rubber plantation. Giant ornate marble columns adorned the front porch that took up two-thirds of the front of the house, soaring three stories high in a semicircle. An incredibly large and intricate crystal chandelier hung in its middle.

The massive porch was mostly white, except for the ornate window casings, which were white marble with so much pink marbling that they, like the columns, gave off a pink hue. Except for the porch and window framing, which were white, the house was pink stucco with stone of the pink shade of the marbling in the columns and window framing.

There were long, single-story buildings on either side of the mansion, which served to display the circular, tree-lined driveway and two-story high fountain and flower garden in the middle of the circle.

Beth gasped at its beauty just loud enough for Dwight to hear. He smiled at her. The house and grounds were undeniably beautiful, but she was so much more so, he thought to himself. *God, is it possible to have such strong feelings for a woman after knowing her for such a short time?*

The driveways and parking areas on both sides of the main house were half full of black Citroens, jeeps, a boxy army ambulance, and two Patton tanks.

Men, in both military uniforms and business suits, came out on the porch to meet them.

Both Dwight and Beth simultaneously realized how ridiculous they must look. Dwight's pants and Beth's jeans and blouse were dirty and had holes in them from the blast. Their faces and arms were smudged and dirty from the residue of the bomb.

They smiled at each other and got out of the car.

Colonel Wetzel met them halfway up the stairs, and Dwight saluted. Wetzel returned the salute and, smiling, extended his hand in greeting, saying, "Damn, son; you're off the base less than an hour and already in trouble!" He then introduced himself to Beth and took her by the elbow, and the three of them continued up the steps to meet the others.

The head of CIA-Vietnam, Michael Lawrence, hugged Beth hello and shook hands with Dwight as Beth introduced them. Five other men, three bird colonels, and three blue-suited CIA men were introduced. The two men who had delivered them stood together beside the front of the car.

Lawrence was a legend in the world intel community; he was known for his bravery and ability to think on his feet but also for his brilliance and high-level connections in several major countries.

His father was of black African descent, while his mother was from Finland and very fair, blond, and tall. The only child of a career diplomat, Lawrence had been raised in France, China, Italy, Spain, and South Africa and was fluent in six languages. He had spent his high school years in Capetown, and during that time, had been the darling of South African society.

His complexion was a light-coffee color, and his square jaw combined with deep-blue eyes and the physique of a linebacker (he had, in fact, been a star linebacker at the Naval Academy, where he had graduated second in the class of '53) made him a breathtakingly striking figure.

After five years as a navy fighter pilot in the Korean Conflict, he had been shot down and received the Medal of Honor for his actions in rescuing another downed navy pilot and fighting his way back to army lines, using weapons taken from Chinese Communist soldiers whom he'd killed. He'd joined the CIA soon after his discharge.

His meteoric rise in its ranks hadn't been hindered by the fact that in Korea, the first American Army officer to see him when he came through the perimeter wire, carrying the other wounded pilot, was then Major George Baxter, now the Commanding General of the 173d Airborne Brigade.

After the war, Baxter was assigned to the Pentagon, where their friendship had flourished, and Agent Lawrence and then Colonel Baxter's daughter Susan had gradually fallen in love.

Suzy, as she was known to her friends, had become an accomplished pediatric surgeon and internist; she had left a lucrative and successful practice in Washington and was currently in Vietnam working with orphanages in both Saigon and Bien Hoa.

She and Beth had met at a diplomatic function in Saigon six months ago and had become fast friends.

It was, after all, a small world.

Wetzel said, "Well, it seems that you two put on quite a show for the Continental Hotel staff, Saigon's citizens, and the enemy today. I can't help but believe that someone besides us now knows of your talents, Lieutenant Johnson."

They all laughed.

Lawrence said, "Let's go inside; it's too hot out here to be wearing a suit!"

They walked into the mansion, which had a large pink foyer with wide twin stairways curving up each side of the room to a mezzanine floor. The stairs were covered in red carpet with polished brass rods across the base of each stair. The ornate railing and support posts, placed five inches apart, were made of the same white with pink marble as that on the porch. Massive two-story-high white French doors opened from the foyer into a gigantic sitting room and ballroom.

Lawrence motioned Beth and Dwight to a large French provincial sofa on one side of a predominantly blue, pink, and red Persian rug, around which were placed various other sofas, love seats, and wingback chairs. The dominant colors of the furniture in this particular cluster were white, red, pink, and blue.

Two male Filipino house servants came in through swinging doors at the far end and side of the room, beside an immense fireplace, carrying neatly folded linen towels over one crooked forearm and, one arriving at each side of the sofa where Dwight and Beth were seated, asked for drink orders.

Beth unhesitatingly asked for a gin and tonic. Dwight and the others did the same.

They made small talk about the weather (a cloudburst had just begun and the thunder was loud and the lightning flashes through the gauzy curtains over the long windows were bright and spectacular) until the drinks came on two silver service tables, each one rolled to either side of the gathering by the two servants.

When the drinks had been served and the linen-draped tables left with attendant ice buckets, gin bottles, and several small tonic bottles, Lawrence said, "Lieutenant, why don't you tell us exactly what happened today, starting with you shooting the sapper through the door."

Dwight turned to Beth. She smiled and, unashamed, winked at him.

He blushed and looked at his shoes. Lawrence and the others tried to stifle their laughter but were unsuccessful.

Dwight said, "Well, I guess *that* part needs no further explanation."

They all laughed, this time without reservation; the ice had been sufficiently broken.

Dwight said, "Well, Mr. Lawrence, I …"

Lawrence, holding up his hand to Dwight to signal him to stop talking, said, "Dwight, you're making me feel like an old man; please, call me Michael."

"Sure … Michael. Anyway, I was in the process of laying GG on a chair, when …"

"Sorry to stop you again, Dwight, but, lest a few of the men's minds are in the gutter, GG is Dwight's grease gun." He motioned to the weapon now hanging by its sling over the arm of the sofa, at Dwight's side.

Dwight went on to describe the events of the morning, with Beth interjecting portions of the story that Dwight either wasn't aware of, such as having to show her ID card to South Vietnamese authorities who had tried to detain her for questioning inside the hotel, or thought might be bragging, such as bagging the sniper with a head shot, at over a hundred yards, firing from the waist.

During the debriefing, they'd all had another drink, and as they finished, Lawrence said, "Well, Dwight and Beth, of course there's a lot more to talk about, but it all has to do with where we go from here, now. Dinner will be at five in the dining room that adjoins this room, over there." He motioned to the doors on the other side of the fireplace from the ones that the servants had used. "That gives you several hours to bathe, rest up, and change. The servants will show you to your rooms.

"There are new uniforms and clothing there for you. Dwight, the uniform of the day is dress khaki, and Beth, there are several dresses and accessories in your room for you.

Suzy (the aforementioned Suzy Baxter, Lawrence's lover and Beth's best friend) made a few quick purchases for us, and they should have been delivered while we've been talking. If you need anything, pick up the phone and an operator will direct your call; any questions?"

Beth said, "Is Suzy still here?"

Lawrence said, "Yes, she will be joining us for dinner. She hasn't slept for forty-eight hours; she's been in surgery all night. Several children were in a bus wreck on Highway 1 last night, so please don't ring her room. I'm sure she's fast asleep by now."

One of the servants had stationed himself beside the sofa to take them to their rooms. They stood and followed him out the front door to their rooms at the front of the west wing of the adjoining single-story structures.

Their rooms were side by side, and there was a connecting door between them.

Both rooms were large and had a separate kitchen with a large refrigerator stocked with food, including cheeses, cold cuts, beer, champagne, other white wines, soft drinks, and bottled water. The pantries contained bread, crackers, condiments, and everything needed for snacks and sandwiches.

There was also a fully stocked liquor cabinet and a fresh bucket of ice on the kitchen table, along with a large bouquet of fresh flowers. A fruit basket was on the counter between the table and kitchen.

The rooms were identically furnished in French provincial with pink-ruffled mosquito netting canopying the queen-sized beds. Plush red carpet adorned the floors, except for pink tile in the bathrooms and kitchens. The window trimming, counters, and kitchen tables and chairs were white. French doors opened onto a small, furnished patio that joined with the patios of the other ten rooms on this side of the complex. Gauzy white curtains covered the glass, allowing the inhabitants to see the main mansion and parking area but obstructing the view of anyone attempting to look inside the cool, semi-darkened room.

Both closets had been left open so that they could see that Dwight's displayed both khaki and fatigue uniforms, covers (hats), and belts, along with a pair of his spit-shined boots.

Beth's contained several evening dresses, pairs of shoes, and some jewelry, which had been left on her dresser along with a note from Suzy stating that the clothing and shoes were Beth's but the jewelry and accessories were not and not to forget where she got them. Of course, Suzy also wished her well; she was glad she hadn't been injured and congratulated her on the acquisition of her new stud, hero, lieutenant, paratrooper. Then she closed, stating that she looked forward to meeting him at supper.

Both dressers contained various undergarments, socks, and stockings.

Suzy had provided Beth a new black silk negligee and robe and Dwight some black silk drawstring pants. These were draped over separate chairs in Beth's room.

Dwight had gone straight to his kitchen, opened a loaf of rye bread, and said, "Hey baby, I'm starving. I'm going to have a ham and Swiss on rye. What do you want?"

"I'll have the same, thank you, sir—mustard on bottom, mayo on top."

"No kidding; that's exactly the way I like 'em!"

"We're made for each other."

"I'll eat to that!"

He heard a champagne cork pop in Beth's room, and, as he was cutting the sandwiches, she walked in with the wine in an ice bucket and two crystal flutes. She poured the wine as he put the sandwiches down on the table and tore open a large bag of potato chips, putting a handful on each plate.

The champagne was a 1951 Dom Perignon. Dwight had never had it before and noted how it went down more like smoke than liquid. Smooth was an understatement, and the taste was delightful. He considered that he could become accustomed to living like this very quickly.

Dwight said, "I suppose you're used to living like this, but I'm certainly not. I'm thankful when a box of C rations yields a can of beef stew rather than beans and franks!"

"This isn't exactly my daily fare either, but I do have it pretty good here. But I'd advise you to live it up, cowboy. HALO school's not going to be a walk in the park."

"Tough as jump school?"

"Tougher; you're going to be doing PLFs from four-foot plat-forms." Dwight remembered that jump school's platforms were two and a half feet high, and, although everyone had been in great shape because the school had come immediately after basic training, they had all been extremely sore for the first four days. "As I said, the canopies are much faster and also have a seven-mile-per-hour forward speed, so you're going to need to train for the faster rate of descent and doing fast forward PLFs.

Also, the morning runs are going to be longer and faster, and you'll be going through the obstacle course every day before evening mess."

Dwight poured them each another flute of champagne. "And where will you be while I'm going through these rigors, my sweet?"

"I'll be teaching you and your men the finer points of high-altitude parachuting, free fall, and navigation under canopy. You'll be taught not only HALO but also to open high so that the airplane can't be heard going over the target and then to fly the parachute to the target while breathing oxygen and fending off the high-altitude cold."

"So, you're not going to be there for the tough stuff?"

"Some of it; I have to stay in shape, just like you do, but I don't think you'll want me there for the runs and the obstacle course, at least not during the first five days or so."

"Why not?"

"How much running and obstacle course work did you do during your stay at Ft. Polk?"

"I ran a mile every morning before chow."

"You'll be covering five miles every morning before chow and calisthenics before that, but you'll have a PowerBar after the calisthenics for energy during the run."

"PowerBar?"

"It's a new thing. Essentially, it's a high-energy candy bar, packed with protein, carbs, vitamins, amino acids, trace minerals, et cetera."

"You're way ahead of me! The only words I recognized were *vitamins* and *protein!*"

"Well, it doesn't matter; you'll be learning all about it during the training."

"You never answered my question."

"What question?"

"Why I wouldn't want you with us during the tough stuff."

"I tried to answer it obliquely, so I wouldn't hurt your tender masculinity and preconceived notions of femininity."

"You can beat me on the runs?"

"*And* the obstacle course."

"Really, now?"

"I do it all the time, sweetheart; it's simply a matter of conditioning."

"And, do you think you're in good enough shape to take a shower with me?"

"Tell you what, cowboy. I'm going to take another flute of this champagne into *my* bathroom and take a nice, feminine bubble bath. Why don't you take a shower and find something to occupy your mind for a few minutes.

There's plenty of reading material, and you can call home on your phone if you like. Just remember that most of what you're doing here is classified, although the enemy probably knows as much about it as you do, at this point. Our rooms aren't bugged, but any calls you make will be listened to—a word to the wise."

"Hey, that's a good idea; the folks will be glad to hear from me. What time is it in Corpus Christi?"

"Oh-six-thirty, yesterday."

"Great; they're both early risers. They'll be up."

Beth drained her flute, poured herself another, and left the room while Dwight sat down by the telephone and slipped off his shoes.

Dwight's father, Jack, had been a highly decorated navy fighter pilot in the Pacific during World War II. He had become an "ace" during the "Marianas Turkey Shoot," shooting down six kamikazes in his Corsair before running out of ammunition.

After the war, Dwight and his mother had joined his father and had lived on Saipan, Tinian, and Guam. Jack was born and raised in Iowa but had fallen in love with Corpus Christi, Texas, during his training, and that's where Dwight had been raised.

Dwight had written them a letter six days ago and had told them that the details were classified but that he had been awarded the Medal of Honor, or would be when he was sent back to the States to receive it from the president. He explained that he had also been awarded the Silver Star and Purple Heart in his first week in country. (They had also received a telegram to that effect, and an article had run in the *Corpus Christi Caller-Times*.) And he told them that, because of events that he was not at liberty to discuss, he had been commissioned an officer and would be placed in a leadership position, as soon as he completed the training for it.

Predictably, his father was proud of him but dying to know "what the hell was going on," to which Dwight had again told him that he could say no more than what he had already told them in his letter.

His mother, Pat (Mattie was her given name, but she had shed it when she became a WAVE, finally getting out of the little town of Elba, Alabama), was glad for him, but her chief emotion was a mother's worry for her only son.

She had been a clerk-typist for the navy at Memphis NAS and had met her dashing young fighter pilot on a blind date to an Officer's Club dance. They had married two months later at St. Patrick's Catholic Church in Corpus Christi, where Dwight had attended school from grades one through eight. The reception had been at the Corpus Christi NAS O-Club, and their honey-moon had been in Monterey, Mexico.

Dwight was born exactly nine months later at the Pensacola NAS Hospital, the nearest base to Pat's hometown, while Jack was shooting down Japanese kamikazes and flying off carriers in the Pacific.

Dwight had joined the army the day after he graduated from high school, to become a helicopter pilot/warrant officer. After basic, his eyes had failed the flight physical, but the army wouldn't let him out to go to college and then come back as an officer.

He and his father both felt that he'd been snookered, but he had no choice but to fulfill his commitment. He knew that he eventually wanted to become either a professional pilot, a physician, or a veterinarian, so he decided to go to medic school at Ft. Sam Houston in San Antonio, where his parents had moved and his father, as had been planned for two years, had started a new air charter company, while Dwight was in basic training.

His father had been angry at both him and the army, but although he'd pulled all the strings he could, he couldn't get the army to let Dwight out.

Dwight's becoming an officer and winning the nations two highest medals for valor were more than enough vindication for Dwight's plight of failing to become a pilot/officer, but now Jack too was concerned for his son's health and well-being.

After he had hung up, Dwight took a shower and was glad to see that someone had left a bottle of Canoe cologne for him. Coincidentally, it was his favorite fragrance, and he had been using it since junior high school. Could the CIA know this much about him?

He had pulled up one side of the elaborately sewn mosquito netting (it had been constructed with layers and folds that looked like bows and flowers, all made of the pink netting material) and tied it and folded the bedcovers down. He had put on the black silk pants that had been left for him.

Lying there on his back, shirtless, his hands clasped behind his head, his idle mind had drifted back to Abramowitz's death. Although he was usually successful in not thinking about it, the liquor had lowered his defenses enough to let him think about it again. He felt himself snuffle a little as a tear ran down his cheek, past his ear.

Beth had appeared by his side as he'd brushed the tear away.

Oh no! I can't let her see me this way! Stop it! Stop it!

"Dwight? What's the matter?"

"Nothing; I've got something in my eye. It happened in the shower."

She was gorgeous, standing beside the bed. She again wore high heels, which lifted her buttocks beautifully, and her widely spaced breasts pouted upward against the gauzy silk of the full-length robe, her oversized areolas shining pinkly through the black silk.

She bent over and gently kissed the corner of his eye, where another tear had been preparing its spill downward, and she simultaneously slipped out of her shoes and settled in beside Dwight, her leg over his, her hand reaching across his chest, and her middle finger touching his cheek and catching a tear as it began its fall from his other eye.

He sat up on the edge of the bed, moving away from her, and put his head in his hands, saying, "I got something in my eyes in the shower. Maybe I'm allergic to something in the shampoo."

I can't let her see me be so childish. She'll think I'm a weakling or maybe even unstable. Maybe I am unstable! What's wrong with me? I can't seem to get Abramowitz and his family out of my head!

Beth sat up beside him, putting her arm around his shoulder and rubbing his forearm with her other hand. Sex was nowhere in her mind now; in its place, a strong, maternal instinct had consumed her. She knew, from the depths of her femininity, that Dwight needed her now, more than ever.

Still, he resisted his own need for her, feeling that to expose his sorrow would diminish his masculinity and strength. He deeply feared that it might serve to weaken the man who had been so rapidly emerging from the boy of only a few weeks ago.

He stood up and walked over to the window, resisting the need to wipe the tears away, now unseen to Beth because his back was to her.

As she came to him by the window, one of the two tanks that guarded the complex had started up and was clattering and clanking down the driveway in front of their rooms. The noise allowed an unstoppable sob to escape his throat, and he coughed to try to hide it.

Beside him now, she pressed her breast to his arm; her arm was around his waist, and her other hand's fingers were in his chest hair.

He turned away but not before she saw the agony on his face as it contorted a little, like a child's who is trying to hold back tears. His bottom lip quivered as he tried to speak, so he abandoned the effort, continued his turn away, and walked back toward the bed.

What in the hell is the matter with me?! I'm right on the edge of losing control of myself! Am I losing my mind?! I've got to stop this craziness! I think I'm cracking up! Nothing like this has ever happened to me before! What can I do to stop this?

He sat back down on the bed and put his face in his hands again, both wiping his tears and hiding the anguish he knew was written there.

Beth too was experiencing emotions that she had never felt before. Her maternalism had emerged with the force of a lioness for her cubs. The realization that she would kill or even die for this man both consumed and astounded her.

The instinct's strength took over her actions as she walked up to Dwight and wordlessly pressed his head against her belly.

He said, "No, Beth," as he pulled away from her and gently pushed her away.

"I just have some personal issues that only I can deal with; I'm OK. Just give me a minute. I have to just push them out of my head again. I don't know what's wrong with me! I guess I'm tired. It's been a long day, and the champagne has caused me to get all sappy or something."

Beth knew the extent of his need for her now. She instinctively knew that he needed her to be there for him in the way that both men and women need each other most. He needed to be able to depend on her. A major test of their bonding had arrived, and it was time for her to take control and for him to relinquish it.

She walked around to the other side of the bed, lifted the mosquito netting, lay down, and moved over to Dwight. She then put her gentle hands on his shoulders and pulled him down to her. He offered little resistance as she put his head on her breast, holding the side of his face with one hand and his shoulder with the other, pulling him snugly against her body, not merely offering him the respite of her being but insisting that he take it.

Dwight could no longer control his emotions; the dam broke. He was at once ashamed and relieved. He was relieved not only that he could feel safe and secure in Beth's arms but also that he could feel her sympathetic, silent tears running down his forehead and into his own eyes, mingling with his tears and then running, together, down his face, past his ear and onto the sheets. She understood; she knew. And it was OK.

She was gently saying soothing words for him—"It's OK, baby. It's OK, sweetie. Just let it out. It's OK. It's OK"—as she gently rocked him.

He was now sobbing uncontrollably. He had no choice in the matter as he let his shame succumb to the power of his emotion, so that shame was no longer a factor in his tumult. He wept with a trust and abandon that he'd never known before.

In this precious moment, they both knew and understood that they were in love, that they loved each other with all their might. They were one with each other now, and they both fervently hoped they could remain so forever.

Finally, his tears began to subside, and he said, "I'm sorry, Beth." And, although he knew better, he needed to hear her soft assurance as he said, "You must think I'm just an immature little boy."

Through her own tears, she couldn't stifle a soggy laugh, "You know better than that, my wonderful, sweet man. You're the most incredible man I've ever even imagined, much less known.

"I love you, Dwight."

"I love you, too, Beth; so much is happening. So much has so recently happened to me, to *us*, it sort of confuses me. I think that I understand better now, what so many of the poets and philosophers meant when they talked about love but, more importantly, when they expressed their *need*. I need you, Beth. Am I being childish? Do you understand what I'm trying to say?"

"Dwight, I not only understand what you're saying. I *am* what you're saying.

I'll try to say it in a different way; it would be silly if a half of something said to the other half, 'I need you,' wouldn't it? My darling, loving, compassionate man, if I feel like you are the other half of me, whom I've been searching and waiting for, then that makes us like one, doesn't it?

"Just look at our bodies for physical proof of this fact. Not only are we made to become physically united, but our brains are hardwired for it too."

He nestled down further into her breast, wiping his tears with the corner of the sheet, which she then took from him and more thoroughly and lovingly wiped his tears, caressing his face with both hands as she did so. The tears had now become only a trickle because they were now tears of joy—these tears that Dwight had never experienced before but was completely unashamed of, with her.

In a way, this woman knew him better than he knew himself. It was her job to lead the half of him with which he was only now becoming familiar, her job to teach him and care for him in these finer parts of their lives, now so completely coupled.

Then, wiping away her own tears, she pulled him closer to her as he crossed his leg to be between hers so that they were now intertwined, side by side, his head still on her breast, her cheek on his forehead.

He said, "I accidentally killed a couple of troopers after the battle last week and …"

"Shhhh," she said. "I know all about it. You didn't kill them. You did the best you could. They both would have died without you being there anyway. The most that could be negatively said about it is that you made a couple of medical mistakes.

We all make mistakes, especially under circumstances like that. You're a very special man, Dwight, but you're not Jesus Christ. Everyone makes mistakes, every day."

"Yeah, but …"

"No buts … Like Colonel Baxter told you, you never get over things like that, but you *do* get through them."

"How'd you know about what Colonel Baxter said to me?"

"It was in his report. You're being groomed for serious command, Lieutenant, and it's necessary that the people whose responsibility it is to groom you know what you're being told and taught.

"But, back to the subject at hand, I have some valuable information for you, mister wonderful. Those won't be the last times that happens. You've become a very important man; you are being taught, right now, how to deal with things like that, and you've got a lot to learn about these kinds of things, in a very short period of time, and I have no doubt that you'll come through it just fine.

"I want you to try to imagine what it feels like to lose a *lot* of men because you didn't make the right decision, because that's going to happen to you. It happens to every combat commander, eventually.

"If you were Genghis Kahn or Hitler, you wouldn't suffer for it. But the fact is, Lieutenant, that you're a good man, as good as there's ever been, as far as this woman's concerned. Yes, you're going to suffer when men die under your command, and that's one of the things I'm here for; it's one of the reasons for my existence.

"You're a very special man, Dwight, in so many very special ways. And I love you so much that I can barely stand it."

"I love you too, Beth." He held her tighter and she did the same as they both tried to merge themselves, feeling the strength of the kind of love that bonds people together for eternity, the strongest emotion known to man and even to God, for he is the essence of it.

As they realized that Dwight was becoming erect against her thigh, they both chuckled. The glee of their bodies sang a softer song now.

Their lovemaking was different this time—slower, more exacting, more caressing, more purposeful, more loving.

Slowly showering each other with kisses, he entered her in the missionary position, moving slowly. She began approaching orgasm quickly and held his tight buttocks in each hand, thrusting him hard into her with the rhythm of the universe, as she merged with it in the second whiteout orgasm of her life.

Beth's whimpers and then scream of pleasure furthered Dwight's excitement, and he was fast approaching his own orgasm now, as he grew larger and stronger inside her and Beth brought her legs up higher and wrapped them around his back, locking her ankles together and pulling him into her in his rhythm and helping him thrust even deeper into her.

She pulled his final, long, powerful thrust as far into her as possible as he exploded in ccstasy, a deep groan loudly rising from deep into his being. As he moved and throbbed inside her, the sheer volume and power of his essence against her cervix caused her to come again; this one was powerful also but more solid and meaningful, like large but gentle waves lapping against a receptive shore.

With him still inside her, they both fell into the soft slumber of eternity.

The telephone operator called them at four to awaken them so they could get ready for dinner.

After he put the phone down, Dwight lay back down and stretched luxuriously.

Beth rolled half onto Dwight, putting her head on his chest, and nestled into his chest hair, languishing in the soft tickle of it on her cheek and nose.

She said, "I don't know about you, cowboy, but I think I'll just stay right here, thank you."

"I'm for that," he said and reached over and picked up the telephone receiver and handed it to her. "Here, ask for President Johnson, and tell him that we are putting the war on hold for a week or so, or, even better, tell *him* to do it; I doubt if that would piss anyone off."

Beth took the receiver and, after waiting a few seconds for the operator, said into it, "Give me Suzy Baxter's room, please."

After a few seconds, she said, "Wake up, Little Suzie; there're things to do and people to eat!"

Then, listening, she laughed and said, "Yeah, there's only one I want to eat too!"

After listening again for several seconds, she said, "Well, you wouldn't have to sit beside your father for every one of these things if you'd marry the man! I mean, everyone knows that you and Michael are an item, but protocol won't allow it unless you at least are engaged to him and …"

Listening again, she furrowed her brow and then said, "Oh, I'm sorry, Suz; I forgot that Dwight didn't know about you two. Don't be upset, Suz. He would have known by dessert, anyway;

he's not stupid. Everyone else knows, and you two sit there all night making goo-goo eyes at each other, and then afterward you mysteriously disappear at the same time!"

"I'll warn you about one thing about Dwight, and you'd better pay attention. You don't want to have any homicidal thoughts toward him. If you ever do, make sure I'm not standing near you."

Beth listened for a minute and said, "Wait a minute, Suz! That's classified information, and you know this phone is bugged! Your dad shouldn't have said anything about him to you!"

After a second, she said, "Not you too! You're going to be working with Dwight's new platoon?"

She listened for several minutes, her mouth opening in surprised gasps now and then.

After she hung up, Dwight said, "What?"

"What?"

"That's what I said, 'What?'"

"What, 'what'?"

"You know what I'm talking about! What does she have to do with my platoon?"

"I can't tell you."

"What do you mean, you can't tell me?"

"It's top secret."

Remembering how Rich had jumped him the night that Dwight had been jerking his chain with the Einstein baloney, he jumped Beth and found himself suddenly on the floor in a choke hold.

Before he needed air bad enough to become uncomfortable, she was off of him and back on the bed, sitting cross-legged, chuckling at him as he struggled back to his feet.

He said, "How'd you do that?"

"It's just simple conditioning and training, lover. Like I said before, I'm trained and conditioned in ways that you're not. Don't be concerned; your training is as a medic. You'll be brought up to speed on that hold and a lot more, before your training is finished.

"I hope you'll never need to use that hold, but, if you do, you'll be able to kill a man without him being able to utter a sound, a valuable tool when you're in close enough contact with the enemy to need to use it. If you stick a bayonet in a man, he's going to scream, so you might as well just shoot him."

"Shit, woman! You really are for real, aren't you?"

"Don't be upset with me, cowboy; you'll appreciate it one of these days. I mean, what if we were going to a play in New York and we were mugged? Who would protect your tender, pink ass?"

She relaxed and let him pin her to the bed this time. They were both laughing, and then she was in his arms again as they kissed and nibbled each other with mirthful lips and teeth.

Beth grabbed Dwight's forearm and turned it so that she could see his watch and said, "Good grief! We've only got thirty minutes before we have to be there!"

They both jumped up and headed for their respective bathrooms.

After a quick shower, Dwight was ready first. He had to admit, he looked pretty sharp in his dress khakis. He put on his cover and looked at himself in the full-length mirror on the bathroom door—one side, then the other, then back to a front view. Then he turned around and craned his neck to get a view of his back. Then, as he turned back to the front, came to attention, and saluted crisply, he saw her out of the corner of his eye.

"Been in town long, soldier?" Beth laughed.

She walked slowly toward him with the exaggerated one-foot-crossing-in-front-of-the-other steps of a runway model.

My God, but she's beautiful!

She wore a tight emerald green dress with spaghetti straps holding her breasts with gentle triangular cups, leaving ample cleavage in front and the hint of provocative swell on the sides. The hem was just below her knees where her tanned, stockingless skin displayed her calves and the fine turn of her ankle. Matching green high heels and her ubiquitous pearls completed the ensemble.

Pouting, she put the cool fingers of both hands on his cheeks and circled them around his neck. He swallowed hard as the Chanel No. 5 completed the sensory input.

Whatever he had, or had access to, was hers. Her power was overwhelming. He didn't have a chance. His white flag of surrender waved against her thigh, and she backed away from it, laughing.

She said, "No, no, Lieutenant! We have another kind of social obligation to fulfill."

She held him at arm's length to examine him.

"You'll be the best-looking man at the ball, Lieutenant, but where are all those medals you've won in the last few days?"

"They haven't been presented yet. There has to be a ceremony, and, for the big one, I'll have to go to Washington."

During cocktails, Dwight began to feel a little self-conscious. He was obviously the center of attention, and he simply had no practice at holding court. Because the guests were everyone from high-level diplomats to junior-officer aides to the senior officers and their wives to news correspondents to the servants, for security reasons he was unable to talk about almost everything that he was being queried about.

The room contained close to a hundred people, with plenty of room to spare. The ceiling was forty feet high, covering two-thirds of the entire bottom two floors of the gigantic mansion. The dining room, kitchen, and outside porches comprised the remainder.

After fifteen minutes or so, Dwight realized that Colonel Baxter and the high-ranking MACV officers were performing a tag team maneuver to be sure that someone of responsibility was continuously at his side to deflect and field questions where necessary, especially with the news people.

The big surprise for Dwight had been him seeing that his squad leaders were all there when he and Beth entered the room. They had rushed up to him from various sectors of the vast living room/ballroom. It was obvious that the men had obviously planned their reception, because when they'd approached him in greeting, they had each put out their right hand to shake his in greeting and then put their left forefinger in their mouths and said, "Airborne!"

Not missing a beat, Dwight had reciprocated in kind. Then, they'd each wholeheartedly embraced him. These were *his* men, and everyone in the room knew it and every officer envied it. The men obviously adored him.

His men tried to not ogle Beth, but it was impossible. To a man, they thought that she was the most beautiful woman they had ever seen. They were almost as captivated by her as Dwight was.

Everyone had a chest full of ribbons except Dwight. That was no surprise, but he had been surprised that his men each had two to three rows of them.

Well, after all, he thought, *they have all been in the army and in country quite a bit longer than I have.* Then he noticed that Rich and Bandy each had their new Silver Star ribbons. *Strange,* he thought. *I feel kind of naked. I'm not only the lowest-ranking officer here, but I don't have even one ribbon on my chest!*

There was a five-piece band in the corner near the servants' door, and they

began playing Julie London's old hit "Please Do It Again," and the way Beth looked at Dwight, put her lovely fingers on his arm, and asked him to dance with her wasn't lost on very many people in the room. Most of the men envied him; and the women, her.

Dwight felt that strong surge of love for Beth again, as he'd felt in bed just a little earlier. His emotion for her was so strong that it choked him, and he felt his chest and eyes well up again. He pushed away from her a little, for self-preservation purposes.

He realized that he was literally choking on his feelings for her!

Beth looked questioningly into his eyes and understood immediately what he was going through.

"Oh, honey," she said. "I love you so much." She kissed his neck and held him close to her, sending a thrill down his entire body.

"Beth, you've got to help me! I swear, this shit is too much for me right now! I'm seriously having trouble with these feelings for you! I've never felt anything like this before; help me, sweetie!"

She said, "Help is on the way, General Custer." Rich tapped him on the shoulder, and he gratefully relinquished Beth to him.

Rich said, "Excuse me, sir, but this is way too fine a woman to have to dance with an FNG lieutenant all evening!"

Before Dwight could reach the edge of the dance area, another beautiful woman had captured him. She had almost black, naturally wavy, shoulder-length hair and classically beautiful facial features; perfectly shaped, expressive green eyes; a flawlessly milky complexion; and a little turned-up nose. Her rich, full lips, made for kissing, were shimmering red, matching the ruby and diamond chandelier earrings dripping from her pierced ears. She had a high, intelligent forehead, high cheekbones, and perfect teeth. Dwight was amazed to see that her teeth actually sparkled in the soft light, marrying them to her warm smile!

Dwight was enthralled by the second most beautiful woman he'd ever seen. He thought, *This must be ...*

"Suzy Baxter," she said. "My, but not only are you quite the talk of the town but handsome too! I'd say Beth's done very well for herself, Lieutenant."

Not having quite regained his composure from his breathtaking encounter with Beth, he said, "Thank you for being so kind, Suzy, but I'm really kind of new at all this." He then looked past Suzy to see Beth looking at him with a mocking pout, as if she was hurt that he was dancing with Suzy.

Suzy thought to herself, *Oh my; he's a little shy and humble too! Quite endearing, considering his fame!*

Sensing what was now occurring between Dwight and Beth, Suzy took the lead and turned Dwight around so that she could see what he was looking at and caught Beth in her pouting pose.

All three of them laughed as Rich, in mid-sentence, stopped talking to Beth and turned them sideways to see what the laughter was about.

Suzy said to Dwight, "The world is full of unhappy young officers tonight, Lieutenant."

Having recovered now, Dwight said, "Oh? Why's that?"

"Well, it appears to everyone in this room and to the rumor mill from Saigon to Washington that one of the most desirable women on the planet has been taken off the market!"

"Please … don't tell me that you're not available, Suzy!"

She backed and looked into his eyes. Dwight thought to himself, *This woman is fully aware of her beauty, and she's really showing it off. I love it!*

"You really *are* a cowboy, aren't you, Lieutenant?"

"Please, Suzie, call me either Dwight … or cowboy."

They both laughed, and Suzy said, "OK, Dwight, but if only half the things I've heard about you are true, I should probably call you 'sir.'"

"OK, then, call me 'Sir Cowboy.'"

When the band ended the song, General Baxter stepped up to them and said, "If you'll excuse me, Suz, I need the lieutenant for a few minutes."

Pouting herself now, she said, "Oh, Daddy, you always spoil my fun!"

General Baxter colored slightly as his daughter, obviously delighted in seeing him brought down a peg or two, laughed a laugh that Dwight knew was reserved only for her father, and anyone could see that the two of them thought the world of each other.

Dwight said, "Excuse me, Suzy."

"You're excused, Sir Cowboy."

As they walked away, the general said, "What was that all about, Dwight?"

"I beg your pardon, sir?"

"Sir Cowboy."

"Oh, it's a long story. She decided to start calling me that because I'm from Texas and that's what Beth calls me."

"Beth calls you 'Sir Cowboy'?"

"No, sir. I mean, yes, sir. I mean, she calls me 'cowboy' some-times, and your daughter got wind of it, and she just added the 'sir' part to it."

"I guess I'd have to have been there to make any sense of it."

"Yes, sir."

"There are a few people I want you to meet before dinner, OK?"

"Yes, sir."

Dwight was introduced to the American ambassador to South Vietnam and his wife; three South Vietnamese dignitaries and their wives; the commanding generals of the Twenty-fifth Infantry Division, the First Infantry Division, and the First ARVN Airborne Division; two MACV generals; one bird colonel; and several other field-grade officers.

Everyone he met seemed truly happy to meet him and stressed that he should feel free to call on them for anything at all.

As they were walking across the room for more introductions, General Baxter said, "They are all sincere, Dwight. They truly do want to be of assistance to you, but be aware that there's no free lunch. Be careful what you ask for, because you'll not only get it but you'll eventually have to pay it back. Try to learn early to be indebted to as few senior officers as possible."

"Yes, sir."

As they crossed the big room, Dwight couldn't help but notice that many eyes were on them. He hadn't yet come anywhere near the realization that he had become a living legend.

Lawrence had stopped the band and was using one of their microphones to announce that dinner was being served.

General Baxter said, "There are a few more people I want you to meet, Dwight, but we're out of time. The chef gets a burr under his saddle if we don't sit when we're told. You'll understand why we put up with him when you wrap your lips around whatever he's prepared."

Dwight said, "Yes, sir" as the general moved away toward some other generals.

Beth had materialized at Dwight's side; his men were on both sides and behind him as they walked into the dining room.

The walls were separated horizontally by chairback-high eggshell-colored wainscoting. Below that was a soft shade of sandy-tan paneling. Above the wainscoting, the walls were painted a lightly pink-shaded deep red.

The walls were adorned with various sized portraits of men, both military and not. The lighting was via a giant crystal chandelier, hanging over the fifty-foot-long table, and candelabra-shaped lamps, spaced at ten-foot intervals at eight-foot height along the walls.

Like the ballroom, the room was two stories high and made for the table or vice versa. The table was covered in eggshell linen, and gold candelabra were spaced every ten feet. The china was eggshell with tiny red and blue flowers with gold leaf circling the centers and adorning the edges.

Placards at each place stated who should sit where. Dwight noticed that his men were seated together, across from him, and he was seated between the wives of the commanding generals of the Twenty-fifth and First Infantry Divisions.

To Dwight's thankful surprise, the two women were professionally adept at making him comfortable. They were near his

mother's age, somewhere above forty, and seemed truly interested in his hometown, what his parents did, and so forth.

Beth was seated between a colonel and the Twenty-fifth
Infantry Division's commanding general, happily making
conversation with them both and laughing freely. As Dwight
looked at her, she sensed it and looked back at him and smiled
for him, almost imperceptibly. He felt his pulse quicken and his
face flush. Rich had been right; he was thoroughly smitten.

He looked at Rich and realized that all four of his men were
watching him. Bandy and Pascone smiled knowingly, and Rich
winked at him. Cargo Sabinski leaned back in his chair, threw his
head back, and laughed out loud as Dwight made a mental note
to try to quit being so obvious with his affection for Beth.

The two generals' wives had the social grace to not embarrass
him, but he could see knowing smiles on their faces also. He
simply *had* to get control of this thing, he thought to himself.

He stole a glance at Suzy and saw that she also was seated
between two generals, one being her father. Lawrence was seated
at the head of the table, and it was obvious that she couldn't
keep her eyes off of him for any length of time.

Lawrence tapped his salad fork on his wineglass a few times to
get everyone's attention; he stood up and buttoned his tuxedo
coat. He said, "Ladies and gentlemen, there is some business to
be taken care of before we eat. Ambassador Studiford has a few
words to say.

The ambassador stood and said, "Good evening, everyone. I'll
make this as short as possible so that we can get on with dinner.
Believe me, you don't want to know what can happen if Pierre
has to wait to start serving his artistry!" There was twittering
laughter, as apparently everyone knew of Pierre's reputation for
perfection and culinary timeliness.

"President Johnson has asked me to make an announcement
and to perform a duty in his stead."

Studiford began walking the fifteen feet down the table toward Dwight, as he said, "Lieutenant Johnson, would you stand up please."

Bewildered, Dwight dutifully stood. General Baxter pointedly pushed his chair back, came to attention, and shouted, "Tensh-hut!" bringing all the military men to attention in a noisy scraping of chairs and clattering of silverware onto plates. The ununiformed men either came to attention also or stood.

Studiford carried a thin, black leather case, ten inches by six inches, to Dwight, who was standing at attention. Studiford softly said, "About-face, Lieutenant."

Dwight spun around in the maneuver, remaining at attention and wondering what was going on.

Oh, shit. I get it! Holy shit; I'm not believing this!

Although he managed to keep his head rigidly ahead, he couldn't help but lower his eyes to what Studiford was removing from the now opened, blue, felt-lined case. The Medal of Honor glittered in the light of the chandelier and candles.

Picking the medal up by either end of its wide blue-with-white-stars ribbon, Studiford said, "By the powers vested in me by the president of the United States of America, I award you, Lieutenant Dwight F. Johnson, Regular United States Army, the highest award for valor of the greatest and strongest nation the world has ever known."

Reading from a note card that he'd taken from his coat pocket, the ambassador said, "Lieutenant Johnson, for extraordinary valor, above and beyond the call of duty on the date of June 4, 1965, having no regard for your own life, you disposed of a live satchel charge, saving the lives of your fellow squad members. You then killed an enemy soldier who was attempting to kill you.

"You then proceeded to the commanding general's quarters and intercepted another enemy soldier as he was preparing to toss a satchel charge into the general's tent. You killed the sapper and then, seeing that the general was exposed to the bomb's blast, threw your body onto the sapper's body and the bomb, to save the general's life.

"The entire country and especially all of us here this evening are very grateful that the charge failed to detonate."

Then he said, "Lieutenant Dwight Johnson, I award you the Medal of Honor," as he clasped the ribbon around Dwight's neck.

Colonel Baxter was now standing beside Studiford with several smaller boxes. He took Studiford's place in front of Dwight and, with similar praise and statements of description, presented Dwight with the Silver Star with oak leaf cluster (i.e., two silver stars—one for his action in the recent battle and the other for his action in the Continental Hotel), the Bronze Star for his action after the helicopter landing when he warned and thereby saved lives in his platoon and then rushed the tree line, and the Purple Heart, pinning each medal on his chest in turn.

He then pinned on, above Dwight's airborne wings, the Combat Medic Badge, an award that medics receive for serving in combat, comparable to the infantry's CIB or Combat Infantry Badge.

Then, a member of the South Vietnamese delegation presented the South Vietnamese Cross of Gallantry to Dwight, also pinning it on his left breast.

When the award ceremony was finished, General Baxter said, "About-face, Lieutenant."

As he spun around, the crowd broke into polite applause.

Dwight was still at attention and couldn't look around, but, from the corner of his eye, he could see Beth wiping tears from her eyes with her napkin.

General Baxter let him stand there at attention for a few seconds, until the applause had died down. Then he said, "At ease, Lieutenant."

Dwight turned toward the general as he shook his hand. He could see the pride and love in the general's face for him.

His eyes glistening, the general, still clasping Dwight's hand, embraced him.

A wild cheer went up. The women were clearly crying with joy and happiness for both Dwight and the general, as the general held their embrace, his fist clenched behind Dwight's shoulder. Many of the men were trying to surreptitiously wipe tears from their eyes with the backs of their hands.

Dwight heard Sabinski shout, "Speech! Speech!" Others picked up the chant, especially his other three squad leaders.

The waiters had been quickly pouring champagne as the proceedings had progressed. There were now full champagne flutes and bottles between each place setting.

Dwight didn't hesitate; he knew what he was going to say. He reached down and picked up his flute and held it high, turning slowly from side to side as he waited for everyone else to do the same and the applause to quiet.

He then lifted his glass a little higher and shouted, "Airborne!"

The house came down! Everyone came to their feet as pandemonium broke out, and even the waiters were clapping and shouting, "Airborrrne!" at the tops of their lungs. Dwight thought his men were going to jump up on the table and cross it to him!

The band, all but forgotten in the other room until now, struck up "Stars and Stripes Forever."

The men had ceased wiping away their tears now as they and their women screamed, Airborne!" as loud as they could. The affair had turned into a party, and nobody gave a damn about Pierre or his food; in fact Pierre had emerged from the kitchen, drinking directly from a champagne bottle and shouting, "Airborne!" with the best of them! (Dwight found out later, from Pierre, that he had been a French paratrooper at Dien Bien Phu.)

Beth was there beside him now, and, laughing and crying simultaneously, she said, "I love you!" and kissed and hugged him.

His men were suddenly there, hugging him and shaking his hand, yelling "Airborne!" and "All the way!"

All around him, people were elbowing their way to him to congratulate and honor him and yelling, "Airborne!" at the top of their lungs.

-CHAPTER FOURTEEN-

HELP IS ON THE WAY

IT WAS A FRIDAY afternoon, and three weeks had passed since the banquet. Dwight was taking a break with his platoon in the shade of a thin tree line fifteen miles west of Saigon. They had parachuted into a location ten miles west of there at midnight and had arrived at the pickup point three hour early, after a recon exercise. They had HALO'd into the area in three groups, joined up at ten hundred hours after separate recon missions, and maneuvered to the pickup point ahead of schedule.

Dwight was the first to see the two black dots just above the horizon that he knew were the two Chinook helicopters, as his mind was wandering to his last night with Beth. Although they were now more accustomed to being with each other, their love and lovemaking had still grown in strength and intensity. Although they had been kept out of Saigon for security purposes, they had spent two more wonderful Sundays together at the secret CIA compound, the second one with Lawrence and Suzy, by the pool during the day and at dinner in the big dining room, joining some army and air force brass who were there for strategy meetings.

The training had gone well, and, since this was the last of the HALO qualification and reconnaissance training jumps, there would be a ceremony this evening to award the men the Vietnamese Airborne wings.

Dwight needed to give no orders as the Chinooks flared and sat down in the field by the tree line; everyone knew the drill by now—first and second squads in the lead chopper and third and fourth in the second, at double-time so as to not leave the helicopters sitting ducks any longer than necessary. There would be gunships circling the perimeter during the real thing, but there were none needed in this, at least today, relatively safe area.

As she had forecast, Beth had been a big part of the HALO training, and she had been correct in supposing that Dwight and his men would be surprised and chagrined that she not only was in better shape than they were but could best them in the hand-to-hand combat techniques taught during the first week. Of course, they redoubled their efforts to rectify this embarrassing situation and soon, because of their superior size and strength, had risen above her capabilities by the end of the week. At the realization of this goal, they weren't so much proud as relieved.

There had been a small problem at chow at the end of the first day of hand-to-hand training when Cargo Sabinski had asked Dwight, in front of his men, what he had been injecting into that woman. The table had gone silent as Cargo had realized his gaffe and immediately apologized. He had had the good sense to quickly defuse the situation, and there had been no hard feelings. In fact, it had been a good thing for his men to see Dwight's response. The men had never seen or even heard an angry word from Dwight, except toward the enemy in combat. This instance served to further their respect and discipline as they witnessed Dwight's body tense as his fork was nearing his mouth and his eyes go from placid to cold steel blue. Although Cargo saw to it that the situation was neutralized in an instant, there was no mistaking the seriousness of stepping out of line in this outfit.

When they returned to their rooms, the new Vietnamese wings had been sewn over the right pockets of their clean fatigue shirts, and instructions had been left to leave today's shirts on their bunks for the same treatment.

Although the lights were out every night at nine, Dwight was surprised to be rousted from a deep sleep at 0330. As his eyes focused, he saw that he was being awakened by none other than Michael Lawrence who, holding a finger to his lips, said, "*Shhh* … Come with me.*"

Lawrence had the tact and presence of mind to turn and walk out of the room that Dwight shared with Rich, his red-lensed flashlight's glow disappearing in the shadow of the closing door as Dwight sat on his bunk for the minute it took to will his erection to recede to an acceptable level.

In the hallway, Lawrence apologized and told Dwight that there was an emergency that required his attention and for him to roust his squad leaders and have them awaken the platoon and fall the men out in formation in full combat gear. Chow was being prepared for 0400, and their briefing would occur after they ate. Ammo and rations would be dispersed beside their gear while they were at chow. Dwight would be eating with General Westmoreland and his staff and the CIA brass at the briefing. He would then meet his men at the staging area, where he would brief them and complete gearing up for the operation.

The briefing was held in the large meeting room at MACV HQ. They were immediately seated in assigned places as the waitstaff brought family-style heaped trays of bacon, ham, eggs, pancakes, biscuits and gravy, oatmeal, and grits. Dwight was both happy and concerned that, as the last people straggled in and were seated, both Beth and Suzy Baxter were among them. His startled expression must have been obvious as Beth winked and crinkled her nose and Suzy laughed out loud. They both wore fatigues and no makeup or jewelry, so Dwight figured correctly that they would be involved. Beth's presence was understandable, but Dwight wondered what on earth could cause Suzy's involvement.

The long tables had been set up in a horseshoe with a large map board and blackboard set up in the open end. They were told to eat quickly but to relax; although the situation was urgent, there would be no immediate danger, so they shouldn't get excited and cause themselves indigestion. They could talk freely among the waitstaff, as they would be sequestered to the base until any danger of a security breach had passed.

After they had been eating for exactly five minutes, General Westmoreland himself entered the room carrying a two-foot-long black lacquered swagger stick made from a chrome-plated .50-caliber shell as its base and a chromed bullet at its point. One of the colonels flanking him shouted, "Tensh-hut!" as, with a scraping of chairs and clanging of silverware, the room came to attention.

"As you were," Westmoreland said and then paused for a few seconds to both raise the cover from the map board and allow the now rapt audience to seat themselves. He said, "As you can see, this is a map of Cambodia. As you are aware, the United States of America's politicians have decreed that its military forces cannot operate inside Cambodia. Well, then, we are not going to 'operate.' We are going on a humanitarian mission to free and evacuate a large group of Laotian Army troops' dependent wives and children. For fear of being misunderstood, this mission is not only top secret but its very existence will be strenuously denied. No matter how this turns out, it never happened. If anyone disagrees with my decision to save these people's lives, they are invited to leave, now." He paused and, slapping his swagger stick in his palm several times, searched the eyes of everyone in the room; he then said, "Are there any questions so far?"

No one moved.

"Now, a division of Laotian Army Regular Infantry has been decimated by the North Vietnamese, captured or killed here in the central part of the country." He pointed to a place on the center of the map. "The remaining prisoners and their families

have been herded to here"—he moved the point of the swagger
stick several inches from the first point—"and not fed for three
weeks. These people are staying alive on weeds and rodents. Our
intel has it that disease and starvation are killing over a hundred
people a day. The good news is that they are only lightly guarded
now that they are too weak to flee. Ladies and gentlemen, I have
no choice in this matter. I am staking my career on the fact that
these people must be helped. I will not let these people die while
I have the ability to save them. As I said, ours is not an act of war
but a humanitarian gesture. I have decided upon this course of
action because by the time Washington came to a decision about
it, it would be too late. There are approximately 1,000 people
remaining out of an initial 4,000, and they are virtually all sick
and dying. I only pray to God that it isn't too late already. If we
are successful, this will be the largest medical evacuation in the
history of mankind."

He went on to describe the mission requirements in both
personnel and equipment. Dwight's platoon would HALO in
from 30,000 feet and land three miles away, in three positions
around the encampment, and secure the perimeter. Then the
medical people and CIA would arrive by helicopter to take care
of the prisoners, stabilize them, and prepare them for evacuation. There would be twenty MACV medics and two Chinooks
full of C rations and medical supplies arriving just behind the
initial team. Dr. Baxter would be in charge of the medical
procedure, triage, and feeding. Her orders were to be followed
without question unless the military command decided that the
saving of life would be better suited to a military maneuver in
any given circumstance.

He then said, "All right; everyone is dismissed to begin preparations, except for Lieutenant Johnson and my staff."

Dwight glanced at Beth, who again crinkled her nose and
winked at him as she noisily slid her chair away and led Suzy,
who was in animated conversation with Lawrence, out the door.
Dwight smiled and winked back.

When the room had cleared of everyone but a few high-ranking officers and Dwight, the general said, "I'm not going to blow any smoke up your skirt, Johnson; this thing could blow up in our faces. You have a promising military career ahead of you, and mine is nearly over; I can afford to take a chance like this. Conversely, this one act could literally ruin your life, not just your career. You know the rules; you're a combat soldier. Your MOS is still 911, in addition to your new infantry MOS, but I don't think you'll be able to hide behind that, should the feces hit the fan. There's been too much water under the bridge for that. You are voluntarily going into a sovereign nation on a military mission. Do you understand what I'm trying to say, Lieutenant?"

"Yes, sir; I think so, sir."

"The reason I've chosen you, Johnson, is that there is still a NVA division in the area, and they, or elements of it, could sneak up on us while we work. We'll have Special Forces and 173d LRRPs waiting in the wings, but I don't want to bring anyone in unnecessarily. The less attention we bring to this operation, the better. We need to be as stealthy as possible, so I need to be able to rely on your perception to both sound the alarm and hold the Indians off until the cavalry arrives; are you with me?"

"Yes, sir."

"You have the right and ability to tell me, right now, that you disagree with this mission—that this is not what you have been trained to do and that mine is an illegal order. It will not be held against you and may even be a positive entry in your dossier. It is up to you to determine whether you are doing the right thing by accepting this mission. I cannot tell you that you may be too young and inexperienced to make such a decision or that, in a court-martial, you would be held harmless in my decisions. In fact, I must go on the record as saying that you have been fore-warned that you probably will not be allowed this excuse. This must be totally your decision, Lieutenant; is that clear?"

"Yes, sir."

Man, what kind of fix have I gotten myself into this time? Oh well, what the hell; as dad said when he got fired, I was looking for a job when I found this one.

The general said, "OK, Lieutenant. I want you to go brief your men and get their OKs also. The CIA and medical people are OK with it, but they don't have at stake what you and I have. We'll be the ones skewered, if Washington decides to do so. I'm sorry that I've had to put you in this position, Johnson, but if we pull it off, your bravery and fortitude will not go unnoticed.

"I also want to apologize for having to jump your platoon so high. It's going to be cold up there, and you'll have to breathe oxygen until you exit and not be able to take a good breath for ten thousand feet, but again, I have no choice. The element of surprise is paramount, and we have to get in there before more innocent women and children die unnecessarily. Do you have any questions or requests, son? Believe me, I'll do whatever I can to ensure the success of this mission or make sure my people have every advantage."

"No, sir. I think we're about set."

"Good to hear it, Johnson. Colonel Wetzel will brief you and your squad leaders on the fine points and issue maps to each of you," the general said as he turned to leave.

"Colonel Wetzel shouted, "Tensh-hut!" as two colonels followed Westmorland out the door and the remaining five men in the room came to attention.

Greetings could be heard out in the hallway as Dwight's squad leaders said hello to the general and entered the room. They shook hands all around and were seated on either side of Dwight.

Wetzel told them that it was an extreme HALO and they would be breathing oxygen before the jump. They had made two extremely high-altitude jumps last week and were unconcerned. They had also separated by squads in the free falls and were well trained in tracking to prearranged positions before opening. They knew that, in a good track position, they could travel one foot horizontally for every two feet of vertical fall; thus 30,000 feet would allow them to travel roughly 15,000 feet or almost three miles horizontally. The weather was forecast severe clear, so they should have no trouble attaining their designated opening points, if they left the airplane exactly over the target.

Wetzel had enlarged aerial photos of the target and each opening point, at each point of the compass. They would exit down the ramp, first and second squads on the starboard side and third and fourth squads to port. Each squad would have a radio, and they would coordinate their attacks to hit the enemy simultaneously.

With any luck at all, they would achieve total surprise and be able to kill or capture the small guard contingent without much trouble. A monitoring command plane would be high above them to coordinate the rescue party and, should the platoon get into more trouble than anticipated, to call in the cavalry, as Westmorland had put it.

It was important to take out the enemy HQ first and destroy the radio. Its location had been positively identified via the radio antenna's obvious position. They would carry a half day's rations and the now beloved PowerBars that they had become so reliant on before their morning and evening runs and obstacle course training. Each man would carry at least one LAW anti-tank weapon to be used as bunker busters, if needed. Anyone not carrying M60 or M79 ammo would hump a second LAW. In this platoon, that meant Dwight and his squad leaders. This is how they'd trained during the last four weeks, so they were ready for the load. And they had each fired at least fifty LAWS during the training and were each expert with it and knew its capabilities.

Dwight thought back on the training he and his men had gone through together. HALO training had been much more than parachute training.

At the end of each day but before running the obstacle course and chow, there had been a thirty-minute weight-training regimen, concentrating on legs, chest, and arms, and, despite the rigorous days, they had each put on at least five pounds of muscle. The food had been protein-rich and plentiful.

Although he had seen Beth every day and gained a new appreciation for her abilities and conditioning, there had no thought of sex. Even if they would have had a chance to be together in the evenings, they were both simply too exhausted to even consider it.

The platoon consisted of fifty-three men, including Dwight. Although a few men had experienced some trouble with maintaining stability in free fall, all had eventually mastered it. They had made five jump-and-pull jumps with the lower-performing double-L parachutes and fifteen with the 7-T-U. (Looking down from above the opened parachute, the Double-L looked like two *L*s, facing out from each other—two panels removed and a foot of the bottoms of four panels removed. The 7-T-U looked like the Double-L except the lower portions of the panels between the two *L*s were removed so that, from above, it looked two *T*s hooked together or a *U* with panels partially removed at its bottom.)

For the JPs, during their first five jumps, they counted, "One thousand, two thousand, three thousand" and pulled the rip cord, which was a two-foot-long, thin steel cable with a D-ring on one end and four pins on the second foot of the cable that held the backpack closed via fasteners.

When the D-ring was pulled, the pins came out of the fasteners, opening the backpack, which opened via a small spring-loaded pilot chute, which popped out, pulling out a sleeve out that contained the parachute. The pilot chute then pulled the sleeve off of the parachute so that it opened slowly enough, as the sleeve came off of it, to not explode the chute or break the paratrooper's back.

Terminal velocity, the speed that a man in a stable position reached in free fall, was about 120 miles per hour. If a parachute were to open without something like the sleeve causing it to open relatively slowly, the shock would be too much for the man or the parachute or both. Even with this method to slow the parachute's deployment, the parachute deployed in only a couple of seconds.

Anyone who failed to hold on to the rip cord, roll it up, and put it in a pocket had to pay five dollars for a new one. This discipline served to cause the men to think about what was going on and keep their wits about them during those crucial moments when a malfunction could occur and be levelheadedly dealt with. No one dropped a rip cord after the third jump.

After the initial J-Ps, they had progressed to twenty-second delays, reaching stability in terminal velocity for about five seconds, before they pulled. Then, when each could maintain a stable spread without turning or twisting, they progressed to more time in free fall until they had done ten free falls of sixty seconds and had passed a baton at least twice.

They then moved on to jumping with full equipment. Free fall under these circumstances would have been nearly impossible because of the uneven and unusual weight distribution and the differences in aerodynamics caused by egressing the airplane carrying their equipment in a bag on their fronts. The solution was to jump actually holding a pilot chute that was only two feet in diameter, attached to the center of the rip cord in the middle of the backpack. Immediately upon leaving the aircraft, the trooper released the pilot chute, which stabilized his falling body. Terminal velocity was thus slowed to 100 miles per hour, and the jumper then only had to stabilize any spinning motion and control any lateral motion as he normally would, using extremity positions. They made another ten jumps in this configuration, but some of them needed a few more jumps to perfect the technique.

Cargo Sabinski, jumping a specially made, larger 7-T-U, needed another five jumps, but the problem wasn't the parachute. Sabinski was having trouble stopping his spinning motion in free fall. The instructors were especially upset with this situation because two of them would have to jump with him to both analyze the problem and stop his spinning by actually grabbing his spinning body by one of his feet, which was dangerous for all involved. They finally stopped the problem by taping a bamboo stick to his back over his spine so that he could feel that he was twisting his body and was thus able to correct the problem.

The men had quickly learned to not be fearful and enjoy the freedom and maneuverability of free fall, but they also enjoyed the ride after the canopies had opened. Unlike the army's standard Airborne T-10 canopy, these could be "flown" via toggle lines, one on each riser on each side of the paratrooper. Pull the right one and the slit on the right side would close, causing the air rushing through the still-open slit on the left side to turn the canopy to the right and vice versa.

Also, when they got good enough at judging their distance to the ground, they could pull both toggle lines to slow the rate of descent by over half, cushioning the fall enough to actually be able to perform a stand-up landing, rather than doing a PLF. The hot dogs among them started doing this as soon as they became capable, and Dwight was among them.

However, this was not encouraged for two reasons; first, one could easily break bones, even if the height judgment was correct, trying to perform a stand-up, and, if the judgment was incorrect and the jumper was too high when he closed the panels, the parachute's rate of descent suddenly became half-again its normal rate and an injury became probable.

When they had advanced to jumping with weapons, ammo, and equipment in a large bag attached to their front, this hotdogging not only was not tolerated but could result in serious disciplinary action. Most of this stuff would be hanging ten feet below the paratroopers via an equipment bag called a Sally bag, which was released via a slipknot when the trooper got about seventy-five feet above the ground or when he was certain not to hit or entangle another paratrooper, sometimes just before impact. The stand-up landing was possible but forbidden. Worse than losing member of the team, having to carry an injured paratrooper would hinder a fast-moving operation, and the chance was not to be taken.

Dwight sat on the deck by the ramp. Despite the thermal coveralls used for high-altitude jumps, he was shivering in the cold hold of the C-141. They had made all of their extreme HALO training jumps from it because the C-130's ceiling was only about 25,000 feet, and it had to struggle for that. The C-141 could climb to over 40,000 feet, but the exit was uncomfortable, to say the least. Being a jet, the stall speed was substantially higher than that of the 130. But because the air was so thin up here, the exit blast wasn't near as bad as it would have been at lower altitudes.

The jump light went from red to orange, and the ramp began to swing to its down position. The men all stood and double-checked each other's equipment, breathing oxygen from wall-mounted bottles. Although the Sally bags were firmly attached to the men, they would hold on to them until after the blast and then put arms and legs out in a stable spread position until reaching stability at terminal velocity; then they would move their arms to their sides, palms down in order to achieve an effective track position, and literally fly to their opening points. Dwight would be with first squad and would track south. It was important to set up the track immediately upon attaining terminal velocity, as they had just enough altitude to reach their respective opening points.

The trick was to release the pilot chute and grab the equipment bag with both arms just as he stepped off the ramp. Otherwise, the loosely secured bag could give him a good whack in the blast.

Tumbling, Dwight saw the rapidly receding airplane go by three times before he got stable, and knew that he'd blown the exit. What the hell; it wasn't the first time. With all this gear, it was more the rule than the exception. The inevitable trouble was that the five-foot pilot chute line had wrapped around him, but, again, he was used to it; he quickly freed it and was immediately stable. He looked up and saw the airplane, turned to a position where it was going away to his left; he entered a track position and began to see the earth moving beneath him as his across-the-ground speed attained about sixty-five miles per hour. He looked to see that his men were tracking properly and saw second and third squads tracking away to his left and right. He knew that Rich and the others of first squad were just above and behind him—so far, so good.

Looking at his altimeter, he saw 25,000 feet and realized that he was breathing too rapidly.

Relax.

Relax.

Don't burn more oxygen than you need.

Thirty more seconds and you're good.

Where's the opening point?

There it is.

There it is.

I got it.

Good.

Dwight spotted the opening point about two miles ahead and 22,000 feet below. It never ceased to amaze him how, at high altitude, there was no perception of descending. Dreamlike, it felt and looked as though he were just hanging there; even in a track position, the motion was barely perceptible. But at around 3,000 feet, look out; there was no question that you were falling like a rock.

The wind was out of the east at ten, gusting to fifteen knots; a back PLF would be needed. At 6,000 feet he was over the point and moved into a stable spread position, slowing from a 150- to 100-mile-per-hour rate of descent. He pulled at 1,500 feet and was swinging under the canopy at 800 feet. He checked his canopy and turned into the wind, seeing the squad do the same above and behind him.

At 50 feet, he pulled the slipknot, dropping his Sally bag, and saw that the DZ had a few large rocks in it but was mostly nice, soft grass—no problem.

Dwight listened to the men talking and shouting to each other: "Watch out for that rock, Murph!"

"I've got it, asshole! This ain't my first jump, dipshit!"

And, "Hey, Peterson, when you gonna drop your bag?"

"Oh, shit; thanks!"

Dwight's rearward speed was only about three miles per hour. The bag hit, and he pulled both toggle lines down. He twisted to the right as his toes hit and made a perfect rear PLF. *Damn, I'm good,* he thought and smiled as he rocked up to his feet from his latissimus dorsi, the large muscle on the side of the back and the last muscle to hit in the PLF. He simultaneously grabbed handfuls of shroud line, collapsing the billowing canopy. Immediately, he looked as the last of the squad did the same.

Everyone's up, looks like.

Looking good.

Looking good.

Rich was rolling up his canopy not fifteen yards to Dwight's side. Dwight said, "Rich, did you see anything after we opened?"

"Nope; it looked like the curvature of the earth and the trees near their camp obscured us. Lassiter was the last one out; ask him."

Both Dwight and Rich began walking to the nearby tree line as they raised their right hands in the air and made a circling motion, forefinger extended—the signal for "form on me"—as the men began gathering Sally bags and rolled parachutes and moving in the same direction. It was important to get out of the open area as quickly as possible.

When they were inside the tree line, they removed the loose-fitting overalls, and, beginning to unpack, Dwight said, "Lassiter, did you open highest?"

"Yes, sir; me and Lopez were about even."

"Could you see the camp?"

"No, sir. I looked as soon as I was under canopy, and I couldn't see anything."

"Lopez?"

"No, sir; I looked too, and I couldn't see nothing."

"OK; good work. Did anyone see anything unusual?" Dwight said as he looked from man to man. Everyone shook their heads no. "Anyone hurt?" The men looked around. All thirteen seemed OK and ready to go.

Rich spread a map out on the ground as he and Dwight took a knee beside it, and the men gathered around. Dwight had taken GG out of his bag and inserted a magazine. The first things unpacked were weapons and ammo. He put GG's barrel on the bottom edge of the map and said, "OK, here we are. As discussed in the briefing, we're going to hug these tree lines all the way to their perimeter." He traced a crooked line with GG's muzzle to the encampment. Then he said to the RTO, "Lopez, how's the radio?"

"Good, sir. Standby is on, and I picked up the static from the airplane when I switched it on to check it." Dwight recalled that the airplane would be broadcasting static for the first fifteen minutes for the teams to test the radios on, and the enemy, if they were monitoring the frequency, would think that an airplane with faulty equipment was passing over the area.

Dwight said, "All right … saddle up. Anyone have any questions?" There was no comment as the men busied themselves putting their gear on and helping each other hook up and drape machine gun belts over shoulders and attach LAWs on rucksacks. No one wanted to be the last to be ready to go. Dwight stepped out into the grassy field as the squad fell in behind him, Rich twelve paces behind and the others maintaining the same separation.

The wind was rustling the leaves above them and blowing gusty waves in the thigh-high grass. Dragonflies darted, and birds sang and flew from tree to tree. Puffy white clouds drifted across a light blue sky, and the dry temperature was a pleasant 92 degrees. Dwight watched proudly as a large butterfly landed on the nose of one of his men, and the man simply watched it, eyes slightly crossed—cool.

They covered the three miles in just under an hour and formed up in the tree line a hundred yards before the tree line that defined the encampment. Dwight told the assembled squad to remove their packs and spread out at twenty-yard intervals and watch for thirty minutes and report back to him. If no one saw anything, he would take two men and recon the area inside and beyond the next tree line. After thirty minutes, he took the handset from Lopez, switched the switch from standby to ON, and double-clicked the mike. He waited as second squad clicked twice, third clicked three times, and forth clicked four times. So far, so good—everyone was set and each squad would now begin their recon. Dwight knew that the communications airplane was passing on the progress of the operation as they heard the mike clicks.

The men began reconverging on his position and reported that no one had seen or heard anything. Dwight hoped that he had the right tree line.

All eyes were on Dwight and the two men he'd chosen to go up with him. He said, "OK, I'm going up. Saddle up and be ready to go. If you hear gunfire, it's party time. Get up to me as fast as you can." He looked in each of their eyes and saw nothing but resolve. *God, I'm proud of these men,* he thought.

"Holy sheet!" Ariza whispered. Dwight, Ariza, and Simone lay in the underbrush at the edge of the tree line, looking at the scene before them. The Hmong tribesmen were a hearty bunch and the core of the American allies in Laos. There were at least a thousand women and children in the field before them, most in grass lean-tos but some lying out in the open. Their bodies reminded Dwight of the photos he'd seen of the Nazi death camps. The stench of death was in the air, and those who were able carried the dead to open pits on the perimeter. Children, bellies distended, chewed on grass, and women held them and silently cried.

The well-fed North Vietnamese walked the perimeter in pairs. Dwight counted thirty. He could see no weapons heavier than a few light machine guns, and those were all surrounding the main structure: a one-room bamboo-and-grass hut with an antenna mounted on a fifty-foot tower beside it. There were what appeared to be about fifteen two- to four-man tents and grass huts around those.

The tree line across from them, about five hundred yards away, erupted in gunfire and grenades. Tracers, both green and red, flowed like spaced lava and then ricocheted upward like sparse desert plumes, disappearing as they cooled. White-orange explosions ripped leaves and branches from trees as grenades thundered behind their telltale gray-white puffs of smoke. Sabin-ski's .50 barked a long complaint as its big tracers began igniting the thatch of the main hut. Someone fired a LAW, and the round went through the hut and exploded thirty yards on the other side. A second one found its mark, and the hut exploded in a ball of red-orange flame.

Dwight saw at least ten NVA soldiers, who had been concealed in his tree line, begin running toward the action. GG put two rounds in three of their backs before Ariza and Simone began firing, each of them cutting down a man before the remaining six or so turned, dropped to the ground, and began returning fire.

Dwight tried to figure out what was happening. Apparently, Sabinski's squad had stumbled into NVA, who had been concealed in his tree line as these remaining six Dwight was now dealing with had been. Small-arms fire was now beginning on the other two tree lines. Dwight suspected that the other two squads had been caught as flat-footed as he had. The attack had been scheduled for almost an hour from now.

Well, Dwight thought, *the good news is that the enemy is as confused as we are, probably more so.* The problem now became whether

Dwight, Ariza, and Simone could hold these gooks off until the rest of the squad arrived.

Ariza and Simone had rolled to their sides about ten feet in order to acquire a modicum of separation. The enemy was firing sporadically as they tried to figure the situation out. As Dwight thought about it, although unplanned, this might just be a good tactic. The enemy must think that this is a coordinated attack and that the main action was on the other side of the perimeter and that Dwight's position was diversionary.

He shouted, "Start raising as much hell as you can. I want them to think there's more of us here! Throw your grenades and lay down suppressing fire!" He had pulled the pin on the first of his six grenades and threw it as far as he could. He didn't bother ducking. He knew that the grass would soak up any shrapnel headed in his direction. Out of the corner of his eye, he saw Simone rear back and throw one forty yards, from his knees. *Damn, that man's got an arm!* he thought.

Come on, GG! Concentrate, baby! Where are they, sweetie?"

Seemingly on her own and on command, GG raised herself over his head and chattered out four rounds. A surprised NVA stood up thirty yards away with his rifle out in front of him, eyes wide and mouth frozen open. Simone knocked him to his back with one AK round. GG pivoted to her left three degrees and cut two more rounds loose. A terrible scream emanated from her victim and continued unabated, except for short, ragged breaths—must be a gut wound.

Gaining confidence, she pivoted again, this time to her right fifteen degrees—two more rounds and another gut wound.

Dwight could hear the rustling vegetation and pounding boots of his squad arriving, and he was quickly on his feet. Two NVA rose up out of the grass with their arms in the air. They should have stayed down; Simone got one and Ariza the other. *What could the idiots have expected?* Dwight thought. *The trigger works a lot faster than the reasoning powers do.*

Rich was suddenly at Dwight's side, and they were running full speed across the field. They all knew that this was a particularly dangerous maneuver. If they weren't careful, they could be killing each other in a four-way cross fire. Luckily, the NVA knew they were beat and began standing, their arms in the air. It was over.

As they ran, they jumped over lifeless Laotians and others either sitting motionless and glassy-eyed or standing weakly as they had been trying to help their friends and families. Some smiled weakly and bowed their appreciation.

Dwight said, "Rich, stay here and start rounding up and disarming the guards. I'll get the others doing the same, Where's the RTO? Never mind. I see him." Then he shouted, "Lopez! Over here!" The RTO was fifty yards back toward the tree line, herding several guards toward Dwight's position. He prodded them in the back with his AK-47 and said, "De-de-mau!" and they all began trotting toward Dwight.

Dwight sized up the situation while he waited for Lopez to arrive. He knew that people were dying and that he needed to act quickly; there was no time to waste. The temperature had risen into the high 90s, and the air was laden with moisture. Dwight could see thunderheads building in the south and west. *Damn*, he thought. *We've got to get some food and medicine in here, right now! This weather's going to be socked in in a few minutes.*

Lopez trotted up and, turning his back to Dwight so he could operate the radio, told his prisoners in Vietnamese to sit down and put their hands on their heads. As Dwight picked up the handset and turned the switch from STANDBY to ON, he saw that the squad leaders had taken the initiative and begun gathering the NVA guards and their weapons and herding them toward the now burning radio hut. He heard Rich shouting for the men to give their food and water to the sickest prisoners first and to search the HQ area for the NVA's food and water. *Jesus, what a mess*, he thought.

Into the handset he said, "Savior, this is Moses; do you read?"

"Moses, this is Savior; I read you five by five."

"Savior, we have secured the area. Come on in."

"What happened, Moses? You weren't supposed to begin for another forty-five minutes."

"I don't have time to explain; just get in here. People are dying all around me!"

"We're socked in, Moses! " Dwight could hear the cracks of lightning and thunder over the radio. "We can't move! We have high winds and rain! We have to wait for this storm to pass!"

"Are all y'all in one place? I thought you were going to be coming from two locations!"

"We were, but the storms are all over the place! The second team was forced to come here! Their staging area has been socked in for two hours!"

OK, just get here ASAP. We've got a really bad situation here!"

"Roger, Moses. We'll get there as soon as we can!"

Dwight said, "Moses out!" and snapped the handset back into its cradle.

Lopez turned and looked into Dwight's eyes and then looked away, as Dwight knew that Lopez had seen his despair. He couldn't let the men see too much of that kind of thing, he knew. He tried to perk up and said, "Get these sombitches over to the compound and then stay close to me. I want to hear anything that comes up on that radio."

"Yes, sir," Lopez said. Then he told the guards to get up and deedee toward the burning hut, again poking them in their backs with his rifle. Dwight considered telling Lopez to take it easy on the prisoners, but frankly he didn't have much love for them right now either. Anyone who treated civilians like this, much less women and children, wasn't going to get much sympathy from him.

He tried to better size up the situation. He knew that he had to start doing whatever he could to save these people's lives. He began devising a plan as he trotted toward the compound. The guards were now all seated in the center of the compound, close enough to the burning radio hut to feel the heat. Sabinski had a cigar in his teeth and was glowering at them, smoke still curling up from the barrel of his big machine gun. They were truly frightened of him, as well they should have been.

Dwight pointed GG in the air and fired off three rounds. As every eye went to him, he raised is arm and rotated it in the circular "form up on me" signal. The men were scattered over the area in varying positions and degrees of trying to aid the dying Laotians. He let his thoughts further jell as the men gathered around him and the prisoners.

He said, "All right, listen up; we're going to have to work fast. The choppers are held up by those thunderstorms, so it's up to us to keep these people alive until they get here. First squad is in charge of guarding the prisoners and finding their food and water. Rich, all you'll need is two guys on guard. I want the rest of you to get these people out of the sun. We're going to move all of them over there in that tree line." He pointed to the closest stand of trees, which were also the tallest and had the sparsest vegetation beneath them.

Then he said, "We're going to divide the area up into thirds; second squad, take this third." He put his arms out at forty-five-degree angles, indicating the area for second squad. "Third squad, take this area." He pivoted to point out third squad's assignment and then did the same for forth squad's area. "Third squad will take the center of the tree line and second and forth squads on either side of them. Each squad will be responsible for the people they gather and bring in. The most important thing is hydration. It's up to each squad leader to be sure his men tend to the most seriously sick people first. Go over your areas with your men, and figure out who needs help the most;

set your priorities, and then get started. First squad will begin bringing water immediately and then food. The medic and I will meet you in the tree line."

Then he raised his voice another decibel, and, looking around the group with a scowl, he said, "If anyone dies under your care, I'm going to damn well want to know why! Now, get moving!"

The men went straight to work. There wasn't a lost motion or moment. The first patients began arriving soon after Dwight and "Brad" Bradbury, the new medic, arrived in the tree line. A woman and two children were unconscious. The kids were both about six years old, Dwight guessed. The woman appeared to be in her late teens. All three were hot and dry—not a drop of sweat on them.

Dwight said, "Get their clothes off, and get some water on them! We've got to get them cooled down!" He tore the clothes off one of the kids as the medic did the same with the other. One of the troopers who had brought them in took the woman's long-sleeved black top off while another trooper pulled her black pants off. Dwight could not figure why most of these people wore black pajamas in this heat and sun. He splashed some water on the now naked child and, handing him to a trooper, poured water from his canteen over the woman, putting two fingers over the opening and shaking it so that the water dribbled over her body. He then sat at her head, cradled it in his arms, and saw that she was breathing rapidly. He opened her mouth and dribbled a few drops into it. She choked a little and her eyes opened and closed again as he dripped a few more drops into her mouth. She sputtered again and opened her eyes for a few seconds this time. He repeated the exercise several more times until she kept her eyes open and she could take small sips of water.

The two children were beginning to come around also, in much the same manner. The woman in Dwight's arms was conscious enough now to be able to lift her hand and place her fingers on Dwight's wrist. He felt a surge of compassion in his chest and smiled at her; she smiled back. He could feel her relax a little and saw the fear and anguish somewhat abate from her face. Both of the boys were sitting now while the troopers gave them sips of water and continued to pour water on their necks and bodies. It looked as though all three of them were going to make it.

Dwight began circulating and triaging, sending Bradbury to fourth squad's area while he worked his way over toward second squad. Within thirty minutes, the platoon had stabilized the Laotians and was beginning to feed them. The NVA prisoners sweated in the sun and the heat from the still-burning embers of the radio hut.

"Well, it looks like your young lieutenant certainly has his shit together, Beth," Suzy Baxter said as she inserted an IV into another patient's arm. Three all-purpose tents, like the ones the squads slept in back at the base camp, had been set up next to the tree line. Four Chinook helicopters sat majestically in the center of the field, their giant twin rotors rocking gently in the gusty breeze. The wind was now quickening as a thunderstorm approached, and the first few drops began to fall. The platoon had set up the perimeter, and Dwight was with his men.

"It sure looks that way, huh, Suz? I don't think he needed us at all."

"These poor Laotians certainly do, Beth, and I'd say he wouldn't be much without you."

"You're giving us both too much credit, Suz; he had these people stabilized and fed before we got here. He could probably march them out of here and have them trained and ready to take Hanoi by early next month!"

"Yeah, right, and then who do you think would take Westmoreland's job when he gets fired for this stunt?"

"Oh, yeah ... I forgot about that! Dwight'll have to be available to run the whole show!" They both laughed.

Suzy said, "We've got everything under control here. Why don't you go find him?"

"Do you think it would be OK; you don't need me here anymore?"

"Not really; we've got everything pretty much under control. You're not a medical person, anyway; you're just in the way, at this point. And the two of you had better start figuring out how you're going to march these people out of here. General Westmoreland said we've got to get the show on the road in twenty-four hours. Bringing these choppers in here was risky enough; if the NVA gets wind of this sooner than we think they will, we've got a problem. He can resupply us, but we've got to march them out."

"Yeah, you're right; I'm outta here. See you later." She set off toward the first paratrooper she could see to inquire as to Dwight's whereabouts and was directed to the opposite tree line, five hundred yards across the field. As she walked she considered the events of the day. They had been grounded by the thunderstorms for three hours and so were now two hours behind schedule. But Dwight and his men had done a masterful job of triaging and caring for the Laotians. And, although the assault had gone wrong, Dwight had been able to pull it out without one American casualty—a remarkable feat.

The sky darkened several shades, lightning cracked into the tree line three hundred yards to her left, and the rain came down in earnest, blowing at a forty-five-degree angle from her right as she caught her fatigue cap as it blew off her head. Holding the hat on her head, she let out a loud whoop, surprising herself and laughing as she broke into a sprint for the tree line, now seventy-five yards in front of her. As she got closer, she saw Dwight standing just inside the trees, hands on his hips and smiling as he watched her. She took a quick look around and couldn't see anyone else. *Why not?* she thought. Instead of slowing up, as she knew Dwight expected, she flew into his arms, and both of them tumbled to the ground, laughing and smothering each other with kisses.

They were beneath a large elephant ear plant, and the ground was still dry. Raindrops filtered down through the trees and hit the three-foot-square leaves with drumlike thumps as they rolled in the grass, delighted in the solitary perfection of their passion. The darkness coupled with the thunder and heavy rain gave them a small room of their own and time for their Adam and Eve moment. *Carpe diem*, she thought as she sat up astride him, opened her shirt, unfastened her bra, and lowered her breast to his face. She moaned as he took her nipple in his mouth and gently sucked-stroked it with the length of his tongue.

He rolled her over on her back and pulled her pants and underwear down with a single motion. Kneeling now, his eyes riveted to her pussy, he pulled his pants down as his penis throbbed out of its painful confinement. Beth moaned and reached for it, slowly rotating her fingers around the ridge of its head, eliciting his moan.

The rain beat hard on the elephant ears as he raised her legs and entered her, his face framed by her boots on either side and her panties under his chin. Neither of them had ever felt such pleasant urgency before as they reached orgasm together, after only fifteen to twenty strokes. She squealed and he moaned as they came together and from out of the corner of their consciousness heard, "Oh, shit!"

They looked toward the source of the sound and saw Rich turning away, a dark crimson blush visible on his chocolate cheek and neck. They burst out laughing as Rich vanished into the woods. Lightning cracked close by, revealing a final, bright glimpse of Rich's back like a flash photo of a wet soldier in full retreat.

The column moved along the riverbank on an established trail. Dwight was a thousand yards ahead with first squad. The morning was bright and crisp with temperatures still in the low 80s. They had been moving for five hours and had covered about ten miles. Thirty of the nonambulatory Laotians and seventy-five children had been flown out in the choppers. Suzy and Beth were with the medical contingent, who had stayed to care for the Laotians on the march. Beth was now the sole CIA operative remaining.

Dwight hadn't wanted to expose them to the dangers of the forced march through the jungle, but it was out of his hands. General Westmorland had decreed that they and the MACV medics would go along to care for the still-sick Laotians. Dwight and his platoon had wondered aloud at the wisdom of marching back to Vietnam, but the scheme was to try to keep this exercise secret, and to have flown everyone out would have most assuredly blown their cover. Walk they would—no matter the cost.

Second and third squads were out on the flanks but had to join the column often as the jungle became too dense to penetrate. Dwight didn't like following the river, but it was necessary because there were no other established trails in this direction. In two more days, traveling at this rate, they would be in South Vietnam and then be helicoptered out to Saigon.

It rained most of the afternoon, and at three o'clock, Dwight decided to stop the column and set up camp in a clearing beside the river. He knew the Laotians were tired, and he couldn't push them too hard in their weakened state. Normally, they could outmarch any American unit but not today. Third squad had been all day on the other side of the river and had set up camp in the jungle there. The troopers had plenty of daylight to set up claymores on ambush points on the trail, and the medics, Beth and Suzy, helped open C rations for the remaining, older children and set up pup tents.

As always, Rich and Dwight sheltered together. As they were joining shelter halves and digging a trench around their tent, Dwight said, "Sorry about Beth and I embarrassing you in the rain the other day, pardner."

"You didn't embarrass me, man. I walk up on people fucking in the jungle every day. I was just a little surprised, that's all.

Anyway, it was such a treat, getting a glimpse of your creamy white ass."

"That's not all you got a glimpse of, my man."

"I don't want to talk about it, brotha'. And I don't want to even mention what a lucky sombitch you are. Shit, man … the rest of us only dream about women like Beth, and not only do you have her but you've got her out in the boonies of Viet-fuckin'-nam, for God's sake!"

"Yeah, I guess you're right; I do have it made. I heard you've got a woman back in Bien Hoa."

"Yep; did you hear how I met her?"

"No. I just heard that you always go see her when y'all go to town. How'd you meet her?"

"There's this whorehouse we always go to, especially right after we get back from an operation. We kind of take care of the girls there, whether we ball any of 'em or not. It's an old two-story French villa, and there's a big tree in the front courtyard, and the whole compound is shielded from the street by a wall in front and two-story apartments on both sides. Lots of nice vegetation around too—makes it real nice and private. Anyway, the whole squad's sitting in chairs under the tree, drinking Beeli and smoking dope when Smythe reaches over and taps my arm. When I looked at him, he points to the upstairs window of the apartment next door. There's this beautiful Vietnamese girl smiling at us, and she waves. We both smile and wave back, and Smythe points to himself and mouths, "Me?" and she shakes her head no and points at yours truly. I point at myself, and she nods her head and giggles. Beautiful little thing, she was—long black hair and wearing a high-collared Ao-Dai."

"What's an Ao-Dai?"

"It's the traditional Vietnamese dress you see most of the women wear when they get dressed up here, usually silk pants and a high-collared silk dress with slits up both sides all the way to the waist."

"Oh, yeah. I know what you're talking about ... makes 'em look like dolls or something."

"Yeah, that's it. Anyway, I picked up my weapon, go out the gate, and go up there, certain that she's just another whore. Now remember, we'd only been in country two weeks, and I didn't know any Vietnamese yet, and she didn't know any English, so I just walked into her apartment, took off my clothes, and then took hers off and did the nasty thing. Afterward, I took out my wallet and gave her 5 or 6 P and started getting dressed, and she started crying and put on a robe and ran out."

"She wasn't a whore!"

"Right-o, old man. I had just raped the bitch! She comes back in with this neighbor chick who speaks enough English to explain this to me. Man, did I feel like a heel!"

"Wha'd you do then?"

"What choice did I have? I dropped another 10 P on her and got my hat! Here I was, a totally stoned rapist! All I could do was tear out the page and start another chapter. I told the guys I didn't feel well and caught the first Lambretta I saw back to the base camp."

"No shit. How'd you end up getting back with her?"

"That night, Smythe told me that she came down there with her friend to translate for her and told him to tell me that she wanted to see me again."

"No!"

"Yes. She hoped that I wasn't mad at her, and she wanted to make dinner for me."

"No way!"

"I ain't selling no wolf tickets, bro. She was warm for my form after I'd treated her like that—hard to believe but true. So I went back the next day and told her that the squad was all going to get our laundry and a haircut and that I'd be back in a couple hours, and she was all excited and said she'd go get food. We did all this talking by pointing to hair with fingers as scissors and my shirt and scrubbing it as laundry and her doing the same kind of things, pointing to mouths to eat and such. Her name's An; it means *peace* in Vietnamese. So that's the story. So An and I are an item and have been ever since."

"So, do you love her?"

"In a way I do, but I don't let my heart get away from me over here. It can not only cloud your judgment, but it can get you killed. I try not to let anything get in the way of the moment, the mission at hand. You start thinking about anything other than what you're doing, you can be put in a bag real quick."

"Yeah, I see what you mean. What're you going to do about this shit when you rotate out?"

"I don't know. I'll think about that when the time comes. I can't afford to bother with it until then. What about you and Beth?"

"We don't really talk about it much. It's just kind of assumed that we'll be together forever."

"That's a pretty long time, pardner."

"Yeah, but sometimes forever is just the moment that we're in."

"That's the attitude, Dwight. Keep that one going. That's how we get through things here. You've led a blessed life so far, but when you get in the shit up to your eyeballs and you think it's going to be curtains, remember what you just said to me."

Dwight finished laying out his poncho in the tent, put his pack at the far end to use as a pillow, stood up and stretched, and said, "I need to go check on the troops. You need anything?"

"No, I'm good. See you before dark?"

"I think so; can't be sure. Keep your guys sharp. There's a hamlet up ahead a few miles, but we could be a lot nearer than that. We're going to have to leave the trail in the morning to get around it undetected. You, me, and Lopez'll leave before dawn to scout it out. See ya."

Dwight finished his rounds and was sure the perimeter was set up properly before he checked on the Laotians and their caretakers. Pascone's squad had rigged a rope across the river—

twenty feet wide over rapids at that point—so he didn't have to get wet going across. His men were doing their jobs well, and there wasn't anything he could suggest or add to their efforts and he told them so. The men were proud of themselves, as they should have been.

Beth was noticeably antsy. After talking to Suzy and some of the medics, she and Dwight walked along the river. The rain, after having stopped for three hours, was beginning again as a light drizzle. This was probably the upper level low that had been forecast to be around for several days. It would keep things cool but at the cost of constant rain. It was moving in from the northwest, and the brown, swollen river portended a big storm. Beth said, "Dwight, Suz and I were talking this morning, and I want to run something by you."

"Uh-oh, I don't like the sound of this."

"It's really no big deal, honey. It's simply a matter of expediency."

"That's woman talk for, 'I want something, and my reasoning to get it is flawless.'"

"Oh, come on; it's just a request and it makes a lot of since. Just listen with an open mind, OK?"

"OK, shoot."

"I'm not a medical person and my talents are just being wasted with the column. I could be much better utilized ..."

"Utilized, is it now? You're not a rifle or a truck, Beth ..."

"Hold on now; just hear me out, OK?"

"OK, sorry."

"I'm in great shape, and I'm trained in weapons, ordnance, and hand-to-hand combat techniques. If the feces hit the fan, you're going to need me with you and your men. I'm no good at nursing people as we stroll along a river! I'm not trained for it, either. I *am* trained for what you're doing: keeping an eye out for the enemy and acting to defeat them, if the time comes to do that."

"I understand how you feel, Beth, but the mission statement says for you to remain with the column. And it would be a distraction for both me and the men for you to be with us in a fight, and we can't afford to be distracted."

"Oh, come on, Dwight. This is something I've wanted to do all my life. My gender shouldn't stop me. It just isn't fair!"

"I know, honey; it isn't fair. But that's life; that's how the cards have been dealt. I can't disobey orders in this instance, Beth. If the risk was the only factor, I would probably do it. But our relationship is the big problem. Everyone from the men to General Westmorland would see it as me being stupid, unprofessional, impetuous, and immature, and they'd be right."

"My, my … don't you have a big vocabulary for a youngster!"

"Now that's not fair, Beth! I was pushed into this position; I didn't ask for it! And you practically attacked me at the Continental Hotel, so don't be bringing my youth into this! Sure, I spend a little time with a dictionary and a thesaurus. I *have* to learn fast and act older than my years! I don't have any choice in the matter. It's expected of me."

Dwight stopped and turned toward the rising river and put his hands on his hips. Chewing his lower lip, he said, "To tell you the truth, I don't think it was such a good idea for you to even be here, either you or Doctor Baxter. There's no place for women in combat. At best, the men will have to carry y'all if the shit gets thick! The medics could have done the job just fine!"

"All right, Dwight; let's stop it right now. I was out of line, and I'm sorry. I'm sorry, honey. Please forgive me. I didn't mean that. You're the finest man I've ever even imagined! Sometimes I just hate being a woman and treated like a weakling and condescended to. I just *hate* it!"

Dwight turned and took her in his arms and kissed her forehead. "I know, baby. I'm sorry too. I shouldn't have said what I did either. But there's a lot of pressure on me, and I've got to be careful. I've got a ton of responsibility here, and sometimes it weighs so heavy on me that I almost feel sick."

"I know, honey; I know. I shouldn't make things any more difficult for you than they already are. I'm sorry."

"Me too."

"I'm sorrier."

"Bullshit. I'm sorrier!" He picked her up and, swinging her around, acted like he was going to throw her in the river.

Beth squealed and said, "Put me down, you large moron!"

"Large moron is it now. All right, now you've gone too far!" He laid her down on the grass and, as he unslung GG, said, "I'm in command here, and I'm going to *utilize* you!"

"No!" she squealed in mock terror, covering her breasts and crotch. "Please don't utilize me!"

He lay on top of her, covering her face and throat with kisses as she laughed and rolled him over so that she was on top. "No, you large moron! I'm going to utilize *you*!" They were both laughing and rolling over and over in the damp grass, and nothing else existed for them but each other.

Walking back, she said, "You know, Lieutenant, you shouldn't be seen holding my hand as we stroll along the river. General Westmorland will hear about it and have your bars."

"Yeah? Well, I'll tell you where old Westy can put his bars."

"Westy is it? My, aren't we getting familiar with the top brass?"

Dwight stopped and let go of Beth's hand as a tremble went up his back and visibly shook him. Beth said, "What's wrong, honey?"

"They're here!"

"Who's here?"

"The enemy; they're here!"

"Where, Dwight; where are they?!"

"I don't know, but I can feel 'em; they're here!

"Dwight, try to relax and concentrate; where are they?"

Dwight was trembling. He bent over and put his hands on his knees. GG fell down his arm, her butt in the mud as the sling, now on Dwight's wrist, held the rest of her out of it. He took deep breaths and tried to relax and concentrate; Beth's hand was on his back. He stood up and wiped the mud off of GG's pistol grip, flipped the safety off, and said, "Talk to me, GG! Where are they, baby?"

He looked around—first across the river, then up and down the river, and then into the jungle. He took another deep breath. "Shit, Beth. I've never felt it like this before! They're not in any direction, but they're here! What in the hell is going on? Am I losing my mind?"

"It's OK, honey. You're not losing your mind. Don't think; relax and just let it happen. You can trust it."

Dwight let his shoulders sag and took another deep breath. He rotated his head around and, as his face went skyward, he said." That's it; they're parachuting in! I've got 'em; I can feel 'em! Let's go!"

They ran down the river, arriving at the perimeter in thirty seconds; he said to the guard, "Go get Sabinski and tell him to meet me at Dr. Baxter's tent! We got trouble; hurry!" The trooper took off without a sound. In a hushed, shouted whisper and through cupped hands directed across the river, he said, "Pascone! Pascone!" One of Pascone's men, recognizing the need for silence, said, "He's not here, sir; he's over there," pointing into the jungle behind him.

"Go get him and tell him we've got trouble! Dinks in the bush! Get the squad over on this side of the river, *now*! Tell him to meet me at Dr. Baxter's tent!"

"Yes, *sir*!" the trooper said as he plowed into the under-brush.

"Beth, grab a weapon and go get Rich! I'll find Bandy! *Go!*" He reached over to slap her on the back, but, at full sprint, she was already out of reach, sliding almost silently through the jungle.

Cargo Sabinski was the last to arrive. Suzy and Beth stood in the background as the five men huddled. Dwight said, "Suzy and Beth, come over here; you're a part of this. We're going to need your help."

Suzy and Beth walked the few steps to join the group as the drizzle turned into a steady rain and the high overcast turned a shade darker. No one bothered to unfurl their ponchos from their web belts; they knew that freedom of motion and stealth would soon be needed. Dwight put his face up into the pounding rain as he tried to clear his head and judge the height of the overcast.

This was a daring move by the enemy. The troops were obviously elite and he hadn't heard any aircraft, so they had to be HALO. Now, how many were there, and how had they known his location? Most European armies didn't even have HALO yet; how did the NVA have it already? Could these be Russian? Probably at least Russian-trained. It was the middle of the monsoon season, and it had been raining and overcast for three days; how could they have known where they were? Then it came to him!

"Suzy! Gather the medics and tell them to strip-search the guards. Go through everything they have until you find a transmitter! It could be as small as a cigarette lighter, so you might have to look in some unlikely places. Then, if you haven't found it, herd the Laotians together and strip-search them! Go!"

"Yes, sir!" she said and hurried off in the direction of the encampment. As the others silently watched, Dwight stepped away from the group and slowly paced down the frothing, eddying river, which had risen at least a foot during the last four hours and was almost over its banks. He paused and looked across at the opposite bank, thirty feet away. He could feel the enemy still, but the feeling was weaker now. They were down and forming up, he knew. He had to wait for their anger. They were busy with other things now. He had to wait.

He closed his eyes and lifted his face up into the warm rain again. *Relax. Wait.* The weight of the world was on his shoulders.

He wanted to yell for his men to leave him alone, to quit being so damn insistent. What did they expect from him, magic? Yes, he realized; that's exactly what they expected. Maybe he couldn't do it this time. Maybe he'd let them down and get them all killed. *Jesus*, he thought. *Please come through for me again, whatever or whoever you are. Relax. Relax.* He bent over again and put his hands on his knees. GG fell down his arm again.

Deep breaths.

Deep breaths.

He thought, *What will it feel like to die? A bullet to the head—that's the way I want it. Instant death—I won't even know what happened. That's the way I want it; the lights go out, and it's all over. I deserve it. What the hell was I thinking, going airborne? It must have been some kind of death wish.*

Try to relax.

The bullet shatters the skull. Maybe that's the beginning of a whole new kind of time conception. People who have come close to death say that your whole life passes through your mind. Maybe the neurons, all loaded with information and memories, flash instant messages with the impact. It seemed like more of a realization than a thought. *By the time the bullet was compressing the complex mass of jellied neurons and synapses, a tremendous last energy would be released.* Memories: his first love, Susan Susser, in the third grade. He loved kissing her little lips. He and his mother on Saipan in '48. His first dog, Pepper. The pleasure/pain of scratching athlete's foot between his toes with a sock in the locker room in high school. Ada, Oklahoma, and getting his first shotgun that wonderful Christmas morning when he was twelve.

He straightened up, threw GG back to her position on his back, and, realizing the absurdity of his thoughts, threw his head back and laughed. Realizing how ridiculous he must look, he turned back to the group. Sabinski was beaming at him; the others, including Beth, stared in disbelief. He couldn't help himself; he pointed at them and, staggering, went into gales of laughter.

It hit him. *Here they come, lots of them. Feels like full company strength: 150 or so. Where are they? Where are they? There! There; I've got 'em!*

He shouted, "They're ahead of us on the river! On this side, about a half mile down! We don't have much time! We'll set up an ambush right here. Fourth squad! Set up across the river, and leave all your claymores here! Third squad, you'll be the blocking force! They have about 150 men, so we're going to have to act like they've surprised us! Rich, first squad will act like we're walking point and start firing like we're disorganized and begin falling back! We've got to make them believe they've got us on the run so we can suck them into the ambush! We've got to make them bunch up before we lay into 'em! Second squad will have all the claymores! Cargo, you take all the LAWs with you across the river. Second squad's going to be too close to use them! Move upriver just a little so you can get a good shot before they get abeam second squad! You're going to have to hit 'em hard before they get to us and drive them further into the trap! Let the other guys blow the LAWs; I want you on that .50 right from the beginning! Do you understand what we're trying to do here, Cargo?"

"Yes, sir; I've got it."

"Go!" Sabinski ran upriver, headed for his men and the rope across the river. The big grin was still plastered to his face.

The rain intensified, equaling the noise of the rushing river. The sky turned several shades darker, and the gusty wind picked up to about twenty miles per hour. Dwight was reminded of a werewolf movie as the wind whistled and the rain slanted into his back. He leaned into it and forced a smile at Beth, Pascone, Bandy, and Rich, each in turn. He could see them relax a little as they returned the gesture. "Bandy, you and Pascone got any questions?"

"No, sir," they said in unison.

"OK; go ahead and get your men and set up. Don, make sure none of those claymores are pointed toward Cargo's guys.

Timing is everything here, boys; be sure your men understand what we're trying to do here. First squad's gonna be beatin' feet back up the trail, so be sure no one shoots 'em. As soon as Cargo's guys hit 'em with the LAWs, hit 'em with everything you've got. Don't worry about conserving ammo; this thing'll be over in two minutes. If it fucks up, everyone scatter and meet at the pickup point day after tomorrow. Beth, go tell the medics and Suzy that I'll fire a flare if we don't prevail. If they see the flare, scatter and hide in twos. Run for a quarter mile and hide for the night and meet us at the pickup point day after tomorrow. Understand?"

"Yes, sir," she said as she turned and ran up the trail. Dwight noticed how naturally she carried herself carrying a full pack, four ammo pouches, and an AK-47. He recalled seeing her hitting pop-up targets at 100 yards in training and was amazed at how quick she had been. Most of the men hadn't been able to pick up the motion, identify, aim, and fire nearly as fast. Like Dwight, she was a natural. That kind of speed couldn't be taught; you either have it or you don't.

Above the clouds, the sun was low in the sky, causing darkness to descend two hours faster than it normally would. Dwight knew that the enemy commander smelled blood and wanted to get it on well before dark, so he probably wouldn't be as careful as he would have been otherwise. Also, the rain and dim light should work to his advantage, the rain providing noise and the rain providing cover. Everything was working in his favor.

After briefing Rich's men, they moved up the trail single file until they found a bend in the river to the left that would allow them to take out at least ten NVA with quartering fire. The enemy knew that their point would certainly take casualties, and Dwight didn't intend to disappoint them. He told the men to aim low to inflict belly wounds and not fire until he did. It would be a frontal ambush, but the enemy wouldn't know that; they'd think that his point had simply spotted them first and got the drop on them. The only problem he anticipated at this stage of the fight was that his men would have to be standing and be twelve paces apart. They had to make the enemy believe that they'd been walking and were surprised. The one-sided casualties wouldn't be a surprise; American soldiers were good shots and had been raised shooting guns. This fact was taken into account in their planning so there would be a lot of troops bunched up behind the point to provide the phalanx of the attack after the initial contact. Dwight had told the men to wait for the NVA bugle to sound the attack before withdrawing and then to run like hell. That would be expected also.

They stood just barely off the trail and waited, Dwight at their head and Rich twelve paces behind him. As expected, the dim light allowed them to hide in shadow, even though they were standing. Small birds twittered in the trees, and the larger ones screamed; they had become accustomed to these noises, but now each new sound caused them to twitch. Sweat rolled down Dwight's nose and mingled with the rain before dropping into GG's open breach as she waited just below—steady. Ready.

Here they come. Don't even swallow. Don't blink. Cautiously, they move. They know! No, they just know that they're close. Did Baxter find the transmitter? He'd not told her to smash it. How many other things had he overlooked? *Shit! Maybe this isn't the best place to hit 'em! There's too many of them! Christ, here they come. Oh mother of God, what have I gotten myself into! What in the fuck am I doing here! Shit, I can see over thirty of 'em already! I shouldn't have picked such an open part of the trail! What was I thinking! Every one of them will be able to see thirteen muzzle flashes when we open up! Oh, God help me!*

GG jumped twice in his arms. Twice more. Twice more. Three men at the rear of the enemy column fell, clutching their bellies and screaming and writhing in the mud. His men's AKs barked in two-round bursts as enemy soldiers fell. Others raised their weapons and began firing. AKs after AKs—the surprise and the sound of what should not have been friendly weapons firing at them had the desired effect on the enemy troops as they panicked and fired high. Most remained standing rather than hiding in the bush or going prone. *Good.*

No! Oh shit! Run!

Dwight shouted, "Run! Goddamn it! They've flanked us! Go! Go! Go!"

He could feel them beside him. How'd they get there? He hadn't felt anything until just now. How had they done this! Why hadn't he felt them until now? *They have intel too,* he thought. *They've been working on this since that incident in Saigon over a month ago! Damn!*

Enemy AK-47 rounds ripped through the trees and jungle. The man in front of Rich staggered and went white with his effort to stay up and his pain. Rich grabbed one arm and Dwight the other, as the man's legs began failing him, blood darkening the right side of his fatigue shirt. GG's muzzle deafened Dwight as she fired ninety degrees to his left, up over his shoulder, behind his back. Two NVA staggered and fell, twenty feet into the bush.

Dwight knew what he had to do, but his mind wouldn't accept it for a second or two. He'd gotten them into this; he had to get them out. "Rich!" he shouted above the din. The enemy had recovered up the trail and was now on a dead run toward them, firing as they ran. The enemy bugler sounded as though he must be only fifteen feet away! Wouldn't he take a goddamn breath? Four RPGs streaked their red flame toward them and slammed into the jungle to the side, killing several of the enemy on his flank. *Thank God for this bend in the river after all,* he thought. "Rich! Go on! I'm staying here with Kohl! Stay with the plan! Go!"

"No!" Rich shouted as Dwight went to the ground, pulling Kohl from Rich's grasp and emptying GG's last four rounds into the chest of a remaining enemy soldier, thirty feet away, on their flank.

"Go!" Dwight shouted. "That's an order! Don't argue with me! Go!" Still, Rich hesitated as rounds snapped by. The rest of the squad was thirty yards down the trail. Dwight twisted to his right, pulled a new magazine from its holder, inserted it, and heard his finger sizzle in the bolt as he burned it again. He didn't feel a thing as, from his peripheral vision, he saw Rich disappear down the trail. Three more NVA fell to GG as Kohl fired his AK down the trail, screaming at the enemy through his pain, "You ain't gettin' the LT, motherfuckers! You ain't getting the LT!"

Beth had never felt an emotion like this one. She felt a murderous rage that would have scared her, had she been in her right mind. She was thankful that it had replaced the paralyzing fear that she had felt only a second before. A scream started deep in her chest and escaped her throat in a hate-filled breath that lasted so long and loud in its exhalation that everyone within fifty yards, enemy and American alike, stopped firing for a second, frozen in terror.

After delivering her message to Baxter, they had found the transmitter in the top shirt pocket of the ranking NVA officer, a young captain. Beth had immediately gathered fourteen medics, quickly briefed them, and told them that they were needed in the fight and to lock and load and come with her. Just about then, the fight broke out. She quickly realized that something had gone wrong by the fact that the ambush hadn't been sprung—no claymores or LAWs, yet.

She immediately reasoned that the enemy had flanked Dwight; she could hear GG fighting for his life, and, like Dwight soon would, she knew what had to be done.

She led the medics through the jungle, thirty yards to the side of the river trail, spinning out of the grasp of the ubiquitous come-along vines and ripping her clothes and skin as she tore through the jungle's defenses like a chainsaw through a bamboo stand.

Bleeding from her face, hands, and the tears in her clothes and a good ten paces ahead of the closest, struggling medic, she had come upon an NVA soldier firing his AK-47 from a crouched position. In full stride, she'd dropped her AK and noiselessly broke the man's neck with her hands.

Picking up her weapon, she saw GG's muzzle flash twenty yards ahead of her. Then she spotted six NVA soldiers firing at Dwight from a crouched position, just on the other side of a twenty-foot clearing that she was entering.

They were trying to kill her love, her life, her reason for existence. There were no thought processes, no decisions. The essence of her femininity took over her very being. She had no choice in the matter as she charged them, the AK now on full automatic; she fired from the waist as she ran, holding the barrel from climbing with a stiffened left arm and hand on its top as she emptied the weapon into three of the enemy soldiers.

Dwight instantly figured out what was happening and where the scream was coming from and was immediately on his feet and charging through the jungle. GG was silent; there was no anger coming from the bush for her to home in on. Dwight's own primal scream enunciated the word, "Airborrrrne!" as he charged, further diverting the now confused and frightened NVA soldiers enough for Beth, her AK now out of ammo, to butt-stroke one of the three remaining troopers in the face and Dwight to shoot the other two before they could recover.

Dwight, on a dead run, threw Beth down and yelled, "Get down!" at the medics as he heard Cargo's .50 go off in a long burst and the LAWs leave their tubes. The last of the medics hit the dirt just as the first of the LAW rounds exploded.

The screams of wounded and dying NVA filled the air, the volume just beneath the shriek of flying metal as the claymores joined the last of the forty LAWs in shredding the ranks of the enemy. They had bunched up and charged past Dwight's position, straight into the ambush.

Dwight yelled, "Follow me!" and ran back toward the trail. The remaining NVA troopers were now in total retreat back down the trail and had already run past his previous position. On the other side of the river, Sabinski led his squad, running along the river bank, screaming, "Airborne!" and firing his glowing, red-hot-barreled .50 in ten-round bursts. *Jesus!* Dwight thought. *That scares me!*

As Dwight, Beth, and the medics arrived on the trail, they were joined by Rich and his men, followed closely by second and third squads. Rich gave Dwight barely a glance as he and his men thundered past, guns blazing and fire in their eyes. Dwight actually pitied the terrified NVA troops as, wild-eyed, they began shedding weapons and anything else that could slow them down. He, Beth, and the medics fell in behind first squad as the remaining enemy troopers entered the bend in the river ahead of them. Cargo's squad had the shorter route and cut them off. The smarter NVA dived into the jungle while the others were mowed down by the concentrated and withering fire.

"Get the sons-a-bitches!" Dwight screamed as first squad entered the jungle behind the enemy soldiers. To his right, he spotted Beth, already spinning through the come-alongs as she charged through the jungle and firing single shot from the waist as she ran, dropping screaming, terrified shadowy figures in their tracks.

Sabinski's men were now in the water and coming ashore thirty yards downstream; then they entered the jungle to cut off the retreat, screaming, "Airborne!" as the feeding frenzy intensified.

Holy shit! Dwight thought. *Maybe I should stop this carnage!* Then after a millisecond of consideration, he decided to let the rout continue to its conclusion. The enemy unit was airborne too. Their pride wouldn't let them give up, and they would attack the platoon and the Laotians during the night in a guerrilla action. *Kill 'em all,* he thought.

He watched in amazement as he realized that he was seeing Kohl entering the jungle and firing two-round bursts as he struggled against his pain and with his rage. "Good grief!" Dwight said aloud as he ran to stop him and lay him back down in the trail. "Medic!" he shouted.

-CHAPTER FIFTEEN-
SOMETHING'S WRONG

IT WAS COLD AT 25,000 feet. The ramp was closed, but the small cargo plane was designed for low-level flight, and the heating was inadequate for high altitudes. Also, the service ceiling of a Caribou was 28,000 feet, so climbing to 25,000 was long and laborious after 18,000.

To occupy his mind, Dwight thought back to the awards ceremony on the parade grounds that the entire brigade had been fallen out for. Every man in the platoon had received at least a Bronze Star and many had received Silver Stars, including Dwight and his squad leaders. There had been five Purple Hearts, all for minor wounds, except for Corporal Kohl, of course. He had been med-evaced out an hour after the battle and was in a hospital in Japan. He had lost a couple feet of large intestine but was already chomping at the bit to get back to the platoon.

After the battle, General Westmorland had ordered virtually every helicopter at MACV's disposal to airlift the Laotians out. The cover had obviously been blown, so he was no longer concerned about what the Laotian government, North Vietnam, or even Washington thought about the adventure. It had been time to get out of Dodge, and he didn't hesitate to make the decision. As it turned out, the entire free world had applauded the effort. Even China and Russia had praised the humanitarian mission.

It had been a week since they'd been back, four days of which Dwight and Beth had been together at the CIA compound outside Saigon. On two occasions, Lawrence had whisked them to Saigon for dinner and dancing at the embassy. Of course, the large security detail had negated their privacy during these trysts, but still it was good to get away from the now too familiar digs at the CIA compound. They had been working on a secret trip to Bangkok when this current emergency had developed.

The Caribou could carry thirty-two troops, so with all the equipment, weapons, and ammo that the platoon carried, they easily filled two airplanes. They flew in formation, side by side, and would disgorge the paratroopers simultaneously.

Each trooper had an altimeter and a stopwatch in a bracket attached to their reserve parachute, just below their chest. They set the altimeter at zero before they boarded the airplane, as they didn't want to read true altitude but rather AGL or altitude above the ground. Normally, since an altimeter is simply a barometer that measures air pressure, all altimeters have to be constantly recalibrated by the operator, to take the local barometric pressure into account. Using their altimeters by setting the altitude at zero on the ground eliminated this procedure.

They would free-fall until they reached five thousand feet and then open, form up, and "fly" to the DZ in formation, landing in a defensive position. Since they were jumping under cover of darkness, they needed this extra time under canopy to form up, find the DZ, and get to it in proper order, machine gunners on the perimeter, squad members together, and so on.

They had made five night jumps in training and had become adept at using light sticks on the parachute backpacks to locate each other in the darkness. During the free fall, the light sticks on the outside of the parachute backpacks guided them, and, after the canopies were deployed, a light stick on the inside of the backpacks could be referenced likewise.

They would then hide the parachutes and coveralls and head out to their objective—in this situation, a suspected POW camp.

If their reconnaissance was correct and the encampment was in fact a POW camp, they would attack and kill the enemy running it, free the prisoners, and call in the First Battalion of the 173d for reinforcements, which would make a traditional airborne attack at dawn. Dwight's platoon would have to hold on until their arrival and before the VC could equip and man a serious counterattack.

If the intel was correct, this was a highly mobile camp that could be moved at a moment's notice. They must act before the camp was moved, which was done often by the enemy, to avoid an operation such as this.

Dwight thought back to the hurried briefing. There wasn't much time, the general had said. Reconnaissance airplanes had seen it; photo experts had fleshed it out. This had to be done quickly. They'd had only six hours to plan the operation, and no other unit was qualified to perform it. The general had no choice but to send his special platoon, even though they were not fully rested from their last ordeal. But no one else could do it. It was too far into Cambodia for helicopters. Anyway, the sounds of them would alert the enemy to the attack, and they'd kill the prisoners. The president himself had called this shot. Dwight supposed that he was emboldened by their success on the humanitarian mission into Cambodia and the world's acceptance of it.

Dwight knew that he couldn't refuse, even if he'd wanted to; however, there was something wrong with the mission that Dwight just couldn't put his finger on, but he couldn't tell anyone how scared and unsure of himself he was, not even Beth. It was a moot point anyway. She was in Saigon, and he couldn't say anything over a telephone from Bien Hoa, even if he'd wanted to.

The general saw it, though; he knew. He didn't like this whole situation either, and he was angry. *Christ!* he thought. *What did they expect of the kid? What in the hell were they thinking?* He'd gone all the way to the top, but even Westmoreland was powerless. *No one in Vietnam thought it was a good idea, but damn it, the kid had been such a wunderkind! Now it was probably going to get him and fifty-two other good men killed, not to mention the prisoners. The kid's too good for his own well-being. I mean, he's good, Mr. President, but he doesn't walk on water!* he heard himself thinking out loud.

Damn the president, he thought. *The idiot honestly thinks he's a brilliant military tactician, along with that asshole McNamara. Who in the hell did they think they were? Military matters in wartime were now far too complex for a damned politician to be in command! The framers hadn't meant for something like this to happen,* he was certain. *Thank God that Roosevelt had understood this. Even Truman could be justified in some of his decisions about how far to go. At least he was wise enough to let military men make military decisions. But this dope sat there in his Oval-goddamned-Office and pored over photographs and maps and made day-to-day military decisions, for Christ's sake! Damn him! Damn that egotistical, ignorant son of a bitch! Commander in chief my ass!*

OK, then; he had to follow orders. He had no more choice in the matter than that poor, gifted, brave young lieutenant had. Damn it! If he'd known something like this was going to happen, he'd never have pushed the kid on the fast track. For God's sake, the kid is … is just a kid! He's only nineteen years old! Oh my God in heaven, this thing just doesn't smell right. We at least need more intel and time to plan it!

Dwight had spent the previous several hours helping the general, MACV commanders, and their aides draw up the TO&E and plan the raid. The tension had been palpable and the brass had tried hard to make Dwight feel at ease, but they had overplayed their hands. Dwight could since their fears and doubt in his ability—as if Dwight didn't have enough doubt himself. Of course, their misgivings just reinforced his as the circle compounded itself.

The DZ was three miles from the encampment, and the four squads would separate a quarter mile away, surround it, and attack at 0400 under cover of darkness, hoping for complete surprise.

Positioning for the attack was especially critical, as one small slipup could jeopardize the mission. A cough or sneeze could prove fatal to everyone involved, including the prisoners.

The men had been flown by Caribou to MACV headquarters for a few hours of preparations and briefing. Dwight and General Baxter had twice shuffled back and forth to the hangar—where the men were preparing and being briefed and supplied—to bring them sit reps and try to keep them calmed down and sharp rather that fearful and nervous. Like bulls before a bull-fight, Dwight had found them practically pawing the ground and snorting as they psyched themselves up for the battle. He knew that he needed to keep them calm enough now so that the adrenaline would peak as they cleared the airplane's ramp into the night sky.

Rumors flew easily and fast. A trooper could make an innocent comment like, "The LT must be sweating blood!" which, after passing from man to man, would become repeated as, "The LT is bleeding from his rectum and may not be able to make the jump, and some MACV captain who has never seen combat and is night-blind will be leading the mission." So the squad leaders had to keep their eyes and ears open and quash rumors before they got going.

Just as a nightmare is capable of causing the dreamer to have a bad day, a rumor in full flight could destroy morale, even after it is dispelled. It was all-important to keep the men in good spirits and in a positive attitude.

The POW encampment was at the foot of a forested hill to the west with grassy plains five miles to the north, separated by thick tree lines. Clearings were a hundred yards to the east and a thousand yards to the south.

The photos couldn't ascertain fortifications, armament, or even if there were guard towers. There were no walls and probably not even wire around the compound, but trees had obstructed the cameras so much that this was all that could be determined, as far as fortifications were concerned. There was a tank inside the perimeter, along with several other tracked but unarmored vehicles. Four small howitzers or recoilless rifles could be seen in the clearing, along with a section of cages, which, according to intel's analysis of the photos, contained American prisoners.

Dwight's brain ran out of thoughts and settled into the lethargy of negativism, and he shook his head to try to dispel the images of the two troopers he had accidentally killed with his bad decisions. The effect was opposite of his intentions, and the imagined memories of their families reentered his consciousness.

Oh shit! This isn't a good time for this stuff to start up again! What in the hell am I doing? There's no time for this!

As the memories began to overwhelm him, he realized that he was more afraid than he had ever been in his life. Suddenly, he could no longer think straight. He felt totally and completely consumed by fear. As if he were suddenly covered with a heavy, wet blanket, it was smothering him. He realized that he was sweating profusely, despite the cold.

I can't do this! I just want to go home! I have no business being here, much less being in charge! This has all happened too quickly. I'm just a kid. This has all been a big mistake! Maybe I should tell Rich that I can't do it. He should be in charge, not me. I'm so fucking scared!

I have a bad feeling about this. We're all doomed! We're all going to die! Or worse, we'll probably be taken prisoner ourselves. This is all wrong! Something really bad's going to happen this time!

Why aren't I thinking about the men? Why am I thinking of myself? I should just quit. Just tell everyone to go back. That's it! I'll go up and tell the pilots to abort the mission! I'm sick. I have the flu ... and diarrhea. Dysentery! I could easily crap in my pants right now. That's it ... I'm sick! I can't go on. I'll get everyone killed! But it's me I'm really worried about. I don't give a shit about these guys! I don't want to die! I've seen too much death already. Jesus God, I'm so scared!

As he wiped the sweat from his face with his sleeve, he realized that Rich was watching him. He forced a smile, but he knew it was more of a grimace. He feared saying anything, as he thought he might actually start crying.

Rich crossed the narrow cargo bay and sat down beside him. Shouting above the engine noise, he said, "What's going on, LT?"

The red lit interior maintained their night vision, but it caused detail to be either distorted or eliminated. Dwight's face reminded Rich of a frightened horse; his eyes showed white all around, and he had actually reared his head back, as if recoiling from the possibility of Rich touching him, his blue eyes black in the dim red light.

"What's wrong, Dwight? Are you OK, man?"

"I'm scared, Rich! God help me, I'm scared to death!"

"We're all scared, man!"

"I know, but I'm *really* scared! This is all wrong, Rich; it's a bad deal, man! It's all wrong! This is a suicide mission, Rich; I think we should abort the mission!"

"Come on, Dwight! Get a hold of yourself, man! The men are starting to look at us, LT!"

Rich moved closer to Dwight and put his arm around his shoulder and put his mouth close to Dwight's ear and shouted, "Dwight! Listen to me, man! You've got to get a hold of yourself! We can't turn back, man! It's too late for that shit! Take some deep breaths, man! Take some deep breaths!"

Dwight saw that a few of the men were watching them; others were feigning sleep. A few appeared to be praying. The noise kept them from trying to converse, so most were in their own worlds and thoughts, as most soldiers are before going into combat.

Dwight took some deep breaths and tried to think of the mission, the job at hand, and he felt a little calmer but not much.

After a minute, he turned to shout in Rich's ear, "Something's wrong, man! Something isn't right! This whole thing is fucked-up, man!"

"So what, man!" Rich shouted back. "Everything's fucked up! The whole fucking army's fucked up! So what else is new?"

"No, man; something's seriously wrong with this whole deal, man! It's not right! We shouldn't be here! It's not right!"

"Bullshit, Dwight! We're trained like a motherfucker, man. We couldn't be any better at this shit! We're cool, man! We're cool! Just relax! Everything's going to be just fine! Think about the mission, man! We gotta free those poor bastards, Dwight; try to think about *them!*"

What's wrong with me! Dad always said that the only way out of the pits is to help someone less fortunate. What's wrong? Why am I so self-centered right now? Maybe I'm just a coward after all! Rich is right; those prisoners are depending on me! But, more importantly, these men right here are depending on me. It's no mistake that I've been chosen as their leader. Shit! The least I can do for them is not let them see how afraid I am! What in the hell is the matter with me?

The amber light between the green and the red one above the rear door came on, signifying that they had three minutes to stand up, check their gear, and exit the airplane when the green light came on.

They stood, checked each other's equipment, and broke each other's light sticks. The hatches opened when there was one minute to go. This is when the fear usually left. There was too much to think about now, too many details to attend to, too many things in the immediate future to think about and to plan for.

Dwight couldn't focus. His left foot was in spasm, the heel jumping up and down on the deck. Try as he might, he couldn't stop it. He saw Rich look away from his foot, concern on his face.

Dwight couldn't get hold of himself. The fear was fogging his thoughts and even his vision as the green light came on, startling him. He felt his chest constrict and knew that he had stopped breathing. He consciously hoped for a heart attack.

Sabinski and Pascone were the first off the ramp, and he and Rich were the last. He noted that Rich hesitated in the door a second, beside Dwight, so he could be above and behind Dwight to keep an eye on him, in case he screwed up his exit, which he did.

Instead of jumping and throwing himself in a stable spread position, he had fallen out the door and his left foot had hung on the edge of the ramp just long enough to cause him to tumble. He saw the full moon, the stars, and then the light sticks on the backs of his men flashing by, over and over, like being on a merry-go-round as a kid, as he tumbled. Then he realized that he still held the pilot chute in his left hand and let it go, but it was too late. The damage had already been done, as he had begun not only tumbling but also twisting over from left to right in a side tumble, compounding the problem.

He finally stabilized after thirty seconds and saw Rich fifteen feet to his right in a stable spread, looking at him. He could see the men below him and their pilot chutes five feet above them, strung out in the order that they had left the airplane, each a little above and beside the other, already forming up to be close when they opened but not in danger of tangling with each other. He and Rich were two hundred feet off to the side, away from the formation.

Dwight's head began to clear as he saw that the cloud bank that was supposed to be at 18,000 feet was beginning to come up to meet them. He knew from experience that while it looked beautiful like snow in the bright moonlight, it would be dark inside and it would be really dark when they emerged from the bottom of it, after only ten seconds inside.

His mind was busy now, and he and Rich began forming up on the others as they entered the cloud bank. The last thing he saw before the darkness enveloped him was Rich smiling and giving him a thumbs-up.

Dwight's mind was focused now as he emerged from the cloud. He could easily make out the light sticks on his men's backpacks and saw that he and Rich had formed up perfectly. They should be opening about thirty seconds after emerging from the cloud. Twenty more seconds. He looked at the altimeter and stopwatch in the bracket on top of his reserve chute and noted that he'd failed to start the stopwatch as he'd left the airplane. *No big deal*, he thought. *I'll just pull when the others do.*

He saw the light sticks began to disappear and realized that the black canopies had begun deploying, obstructing them. *Shit!*

Pull!

He and Rich had fallen past his men, and he was now looking at them about twenty degrees above him and to his left. He could see the light sticks on the backs of the several men whose backs were to him.

Rich had been waiting for him to pull and was now swinging under canopy twenty feet beside him. Dwight was thankful that Rich had the presence of mind to turn away from him, showing him the light stick on his back, to be sure that Dwight could see him and also further separating them, to ensure that they didn't become entangled.

Instinctively, he rolled the rip cord up and put it in his pocket. As he pulled it back out and dropped it, he wondered how many of the other men had done the same.

Dwight pulled his left toggle line down halfway, initiating a gentle turn that showed him several light sticks to his left. He straightened the compass on the reserve chute to be sure it swung free and pulled his right toggle line, turning west, into the wind. The altimeter read three hundred feet. He couldn't see the ground, but his fear was now in check.

He pulled the slipknot on his Sally bag, releasing it to hang ten feet below him. He waited for the sound of it hitting the ground to ready himself for the PLF. He glanced at the soft red glow of the altimeter and saw that it read fifty feet just before he saw the ground. He was moving forward at about five miles per hour and saw that he was landing in high grass. *Good.*

Forward PLF! Perfect. No sweat.

He stood up and, pulling the right riser and then shroud lines, collapsed the billowing canopy and twisted the breakaway fastener on his chest to the release position and hit it with the heel of his hand, releasing the harness.

Rich was releasing his harness twenty feet away, and Dwight heard the rather loud, metallic clap of the harness releases as the others were doing the same, as still others were in varying degrees of landing with the grass-muffled thumps of Sally bags and then the following grunts of well-executed PLFs.

Off to his left, the troopers from the other Caribou were landing in a separated cloud of gray shadowy canopies, punctuated by soft-white light sticks.

The ground and grass were wet with dew, but the earth was dry and firm. A three- to five-knot breeze wafted steadily from the west, carrying the jungle smells of decaying vegetation and both plant and animal life on its breath.

He took his overalls off, and GG was first out of the bag, none the worse for wear. He chambered a round, set the safety, laid her on the parachute, and saddled up in less than a minute.

He removed his compass from its bracket on his reserve chute and pulled out the red-lensed flashlight clipped to his web belt, snapped it to the first click, and, pointing it at each eighth position around him, pushed the button twice at each position, signaling the men to form on him.

Machine gun crews and M79 men began setting up a perimeter around him in a fifty-yard circumference.

Men were gathering and forming into their four squads as the squad leaders made a head count and checked for injuries.

The jump had been perfect in all respects. The intense training had paid off, again. No injuries on a night jump was unusual.

Sabinski was last to report as the arrangement and rigging of his big machine gun was more complex and time-consuming than for the others. Dwight felt the contagious reassurance of his gigantic smile as Sabinski put a fresh cigar in his teeth as he arrived. "What's happenin', LT!" he said in a low, gruff whisper.

A communication/command post airplane would be passing over at 40,000 feet every hour on the hour. Dwight looked at his watch and told the radioman to be sure to warm up the radio and at exactly 2200, turn it on and click the mike button twice to tell General Baxter, who was aboard, along with his staff and several MACV commanders, that everything was proceeding as planned. The radioman told Dwight that he had already switched the radio to STANDBY and that it was ready.

Dwight had unfolded the map and was looking at it under the red light. He said to his squad leaders, "OK guys; it looks like we're right here." He tapped a large open area three miles west of the camp with the edge of the lens. "Agreed?"

He looked to each of them as they affirmed his assessment with a nod.

"Pascone, put that Seeing Eye cat of yours at point." Dwight said, referring to an Apache corporal named Brokenfeather who had extraordinary night vision, "Be sure he has his reflectors on." Each man had been issued white reflectors on elastic straps to be worn on the backs of their hands to give hand signals with. Only the point man, squad leaders, and Dwight would wear theirs during the march, and the others would wear theirs inside out, to avoid inadvertent signals or enemy detection.

They headed out with Dwight walking thirty paces behind the point, Pascone and his squad behind him, and the other three squads in an unbroken line behind, at five-yard intervals so that each man would not lose sight of the man in front of him.

They covered ground rapidly and arrived at the clearing behind the tree line before the encampment clearing at 0340.

Dwight's foreboding feelings began to emerge again as soon as the monotony of the march had settled in. By the time they had stopped at the edge of the tree line, he had developed a twitch in his left eye. His biggest fear—the fear that he was becoming a coward—had settled firmly in on him by now. He knew that his breathing had become too rapid and that he was sweating too profusely for the circumstances. He considered the possibility that maybe he really *was* getting sick.

The POW camp was lit up by two campfires, and a lantern shone through the bamboo sides of a thatch-roofed main hut. There were no guard towers, and two sides of the clearing were open. There didn't even seem to be any wire or even a pungi pit dug around the encampment. Could the enemy be so confident in themselves and their location this deep inside Laos that they weren't even taking basic precautions?

The men formed up by squads in the tree line, as had been practiced on the tarmac at Tan Son Nhut Air Base yesterday. Everything was going perfectly; their planning and training had paid off in spades.

Dwight led his four squad leaders to the rear of the tree line, about fifty feet, so they could talk.

"Shit, LT!" Sabinski said. "This is a fuckin' cakewalk, man! Let's just walk in, kill 'em all, and leave! Shit! Beaver (referring to his big .50-caliber machine gun) and me can do it all by ourselves!"

The four of them were standing in front of Dwight, looking at him for instruction. As he unlatched his helmet and took it off with his left hand, he wiped the sweat from his eyes with the inside of his right arm, which held GG.

"Fuck!" he said.

Pascone said, "What's wrong, LT? It don't get no better 'n this!"

"That's what's wrong!"

Bandy said, "What the fuck you talking about, LT?"

"It's too perfect, man; it's gotta be a setup!"

Rich said, "Bullshit, man! What the fuck you talkin' 'bout? The stupid bastards just don't expect us, man! It's a layup, Dwight; let's get the job done and get outta Dodge, man!"

Pascone said, "Maybe Dwight's onto something, guys. Let's think about this for a minute!"

"Oh, bull*shit*!" Sabinski whispered, a little too loud.

Pascone said, "Shut the fuck up, you stupid Polack! Keep your mouth shut, for a fuckin' change!"

"Shhh!" Rich said.

"Quiet!" Dwight said. "Let's think about this for a minute. These are the same fuckers who tried to kill me with a bomb in Saigon a month ago and had a sniper on the roof across the street as a backup. They're painfully aware that we kicked their asses in a major battle and beat them at their own game in the refugee ambush.

"Do you think that they just might have some intel about our training and be just a bit smarter than we're giving them credit for? Is it a coincidence that the CIA gets a shot at saving a bunch of POWs via a rather too-fortunate spy photograph? Then the fucking POW camp is lit up like a Christmas tree, and there's no concertina wire or pits or walls? All we gotta do is grease the guards and free the prisoners and everyone lives happily ever after?"

The men looked at one another.

"Oh, shit!" Sabinski said as he and Bandy simultaneously dropped to a knee. Dwight and the others followed suit. The moon broke out from behind a wispy cloud for just long enough for them to see the alarm on each other's faces, just inside the tree line.

Dwight said, "Rich, this is the reason for all this seemingly irrational fear I've been experiencing. I've been picking up on it since we were told about it three days ago! It's coming clear to me now. The whole United States of fucking America has been successfully set up!"

"What are we going to do, man?" Pascone said as the moon slipped out and back in again.

"OK. I'm just going to think out loud for a minute. Feel free to chime in wherever you want to.

"If they're smart enough to have snookered the CIA and MACV, they're smart enough to know exactly where we are and what we're doing, right now. All they have to have done is set up some radio-monitoring equipment. They know that we use mike clicks to communicate. A PRC-25 is no secret fucking radio. Shit, they even use captured ones themselves! All they have to do is triangulate the signals and they know where we've been, every hour, on the fucking hour!"

"Shit!" Rich said, looking at his watch. He started to get up and said, "I gotta go stop the radioman!"

Dwight grabbed his sleeve, "No! Let him do it! We don't want the bastards to suspect anything!"

Rich went back to a knee as they waited for Dwight to begin speaking again. He thought for a minute.

"OK. They know that I can pick up on them when they start their attack. Their brass probably hasn't even told the troops what's going on. They're probably camped a thousand yards into that hillside over there. Their radio triangulation units have been reporting to the brass for three hours. The troops are all awake, fed, and armed. As soon as we hit the camp, they'll be told what to do, and they'll run us down like dogs.

"But, they're not going to be very organized because the brass can't risk getting them fired up because they know I'll feel it and probably figure it out.

"The troops have probably been told that they're moving out. As long as they don't get pissed and go into combat mode, I won't know anything about it."

He opened the map and spread it out on the ground, the five of them kneeling around it. "All right; here we are." He touched GG's muzzle to the tree line a hundred yards to the east of camp.

"They're going to be right here." He touched the muzzle to the base of the hill to the west.

"We're not going to surround the camp, as planned. Sabinski, you, me, and your squad will stay right here."

"Do you guys remember that ravine we went through a mile or more back?" He looked up at them.

They each affirmed that they did.

"OK. We've got to assume that they've got at least a company and probably a battalion, anywhere from two hundred to a thousand men. We're going to have to feed 'em into that ravine, let half of 'em through, and then hit the middle of the column with the claymores and hit the last half with rifles, grenades, and M79s. You'll have good range from the tops of the ravine with grenades.

"Go ahead and burn up all the M79 ammo and hand grenades on the back third; they'll be all bunched up as they stop for the claymores. Fire single-shot; if it's a full battalion, we're going to need every round.

"Me and Cargo's squad are coming through first, so be sure your guys are well briefed; if anyone blows a claymore on me, I'm gonna be really pissed!"

A few chuckles broke out as the tension began draining and confidence began returning. They were getting cocky again, and they could feel that Dwight was back on his game.

"If I'm wrong, then Cargo's right. He and Bucky there ..."

"Beaver."

"That's what I said."

They were all smiling at him. He winked at Rich, who smiled wider.

"We're not going to cut Beaver loose if this is what I think it is. We'll open up with GG and the AKs and a few M79 rounds and a bunch of hand grenades to make as much noise as possible.

"We'll save Beaver for the ambush of the head of their column, after we get through the ravine, but we're going to need your help." He looked up at the other squad leaders.

"Their strongest men and their best officers are going to be in front, so don't worry about mopping up the back of the column. As soon as they start their retreat, get your asses up front with us. With any luck, we'll have the front of the column in retreat too and we can close flanks on them, but they'll probably run north, rather than back through the ravine, through that flat grassland. We're going to have to flank 'em on that side then, before they get in that high grass and get away.

"If we get lucky, we'll be able to go back and run down the retreating rear of the column before they counterattack. Remember, single-shot only! We're going to have to be cool if we're going to pull this off. If you run out of ammo, get it off the guys you kill with the claymores. In fact, we'll be going back through there if we go after what's left of the column, so be sure to tell your guys to pick up the dead NVA's ammo on the way by.

"Any questions?"

Rich raised his hand and they all looked at him. He said, "What's the capital of Nebraska?"

"Fuck you. Lincoln, asshole."

"Shit! No one knows that!"

"All right. Let's go."

-CHAPTER SIXTEEN-

GOTCHA

IN ORDER TO MAINTAIN silence, Dwight told Pascone, Bandy, and Rich to get their squads into the next tree line, about a thousand yards away, before briefing them. He told them to gather all three squads and for Rich to conduct the briefing so that everyone heard the same plan and the reasons for it—this to ensure that all three squads worked as a team and that nobody got their signals crossed. Also, they would be working as two squads rather than three, one on each side of the ravine, so it was important that everyone was on the same page.

In addition, Dwight wanted everyone to know about the plan before they headed out to the ambush destination so that they could consciously recon the area between the camp and the ravine in case of changes in planning and to be as familiar with the area as possible in case they came back through it, chasing the retreating NVA.

The initial plan had been to use the cover of darkness to attack the camp and free the prisoners. Dwight had decided to attack at first light so that it would be dawn by the time he led the enemy into the ambush. The paratroopers would need plenty of light for accuracy, firing single-shot.

Besides twenty-eight claymore mines (one carried by each trooper not carrying an M60 machine gun or M79 grenade launcher), they each carried a LAW.

Dwight and all of Sabinski's squad stripped down to just essential weapons and ammo. The other three squads would carry the extra LAWs, claymores, rucks, and any other weight Sabinski's squad could shed so that they would be able to stay well ahead of the attacking enemy. They would also need to be stripped of nonessential weight in order to carry disabled prisoners, if there were any.

All of their AK-47 and M60 ammo were AP rounds and the small tank in the center of the clearing could be taken out with that, if it turned out to not be a dummy or decoy, as Dwight suspected. Once enough AP rounds start rattling around inside an armored vehicle, anything inside is going to get fairly well chewed up. As had been demonstrated to them in their training, the trick was to concentrate AP fire on a portion of armor that is least likely to ricochet the rounds, and if you're within a hundred yards of it, the tank will soon stop operating. But, just in case, Dwight decided to keep two LAWs for the tank.

All of the remaining LAWs would be positioned to the rear portion of the ambush at the ravine to take care of enemy armor, but they would probably be at least five minutes behind the lead enemy troops; with luck, they wouldn't have to be dealt with until after the main body of enemy troops had been. Although faster than ground troops, the tracked vehicles would have to go around the tree lines to get to the ravine, so they would be far to the rear when the action started.

Dwight had sent Sabinski's two M60 men back with the others and taken two of Rich's riflemen in their places. He would keep the RTO with him and call the general after the enemy launched their attack. The problem was that the entire First Battalion of the 173d was planning to jump into an open area one mile to the east of the POW camp at dawn plus thirty minutes. If Dwight told the general that they were heading north to the ravine instead of west to the DZ—the only area big enough to drop a large concentration of men and equipment—the enemy could easily figure out that he had set up an ambush for them, if in fact they were monitoring the net, which he was certain they were. He hoped that the general would figure out what was happening when he was informed of the action from air reconnaissance.

Thinking about it, he realized that it probably didn't make any difference. They were going to be either victorious or dead by dawn plus thirty minutes anyway. Dwight was certain that the enemy had planned for the big jump at dawn and probably intended to be gone by then.

He just hoped that they wouldn't figure out that something was wrong by analyzing why Dwight had decided to attack at first light. He knew they'd be expecting a night attack and would be pretty nervous when nothing had happened by 0420. Hopefully, they'd think that the bumbling Americans were having trouble getting in position in the cloud-covered darkness and had fallen behind in their plan.

Dwight had briefed Cargo's squad himself and had stressed that it was all-important that the enemy believe that the attack was real and in force. Like a screen pass in a football game, the defense had to buy that the offense was running something other than a screen. If they could sell the enemy that they were attacking to free prisoners and then sell that they were panicked and retreating from a superior force, the plan would work.

As previously planned, they would sneak up on the camp and kill the enemy guards with small-arms fire and both hand and M79 grenades, but first Dwight sent out two three-man patrols, one in each direction around the camp, to be sure none of the surprise attack enemy troops were close enough to cause any damage during their assault on the camp to free the prisoners.

He was fairly sure they wouldn't find anything, but it was better to be safe than sorry. If, as he expected, the enemy knew they were here, they'd be foolish to tip their hand by being in the way of Dwight surrounding the camp before attacking. This should work in his favor and give him some room to operate and set up the ambush at the ravine.

If, on the other hand, the enemy was, as Cargo had been so certain of, overconfident and hadn't prepared a more secure camp, they wouldn't be cautiously guarding the camp from outside, uncomfortable night after night in the bug- and mosquito-infested jungle.

The patrols returned after thirty minutes or so without any contact.

Dwight decided to keep up the two-mike-click communication with the general every hour, even though he knew that H-hour would have come and gone for three hours before the action actually began. He knew that the general and virtually all the brass involved, including Lyndon Johnson, would be climbing the walls wondering what had gone wrong.

Dwight had to smile at the thought of LBJ, McNamara, and the Joint Chiefs storming around the White House Situation Room, prognosticating about the new platoon's situation and the recriminations that would be flying about putting a nineteen-year-old medic in charge of such an important and complex operation.

Beth had sworn him to secrecy about what Suzy had told her about General Baxter's dislike of the two politicians. Actually, it was no secret that virtually all of the brass disliked them and their smug, arrogant, and unprofessional management of the war.

Dwight's biggest fear was that the president would panic and do something stupid, thinking that the mission had failed. All he needed was the dope sending air strikes, artillery or napalm runs, or just about anything that would not only ruin the plan but cause casualties to his platoon. He knew the general was a pro and would maintain his cool, so, as long as the mike clicks kept coming, he'd hold his horses; at least Dwight hoped he would.

He had sent both of his medics back with the other three squads. If there actually were any POWs and if anyone needed medical care, he could do whatever needed to be done until they got back. If the enemy was as smart as he thought they were, there would be American POWs in there. If the Americans had fallen for the ruse and then found no POWs, they might smell a rat and take off before the enemy could spring their attack. The POWs would take time to set free and then would slow the American's retreat. It would be wise of them to have POW'S there.

Using their binoculars, Dwight and Cargo agreed that there were at least five men in three cages, but nothing could be determined for sure as most of the guards and prisoners were asleep, or appeared to be. They couldn't estimate how many guards there were, but the two hooches that were dark were probably barracks and looked to be able to sleep six or eight each.

There had been one changing of guards, and only two had replaced the two in the main hut with the lanterns and radio equipment. The two guards, like the two before them, played cards at a small table and appeared to be drinking, as they were both boisterous and staggered noticeably when they checked the cages every thirty minutes and urinated.

Dwight thought that they had probably been told nothing of the enemy buildup in the trees at the base of the nearby hill, if indeed there was one. His plan's working well depended on the enemy leadership being careful that no one who absolutely didn't have to know their plans knew anything at all.

"Cargo, look!" Dwight pointed to the tree line at the base of the hill.

"Yeah, I saw it, LT!"

Thank God, Dwight thought. *So far, so good.* Someone had lit a cigarette and, Dwight was sure, was now getting his ass reamed, royally. Dwight considered how difficult it must be to not let the enemy troops in on what was going on and make them be quiet and stealthy too.

"Oh shit, Sabinski! I can feel it now. Some of them are starting to put two and two together. Damn!"

"You want to hit 'em early, LT?"

"No. We've only got twenty or thirty more minutes to first light; let's try to hold off. Our guys got to be able to see good when the dinks hit the ambush at the ravine."

Dwight could feel the enemy's negative energy growing exponentially now. *Ten more minutes! Just give me ten more minutes!*

"All right, let's go!" Dwight whispered. The difference in light was almost imperceptible. Dwight, the RTO, and Sabinski started creeping toward the guard shack. Sabinski's "Beaver" was slung on his back, and he carried an AK-47. They reached the trail that encircled the camp and breathed a sigh of relief—no mines.

Dwight heard the bolt cutters snap and an accompanying grunt of surprise from a prisoner off to his left, telling him that the first cage had been broken into by the RTO, who had left the radio at the tree line, to be retrieved on his way out.

As Dwight and Cargo approached the main hooch, they noticed that the two guards wore green NVA uniforms and chattered in Vietnamese as Sabinski silently and slowly pulled the door open, his K-Bar knife in his right hand and the bayonet-fixed AK-47 in the other. Sabinski rushed the guard facing him, passing the one with his back to him and simultaneously knocking the table over and plunging the bayonet into the guard's heart, pushing him to the ground as the NVA soldier emitted a high squeal of pain and fear as he died.

The other guard turned but didn't make a sound until Dwight's K-Bar plunged from the base of his neck beside his collarbone into his heart. He yelled loudly before Dwight levered the knife back and up, severing his larynx. His life left him quickly as blood spurted from the wound over Dwight's chest, arm, and lower face. Dwight held him to his body for the few seconds that it took for his motion to cease.

As they turned toward the door, they simultaneously saw and heard several grenades explode inside the two barracks huts. Dwight had closed one eye before he released his man and turned and hoped the others had remembered to do so also.

A grenade's flash could destroy night vision almost as well as a flare could.

The incendiary grenades had flamed the bamboo-and-thatch shacks immediately, and now the fragmentary grenades were taking their toll. Men were going down with the blasts, and Dwight saw one actually blow through a flaming bamboo wall.

The tank had been a decoy and was now a pool of burning rubber.

Knowing the grenade attack was finished, they ran toward the second barracks, GG jumping in his hand with two-round bursts; the guards were being mowed down as they emerged.

Americans would never sacrifice men like this ... or would they?

Dwight looked back to the cages, opened his other eye, and saw five prisoners standing together as the bolt cutters were being wielded on their shackles. They wore nothing but shorts, and even from twenty-five yards away, Dwight could see that they were filthy and skinny but mobile. *Good.* They each had on flip-flop sandals.

He then looked past them to the base of the hill, now two hundred yards away. He saw several flashlights come on and movement, but there was no firing yet. *Good,* he thought again. *They don't quite know what's going on yet, and their training won't let them take individual action. Orders have to come down.*

"Sit rep!" he shouted.

He heard men yelling "OK!" as they ran toward him.

From fifteen feet to Dwight's left he heard Sabinski say, "All present and accounted for, LT—plus five POWs!"

The crackling of the flaming buildings and his and his men's pounding footsteps were all they heard until they got to the tree line. Just as the RTO scooped up the radio, they heard the bugle, and then, almost simultaneously, the air was full of lines of green tracers, which went in all directions as they hit the trees and earth without specific aim.

Sabinski was carrying an emaciated POW over his shoulder, and the other paratroopers had teamed up as planned; one stood on each side of a POW, his arms over the POW's shoulders, enabling him to lift his feet off the ground—again, as had been planned. They were wearing rubber flip-flops, ubiquitous in Vietnam and all of Southeast Asia for that matter, and were able to run on their own, at least partially under their own power.

As they entered the next tree line, Dwight called a halt.

Shit! Things are going too well! We're going to have to slow down for 'em!

Sabinski came running back to him and said, "What the fuck you doin', LT?"

"They lost us in the woods, Cargo; I think they're heading toward the DZ! Their intel's good, just like I thought! We can't let 'em go that way; in thirty more minutes, First Battalion will drop right in on them and get cut to pieces!"

He thought for a second. "I want you to drop that guy, run fifty yards over to that side of the tree line, and fire a ten-round burst from Beaver at that tree line over there." He pointed across the clearing, in the direction of the firing that was now a hundred yards beyond and becoming fainter. "Then run back here and do it again, and then run fifty yards that way and do it once more!"

Without a question but with a look on his face that said that he wasn't comprehending why he was doing this, Sabinski put the man down and took off, dropping his AK-47, swinging Beaver around to his grasp, and chambering a round as he ran.

The jungle off to Dwight's left was alive with tracers, grenades, and now exploding mortar rounds. The damned enemy was going in the wrong direction!

He yelled for the other men to put down their prisoners and fire into the tree line that they had left not forty-five seconds ago, when Sabinski started firing. Dwight knew that Sabinski loaded Beaver with all tracers and that the show would be spectacular. He wasn't disappointed.

Dwight grabbed the handset off the radio, keyed the mike, and said, loud and slowly so that the listening enemy wouldn't get it wrong, "It's a trap, General! The enemy had at least a battalion of infantry waiting in the woods at the base of the hill to the west of the POW camp! We don't have a chance!"

He wished he could tell the general the truth. He could picture him and the others, sitting in that command post airplane, knowing that Dwight and his men would be dead in a few minutes and there was nothing they could do about it. He thought about clicking the mike button twice but decided against it. He couldn't afford to risk it. The message was really for the NVA anyway; the general would just have to suffer.

Dwight heard Sabinski's big feet pounding back toward him. Dwight and the other men had begun laying down fire when Sabinski had started his show. Dwight yelled, "Cease-fire!" as Sabinski approached. As ordered, Cargo stopped in front of them and did it again. Again, the tree line, just seventy-five yards away at this point, was lit up with red-orange tracers, and Dwight could distinctly hear pieces of trees and jungle falling through the underbrush.

Apparently Sabinski had figured out what Dwight was trying to accomplish. A good machine gunner knows to fire short bursts and only move the aim to the correction given by the tracers. After all, that's what tracers are for. Sabinski held the trigger down for a full three seconds, a long time, especially for a .50. Also, rather than holding the fire on target, he sprayed the whole sector of tree line. The big, noisy rounds also had the added advantage of traveling at supersonic speed, making the glowing rounds look like extremely fast-moving, ten-foot-long, three-inch-diameter orange-red neon lights, as they streaked into the tree line and ricocheted crazily in all directions.

These rounds were made for airplane machine guns and were made of magnesium so that they made a flash at impact, but also they, along with the glowing phosphorus of the tracer, ignited anything flammable in the trees. There were two reasons for this: mainly, it allowed pilots to see where their rounds were hitting, but also the flash served to ignite gasoline or any other flammable materials in the object being fired at.

For Cargo Sabinski, the rounds were even more spectacular both because of the initial flash at impact and because he could hear pieces of trees falling through the jungle and hitting the ground as small fires flashed in the trees and jungle undergrowth.

Dwight and the others began firing again as Sabinski cleared their line of fire and ran to his next position, fifty yards to the right, to continue the ruckus.

Shit! I hope I didn't screw up! The enemy's going to think we've got three tracked vehicles over here! If they don't come after us and right now, we've got a problem!

It does look like they've got a full battalion, though. Maybe it'd be best for us for them to stay around here for a while. No; if just one platoon of 'em is in the DZ, First Battalion will be cut to shreds. I've got to get 'em to come after us!

Just before Sabinski started firing again, the enemy's firing had all but ceased. As soon as Sabinski finished firing in his third and last position, Dwight yelled for the men to cease fire. He noticed that one of the prisoners had picked up Sabinski's AK-47 and had been firing it, doing what he could to help.

In the relative quiet, Dwight could hear the enemy troops running to form up in the tree line that Cargo had been firing into.

"Let's go!" he said in a loud whisper. They melted into the jungle and had emerged thirty yards on the other side of the tree line before he heard the bugle again. The firing started back up, but he could tell that the enemy wasn't advancing yet.

I hope I haven't overplayed my hand with that .50. Those sombitches must be shaking like dogs shittin' bones!

The light was gray now, and the squad had covered nearly a mile. Birds were beginning to stir and chirp. Coming out of another stand of trees, Dwight could make out the sharp rise

in the topography a thousand yards ahead; that would be the
ravine. He hadn't realized how open this area was in their initial
trip through here, in the dark. Nineteen men would be exposed
to fire from the rear if he didn't get them to the ravine before
the enemy came out of the tree line he'd just left and spotted
them. The distance could be covered in ten minutes, maybe a
little less.

The advancing enemy troops were still firing, so they were
probably still spooked by Cargo's .50-caliber demonstration, but
Dwight could hear them coming. He could feel them also. The
eager beavers among them were out in front of the main body
of enemy troops and moving fast.

The squad had a chance of making it to the ravine before
the enemy broke out into the open and saw them but, damn,
he was cutting it thin!

After six or seven minutes, Dwight shouted, "We gotta hurry
guys; if they catch us in the open, we got a problem! Let's go!
Go! Go!" He began waving them past and then began trotting
along behind them. Too slow—the POWs were slowing them
down.

The grass was shorter than he'd remembered it on their way
in; it was only knee-high. *Not good,* he thought. *They'll be too easily
seen. Two hundred yards to go—two football fields. The men are tired,
sucking wind.*

Shit! Here they come!

"Cargo! Hold up!" Sabinski stopped, pivoted, and started
running back to Dwight, who was running toward him at full
speed. Green tracers arced over their heads. They were out of
small-arms fire range, but the enemy machine gunners were
lobbing rounds at them, in low arches. The squad was five
hundred yards beyond the enemy machine gunner's effective
range but they knew that they could inflict damage if they lobbed
enough rounds in their general direction. They could walk their
tracers around in the group of Americans and score some hits.

"Spread out!" Dwight yelled. "Line abreast! Line abreast!" He saw the men following his orders without hesitation or question, even though running laterally to achieve a line-abreast formation cost them precious seconds in their quest for the ravine, now only seventy-five yards away.

Sabinski pounded to a stop three feet in front of Dwight, leaning back for his last three steps to stop his forward momentum. Cargo knew exactly what Dwight's intentions were. He put the prisoner down and, almost with the same motion, unslung the big machine gun, handed the back end to Dwight, and went to a knee, holding the front handle in his right hand, his elbow on his knee.

"Good man, Cargo!" Dwight said as he squeezed off a three-round burst. Two and a half seconds later, he saw the chests of two enemy soldiers explode as two of the big tracers found their marks, a thousand yards away.

Don't be jealous, GG!

The least number of rounds the big gun would fire at a time was three, and he felt, rather than saw, all three of the next burst tear apart the two-man crew of a heavy machine gun.

Five rounds, this burst. The four-man crew of a recoilless rifle and a field artillery piece that could have reached the squad with disastrous results all fell.

"Let's go!" Dwight released the big machine gun and started for his men, who were only twenty-five yards from the ravine now. Cargo slung Beaver and the prisoner over his shoulders and was close behind him.

The enemy was in a stunned silence but only for several more seconds.

Only a few green tracers arced overhead now. Dwight could see, in his mind's eye, enemy soldiers, frightened by what they had just witnessed, firing short bursts and then taking cover. He had seen up close what a .50-caliber round could do to a human being. He could only imagine the fear that the big, well-placed tracer rounds had instilled in those among the enemy troops who had witnessed it.

Twenty-five more yards!

He knew that NVA officers were screaming at their troops to fire and especially for them to man the recoilless rifle, which now had four badly torn NVA troops lying around it.

They heard the bugle again. Dwight knew that the enemy column had closed up and was beginning to enter the open area. He hoped that his men wouldn't spring the ambush too early. Close to a thousand enemy troops in the open would be a tempting target, especially considering the fear that so many charging troops would cause them, or any man for that matter.

The light was plentiful now. The gray had turned a dull yellow, but the sun was a long way from clearing the horizon yet. It would be another fifteen minutes before that, and this should be over by then.

The colors around him were obvious now, and there were no shadows. There were all the shades of green that he'd become accustomed to in Vietnam, but there were more grays here. The rocks were gray, and much of the brush was grayish, like in parts of west Texas and New Mexico.

Dwight looked for his men on the hillsides of the ravine the squad was beginning to enter but could see nothing. *Good.* They had learned their camouflage lessons well. He knew that if the hidden men were to stand up, they would look more like trees than men. Branches of bushes and grass had been stuck into belts, helmet bands had been made for this purpose, and boots and slits had been hastily cut into shirts and pants with bayonets and K-Bars.

He knew that he had to keep himself and the first squad exposed until the enemy got into the ravine, and, in fact, the three ambush squads had to let some of the enemy through in order to get most of the enemy column into the ambush. He now needed to decide where to stop. It had to be where he could fight well but also make the enemy think that it was a desperation move—a last stand.

With an adrenaline-fueled burst of speed, he ran up to the RTO and plucked the handset off of the radio, maintaining a dead run.

They were halfway through the ravine now. He looked from side to side, first for the claymore mines sitting on their little tripods and then further up the hillsides for the men waiting in ambush. Still, he saw nothing.

He keyed the mike and shouted into the handset, "General Baxter! We're out of steam! We've been running from them for over a mile! We can't run no more! We're going to have to stop and fight! There's at least a battalion of 'em! I'm sorry I failed you, sir! I'm sorry! They outfoxed us, sir!"

The RTO was looking at him when he put the handset back on the radio. Although running full speed and exhausted, he laughed out loud and said, "Airborne, sir!"

Dwight slapped him on the back and dropped back to the rear of the column.

They had abandoned their line-abreast formation and bunched up somewhat in order to get through the ravine, so they were exposed and in too much of a clump, but the incoming fire wasn't heavy because the enemy, sensing eminent victory, was in full attack, running and firing from the hip. There were now at least three bugles, all of them blaring excitedly for all-out attack.

Great! Their radio interceptors are right up front!

The squad was through the ravine now and the men, fatigued, were beginning to slow down.

"No! Keep running! Keep going! Fast! We've got to make sure they keep coming after us!"

Dwight could feel all of the attacking enemy troops now. Victory was in their hearts and blood in their eyes. He was damn glad that they couldn't pick up on *his* vibes!

There was a grouping of rock outcrops thirty yards ahead. *Good; this is a logical place to make our last stand. The enemy will understand why we decided to stop and fight here. Perfect.*

"Cargo!" he yelled, but before Dwight could say anything more, Sabinski, who had retaken the lead, unceremoniously dropped the POW he was carrying, unslung Beaver and his AK-47, and dropped down behind the first rock, which was gray and round, three feet high and four feet at the base, like the rocks that were always in the "Nancy and Sluggo" cartoons in the Sunday funny paper.

The rock that Dwight and the RTO chose was four feet high and six feet at its base and looked more like a slab that had been stuck into the ground at a forty-five-degree angle than the rounded gray rocks like Sabinski had chosen.

The other men slid into positions behind other rocks as they arrived. The outcropping was about fifteen yards deep and thirty-five yards across. Dwight stood up and repositioned a few of the troopers to maximize the effective field of fire and yelled for them not to commence firing until he told them to.

Dwight realized that a song was running through his head as the enemy began entering the ravine:

Life could be a dream, shaboom
If I could take you up in paradise up above, shaboom
Hello hello again, shaboom
Hello we meet again, shaboom

The enemy officers didn't suspect anything but glorious victory. Their men were bunching up in the valley of the ravine and slowing down significantly because of it. The leaders began emerging and fanning out as they prepared to annihilate the squad and the freed POWs.

Dwight heard the prisoner who was with Cargo, fifteen feet to his right, blubbering about their imminent death and only then realized that they hadn't been told of the ambush. He heard Cargo say to him, "Not to worry, pardner." As he motioned with his head at the advancing enemy, he said, "Watch this shit."

Dwight looked back forward just in time to see both sides of the ravine explode in what seemed like one gigantic white, yellow, and red flash!

The gray-white smoky air of the valley was full of flying helmets, equipment, weapons, arms, torsos, and shreds of clothing and flags. Rich had rigged all of the claymores in a daisy chain that effectively made them all go off simultaneously. *Good man*, Dwight thought.

There was just a second of terrible silence before the screams of terror and pain mingled to a crescendo along with grenade and M79 explosions, which were then punctuated with M60 machine gun and AK-47 fire from the high hillsides, above the lower hillsides, which were now cleared of grass and brush.

Dwight could see that the enemy was already in total disarray and in full retreat beyond the ravine; they were being cut down as they ran.

The two hundred or so enemy troops who had been let through the ravine were a hundred yards away and standing up, facing the carnage behind them. Hearing Dwight's order to commence firing brought them back to their own perilous situation.

GG began bucking in his hands as enemy soldiers began falling and running for the high grass three hundred yards off to Dwight's right, past the base of one of the hills making up the ravine. Dwight hadn't planned on or thought of what now burst out of his mouth; from the depths of his soul he screamed, "Charge!"

Even the prisoners were running after the fleeing enemy troops, flip-flops flying off their feet. Dwight heard Sabinski yell, "Airborne!" before firing a ten-round burst from Beaver, giant tracers chewing up the enemy from behind. Suddenly everyone, including the prisoners, was yelling "Airborne!" in their blood-lust charge.

Dwight had pulled the large black crucifix out of his shirt, and it was flapping against his chest as he pulled a spent magazine out of GG, slipped a full one in, grabbed the crucifix in midair, cocked his weapon, and began firing again, all within ten running steps.

Dwight saw Rich and his men running down the hillside to cut off the retreat and also saw that the enemy troops hadn't seen them yet, as their attention was on Sabinski's squad. Some were dropping weapons and equipment to lighten their load to be able to move faster and hide better, but before they could reach the high grass, Rich and his men had cut them off. They didn't have a chance, and Dwight felt himself change from bloodthirsty to pitying.

Shit! Give up, you idiots! Throw your guns down and put your hands up, you stupid bastards! Jesus Christ! Stop it!!!

As if on his orders, the remaining enemy troops stopped, dropped their weapons, and threw up their hands in surrender. There were only fifty or so left, spread out over a hundred yards.

Dwight yelled, "Cease-fire; cease-fire!" Then he yelled, "Cargo! Come with me!"

Dwight and Cargo began running through the frightened and dismayed enemy soldiers to Rich, Bandy, and Pascone, whose men were surrounding the enemy troops.

Dwight yelled, "Squad leaders! Sit rep! Casualties!" They all answered "None" as they came running up to him. "Prisoners!" "None except these."

"Herd the prisoners together; hurry! We gotta go after the rest of 'em!

As the squad leaders began barking orders, Dwight, thankful that the RTO had stayed with him, grabbed the handset, keyed the mike, and said, "General Baxter! Come in General Baxter!"

"Dwight! Is that you?"

"Yes, sir; we got to move fast!"

"Dwight! I thought you were dead!"

"I don't have time to explain, General! We kicked their ass, but a few hundred of 'em are in full retreat and we have to get after them before they can recover! Has the First Battalion jumped yet?"

"A few hundred are retreating from *you?*"

Yes, sir. I don't have time to explain! Has the battalion jumped yet?"

"They're in the process right now! Why were you giving me all this bullshit about your imminent death?"

"Had to, sir; they're monitoring the net! There's no time to explain! Have the battalion do what they were going to do before, but double-time it! Do you read?"

"I read, Dwight. What is your casualty situation?"

"None, sir!"

"None?"

"None, sir, but we've got to get moving!"

"Yes, *sir!*" General Baxter said, mockingly. Then he said, "Stay in touch!"

"Roger; out!"

Dwight yelled, "Who speaks Vietnamese well?"

One of the freed prisoners raised his hand and said, "I do, sir!"

"Good." Then he said, more for his men's benefit than the translator's, "We have to make the platoon look as big as we can. If the enemy sees that just one platoon is kicking one of their battalion's asses, they're liable to grow some balls.

"Tell the prisoners that we're going to counterattack and that they are going to be running in front of us. If any of them balks—tries to turn back, stops, or does anything else to fuck us up—they will be shot on the spot. Do you understand what I said?"

"Yes, sir, but the Geneva Convention …"

"The Geneva Convention don't say nothin' about how to transport prisoners. Now get on with it!"

"Yes, sir!" He turned to the prisoners, who were being herded together behind him, and began speaking loudly in Vietnamese. The frightened prisoners began looking at each other in amazement, but none protested. They had just been thoroughly whipped by a vastly inferior force, and they weren't about to argue with any of them, least of all their fire-eyed young officer or the giant standing beside him holding a machine gun that would take three of them to carry, much less shoot.

Dwight ordered that each NVA prisoner be given an AK-47 but not before a round had been fired through the receiver, rendering it inoperable.

They formed up in a column, two captured NVA in front of each paratrooper, while the freed POWs put on dead NVA's uniforms and armed themselves with AK-47s.

As the last of them stood up from lacing up boots, Dwight yelled, "Move out!"

He could hear the drone of C-130s in the distance and knew that they were disgorging the First Battalion of the 173d. With any luck at all, they could mop up and be back at base camp by this afternoon. The sun was still below the horizon.

The carnage and destruction in the ravine was awful. The effect of twenty-eight claymore mines exploding simultaneously in an interlocking cross fire was devastating and complete. Many of the bodies were in pieces, and Dwight could only take comfort in knowing that none of the enemy soldiers in the kill zone had felt any pain.

Although there was plenty of AK-47 ammo to be cannibalized, many of the magazines had been damaged by the claymore blasts.

Several of the enemy prisoners became physically ill at the sight of their fallen comrades. All were glad to leave the valley and begin coming upon the individual and still intact bodies of the retreating enemy, many of which had been killed by a single bullet from behind. There were at least two hundred of these, becoming further and further apart, as the lucky ones had finally got out of range of the sharpshooting paratroopers and gotten away.

After they'd past the enemy bodies, Dwight ordered them into a line-abreast formation with the prisoners walking ten paces ahead of the paratroopers and on either side of them. The twelve- to fifteen-pace separation served both to guard against a single machine gun burst or artillery shell hitting more than a few men at once and to make the force look as large as possible.

Also, Dwight had the enemy troops leave their helmets behind, as their pith helmet shape and red disk with a white star in the middle on the front would be identifiable, even at a thousand yards. Instead, he ordered his men to put their boonie hats on the NVA prisoners to somewhat negate the difference in the men's size and the color of their uniforms.

As they approached the tree line, Dwight was anticipating action, but he felt nothing. If their advance was being watched, there was no thought of combat on the part of the observers. Either the fight was gone out of them or there was no one there.

There had been no problem with the NVA prisoners, either. They were thoroughly beaten, and marching them through the torn bodies of their comrades with the accompanying smell of death that was still in everyone's nostrils had taken away any fight that may have been still in them. Truthfully, they were just happy to be alive.

Dwight was hesitant to report to General Baxter because he felt certain that the enemy's radio triangulation equipment was still operating. He still had that eerie feeling that the enemy knew exactly where he was.

-CHAPTER SEVENTEEN-

TRICK OR TREAT

THERE WERE LIMITS TO his powers, but he knew that the enemy didn't yet know what they were. How could they? He himself didn't know! He considered that he should try to tap further into whatever they were.

He halted the column at the tree line, told everyone to take a break, and sent a three-man recon patrol into the woods. They had filled their canteens from the dead enemy's and put water purification tablets into the water, so he knew the men had plenty of water, but that was the least of his problems.

He decided to separate himself from the situation for a few minutes to see if he could get some insight into the situation. He told his squad leaders to relax for a few minutes; he'd be right back.

There was a slight breeze, and cumulus clouds were already beginning to billow, promising rain by late morning. The jungle was still, cool, and wet in the morning dew but alive with birds and insects as Dwight sat with his back against a tree trunk and closed his eyes.

His previous feeling of dread was gone but so were the anticipation of victory and the elation of its realization. He couldn't define his feelings as empty exactly, but there was definitely something missing in his continuum of emotions or insight, or whatever it was that had been driving him since the initial combat—the defining moment of this whole phenomenon that he still had no memory of.

What had happened back then? What had occurred in his head that enabled him that night and henceforth to feel what the enemy was going to do and where they were? He wondered if there was any way that he could sharpen this skill so that he could tap into it at will. Was there a trigger of some kind? Could he learn to call it up and use it at his own behest? Thus far, he'd had to take these things—insights, feelings, whatever they were—as they came.

He tried to clear his mind and, at the same time, ask whatever this power was what the enemy was doing and what they were planning to do. Had they given up, and were they now in flight for their lives? Were they planning a counterattack? Where? How? What sort of equipment did they have? How many men did they have?

Men! Damn! You stupid idiot! What the hell are you thinking!

Dwight sprang to life, jumped up, and, running full speed back to his men, heard a startled voice shout a high-pitched, "Halt! Who's there?"

"Hold your fire! It's me! Lieutenant Johnson!"

A nervous young paratrooper said, "Shit, LT; what the fuck're you doin'? Tryin' to get yourself killed?!"

Dwight recognized one of his new medics. "Sorry, Bradbury. Thanks for not killing me."

"My pleasure, LT," he said, laughing.

"Give me a roll of wide adhesive tape and an IV set."

Unquestioning but with a puzzled look on his face, the medic opened his aid bag and complied.

Dwight pocketed the items and hurried down the line; he told his squad leaders to gather the prisoners together with the interpreter. He paced between two trees, fifteen feet apart, deep in thought as the orders were being carried out.

The prisoners were sat in the grass, just outside the tree line; they watched him curiously as the last of them were being gathered and seated. The interpreter stood between them and Dwight, as curious as the prisoners.

After he was certain that he had everyone's undivided attention, he stopped pacing and stood before them, smiling congenially, and said, "Good morning, officers and men of the North Vietnamese Army."

He looked at the interpreter, who was standing beside him with his mouth slightly open, wearing an ill-fitting North Vietnamese sergeant's uniform. Out of the corner of his eye, Dwight could see Sabinski and Pascone smiling like Cheshire cats. He knew they were wondering what the hell the LT was up to now.

"Well?" Dwight said to the interpreter; who turned to the rapt audience that now included his platoon and repeated Dwight's greeting in Vietnamese.

Everyone had gathered around except those posted to guard positions, and even they were straining to hear what Dwight was saying.

"You have been through quite an ordeal today and have fought bravely and admirably. You have nothing to be ashamed of, and I have the highest respect for you as honorable soldiers."

As the interpreter spoke, the prisoners visibly relaxed and a few even smiled slightly.

"We have in common that we are all soldiers, and I am sure that, even though you may not like us, you understand that we, like you, are professionals and must follow the orders of our superiors, just like you do. We soldiers have had to do this since the beginning of recorded history."

Dwight watched their faces while the interpreter, who had clearly warmed to the task, eloquently relayed Dwight's words and thoughts.

"Although you have been captured and your battalion has been destroyed, this battle is not yet over. There is still much to be done and more fighting and dying to be suffered."

Many of them shifted uneasily as they waited for whatever this brash, young military genius had in store for them. Not a single one of them had any doubts about his tactical prowess, bravery, or nerve. Dwight could feel their fear begin to build.

Still smiling and relaxed, he said, "I want to ask you to do something unusual but easy for you, as fellow professional military men, to do. I want you to try to put yourself in my position."

They relaxed a little at this. The young lieutenant wasn't such a bad guy. He was, after all, simply doing his job to the best of his ability. A few nodded their heads in understanding, and a few took on an even more relaxed posture, some even lying back in the grass on one elbow.

"Now, I ask you to try to understand that these are *my* men." He swung his free hand, the one not holding GG, around to signify an appreciative embrace of his platoon, and he noticed his men smiling appreciatively back at him.

As he waited for the interpreter to finish, he knitted his eyebrows, a look of consternation on his face as he tilted his head back and looked thoughtfully up at the sky.

"If I am to do my job properly, if I am to continue to be victorious, if I am to protect these men whom I dearly love, I need to know what you know about my enemy, the people who want to kill me and my men!" When he came to the "my enemy" part, he shouted it at the top of his lungs, meeting as many of the startled prisoners' eyes as possible and glowering at them with hatred and blood in his eyes. Even the interpreter was visibly startled and took a second to compose himself to convey the thought.

They have to think I'm as crazy as Hitler for this to work.

Again, at the top of his lungs and pulling his K-Bar from its sheath and shoving it in front of his face, he screamed, "I would just as soon cut each of your throats as look at your ugly faces!" Spittle atomized from his mouth in a fine spray with the *c* and *s* in *faces*. His eyes were ablaze with fury as he stalked several of the prisoners with his eyes.

Dwight reckoned that he must have been quite a sight: vicious little machine gun in one hand, big knife in the other, blood in his maniacal eyes, and a large crucifix with a pale white Jesus on it hanging from a big black chain from his neck. *Jesus,* he thought. *He was scaring himself!*

He stopped, as if in thought, and stole a glance at the cluster of his squad leaders. Except for Rich and Sabinski, they looked as shocked as the prisoners did. Dwight could tell that Rich understood what he was doing, but he wished Sabinski would take that shit-eating grin off his face; he was loving it.

Dwight rubbed his temples, machine gun in one hand and big knife in the other, as if he had a maniacal headache. Then he turned back to the now tingling-with-anticipation prisoners, smiled almost apologetically, and said, "To ensure my success and my continuing victory today, I am going to have to sacrifice some of you. How many of you are to die for my purpose is entirely up to you."

He watched the blood drain from their faces as the interpreter nervously translated, his face as ashen as the enemy's.

"We are going to have to hurry, for time is my enemy. I am going to take some of you individually into the woods and ask you some questions about your superiors and the enemy who is still alive and wishes to kill me and my men. I need to know strength, location, and plans. Each of you had better give me the same story."

Holding his K-Bar out in front, knuckles white with the effort, his countenance changed again as he screamed, "The throats of the men who's story differs from the other's will be cut, and I will happily watch his lifeblood gush out onto the jungle floor!"

He pointed the big knife at a captain in the second row and snarled low and loud, like a large dog, "*You ...* get up!"

Sabinski appeared behind the hapless, ashen-faced officer and jerked him completely off the ground by the collar of his shirt and carried him, his feet six inches off the ground, through the front prisoners, knocking three of them to the side and stepping on the thigh of another, who screamed in pain.

After they had gone ten feet, Dwight noticed that the interpreter wasn't following. He turned back and, with his most impatient scowl, shouted, "Well … what the fuck're *you* waiting for?"

Dwight dropped back, grabbed the interpreter's upper sleeve, and, for the benefit of the audience, jutted his jaw, stuck it into the interpreter's face, and snarled low, as if in admonition but so the others couldn't hear, "Play along with me!"

The interpreter stumbled along in Dwight's grasp, confusion in both his face and his motions.

When they'd come to a clearing, out of sight of the others but well within earshot, Dwight stopped, and he and Cargo forced the prisoner to his knees and bound his hands behind his back with the tape.

Dwight, looking as angry and as crazy as possible, screamed, "How many men await us!"

The frightened prisoner looked back at him, uncomprehendingly.

As loud and maniacally as he could, Dwight screamed, "Answer me, goddamn it!"

The interpreter stammered, "He-he can't understand you, sir!"

Changing again, returning to calm reasonableness, Dwight said, "Oh … of course not. What was I thinking?" Then, screaming insanely again, he shrieked, "Maybe *you* should tell him then!"

Thoroughly confused now, the interpreter stammered to the prisoner in Vietnamese, "He wants to know how many enemy soldiers await him! I fear the young officer has gone insane; I think you should tell him what he wants to know!"

The NVA captain spilled his guts, and Dwight could tell he was telling the truth. Dwight felt sorry for the distressed man; he had indeed been through a lot today. He was so frightened, Dwight was afraid the poor bastard was going to expire right there on his quivering knees, in the jungle clearing.

There was a battalion of NVA Regulars in reserve. In fact, their brass had thought that running down and killing Dwight's platoon would be so easy that they had hesitated in sending as many men after them as they had.

There were four light tanks but no other vehicles of any kind. Their only artillery consisted of seventy-five-millimeter recoilless rifles. They had five of these and twenty heavy machine guns. Most of the men were elite infantry.

To be sure the man was on the level, Dwight asked him if there were any intel troops with them. There was an intel platoon, and they *did* have sophisticated radio signal–finding equipment.

Dwight walked around behind the man, removed the tape from his pocket, tore off a foot-long strip, placed it over the terrified man's mouth before he could make a sound of surprise or protest, and wound it securely around the back of his head.

He then removed the IV set from his pocket and cut the tube just below the bag, uncapped the big needle, and, holding the prisoner securely in a headlock, shoved the needle in his jugular vein.

The man tried to scream but only emitted a squeak from his nose as blood, pressured by the man's frightened, hard-pumping heart, squirted through the tube, which Dwight directed all over his face, chest, hands, arms, and knife.

Dwight figured that only about a half-pint would be needed, and the man's body wouldn't miss that small amount.

Sabinski held his hand over his mouth, trying to stifle his laughter enough so that no one back with the group could hear him.

"Shut up, Cargo! They're going to know, man!" Dwight hissed as he pulled the needle from the man's neck and pressed his collar against the hole to quell the dripping blood.

Cargo dropped his weapon, covered his mouth with his other hand, and stumbled off into the jungle, mirth filtering through his fingers, his face red as a beet.

Like the time when he was twelve when he and his father had had to stumble out of church when, in the pew in front of them, a little girl in her Easter finery had noisily passed gas, Cargo's laughter infected Dwight and he had to go stumbling after him.

They finally got control of themselves and came back to the clearing and the prisoners' and the interpreter's amazed faces. Dwight then took a deep breath and, remembering seeing a pig slaughtered on his cousin's farm in Iowa and the bloodcurdling scream when the pig's throat was cut, let out a high-pitched, gurgling scream and let it die out as he ran out of breath.

Cargo stood there, smiling and nodding his head in approval as Dwight called for Rich to come help him.

As Dwight suspected he would, Rich knew exactly what had happened and took the dismayed prisoner away as Dwight and Cargo and the now approving interpreter went to get another prisoner.

Dwight's psychopathic behavior, along with the blood spattered over his upper body, had the desired effect. They chose another captain, who immediately began screaming in hysterical fear and told the interpreter everything he knew before they'd even reached the clearing. The information jibed perfectly with the previous officer's, and they didn't even have to put the man on his knees or tie his hands behind his back.

When the five of them walked back into the throng of men, his troops were all smiling in respect and admiration, and the enemy troops looked sheepish and relieved.

While he removed his shirt and washed the blood from his body with water from a canteen, Dwight and his squad leaders discussed their next move. Dwight was considering calling General Baxter and discussing strategy, even though he knew that the enemy would be listening.

Wait a minute! I wonder how long it would take for a jet fighter to be deployed and parachute-drop a scrambled radio to me.

He plucked the handset off the radio, keyed the mike, and said, "General, do you read?"

"I read you loud and clear."

"I've interrogated NVA officers and have reliable information about troop strength and equipment. The enemy is listening to us, and they have triangulation equipment; they know where everyone who keys a mike on the battalion net is, so they know my location, but you need to know this, sir."

"How do you know your information is correct, Dwight?"

"Let's just say I tricked them into believing that I was insane and that I was systematically killing anyone who didn't tell me the truth about what I was asking them. I'll tell you all about it later, but my intel is reliable, as far as it goes."

"What do you mean, 'as far as it goes'?"

"Well, sir, I don't think I should discuss this unless it's on a secure radio."

"Yes, *sir. Jesus.* All right, Dwight, tell me what you've found out."

"They have a battalion of elite NVA infantry in reserve plus around two hundred who got away from us. They have four light tanks, but the only artillery is some seventy-five-millimeter recoilless rifles. I've taken valuable time interrogating prisoners, so I don't think I can run them down before they get to the main body. I was wondering if we can get a jet to parachute a secure radio to me."

"No time for that, Dwight. Do you know where their reserve battalion is?"

"No, sir. They were at the base of the hill by the POW camp when we hit it, but no telling where they are now."

"I have an idea, Dwight. Where are you now?"

After Dwight gave him the grid coordinates, the general said, "Stay put for a few minutes. I'm going to assign you a code name. The enemy's probably going to assign its radio-finding equipment to the battalion's radios and follow their activity. You're going to be on a secure net in a few minutes, but the code name for your old radio will be what you cock your gun with, do you understand my meaning?"

"Roger."

-CHAPTER EIGHTEEN-

FLIGHT

TEN MINUTES LATER, DWIGHT heard the distinctive sound of an L-19 spotter plane, known as a "Birddog." Before it could be seen, the pilot came up on the net, which was now active as the First Battalion was forming up after its drop, and asked Dwight, using his code name, 'Crucifix,' to pop smoke and tell him what color it was.

The enemy was known to pop smoke to try to lure aircraft to its position and shoot it down, so the RTO would tell the pilot what color to look for *after* it could be seen by the pilot and too late for the enemy to duplicate it.

Dwight popped a smoke grenade and tossed it twenty feet from the edge of the tree line. When the smoke was fifty feet in the air, about fifteen seconds, he told the pilot the smoke was yellow.

Dwight gathered his squad leaders again and told them that he was pretty sure what the general had in mind: that he would be guiding them from the spotter plane.

The L-19 appeared from the east, skimming the treetops at full speed: 150 miles per hour. The pilot pulled the power off, lowered full flaps, to both bleed off airspeed and increase lift for a lower landing speed, and sped almost noiselessly past them, the wind whistling in the struts and open windows. The smoke told the pilot what he needed to know regarding wind speed and direction.

The smoke was going in the same direction as the airplane, from east to west, and the pilot climbed from ten feet off the deck to seventy-five feet to both bleed off airspeed and make his 180-degree turn to final approach, to land twenty feet to the other side of the smoke. The calf-high grass was perfect for the little tail-wheel airplane, and it settled in and came to a grass-aided stop beside the grouping of troops.

Dwight knew the airplane well. In fact this airplane was essentially a Cessna 170. The wing and tail were the same, but the fuselage was a tandem-seat two-place rather than a side-by-side four-place, so it presented a thinner profile from the front.

The L-19 had a stick control system, whereas the 170 had two control wheels in front. There were a few other things such as the rocket hard points, different radio/navigation equipment, stronger landing gear, and larger tires on the L-19, for landing circumstances just such as these. Unlike the 170, this particular L-19 had a more powerful motor and a constant-speed (adjustable) prop, so it could carry more fuel and the extra weight of the rockets and remain on-station longer. Also, rather than two doors, one on either side in the 170, the L-19 had just one on the right side so that the pilot or rear passenger had to slide the pilot's seat forward to get in and out. Dwight's father sold Cessnas for a living, and Dwight had over a hundred hours in the Cessna 170.

Dwight and his squad leaders ran the fifty feet to the airplane as the pilot cut the engine, got out of the airplane, and met them at the end of the wing.

After brief introductions, the pilot, a tall, tan, good-looking man of about thirty with a square jaw and hooded blue eyes who's name was Major McCutcheon, said to Dwight, "General Baxter sends his regards, and everyone in the United States Army and Air Force wants to know how your platoon kicked an entire NVA battalion's ass!"

"It's a long story, Captain; what are your orders?"

"The general wants you to fly with me to coordinate the attack. The airplane has a secure radio to talk to him on, and you can flip-flop frequencies back and forth from his to the net frequency that your men and the First Battalion are using."

Motioning to the airplane, McCutcheon said, "I've got eight Willy Pete [white phosphorus] rockets to mark targets for artillery or airplanes. The general wants to discuss strategy with you as soon as you get aboard. I'll be climbing to three thousand feet to get out of range of small-arms fire, but we'll be getting down low to fire the rockets. The general wants us to stay out of harm's way as much as possible.

As he took off his web gear to be able to sit comfortably in the airplane, Dwight said to his squad leaders, "Form up and be ready to move out. I'll talk to you as soon as I know anything."

He had given them code words to use in their communications. First, he had marked each grid on the battle map with letters. Therefore, each grid now had a name, rather than coordinate numbers, which became the phonetic alphabet names (e.g., alpha, bravo, charlie, delta, echo, foxtrot). Then, because he'd be broadcasting to the platoon on an unsecured radio, the points on the compass were to be reversed (e.g., east ninety degrees would become two-seven-zero, north would be one-eight-zero, forty-five would become two-two-five).

Dwight put GG on his lap and belted himself into the backseat as the pilot turned the airplane around and took off. There was a PUSH TO TALK button on the floor, between the stick and the left rudder pedal, which he pushed and said, "Blue leader, do you read Crucifix?"

He heard the general's voice say, "Roger, Crucifix. I read you five-by-five. Have you departed yet?"

"Roger, we are currently leaving the area."

"The pilot has orders to maintain at or above three thousand feet AGL, unless marking targets. He is now in your command, but do not, repeat, do not order him below that altitude unless you feel that it is absolutely necessary."

"Roger; at or above three thousand AGL."

"He is going to take you over the First Battalion's DZ and then over the battalion in the direction which they are moving; they are heading toward the POW camp. Your intel tells us that the enemy is dug in on the hill. Can you tell your men where to go in code?"

"Roger, sir. I designated each grid coordinate as a letter of the alphabet. The hill is Kilo."

"Good work, Dwight. Can I mark my map starting with Kilo at that grid square and then go through the alphabet back around to it in a logical progression? If something happens to you, I may need to talk to them directly."

"Roger, sir. The square before Kilo will be Juliet."

"Roger; I've already done it and it comes out right. I'm dying to know how you managed to beat such a superior force, Dwight. Is there a fast answer?"

"I figured out that it was a trap and lured them into an ambush, sir."

"Good work; I can't wait to hear all about it. What was it that you wanted to wait until now to tell me?"

"Well, sir, it's about our planning and what I found out about the enemy's strength and all."

"Go ahead, Dwight."

"The enemy knows that I've got whatever this thing is that I can do, so they may not have told even their higher officers exactly what they're up to. They could have a whole division back in there somewhere, for all we know. This trap may be more extensive than we realize."

"You mean you think they may have laid a trap for the whole brigade?"

"I don't know, sir, but they've been pretty shrewd so far. Both you and the MACV brass, not to mention the president and Joint Chiefs, fell for that POW camp bullshit."

There was a moment of dead air as General Baxter ingested the thinly veiled admonition. Then he said, "What are your thoughts, Dwight?"

The pilot looked back at Dwight and pointed down. Dwight looked down out of the right window. He saw that the main body of the battalion was entering a wooded area.

Keying his mike again, he said, "We're over the battalion now, General. I'll be back with you as soon as I get my men moving."

"Roger. Call me back as soon as you can."

"Roger."

Then Dwight said over the intercom, "Major, I'm going to be asking you to go back and forth between the battalion net and the general's frequency. Do you have a flip-flop radio [a button on the radio that flip-flops it back and forth from an active to a standby frequency, like going back and forth between two radios]?"

"Roger, I have two of 'em. I'll have one standing by to talk to air traffic, fast-movers, artillery people, et cetera. Your two freqs are in the other one."

"Good. Is it OK if I just say 'flip' when I need the other freq?"

"Certainly, Lieutenant."

"OK, flip."

Dwight saw the pilot's finger punch the panel, and the radio immediately began picking up the battalion net. He waited until he heard the end of a transmission and the "out," indicating that it was over, keyed his mike, and said, "Buck-o, this is Crucifix, do you read?"

There was silence for five seconds and then, "Crucifix, Buck-o reads you five-by-five."

"Buck-o, begin normal march to Papa and prepare to enter Kilo between Lima and Oscar; report when in position."

"Roger, Crucifix; on the way."

He said to the pilot, "Can I have the airplane for a minute?"

"You know how to fly?"

"Yeah, my father is a Cessna dealer; been flying all my life."

The pilot put both hands at shoulder height, palms out indicating that he was off the controls and that Dwight had control of the airplane, and said, "Sure; go ahead."

Dwight took the stick and immediately kicked hard left rudder, not significantly changing the direction of the airplane but putting it into a drastic skid, presenting the right side of the airplane to the slipstream and showing the panorama of the battalion below them and everything ahead through Dwight's side window, eliminating the engine cowling being in the way of the view. Dwight could see the POW camp a mile ahead and the hill where the enemy was thought to be, just beyond.

In this unnatural, high-drag, sideways position, the airplane dropped airspeed rapidly, and Dwight instinctively applied full power so that he wouldn't have to lower the wing to maintain airspeed and thereby obstruct his view.

McCutcheon said, "You *do* know how to fly this thing! Do you have any time in type?"

"Just one second, major." He was analyzing the situation, terrain, and distance before the battalion came into small-arms range of the suspected enemy positions. He reckoned that they were already in range of the light artillery and tank's cannons and that the enemy was holding their fire to try to achieve at least some element of surprise. He wanted to get in closer and get a look in the woods, both on and at the base of the hill.

He said, "Yeah, I've got over a hundred hours in a 170, which is the same thing as this airplane, essentially—same wing and tail."

"You got any time with stick controls and a constant-speed prop?"

"I learned to fly in an Aeronca Champ [a basic stick-and-rudder tail-wheel trainer with no electrical systems, which meant that it had to be hand-propped to start the motor and had no lights or radios], and I have quite a bit of time in Mooneys [a fast, low-wing, complex four-seater with a constant-speed prop and retractable landing gear] and 182s [Cessna's largest and fastest fixed-gear four-seater, with constant-speed prop but fixed landing gear]. I got my private ticket when I was sixteen. Dad was a navy fighter pilot in the war. We're both tail-dragger lovers."

Dwight had straightened the airplane out and, since the airplane had lost about three hundred feet in the slip, climbed back to three thousand feet AGL.

He said, "You've got the airplane; can we circle that hill in front of us? We think the enemy's there and at its base. Excuse me a minute; I've got to talk to the general."

"All right; I'm going to have to maintain three thousand above the hill too, so I don't know how much we'll be able to see. They're going to have everything pretty well camouflaged."

"OK; well, let's just do the best we can."

"Roger."

"Flip." Dwight saw the pilot's finger immediately hit the button and, after listening for a few seconds to be sure not to interrupt an existing conversation, said, "Blue leader, this is Crucifix, do you read?"

"Roger, Crucifix; go ahead."

"We're approaching the hill, but the pilot has orders to maintain three thousand AGL. I need to get in closer to see anything; permission, sir?"

"Negative, Crucifix; we can't afford the risk. They could reach you with a fifty but the pilot would have enough time to dodge tracers at three thousand AGL. Don't go any lower; that's an order."

"Roger, sir; what's your plan?"

"I'm going to drop a company of dummy paratroopers on the other side of the hill to see if we can flush them out a little and see what they've got. I've got two LRRP squads on the way over there now, coming in from opposite directions. They should be in position in another fifteen to thirty minutes. How long can you remain on station?"

The pilot, who was listening to the conversation, said over the intercom, "Four hours … more if someone down there's got some gas."

Dwight keyed the mike and said, "Four hours; more if there's Av gas on the ground."

"Roger; I'll have some dropped into battalion."

Dwight kicked hard left rudder, grabbed the stick, threw it in the same direction, and screamed, "Look out!"

The pilot instinctively resisted the sudden motion of the stick and rudder controls as big .50-caliber rounds tore through the cabin, killing him instantly. Dwight had rocked his body to his left as two rounds punched through his seat, one grazing his thigh and the other missing him entirely.

The pilot's harness held him in position as his head lolled on his shoulders. Dwight shoved the left rudder pedal all the way to the floor and continued the now unresisted left-stick motion all the way to the side, rolling the airplane inverted and diving.

The big machine gun was directly beneath him, spewing green tracers, which were swinging to adjust to the sudden sideways and downward motion of the airplane.

Dwight, knowing from experience that the rudder worked oppositely when the airplane is inverted, kicked right rudder and continued the roll, keeping the nose almost straight down and rapidly approaching the airplane's Vne [never-exceed speed; the speed where the airframe is in danger of breaking up]; he pulled the throttle all the way off and jammed the propeller control to fine pitch.

The hillside was rushing up rapidly, and he could see that he could reach the rocket-firing switches with his left hand; unbuckling his harness and leaning forward in his seat, he flipped the red ARM switch and put his index finger on the rearmost of the eight switches.

Five hundred yards, now—the machine gun rounds didn't have far to travel, and they were on him in an instant. Using rudder, he jinked back and forth, dodging the rounds as a running child would dodge water coming from a garden hose.

After a quick glance at the ball to make sure it was centered (the ball is a turn-coordinating instrument that sits in a curved glass tube filled with liquid. If the ball is in the center, it indicates that the airplane is balanced, in that it isn't in a skid and therefore in a coordinated turn or, if not in a turn, pointed straight ahead), he fired the first rocket. He had enough time to see the rocket hit the center of the gun and scatter the crew. He knew that the gun was destroyed and the crew members were either dead or wishing they were. Burning phosphorus gains heat and energy when it contacts moisture—in this case, blood.

Glancing at the airspeed indicator, Dwight saw that he was now a little below Vne, so he shoved the throttle full-forward and hauled back and to the right on the stick; he fed in right rudder, turning right to avoid crashing into the trees on the hill.

At treetop level, he could see that the woods were full of troops and equipment. Muzzle flashes were so numerous they were almost blinding! But, just as before, Dwight's senses were at a premium. Like a pro quarterback in his prime, Dwight could see the whole field. He counted twelve tanks and a battery of eight howitzers as he whizzed over them. This close, all the camouflage in the world wouldn't keep him from seeing them, and at over two hundred miles per hour, none of the enemy gunners were leading him enough to hit him.

He turned right again, diving down with the contour of the hill, feeling the airplane quiver as he was over the edge of the envelope of the airframe's design limitations for high-speed maneuvering. He knew the strong little Cessna could handle it and kept the throttle wide-open as the airspeed indicator reached well into the red again.

In an instant, he was over the advancing First Battalion, the airplane well in excess of Vne. He lifted the nose ten degrees to bleed off airspeed but kept the throttle open as he performed a slow roll.

In his headset, Dwight heard the general shout, "Major McCutcheon! What in the *hell* do you think you're doing?"

"The major's dead, sir."

"Dwight?"

"Yes, sir?"

"Do you mind explaining to me just what the hell's going on, Lieutenant?"

"Fifty-caliber rounds came up through the floor, sir. I felt them coming but couldn't move the airplane out of the way in time. I was in an inverted dive by the time I got control of it, so I went ahead and completed the roll and took the gun out with a rocket."

There were a few seconds of dead air, and then the general said, "You know how to fly an airplane?"

"Yes, sir. My dad's in the business; I've been flying all my life."

"Lieutenant, you had a direct order not to go below three thousand feet AGL! Do you know what the penalty is for disobeying a direct order in combat, young man?"

"Yes, sir, but we were in a dive, and the .50 had us. I had to fire; it was either me or him."

"It's out of my hands, Lieutenant. All of MACV command is monitoring this frequency. There will be a mandatory board of inquiry regarding this incident. Do you understand me, Lieutenant?"

"Yes, sir, but we've got bigger fish to fry right now."

"What do you mean?"

"After I took out the .50, I was at treetop level, and that whole hill is alive with men and material."

"We were planning on them being there, Lieutenant; that's no surprise."

"Could you see my flight path, General?"

"Yeah, I saw it. There's a thin overcast, and I'm at forty thousand feet, but the equipment allowed me to keep a pretty close watch on you. Why?"

"Well, I was right down on the deck, sir, and going over two hundred miles an hour, and even at that speed and limited view of the area, I saw a battery of eight howitzers and twelve heavy tanks."

"That's impossible, Dwight! How could they have heavy tanks and artillery in there?"

"They've known about me for over a month, sir. I think they've been planning this thing all along. They're set up to be able destroy the entire 173d Airborne Brigade."

"You mean they expected you to be able to defeat one of their best infantry battalions with your light platoon?"

"No, sir, but I think they planned on you coming in after they whipped me. We know their intel is good. They may have factored in that you'd want to back me up with a full-scale assault if I got whipped or maybe for show, if nothing else."

"Jesus Christ!"

"Sir, can I make a suggestion?"

"Go ahead."

"They're probably discussing right now what to do if I saw their heavy artillery and armor. If they think I saw it, they're getting it out of there as we speak and probably moving their timetable up before you have time to replan your attack."

"Go on."

"That victory roll I did may make them think that I didn't see anything. It wouldn't be logical for me to be behaving like that if I saw that we were about to get our asses kicked."

"I'm with you; go on."

"Well, we know that they need some time to reposition all that stuff, in case I did see it. I'm sure they're moving it right now, expecting us to bring in fast-movers and targeting the positions in a few minutes."

"Yes; in fact, the fast-movers are on the way, right now."

"What's their ETA?"

"Three to five minutes."

"Call 'em off quick, General! We don't want the enemy to think that we're even considering sending fast-movers, at this point!"

"Dwight, can I remind you that you're an FNG Second Lieutenant and that this is a coordinated effort, involving all of MACV and generals with several more stars than I possess!"

"I'm sorry, sir; I don't mean to be impetuous, but please don't think that I'm out of my depth here. I've been up close and personal with these people all day, and I've kinda got a feel for the situation—especially after that last encounter with the .50 and this dead pilot sitting here in front of me. And then there's the attack on the POW camp and me leading the enemy into the ambush in the ravine. You'll have to admit, sir, I'm batting a thousand, so far."

"OK, Dwight; tell me what you're thinking."

"They're not telling their commanders what's going on, to keep me from figuring them out. For instance, I wouldn't have found out that they have a superior force if I hadn't taken out that .50. We have a leg up right now because they don't know that I'm in this airplane, not to mention that I'm flying it; we have to be unconventional and outthink 'em if we're going to prevail.

"Even if I'm wrong, those fast-movers are just going to be dumping napalm in the woods. The tanks and guns will be successfully repositioned by the time the jets arrive, and we may be needing those jets and their ordnance soon and they will have been wasted.

"You're just doing what they expect, sir; if we're going to win, we can't do that! We need to get those jets turned back, refueled, and ready to go so we can have some time to discuss strategy.

"Also, the battalion is getting too close to the enemy. We don't want to engage until we have the probability of victory.

Right now, with those tanks and artillery, they can kick our ass! Tell the battalion to take a break; I have a plan."

"Stand by, Lieutenant."

"Yes, sir."

Dwight unbuckled his harness and seat belt, stood up, and hit the FLIP-FLOP button on the radio.

"Buck-o, this is Crucifix; do you read?"

"Roger, Crucifix; go ahead."

"What is your position?"

"We're in the tree line five hundred yards from Kilo, between Lima and Oscar."

"Roger; hold there. Get some chow."

"Roger on the chow."

"How many LAWs we got left?"

"Fifteen or so."

"Roger; get them together. How high is the grass in the clearing behind you?"

"Calf high, like the other."

"Roger; I'll be there in ten minutes."

Dwight flipped the radio back to the general's frequency, sat back in his seat, and fastened his seat belt. Then he trimmed the airplane for level flight, pulled the prop control back to 2,000 rpm, and set the throttle to twenty-two inches of manifold pressure to bring the power and prop angle to set up for an efficient cruise; he took a deep breath and took his map out of the seat-back pocket in front of him.

He was three miles past the battalion now; another five miles and he would be out of sight of the enemy. He banked left to turn ninety degrees to the battalion, brought the airplane back to level so the wing wasn't in his way, and looked the area over.

The battalion was clear of the big DZ now, and he couldn't see any movement at this distance. He looked for his platoon's position, saw the tree line he was certain they were in, and looked at the position on the directional gyro; he found where they were, in relation to the airplane, and then he headed in the opposite direction, letting the little airplane lope along, as if it were exiting the area.

Dwight knew that if he gradually decreased altitude as he headed away, it would appear to the enemy that the airplane was gone over the horizon, and, while that was in fact a factor, settling down to treetop level enhanced the illusion. He didn't want them to suspect that he was coming back. After all, they had seen the little airplane take hits from the big .50, so he was sure that they thought that it was damaged and headed home.

"Crucifix, this is Blue Leader; do you read?"

"Roger, Blue Leader; go ahead."

"The jets have been turned back, and the battalion's advance has been stopped; what's your plan?"

"First of all, what was the enemy's reaction to your dummy paratrooper attack?"

"No reaction yet; the LRRPs are in the area and report no activity."

"They didn't fall for it."

"Doesn't look like it, genius; what's your plan?"

Damn. The general's gettin' the ass. He's got to be under a ton of pressure. His superiors are watching him like hawks, and he's taking orders from a hocus-pocus, clairvoyant, nineteen-year-old lieutenant. I'd better tread lightly.

"Well, like I've said, sir, I've been engaging this enemy force all day, and I think I've developed a feel for the situation. I think they're set up to whip us, sir, unless we can pull a rabbit out of the hat."

"What makes you think they can whip us, Lieutenant? This ain't exactly the North Dakota National Guard down here, you know."

"No, sir; I understand that, but they've had a long time to think about this, and they've chosen this battleground for a reason; the terrain is made for a tank and artillery duel. The problem is that we don't have any tanks or artillery; do you see what I mean, sir? Remember, I saw a bunch of tanks and howit-

zers, but I doubt that I saw all they have. With just the tanks and
artty I saw, plus a battalion of infantry, they could tear us a new
one."

"OK, Lieutenant, I'm with you; what are your thoughts?"

"OK, General; let's assume the worst and see if we can get
inside their heads. If they have been planning this thing for a
month, we have to assume that they've got enough men and
equipment in the area to take out the entire 173d Airborne.
That's the bad news; the good news is that they don't know I'm
in this airplane, that we've found out that they have tanks and
artty and that they're laying for us"

"I thought that you thought that they moved the tanks and
artty in case the spotter plane saw them?"

"True, General, but since we didn't hit them with the fast-
movers and since the spotter plane left the area, they're back
to plan A now. Heretofore, our forces have always hit them with
the fast-movers when we get intel like that. Also, no matter how
damaged the spotter plane was, they know it would have stayed
on station to get more intel if it had seen the tanks and artty
that it flew over."

"OK, Dwight; I'm following you. What do you recommend?"

"The way I see it, sir, they're going to wait for us to get out
in the open and then hit us from three sides with the tanks and
artty and then follow up with infantry. Do you have your map
in front of you, sir?"

"Yes, Lieutenant; I have my map in front of me!"

Whoops! Be careful, kid; take it easy!

"Sorry, sir; I figure they're waiting for us in Sierra, Romeo,
November, Golf, Zulu, and Alpha. I recommend that we hit
them in the woods coming from Tango and Victor to Sierra
and Romeo. I'll need for you to lob some recoilless rifle rounds
in there from Tango to get them wound up so I can tell where
they are; then I'll take out the tanks, and you can flank them
through Romeo and November."

"You're going to take out the tanks? Just how do you propose to take out tanks with marker rockets, Lieutenant?"

"I'm not going to be using marker rockets until you start capturing their artty and we start using it against them, sir."

Knowing that the general couldn't interrupt him while he kept the mike keyed, he held the button down while he took a deep breath and let his ideas sink in. After a couple of seconds, he said, "I'm going to take the tanks out with LAWs, sir."

"You're *what!*"

"I'm going to punch a hole in the deck of this airplane and put fifteen LAWs and the lightest trooper I've got in the back, and he's going to pull the triggers on the LAWs when I tell him to, and we're going to kill the tanks from straight above 'em, where their lightest armor is, sir."

"You're insane, Lieutenant! Just how do you think you're going to get above the tanks, and, if you can, how're you going to know when to shoot? The LAW will be at a ninety-degree angle from your direction of travel at over a hundred miles an hour, right on the deck! We don't even have bombsights in fast-movers that can do that! Also, a LAW is a recoilless weapon, which means the backblast will be in the airplane! It'll blow the roof out of the airplane, not to mention killing both of you!"

"I'm going to cut the top out of the airplane."

"You can't do that, Dwight! That will ruin the structural integrity of the airplane!"

"No, sir, the roof of this airplane is mostly Plexiglas. That's why it has such big struts. The wing, strut, and side of the fuselage make up a triangle, the strongest structure in nature. I'm not going to take out any of the tubing that makes up the strength of the fuselage.

"As far as my being able to aim and fire the LAW straight down, taking airspeed into account—that's what I do when I shoot people, essentially. I don't really consciously aim; my intuition takes over and aims and fires the weapon. That's how it's always worked with GG, and it worked with the rocket I hit that machine gun with a while ago.

"I should be able to do it with a LAW too; that's why I need for you to lob recoilless rifle rounds at them. All you have to do is get them pissed off and firing at you, and I'll take it from there.

"Look, General, what's the worst that can happen? If I'm wrong, you've at least got them committed and firing at you before they intended to. And you can still follow the plan I've outlined; you won't be walking into their trap and will have at least a chance of completing the flanking movement.

"On the other hand, if I'm right, we'll kick their asses all the way back to Hanoi. Remember, the NVA brass isn't telling their commanders what the big picture is because of *me*. Once we get them in disarray, one hand won't know what the other one's doing, and we can start ripping them to shreds."

"Stand by, Dwight."

"Roger, sir."

Dwight was fifty feet off the treetops now. He pushed the prop control to fine-pitch, pushed the throttle full-forward, pulled the stick back and to the left, kicked left rudder, and made a quick 180-degree turn, back in the direction he had come from. He put the airplane on a heading two-seven-zero, straight to his platoon at full throttle; setting the prop at 2,500 rpm, he saw the airspeed indicator settle on 160 knots. *Good bird.*

He climbed to fifty feet above the trees, undid his seat belt, and, standing to reach past the dead pilot, flipped the radio back to the battalion net in time to hear coordinates being given to begin his suggested flanking movement. *Good general.*

Strapping himself back in, he keyed his mike. "Buck-o, this is Crucifix; do you read?"

"Roger, Crucifix. Go ahead."

"I'm coming home. Get the LAWs together and try to get a hold of something I can saw holes in aluminum with. Roger?"

"Roger; come on home. We'll greet you in the field."

"Roger; out."

Dwight's reckoning had been off by only 300 yards, putting the clearing that was behind his platoon to his right and ahead. He pulled the power off, pulled carb heat, dropped all sixty degrees of flaps, and hauled back on the stick to counter the pitch-down caused by both the power reduction and especially the big flaps suddenly lowering into the slipstream from the back of the wings; he trimmed the airplane for its new angle of attack.

Over the trees, he could see the top half of the enemy's hill, three-quarters of a mile ahead, but he figured they had vacated it, in anticipation of the napalm attack by the fast-movers. With any luck at all, they couldn't see him.

He made the turn parallel to the platoon's position in the tree line, unbuckled his seat belt, and stood to flip the radio back to the general's frequency, just in time to hear him say, "Crucifix! Do you read? Crucifix! Come in!"

"Roger, Blue Leader. I just got back on the channel from the net. I'm in my landing pattern to the platoon's position. I'll call you as soon as I get down."

"What makes you think your plan is approved, Lieutenant?"

"I don't figure we have much choice, sir."

"Roger. Call me when you're down."

"Roger."

Out of his left window, Dwight could see his men out in the grass beside the tree line, waving to him to be sure he could see where to land.

There was a high overcast and no shadows. The shades of green were tinted a slight gray from the dark cloud bottoms, and he could see the wind gusts blowing the short grass in waves, toward the platoon. He would be landing in a direct crosswind. He knew that the crosswind component was fifteen knots in this airplane and ground looping this little sucker right now would be the worst thing he could do. Bending a wingtip or two he might be able to deal with. However, if he lost control bad enough to nose over and bend the prop, the airplane would be finished.

He considered coming in against the wind like it should be done but immediately discounted it; the clearing was too narrow. He counted on being able to skid sideways on the grass if the wind was over the crosswind component. He knew he could manage it in even an eighteen-knot crosswind, but anything over twenty might present a problem.

Raising the nose fifteen degrees, he climbed a little as he made the turn from downwind leg to base leg to final approach, in one sweeping turn, adding power to maintain a seventy-knot approach speed in the tight 180-degree turn. The platoon was now ahead and to his right five hundred yards. The airplane, controls in neutral positions, was flying straight ahead but at a forty-five-degree angle to the left, tacking into the wind to maintain its stability.

Dwight cross-controlled the airplane by putting the right rudder to the floor and feeding in left aileron with the stick. This made the airplane track straight but with its left wing down to counter the wind coming from the left. *Good—no drift.* The airplane was barely within the crosswind component. He added power to maintain a sixty-knot final approach.

Because of the gusting wind, he was making constant corrections in both aileron and rudder, but he had good control; he cut the power. Two feet off the deck now, he could feel the solid feeling of ground effect and the longer grass licking at the landing gear, making a hissing sound like a lover urgently whispering her needs in his ear. *Got to be cool now; hold her off! Hold her off! Try to let her stall the last few inches into the grass.*

Come on, baby! Come on, baby! Settle in there! Come on, sweetie! There we go! There we go! Good girl! Good girl.

Stay with it! Stay with it! The left wheel and tail hit at the same time. *Perfect!* Now the right wheel settled in.

"Whispering Bells," an old doo-wop song by the Del-Vikings, was running through his head: "Whispering bells, whispering bells, bring my baby ... bring my baby back to me."

Now he was dancing on the rudders and keeping the tail wheel pinned to the ground by holding the stick full back and left as the little airplane tried to become a weather vane and turn into the wind. This would cause the right wing to strike the ground as the wheels bit; like a car entering a corner too fast, the airplane would spin around into the wind and try to flip over, striking the wingtip and maybe the prop—a classic ground loop.

Good! As he'd hoped, the wind hitting the side of the airplane caused the wheels to skid on the grass and not bite hard enough to afford enough traction to start the hard left turn that could cause a ground loop—no problem. Truth be known, Dwight knew he could have handled this one on a concrete runway! He came to a stop right beside the platoon. *Cool.*

Dwight unbuckled and stood up, pushed the carb heat off, put the flap lever in the up position, turned off the transponder, pulled the mixture all the way back, killing the motor, and then turned the magneto switch to BOTH OFF, leaving the master switch on so he could keep the radios on; he pushed the floor mounted lever to push the pilot's seat forward, unbuckled the dead pilot and opened the door.

Rich was the first one at the door and, seeing the pilot fall halfway out, Dwight's hold on his collar keeping him from tumbling all the way to the ground, said, "Jesus, LT! Don't tell me you just landed this plane!"

"Yeah. You know my dad's an airplane salesman. I've been flying all my life."

Rich dragged the body clear of the door and said, "What the hell happened?"

"A .50-caliber machine gun was right under us; he never knew what hit him."

"What happened to your leg?"

In all the excitement, Dwight had forgotten about being grazed by the .50-caliber round that he'd barely managed to dodge as it came up through his seat. There was quite a bit of blood, but it looked worse than it was. He said, "The .50 grazed me; I'm going to need a few stitches."

A full second hadn't gone by when Rich yelled, "Medic up!"

PFC Bradbury, the medic Dwight had taken the tape and IV set from, was there in an instant. Dwight asked him for his bandage scissors, and he cut a four-inch hole in his pant leg, exposing a three-quarter-inch-long wound that hadn't reached into the muscle. He dabbed it with a piece of the cloth he had cut away to be sure it was only capillary bleeding and no large veins were involved.

"Brad, give me five stitches, one in the middle and two on each side. Don't worry about gloving and sterile field. Wash the wound and your hands with Physohex, and be sure to wash it deep enough to get it good and clean. Don't spare the Xylocaine; I don't want to feel what you're doing."

"Yes, sir," Bradbury said as he took a knee, opened his aid bag, and removed a suture set, Physohex soap, and his canteen. He was already lathering his hands when Dwight asked Rich what they had figured out on how to cut open the airplane. He winced as the medic began washing the wound with soapy four-by-four gauze.

"Sorry, sir."

"Don't worry about it and work fast."

"Yes, sir."

Cargo said, "These pilots all carry big knives that have a serrated edge on the back, made for cutting themselves out of wreckage, but this guy don't have one on him."

Dwight said, "Look in the airplane; there's pockets on both sides in front and back."

Sabinski found it in the first place he looked: the elastic pocket beneath the instrument panel, on the left side of the pilot's seat.

Dwight winced again as the medic began injecting Xylocaine into the sides of the wound. "Shit! That burns!"

"Yes, sir; sorry, sir."

Don't call me, sir, Brad. I *work* for a living!"

"Yes, sir; I mean LT."

"Call me Dwight, Brad."

"Yes, sir. I mean, right, Dwight." They both laughed.

"I've got to get on the airplane radio, Brad. I'm going to sit on the seat with my right side hanging off. Can you work OK like that?"

"Yes, sir; I believe so, sir."

As Dwight stepped over to the seat and put his left buttock on the seat and foot inside, he thought to himself how difficult it must be for Brad to call him by his first name. A lot had happened in a month and a half.

Brad said, "Do you feel that, sir?" as he probed the wound with the syringe needle.

"No; it's dead, Brad. Go to work."

"Yes, sir."

Dwight then said to Sabinski, "Cargo, unscrew that inspection hole cover on the floor, and if there's nothing directly beneath it, cut a hole in the bottom of the airplane beneath it so I can stick a LAW down through it. Then cut a big-assed hole in the roof so the backblast can go through it." Twisting around in his seat and partially standing on the leg that Brad was suturing, he indicated a six-inch round plate screwed to the deck. Cargo unscrewed the plate and said, "There's cables to the side and a big rod down the middle, but you can stick a LAW through there OK." He then stabbed the knife through the middle of the hole so he could see where to saw the hole, got out and lay on his back under the airplane, and started sawing in big, mighty thrusts. The hole was open in less than a minute. He then got back in the airplane and began cutting the Plexiglas out of the roof, sweat rolling down his arm and onto Dwight.

Dwight turned back to the front, put on the pilot's headset, keyed the PUSH TO TALK button on the throttle, and said, "Blue Leader, this is Crucifix; do you read?"

"Go ahead, Crucifix."

"Are you positioning to hit their left flank?"

"Roger; we should be ready in fifteen minutes. How do you intend to attack, Dwight?"

"I'll call you when I'm ready to go, and then you can commence your attack. Try to get them as riled up as you can so I can feel 'em. I'm going to shoot 'em from treetop level at a hundred fifty miles an hour, when I locate them. I'm putting Richardson in the back, and he's going to fire LAWs through a hole the floor on my command."

Rich said, "You're *what*!?" as Dwight waved him off, listening to the general say, "You'd better be sure you've got a big hole in the roof; a LAW's backblast is as powerful as it is out the muzzle."

"Roger, sir; I've got it covered."

"OK; call me when you're ready."

Twisting again to see Sabinski's progress, Dwight saw that the hole was almost complete, as the big paratrooper's sweat now poured onto him, both seats, and the floor.

"We should be ready in thirty minutes, sir."

"Roger."

As Sabinski started sawing the second side of the big hole, Dwight noticed that the LAWs had been stacked under the wing.

Damn, those little suckers are short! That's all I need is to blow myself up with that backblast bouncing around inside this little airplane.

He could hear his father bragging to his friends that his son had shot himself down with an antitank weapon!

He said, "Cargo, go ahead and cut out the whole roof back there; can you do that?"

"No sweat, LT."

Dwight hung the headset on its bracket beside of the windshield, switched the master switch to the OFF position, and listened to the gyros wind down as he tried to think.

Something's not right. I can feel it. What is it?

Opening the map in his lap, he began going over the plan in his head, starting with the sectors. Hovering around him, Rich, Bandy, and Pascone knew not to say anything while Dwight pondered the situation. Although Dwight was not really very comfortable with it, he knew that his thought processes had become sacrosanct for them. His brilliance in battle had become legendary, especially among those closest to him. He tried to conceal a shudder as he realized the weight of the responsibility on his shoulders. Brad felt it and stopped his work, looking up at Dwight and, thinking that maybe he'd hit a spot that wasn't deadened, said, "You OK, LT?"

"Yeah, Brad; a little nerve wasn't quite dead. No sweat, go ahead."

The fear was back; something was wrong. He was doing something wrong. He had no doubt about it. He knew the feeling now; he knew he could trust it.

What the hell is wrong!? I've made a wrong decision somewhere. This isn't going to work. What have I done wrong?

It came to him in a rush of realization; like waking in the night with the answer to a problem that had been plaguing him for days.

Dwight looked up at Rich and said, "Rich, have you ever flown an airplane?"

"Bullshit, Dwight! I don't know nothin' 'bout no airplane! I ain't never even *sat* in the front of one! I can't fly no airplane, man!"

Dwight couldn't help but laugh out loud. Rich had turned as white as a black man could come to doing so.

"Don't sweat it, man; you're not going to be really *flying* it. All I need you to do is hold it steady for a minute while I fire the LAW."

"Bullshit, man! You think that because *you* can do anything, everyone else can! Well, you wrong, man! The rest of us ain't like you, man!"

"Hold it! Hold it, Rich. In the first place, I ain't no superman, man. I've got some kind of gift that allows me to feel people's anger toward me and know where they are, and I just happen to know how to fly an airplane too.

"Now listen to me. I have to be the one to fire the LAWs. I shoot by feel; if I'm not pulling the trigger, we ain't gonna hit nothing. All you gotta do is hold the stick steady when I tell you to. It won't be but for a couple of seconds, each time I shoot.

"I'm not going to order you to do it; if you're too scared, I'll find someone else."

Then turning to Pascone, he said, "How about it, Don; you ever flew an airplane?"

Before Pascone could answer, Rich did what Dwight knew he would; he said, "Hold on there, cowboy. Who you calling scared? If you think I can do it, I'll do it."

"You know I wouldn't ask you to do anything I didn't think you could do, pardner. Trust me; there's nothing to it."

Then he smiled, glanced conspiratorially at the others, and said, "Anyway, any idiot can fly an airplane; you just push all the levers forward and turn all the knobs to the right. Pull the stick back and the trees get smaller; push it forward and the trees get bigger."

They all laughed, including Sabinski, who, soaked and dripping with sweat, was just finishing cutting away the entire roof behind the front seat.

Martinez, who was standing behind Rich, slapped him hard on the back and said, "Pilot Richardson! Simone!"

Brad was slathering the neatly stitched wound with bacitracin ointment, and Dwight watched as he taped a bandage to it. *Good medic*, he thought.

Dwight took the four steps to the stack of LAWs, picked up two of them, and began placing them in the cargo area behind the backseat. When he turned around to go back to the stack, Rich, Bandy, and Pascone had formed a line and were passing them to him. Being only about a foot and a half long unextended, all fifteen fit easily in the small area.

When they finished loading the LAWs, Dwight took a knee and spread the map out on the grass, which had been sufficiently trampled around the right side of the airplane to make a reasonably flat surface. His four squad leaders settled around the map, holding it down in the gusty breeze with the butts of their weapons,

Dwight explained the situation and the plan of attack. The platoon was to move out toward the base of the hill when they heard the firing begin. If the battle went as planned, their job would be to cut off the enemy's retreat. If communication was lost, they were to hold a position in a tree line 400 yards north of the hill, as the enemy knew their general location and would expect them to be east of the hill, near the POW camp. Bandy would be in charge, and Dwight stressed that Bandy's word was law, meeting the other men's gazes as he said this, for emphasis.

He told Sabinski not to use his .50 until the action got hot and they needed its fear factor. The enemy had underestimated them before and probably would be overprepared if they had to meet them again. Also, they had attempted to make their platoon look more like a company or even a battalion, so they should try to make the enemy miscalculate their exact position, causing glancing blows to the platoon by the enemy units rather than direct encounters. Out of fear or anger or both, the enemy could be counted on to hit hard and in force, so they were to try to be elusive rather than directly confrontational.

Finally, Dwight told the RTO to put a fresh battery in the radio.

Dwight said, "Any questions?"

Rich raised his hand and said, "Yeah, how do you fly an airplane?"

There was slight laughter as Rich said, "No, I'm serious; do you think you could give me some basic instruction? Like how does it work? What are the concepts behind the actions of the thing? What's going to happen when I do stuff—that kind of thing."

Dwight said, "OK, valid question, Rich. Strap into the front seat, and I'll explain it to you."

Rich was now calm, and Dwight watched him closely as he talked, being fairly certain that Rich understood what he was saying. He explained how the stick worked—that it controlled both up and down pitch and turning side to side, called roll, and that if he ever had to make turns, the rudder pedals would kick the rear of the airplane out to coordinate the turn.

Rich was noticeably gaining confidence as he further understood how things worked in the world of aerodynamics. Dwight noted that the perspiration previously beading on Rich's forehead had dried in the breeze. Rich worked the stick around, noting the movement of the ailerons on the wings and the elevator on the back of the horizontal stabilizer, on the tail.

"There's only one gauge you need to be aware of." Pointing to a large, round gauge on the upper-left corner of the panel, he said, "This is the airspeed indicator. Airspeed is everything in an airplane. If there's not enough air blowing over the wings and control surfaces, we lose control of the airplane and fall out of the sky. She'll fly at fifty but just barely; we want to keep it above sixty-five. You can gain airspeed by giving it more gas or lowering the nose, or both. Lose airspeed by letting off the gas or climbing, or both. Just like a car going uphill or downhill, it's going to go faster downhill and slower uphill; you with me?"

Rich nodded assent.

"There's one more thing you'll notice about airspeed. When we put the airplane in any attitude besides straight ahead, like in a turn, the airplane is hitting the air differently, and that bleeds off airspeed too. You'll notice that when we turn, I'll add throttle and/or I'll dive to maintain airspeed. Where most people get into trouble with airplanes is not watching their airspeed in a turn and suddenly there's not enough air blowing over the wing and it stalls, and, because the guy is in a turn when he stalls, the inside wing stalls before the other one; the airplane spins, and he makes a lasting impression. You with me?"

Rich nodded again.

"As a general rule, for what we're going to be doing, nail the throttle in the turns and keep glancing at the airspeed. Again, like a car, if you're coasting along at forty and make a sharp turn, you're going to bleed off a lot of speed. A shallow turn won't have as much effect.

"One more thing ..." Pointing to the radios, he said, "This group of instruments is called the radio stack. We're going to be using just this top radio. It's called a flip-flop radio because of this button here. It allows us to flip-flop between two frequencies. One of the freqs is the brigade net, and the other is the general in the command plane 40,000 feet above us. During the battle, he'll be down around ten thousand. When I say, 'Flip,' I want you to hit that button, OK?"

"I got it, Dwight."

Dwight stepped from under the wing, straightened up, and stretched, arms above his head. Then he twisted from side to side, both to limber up and to display an everyday calmness that he didn't even come close to feeling. He knew that everyone was tense and fatigue was beginning to replace adrenalin. All eyes were on him.

He shouted, "All right; listen up!" and waited for the platoon to gather in a semicircle around the right side of the airplane, prisoners and their guards at the rear.

"First Battalion is on the ground. Second Battalion is on the way. A coordinated attack will commence in a few minutes. You will be in position to either attack a retreating enemy or press the attack, depending on how the initial phase of the battle goes.

"Sergeant Richardson and I are going to be killing armor and artillery with this here tank-buster airplane!" Nervous laughter ensued.

"Your squad leaders will brief you further. Save any questions for them."

Then, thrusting GG above his head, he screamed as loud as he could, "Airborne!" Dwight could feel his men surge with pride and adrenalin as they replied with shouts of, "All the way!" and "Airborne!"

Dwight handed Rich his headset and instructed him on the intercom use and then said, "All right, Cap'n; let's rock 'n' roll!"

Dwight leaned into the front of the airplane, pushed the mixture control to FULL RICH, flipped the red master switch to ON, turned the magneto switch to BOTH, and opened the throttle a quarter inch. He then had Rich apply the brakes by pressing on the tops of both rudder pedals and, from force of habit, shouted, "Clear!" and pressed the starter button. The prop turned twice, and the big motor roared to life as he adjusted the throttle to a thousand rotations per minute, turned on the radio and transponder, and strapped himself into the backseat.

He said over the intercom, "I've got it," moved the controls to be sure Rich was off of them and they were free and clear, and pushed the throttle all the way forward. As they began to roll, he pushed the stick full forward to lighten the tail, minimizing the grass resistance on the tail wheel and, at about thirty, lifting the tail off the ground; he held full left stick and right rudder to again counter the crosswind. He trimmed for level flight, and in another fifty feet the airspeed gauge read fifty-five; he pulled the stick back, and the little bird dog freed itself from the earth and quickly gained speed, pointing itself into the crosswind but climbing straight out. Dwight hoped that Rich was taking note of the airplane's flying in the air rather than the air's relationship to the ground.

The first lines of the famous airman's poem that had been written by a British Spitfire pilot during the early days of World War II in England ran through his head: *Oh, I have slipped the surly bonds of earth and danced the sky on laughter silvered wings.* The man had been shot down and killed on his next flight. Dwight considered that he wished he hadn't thought about that part of it.

"Rich, we believe that the enemy is at the base of that hill at four o'clock. We're going to fly away from it and stay on the treetops for about five miles; I don't want 'em to know I'm here yet. I'm going to give you the controls in a minute, but in the meantime, I want you to put your hands and feet on the controls and just follow what I do. Believe me, I'm not going to tell you to do anything that may cause my imminent demise, OK?"

"Roger, Dwight."

Dwight made some gentle climbing and diving S-turns to the left and right, maintaining their general heading away from the hill.

"OK, when I give you the airplane, I'll say, 'You've got it,' and when I'm taking it away from you, you'll feel me move the stick against your hand and I'll say, 'I've got it.' OK?"

"OK."

Dwight said, "OK, you've got it." and he released the controls. The nose lifted a little, but Dwight decided to let Rich figure it out for himself as they climbed a good fifty feet off the tree-tops.

"Don't take us too high, Rich. I don't want 'em to see us."

Rich didn't say anything but lowered the nose, a bit too sharply. Dwight, hand poised to grab the stick, again decided to try to let Rich figure it out for himself. Sure enough, he leveled off twenty feet above the trees.

"Good man, Rich; you're a natural. Now I want you to hold the stick with the pads of your fingers and thumb. I can tell you've got a death grip on it. Good; that's it. Now do some of those gentle S-turns like I showed you. You're not going to need hardly any rudder. The sharper the turn, the more rudder you'll need."

Rich performed the turns beautifully. No sweat.

"You know something, pal? I said you were a natural back there mainly to give you confidence, but, I swear to God, I think you've got the gift; no shit!"

"Go to hell, man!"

"You know something, Rich? I would normally say something in retort, but I know you pretty well. You know you've got it too, don't you?"

"You know? I'll have to admit, I feels good!"

They both laughed out loud.

Dwight said, "Do a three-sixty."

"Do what?"

"Start a gentle left turn and take it all the way around until we're going in this direction again and then straighten her out."

"Aren't we kinda low for that kind of crap?"

"Yes, but you need a little humility after that little display of natural flying skills. I'll probably have to take it away from you, but go ahead and give it a try."

Rich gave it some left stick and instinctively fed in some rudder when he felt the slip, maintaining his altitude with just a smidgen of back stick.

Damn! He does have the gift!

Rich brought it all the way around to their original heading and straightened out perfectly. He had gained about fifty feet, but it had been a damn good turn.

"Do you have any idea what you just did, pardner?"

"Yeah, I turned the airplane around. No big deal."

"You are what we call an instinctive pilot. You did it by feel! You initiated the turn, and that's where I would have had to take the airplane away from a normal person. You pulled back on the stick to keep from losing altitude and fed in rudder to stop the airplane from skidding. Then you neutralized the controls so that the airplane maintained its attitude and then rolled the airplane out of the turn using right rudder and a little up stick!

"You've got it, my man! You've got the *gift!*"

Rich said, "Bullshit, man," but Dwight could see the smile from the back of Rich's head.

"All right, hotshot; you see that big, round white gauge in the top center of the panel?"

"Yep."

"That's a directional gyro, a compass. I want you to turn right and roll out on a heading of two-four-zero. That's almost west but not quite."

"I know how to use a compass, man!"

"Oh, excuse me, Mister Chuck Yeager! I forgot."

Rich executed a quick, sharp, coordinated turn and rolled out a little too late, but that was expected; experienced pilots did that all the time when checking out in an unfamiliar airplane. Dwight gave him a new heading, and he rolled out perfectly, this time coordinating his rollout to end up on heading.

"Show-off!"

Almost under his breath, Rich chortled, "Heh, heh, heh."

"All right, one last exercise to get you really grooved in. See that tree sticking up fifty feet higher than the others a half mile ahead?"

"Yeah, I see it."

"OK. Off to the left of it about two hundred yards is another one sticking up but not as high; see it?"

"I see it."

"OK, I want you to fly to the right of the big tree about fifty yards, then turn left and go halfway around it, and then head for the other tree. You're going to try to do figure eights around those two trees. There's a lot of wind, so you'll screw it up the first time, but you'll see what it takes to maintain your distances as you have to make corrections for the wind. You'll be banking hard when the wind's trying to blow you away from the tree and shallowly as it's trying to blow you toward it; you with me?"

"Yeah, I understand, but I don't remember which way the wind's blowing."

"Tough shit, hotshot. That's one of the things all this natural flyboy ability you so obviously have is going to help you with."

Rich had correctly lined up to the right of the tallest tree and was now passing it on his left. Dwight pushed the prop control lever to fine pitch and poised his left hand over the throttle and his right by the stick.

Rich entered the turn sharply and with confidence. The airplane turned into the wind with the wings at a forty-five-degree angle; so far, so good. Then, as he came around, the wind began blowing him toward the tree, and he correctly compensated by decreasing the angle of his turn.

The airspeed quickly dropped from 120 to 65, and the big tree was rapidly approaching the left side of the airplane!

"I've got it!" Dwight said as he grabbed the stick, threw it hard right, and nailed the throttle. The airplane responded immediately, and they were heading back in the direction from which they'd entered the maneuver.

Rich said, "Holy shit! Man, did I screw *that* up!"

"You were getting too cocky, man; you just got your head handed to you. Do you know what you did wrong?"

"I think so. I didn't add power in the turn, and I didn't feel for the wind and correct the angle of the turn. I can do it now. Let me try it again."

"OK, you've got the airplane."

Rich immediately banked hard left, kicking left rudder and fire-walling the throttle, as if he were in a barroom brawl and had pushed an adversary up against the wall, his throat in one hand and his testicles in the other.

That's it, my friend. Kick its ass!

Rich eased back on the throttle as he came out of the turn and reentered the arena, the big tree coming up on his left, a hundred yards away.

As the tree began reaching eight o'clock, he began the turn with a bit less angle this time, like a boxer in the first round, sizing up his opponent as he opened the throttle more, feeling his way into it. *Easy now*, he thought. He flattened the turn out and started right stick as the wind tried to blow him toward the tree. He made a sharper right turn now as the wind tried to blow him away from the other tree; it was beginning to approach at two o'clock. *More throttle, less angle*—he applied less throttle as the tree started to pass at four o'clock.

He applied shallow right stick now as the wind tried to blow him into this tree. More throttle, stick, and rudder now, keeping the tree at three o'clock. More stick and rudder as he came around it, into the middle of the "eight"—*more!* He knew that the big tree was now directly to his left, but he couldn't see it because the bottom of the airplane was in the way as he was at a forty-five-degree angle to the ground, throttle nailed, pulling three *g*'s. Now, stick back left, hard left rudder as the rear kicked out; he pulled the throttle back, entering downwind. The big tree appeared at nine o'clock—*perfect!*

"Do it again!"

"Roger!"

Rich entered the first turn with the throttle already wide open, daring the wind to challenge him. He had become one with the airplane—the brains of the bird. A tear ran down Dwight's face, and he had to blink hard to clear his vision. He had never been more proud in his life as the two men shared something few men have: the delight of flight.

The poem entered Dwight's head again: *Hovering there, I've chased the shouting wind along and flung my eager craft through foot-less hauls of air. Up, up the long, delirious, burning blue I've topped the windswept heights with easy grace where never lark or even eagle flew.*

And while with silent, lifting mind, I've trod the high, untrespassed
sanctity of space, put out my hand and touched the face of God.

"Amazing, Rich—seriously, absolutely, amazing."

"I can fly an airplane, man!"

"You damn sure can, my friend—not much doubt about it.
Like I said before, you got the gift. Give me a heading of two-
seven-zero."

"Roger."

Rich nailed the throttle, threw the stick hard right, and
kicked hard right rudder, whipping the little airplane around
to the heading in two to three seconds.

"You like manhandling her, don't you, buddy?"

"She's a part of me, man."

"I know it. What you're doing is the second biggest thrill
known to man."

"Right now, I think it's the *biggest*!"

"You don't know what the biggest is yet, my man."

"Weren't you talking about getting laid?"

"Nope."

"What is it, then?"

"Landing."

"I can't wait!"

"I'm sure you can't, but eights around pylons is a walk in the
park compared to landing, especially a tail-wheel airplane. You'll
be humbled, believe me."

"I still can't wait."

"I know. Do you see the hill up there, about ten miles?"

"I've got it."

"OK, head for it. You'll note that the wind is going to be
blowing you to the left, so you'll have to set a heading of three-
zero-zero or more. Underneath the throttle are two other levers.
The middle one controls the prop. Do you see the gauge on the
bottom left that says MANIFOLD PRESSURE?

"Yep."

"See the one on the left for rpm?"

"Yep."

"OK, the prop and the throttle work together like an automatic transmission on a car. The prop seeks a certain rpm that you tell it to establish. The best settings for this airplane to go at a fast cruise are 2,200 rpm and twenty-four inches of manifold pressure. So, set the prop to 2,200 rpm, and then bring up the power till you have twenty-four inches of manifold pressure."

"Roger," Rich said as he performed the task perfectly.

"The settings for different conditions are on the back of your sun visor. Just remember, in case I forget to tell you: when we're maneuvering, always have the prop on fine pitch, full forward. The same goes for the mixture control—full forward at low altitudes."

Then, to see how grooved in Rich really was, he said, "Flip." In a millisecond, Rich reached up and hit the FLIP-FLOP button on the top radio.

Dwight couldn't help but smile as he said, "Blue Leader, this is Crucifix. Do you read?"

"Roger, Crucifix; go ahead."

"I'm ready to go. When can you start firing?"

"We're good to go."

"OK, I'm ten miles out. I'll be coming from the southeast at 150 miles an hour. The more riled up you can get them, the better. I'll need to see muzzle flashes and smoke from the tank cannons so I can see their general locations and pattern of deployment. When I say, 'Cease-fire,' please be sure they stop firing. I don't want my own incoming blowing me out of the air. OK, General, let's get it on."

"Roger, Crucifix. We're going to commence firing right now."

Five seconds later, Dwight and Rich saw the flashes from the battalion's 106 mm recoilless rifles and the resultant explosions. They were firing as quickly as they could reload, and there looked to be at least twenty-five guns, firing along a quarter-mile front to the left of the hill, into the woods to the left of the hill in a pattern stretching from the southern base of the hill to a quarter mile from the base of the hill toward the battalion's gun positions.

Just as they'd hoped, the woods were full of tanks and artillery, and they started returning fire immediately. The North Vietnamese had started their attack.

At this distance, about five miles now, the flashes from the guns were yellow with red edges and gray smoke. The explosions of the shells were mostly deep red with black and gray smoke.

Dwight reached back and grabbed a LAW, extended the telescoping barrel, and pointed it down through the hole in the floor.

He took the stick in his right hand, holding the LAW by its handle in his left and said, "OK, Rich. Here we go! I've got the airplane. I'm going to pass over a tank and shoot straight down at it. I'll just say 'Now' when I want you to take the controls and 'I've got it' when I'm taking them back. I'm going to keep going straight after I fire and get above the side of the hill before we turn around to make another run. I think they vacated the hill when they thought the fast-movers were coming, after I saw the tanks. We're going to be most vulnerable when we turn. Remember that when the shit gets hot and you're flying. Try to get over friendly territory before you make any turns.

"I'll be making exaggerated, crop duster turns, so pay attention so you can see how it's done. The object is to stay down on the treetops so they don't see us 'til it's too late."

"Roger, LT."

"Cease-fire!" Within five seconds, the battalion's firing stopped, just as Dwight flew over them. Ten feet below, Dwight saw the gun crewmen scampering into foxholes, joining the infantry troops, who were waiting to move out.

Dwight jinked the airplane to the left as an artillery round passed under the right wing. He had the tank zeroed in five hundred yards ahead. Good! He felt the tank crew!

"Now!"

He held the LAW with both hands, tilted it a little to the left, and pulled the trigger, being sure his head was below and to the side of the rear of the tube opening. He had fired LAWS many times during the month of training at MACV but was unprepared for the noise generated inside the little airplane, especially since his ear was so close to the rear of the tube. The rocket motor burned out before the round left the barrel, so, even though the noise was technically a whoosh, it was really more of a boom. Call it a deafening *boosh*. The inside of the airplane lit up a bright orange, and Dwight could tell that Rich wasn't ready for it either, by the way the airplane jerked upward for an instant.

Dwight looked out the back window just as the round hit the front deck of the tank, penetrated the armor, and exploded in a little white flash that Dwight thought may have been a dud, until he realized that it had gone off inside the tank. Then the tank's ammo exploded, sending the turret and gun twenty feet into the air.

He threw the tube out the window, grabbed another LAW from the stack behind him, and extended the barrel as he turned back forward. Rich was on the treetops, heading for the hill.

Dwight pointed the LAW through the floor and, thankful that he'd had Sabinski cut out most of the roof, tilted the weapon to the right and pulled the trigger. They were both ready for the noise and flash this time as Dwight saw another tiny white explosion in the open turret of the tank passing ten feet to his left and below him. He saw smoke and flame come out of the hatch and the barrel of the cannon and knew it was finished.

Dwight said, "I've got it!" and grabbed the stick. They were climbing up the side of the hill at 170 miles an hour as Dwight hauled back on the stick as he looked under the trees to be sure he was right about the enemy having vacated the area. Apparently, he was. He saw nothing but forest floor.

The airspeed dropped radically as they headed straight up. He kicked hard left rudder, holding the stick in a neutral position. The airspeed was around seventy as the airplane pivoted around from straight up to straight down, as he pulled the power off. He again applied full power and hauled back on the stick as they neared the treetops, again approaching 170 miles an hour, heading back down the hillside.

"Hot shit!" Rich shouted into the intercom. Both tanks were now burning dead ahead and a quarter mile. Dwight saw the muzzle flash of another one off to his right, fifty yards from his nearest victim.

"See it, Rich?!"

"Tallyho!"

Where'd he get that crap? War movies, I'll bet.

Dwight shouted, "Now!" and felt Rich take the stick.

Dwight extended the barrel of another LAW, pointed it down through the hole, and concentrated. "Got 'em," he said as he pulled the trigger and saw the round hit the rear deck of the tank. This time there was an immediate explosion of red flame and black smoke as the tank's fuel tank exploded. The little airplane was buffeted but not wildly. *Thank God that diesel fuel doesn't explode violently,* Dwight considered.

They were over a clearing now, headed for the battalion. Rich was five feet off the deck at 170 miles an hour. Dwight first saw the recoilless rifles, mounted on their tripods. Then he saw the paratroopers scrambling out of the foxholes, jumping up and down, pumping their fists, and, although he couldn't hear them, shouting, "Airborne!" A few men in their direct path dived for the ground as Rich screamed right through them.

Dwight could hear him laughing over the intercom and he said, "I've got it!" as he took the stick and pointed her straight up again, leaving the power on this time, for theatrical effect.

Might as well give 'em a show.

The big motor clawed at the air as Dwight let the airspeed bleed off, climbing to over 500 feet. But this time, he let it go to almost zero airspeed before he kicked left rudder, the straining propeller blowing enough air over the control surfaces to cause the airplane to pivot around to a nose-down attitude, a classic hammerhead stall. He pulled the power off on the way down.

Now the airspeed went from zero to over a hundred as he pulled out of the dive, pulling around four g's, power back on.

"Hot shit!" he heard Rich say again as he leveled off just above the ground, heading back over the cheering troops at ten feet and through the no-man's-land between the opposing forces. He knew that he didn't have much more time before the enemy brass figured out that he was homing in on muzzle flashes and call a cease-fire so he wouldn't find the tanks so easily.

"Rich, do you see those two tanks on a line from left to right?"

"I see 'em!"

"OK, here we go!"

He turned sharp left for five seconds and then back sharp right to a heading that he figured would take him over both of them.

"Now!"

As Rich took the airplane, Dwight knew he'd have to work fast as the two tanks were only about a hundred yards apart. He pulled two LAWS out of the back, extended both barrels, and, holding one in each hand, put one through the hole and held the other beside it.

Perfect! He pulled the trigger on the first LAW, pulled it out, pushed the other one in, and almost immediately pulled the trigger on it. The two tanks exploded, one just after the other, both burning fiercely.

Rich turned sharply toward the hill, a quarter mile away.

Shit! I told him not to make any turns over the enemy!

Sure enough, at least five lines of green tracers arced up at them. Luckily, the enemy hadn't lead them enough and the arcs, an optical illusion caused by their relative motion, fell away behind them.

"I *told* you not to make any turns over the enemy, Rich!"

"Sorry; I forgot."

Dwight grabbed another LAW, extended it, and barely got it in the hole when he pulled the trigger and looked out the back as there was a large explosion, this time because the round hadn't penetrated into an enclosure but went off in the open. Dwight knew he had hit the enemy's command center. Bodies flew in all directions as the LAW exploded as it hit the ground in the center of a fifteen-foot square of sandbags, with about ten uniformed men inside. Dwight had seen several men holding binoculars, just before the explosion.

"Rich! I take it back! You just took us directly over their command post. We just killed their brass! I've got the airplane."

Dwight continued up and over the hill and turned left in order to come up behind what he was sure would soon be a retreating enemy. After he was sure he couldn't be seen, he keyed the mike.

"Blue leader, this is Crucifix, do you read?"

"Roger, Crucifix, You're doing a great job! You've hit a tank every time you've fired, except for that last one!"

"That last one was their command post, sir. You can attack now; they're going to be heading the other way."

"How do you know that, Dwight?"

"I don't know, sir! You know how it works as well as I do! I could *feel* them. I *know* that's what it was. We center-punched their command post, General! You can take that to the bank, sir!"

"OK, Lieutenant; I hope you're right!"

"I'm right, General. I've flown over the hill, and I'm going to head south for about five miles while I climb to a few thousand feet, so I can take a good look before I attack again. I think I'd be pressing my luck if I were to come back down the hill at them again; they'll be laying for me. I'll attack from the south, next run. Roger?"

"Roger, Crucifix. You appear to be right; it looks like the enemy is in retreat. There are a minimum of eighteen more tanks—at least we have picked up eighteen more—all headed north. It appears that their artillery pieces are being abandoned."

Damn! My platoon's right in their path!

"Has my platoon been alerted?"

"Roger; they are positioning now. Who did you leave in charge?"

"Sergeant Bandy, sir. I'm leaving the frequency, sir!"

"Not yet! Dwight! Are you there?"

"Yes, sir."

"Stay low over the target. Second Battalion's on the way into the DZ, and the air's going to be full of C-130s heading east to west."

Dwight looked to the east and saw twenty or more black dots, low on the horizon.

"Tallyho; I've got 'em. Crucifix is out."

Damn, Rich has me saying it!

"Flip!"

Rich hit the button, and Dwight waited for a break in the radio traffic, which was difficult, as the battalion was beginning their attack. Finally, he keyed the mike: "Special Platoon, this is Crucifix. Do you read?"

"Roger, Crucifix; go ahead."

"Bandy?"

"Roger."

"They're heading straight for you, Glen; they're retreating! Get in that tree line to the east of the hill, where we changed the plan in the dark this morning! Do you get my meaning?"

"Roger, LT, but I have orders from battalion to stand in their path!"

"Negative, Glen. Battalion don't know that you don't have any LAWs. There's a bunch of tanks coming your way. You're going to have to let them go by and hit the infantry that'll be behind 'em!"

"Roger!"

Another voice came up on the net. "Crucifix, this is Colonel McMullen. Are you countermanding my order?"

"Sir, an armor-fortified NVA battalion is going full speed through there! My platoon'll be overrun and wiped out!"

"Your platoon's job is to slow them down so we can catch them, Lieutenant. This thing's a lot bigger than you and a few of your friends. Now get off the net!"

Over the intercom, he said, "Rich, it's up to us to save 'em. We've got to stop those tanks and demoralize the infantry enough so they'll surrender when the platoon opens up on 'em. I hope the enemy's as scared of us as I think they are."

Dwight kicked hard right rudder and laid the stick all the way right, doing a hairpin turn back to the north. They were at 1,500 feet, the hill just off the nose and to the right, the battlefield at one and two o'clock.

The enemy tanks were clearly visible now, raising dust and vegetation in their wakes in their haste to get away. Tree limbs that had been used for camouflage were bouncing and blowing off their decks and turrets.

"Rich, we're going to have to sneak behind the hill and hit the lead tanks as we blow across from left to right. Each of those tank commanders has a .50 on the turret, and they'd kill us if we went by from south to north. If we're going fast from across in front of them, they'll have to lead us exactly right, and that's going to be hard to do in a bouncing tank. Do you understand what I'm saying?"

"Roger; I understand, Dwight."

"You're going to have to do most of the flying, and we're going to have to put on one hell of a show if we're going to stop 'em. I'm talking blasting three tanks on each pass, and you're going to have to do the crop duster turns while I'm getting out three more LAWs and getting 'em ready."

"I can do it; I've got it covered."

"OK, let's go over it. I'll set up the first pass. We don't necessarily have to go after the first three tanks, just the first three that we can hit in a line. Everyone with a gun is going to be shooting at us, so stay on the deck and get outta Dodge. You'll be able to tell when you're out of range when you don't see no more green tracers going by us from behind. If you're low enough, it'll only be a few seconds; you with me?"

"Roger, I've got it."

"OK, when you're going to do the crop duster turn, pull the throttle off and point the nose up at about forty-five degrees. Don't try any fancy straight-up shit. I'm serious, man; don't do it! I don't care how good you think you are; you'll kill us if you try it. Don't even *think* about it, OK?"

"OK, Dwight."

"Forty-five degrees is halfway to straight up, and that's plenty. Watch your airspeed; as soon as it gets below a hundred, kick it around, open the throttle, dive at a forty-five-degree angle, and pull out as you see the ground come up. You're gonna have to get a feel for it because you don't come out of a steep dive all at once, so be careful. OK?"

"I understand."

"OK, here's the tricky part. While you're doing all this, you're going to have to be picking out the next three targets and lining up on 'em."

"I can do it."

"You be cool?"

"I be cool!"

They were at five hundred feet, the hill passing on their right, fifty feet beside and below the wing; Dwight and Rich were both looking intently out of the right side of the airplane.

They saw the tanks at the same time as the hill passed to the right. Dwight said, "There ... at four o'clock. See 'em?"

"Roger, I see 'em."

There were ten tanks heading north in no particular formation. The first two were only about twenty yards apart, one behind the other. The next one was to the second one's right about two hundred yards and behind him a hundred yards, and then a third tank was a hundred yards behind him and to his right three hundred yards.

Dwight started his dive to treetop level before he turned to make his run. He said, "Rich, I'm going to line up on three of them. You'll see which three when I do it. It'll make since to you when you see it, OK?" I'm going to let the first tank go for now.

"Roger."

Coming out of the dive, he banked around to his four o'clock, lined up on his three targets, and said, "Do you see my plan?"

"Roger, I see the three you're after."

"Now!"

Rich took the controls as Dwight pulled out three LAWs and extended their barrels, saying, "After you go over the first one, jog right to the next and then back left to the third. Got it?"

"Roger, I've got it."

"OK, Chuck Yeager. Lock and load."

"Lock and load."

Suddenly they were over an open clearing about a half mile long. Beyond that was a tree line that went for about three hundred yards and then the big grassy plain that the tanks were in.

Rich jinked down to five feet off the grass, airspeed at 180 but beginning to bleed off some as the momentum of the dive dissipated. Dwight felt a tingle in the hair on the back of his neck as Rich waited until the last second to come back up to treetop level, as they got to the tree line.

Jesus! I hope he's as good as he thinks he is!

Rich adjusted his approach a bit to the left as the tanks' forward speeds had brought them further left, while Rich couldn't see them because of the trees that he'd just jinked over.

Concentrating, Dwight held the LAW in the hole with his left hand by its pistol grip, another one by its grip in his left hand, and the third between his knees.

There. Got him! He pulled the trigger, threw the tube out the window, and shifted the second LAW. *There!* He pulled the trigger, threw it out the window, and pushed the third one in position. *Wait …wait … now!* He pulled the trigger and looked out the back.

The first tank was burning furiously; the second exploded as he looked, tossing the turret in the air as its ammunition ignited, but the third kept purposefully moving at its maximum speed of about thirty miles an hour.

Damn! I finally missed one! I wonder what I did wrong.

Then, almost imperceptibly, the big tank began a slight turn to the right, plowed into a stand of trees, and came to a halt twenty yards into the stand and began smoking. Dwight realized that the LAW had killed the crew but hadn't ignited the ammo inside.

Dwight was abruptly aware of a line of green tracers in front of the airplane as Rich jinked downward to dodge them, the tires actually hitting the ground as Rich bounced the airplane back to twenty feet off the ground and then back to the wheels, which hissed against the grass like an angry tomcat, as the enemy gunner overcompensated and the tracers arced over the top of the almost out-of-range airplane.

It was Dwight's turn to say, "Hot shit!"

They were over trees again as the machine gun fire abated. They went down into another clearing, and the two warrior's hearts leaped into their throats as they saw troops running toward them. Then, just as suddenly, they realized that the soldiers were American paratroopers, on the attack; they shook their weapons in the air at the screaming at the little airplane, "Airborne!" on lips, which were drawn back in both anger and joy.

Dwight twisted in his seat to pick up three more LAWs as he felt the *g* force of Rich entering his climb, and he could hear the airspeed rapidly decrease as the wind noise through the holes in the floor roof and windows diminished. He couldn't help but look up as he began extending the barrel of the first weapon, to see Rich make a well-executed left turn using little aileron and almost all rudder and begin his power dive back to ground level, building airspeed.

Dwight glanced ahead as he put the first LAW between his knees and began readying the second. There were three tanks at just about the same angle back the way they had come, but the last one was way behind the first two. They were going to have to shoot the first two and then make a hard left turn to get the third one. He knew that every enemy gun that could would be frantically firing at them. He watched as a rivulet of sweat run down Rich's neck.

"Be cool, Rich; they almost got us last time because we were going away from them. Not much deflection in their aim. This'll be different; we'll be perpendicular to their guns and going like hell. They won't lead us enough, and you can dive down behind those trees as soon as we shoot the third tank."

"Roger, LT; I'm cool."

They were almost on the first tank when they realized they had a problem. The tank commander had had the presence of mind to rotate the turret around to be able to shoot at them on they're way back. He opened up with his .50 as Rich jinked left and down and then back right, both the wheel and wingtip hissing in the grass; he then shot up ten feet and left, in a sharp turn over the tank, as Dwight pulled the trigger. The tank exploded violently, knocking the bird dog sideways and up. Rich instinctively stabbed right rudder and aileron, bringing the airplane back on track.

Thankfully, the next two tank commanders hadn't turned their turrets toward them as Dwight threw the first tube out the window, positioned the second one, and pulled the trigger, again only ten feet above the target. He threw that tube out and took the third one from between his legs, almost dropping it as Rich pulled three *g*'s in the quick left turn to the third tank. Just as Rich leveled the airplane, Dwight pulled the trigger and felt the tank's fuel explode beneath and behind them.

Green tracers were arcing behind them as Rich shoved the stick forward to enter the safety of the tree line, again skimming the grass.

Dwight said, "Hey, pardner, you know you almost stuck a wingtip in the ground back there dodging that machine gun on the first tank?"

"I know what I'm doin', cowboy!"

"Let's go on around the hill and get a little altitude and take a look at the situation. We'll be pushing our luck to make another pass right now.

"Gladly, LT; those gunners are starting to catch on!"

Dwight let Rich continue to fly the airplane; his learning curve was flattening out, and he was doing fine. Rich was climbing and making the turn behind the hill, and they were soon safely out of range of the enemy guns, for now.

Dwight said, "The best rate of climb is seventy, Rich. Hold the nose up at whatever angle holds the airspeed on seventy." Rich immediately found the correct angle, the airspeed nailed on seventy. *Good man,* he thought.

Then Dwight said, "Flip," and Rich hit the switch, practically before the word was out of Dwight's mouth.

"Special platoon, this is Crucifix, do you read?"

Bandy answered, "Roger Crucifix; go ahead."

"What's your status, Glen?"

"It looks like the tanks are no longer a factor, but we've got hundreds of ground troops headed our way on a dead run!"

"The tanks are no longer a factor? What do you mean, the tanks are no longer a factor?"

"Didn't you see what happened after your last pass?"

"No, the gunners were starting to zero in on us; we got outta Dodge. There're at least ten tanks left; what's going on?"

"Roger; the remaining tanks have stopped and are being abandoned! You guys put on quite a show! We got a *big* problem with the retreat, though. They're going to be on us in five minutes, and they'll run right through us; there's too many of 'em!"

"How many does there appear to be?"

"Five hundred, at least—maybe more!"

"You've got to get out of the way, Glen!"

"Negative, Crucifix! Special Platoon, you hold your position!" It was Colonel McMullen again. Lieutenant Johnson, do I have to remind you again who's in charge here? Now get off the net! Special Platoon, you hold your position at all costs; reinforcements are on the way. Second Battalion is moving out from the DZ for your position as we speak."

Dwight keyed his mike and said, "Colonel, they're twenty minutes away! This thing'll be over in seven minutes!"

"I told you to get off the net, Lieutenant!"

Dwight spoke into the intercom: "I've got the airplane!" As he took the stick and shook it to free it from Rich's hand, he threw the stick hard left and kicked hard left rudder, reversing course. They were headed for the hill and already had enough altitude, about a thousand feet, to easily clear it. He set the prop for 2,200 rpm and fire-walled the throttle for maximum speed and began a shallow descent to barely clear the hilltop; he knew he didn't have a second to spare.

He said into the intercom, "You ever drive a tank, Rich?"

"Oh, shit, you crazy bastard! You're *not* going to do what I think you're going to do, are you?"

"No choice, bad-ass-tank-buster-pilot! But first, we're going to see if we can slow 'em down a little bit. We've got eleven white phosphorous marker rockets and five more LAWs. We're going to make a run on the front of their column and throw as much shit as we can at 'em. I'll fly the airplane and fire the first LAW from a half mile out. Then you fire the other LAWs just as fast as you can shoot 'em, and I'll fire the rockets. This little Birddog's going to be lit up like a Christmas tree! Then we're going to land and get a tank and see if we can help the platoon."

"Whatever you say, you crazy fuck; you're the boss!"

"Flip." Rich hit the button and Dwight said, "Blue Leader, this is Crucifix. Do you read?"

"Roger, Crucifix; go ahead."

"Do you know what Colonel McMullen is doing, sir?"

"I'm aware of what's going on, Lieutenant, and I don't have time to justify things to you. You're doing a great job, but you're not a field commander."

"Roger, General; OK, I'm going to make a pass at the front of the enemy column and use the twelve Willy Pete rockets and five remaining LAWs to try to slow 'em down.

"They've abandoned about ten tanks. I'm going to try to commandeer one of 'em and see if we can use it against them. May I suggest that you order the lead elements of the First Battalion to do the same? Those tanks should be fully operable and may even still be running."

"Good idea, Dwight; I'll call them right now."

"Also, General, please make sure no one shoots at enemy tanks from here on."

"No guarantees there, Dwight, but we'll do the best we can."

"Roger; out."

"Flip." Rich hit the button.

Dwight keyed the mike and said, "Special Platoon, do you read Crucifix?"

"Roger, Crucifix; go ahead."

"How close are they, Glen?"

"A quarter mile, at the most!"

"Tell Cargo to open up with his .50, *now!* Try to slow 'em down until I can get there. We're going to hit 'em with the LAWs we have left and the Willy Pete marker rockets we have left in the airplane and then land and try to use at least one of their tanks on them from their rear! *Do not*, repeat, *do not* fire on any enemy tanks. Americans are going to be driving them; do you read?"

"Roger, I've got it; out!"

Dwight and Rich were five miles from the front of the enemy column now, which was at the airplane's four o'clock, and they went back down on the deck to try to remain unseen as they approached.

Dwight began a right turn toward the front of the enemy column and said into the intercom, "You've got the airplane, Rich. I'm going to extend four LAWs and put them in your lap."

"Why don't you just put them between my seat and the door, on my right?"

"Because the dough ain't gonna be there no mo."

"Oh."

Dwight unlatched the door and pushed it open against the slipstream with his right foot and then put GG's muzzle as close to the bottom hinge as he could get it and blew it away with three rounds, being careful not to hit the propeller or wing strut. Then he did the same with the top hinge, and the door flew away. He then began preparing the remaining LAWs, putting four in Rich's lap and leaving one for himself.

He then threw the red rocket-arming switch on the console between the two seats, on the left side, between the front and rear throttle quadrants. The firing switches were in two rows of four.

"We're going to do this all at once, Rich. The rockets have the most range, so I'm going to fire them first; then I'm going to fire my LAW. Then I'll take the airplane, and you lean out the door and fire those LAWs as fast as you can. Remember, the blast out the back of these suckers is as bad as out the front. Make sure to fire clear of the airplane, in both directions, and be sure to lean hard forward; that wind out there is 150 miles an hour!"

"Roger, I've got it."

"OK, here we go, pardner."

The front of the enemy column was seven hundred yards from his platoon's tree line and coming to a stop as Sabinski's .50-caliber tracers sprayed their two-hundred-yard-wide front. Luckily, the ground was rocky, so the tracers were ricocheting in all directions, making the volume of fire seem more than it was.

The enemy's return fire toward the tree line was seen as green tracers and was beginning to build in intensity. They hadn't seen the little airplane approaching from their left, just above the grass, yet.

Dwight pulled the first two switches toward him, and a rocket ignited from each wing in a straight trajectory of red exhaust and white smoke.

Perfect—the first two rockets landed on the front edge of the enemy's left flank. Dwight pulled the remaining toggles two at a time in close succession and then leaned out the door and fired his LAW, just missing the propeller and the tail.

The marker rocket's white phosphorous explosions were spectacular, especially since they had been fired so close together. The entire front of the enemy column was obscured in thousands of white smoke–producing pieces of phosphorous, some still traveling up and out while others were raining back down. The airplane would be in the smoke in three more seconds!

"Hold your fire, Rich!"

Too late—Rich was already leaning out into the slipstream and didn't hear him. The exhaust flash of the LAW temporarily blinded Dwight as it barely cleared the fuselage beside him. Coupled with the phosphorous smoke they had now entered, it totally disoriented him and he hauled back on the stick, causing Rich to drop the next LAW on the deck, where it clattered around and then jammed the rudder pedals!

"Rich; be careful! That thing goes off in here, it'll kill us both!" Dwight said as Rich grappled with the armed tube on the deck.

They had broken out of the smoke on the other side and were climbing at a forty-degree angle. The airspeed had bled off to 110. Green tracers were all around them, and the airplane was making pinging noises as little pieces of it flew away, framed by the streaming green tracers.

Dwight dived for the treetops and in five more seconds was finally out of range of the enemy machine guns. He kicked hard right rudder and threw the stick to the right stop as the little airplane wheeled around, its prop clawing the air as he pushed its lever to fine-pitch.

No good! Dwight threw the stick and rudder back hard left as the enemy troops, now fully aware of their presence, threw everything they had at the little airplane. They had fired early and didn't quite have the range, so nothing hit the airplane, this time.

"We're done, Rich. We can't get close enough anymore. You got any ideas?"

"I just work here, man. You're the brilliant tactician and shit; that's why you're making all that money and got gold bars on your collar, *sir*."

"Come on, man. I'm out of ideas; the platoon's going to be overrun if we can't stop those assholes awhile longer!"

"Well, this might be a really stupid idea, but we still go three LAWs; why don't we climb up above them? You be such a dead-eye and shit; you should be able to shoot 'em from up there."

"Brilliant! Why didn't I think of that!"

"Cause you ain't black enough, cowboy."

Dwight pointed the nose up and began a climbing turn, back toward the action.

Once again, they were over the oncoming charge of the lead units of the First Battalion, who were waving and shouting. They should be overtaking the enemy in another five minutes or so. With just a little luck, Dwight and Rich could hold the enemy down for that long.

Dwight knew that the airplane's best rate of climb was seventy miles per hour, but he could see by the rate-of-climb indicator that it was struggling for just over a thousand feet per minute and they had just started their climb. The absence of a door and the holes in the roof and deck were causing too much drag. It would be a full two minutes before they were high enough to be out of range of the enemy's heavy machine guns.

"Flip," Dwight said into the intercom, and he saw Rich hit the button to change the frequency.

"Special Platoon, do you read Crucifix?"

"Roger, Crucifix; go ahead."

"Get Sabinski back on that .50. You gotta hold 'em down until I can get back in the fight."

"Negative, Crucifix; he's out of ammo."

Dwight could see the enemy column beginning to move again as green tracers arced up toward him but fell away below because the range was too great. He saw that he couldn't get the angle necessary to lob a LAW round without hitting some part of the airplane—wing, propeller, strut, or landing gear. *What now?*

"Rich, in just a few more seconds, those assholes are going to figure out that Cargo's .50 ain't no mo'. It'll be another two minutes before we have enough altitude. You got any more ideas?"

"Yeah, cowboy; as a matter of fact, I been pondering that exact sitch-e-ation. Why don't I jerk the stick back and point the airplane up, and, before the airspeed goes away, you fire a LAW through the floor. Does that Norden bombsight you got in your head say we got enough altitude to do that yet?"

"Shit; brilliant *again*! But we'll fall out of the sky because you're going to have to go around beyond straight up for me to get the angle. You're about to do your first loop, pardner!"

"No way, man! If I fuck it up, those armed LAWs'll be clanging around in here and might go off!"

"A chance we gotta take. You'll do just fine; just keep positive *g*'s so the LAWs stay on the floor. I'll get it started; when I say, 'Now,' you just keep it coming around. We don't have time to do a practice one, but you can do it. Just keep back-pressure on the stick, and look for the ground to come up through the Plexiglas in the roof. Don't worry; all you gotta do is hold it through the back half of the loop so I can fire the LAW."

"OK, bro; whatever you say."

Looking through the yawning space where the door had been, Dwight could see the leading edge of the enemy column approaching his platoon's position. The big muzzle flashes of his men's AK-47s winked like flashbulbs at a football game, as they fired single-shot to conserve ammo. Then he saw the larger muzzle flashes of the M79s and their resultant explosions in the enemy's ranks, slowing the advance for a few more precious seconds. Green tracers arced up at the airplane, falling barely away before reaching them.

Rich said, "Showtime, cowboy! They don't got but a few more minutes down there!"

"OK, Rich; we're almost in range! Get ready! Not yet! Not yet! Hold it! Hold it!

"OK, pardner; here we go." Dwight put the nose down to build airspeed and then hauled back on the stick, watching the horizon rotate out the side. At a little past vertical, he said, "Now!" and let go of the stick, grabbed a LAW, stuck it in the hole, and pulled the trigger. Rich had done beautifully, holding enough back-pressure on the stick to keep positive g's and the remaining two LAWs from clattering around the cabin.

Coming out of the dive, they'd lost sight of the small round but saw it explode in a group of enemy troops near the front of the column.

The explosion was twenty yards behind the leading enemy troops and right in the middle of a large group of them. They saw bodies flung into the air as the other enemy troops dropped back to the ground and looked up. Dwight could both see and feel their confusion. The anger that he needed to feel from them in order to fire was beginning to dissipate. He could feel that their fighting spirit was rapidly leaving them.

"Again, Rich! This time I'm going to fire twice, but we're not going to complete the loop. When I bring it past vertical, just hold it there; it'll fall out of the sky, but I'll have enough time to fire two LAWs; then I'll have enough altitude to recover from the resultant spin. Try to hold it straight so it'll snap-stall, but it'll be almost impossible; the rudder's going to work oppositely because we'll be sliding backward, but give it a try."

OK, cowboy; I hope you know what you're doing."

"So do I, but the enemy's just about ready to give up; we gotta give it a shot!"

Dwight positioned one LAW in the hole and another between his knees.

"OK, Rich; here we go!" He was now in range and had enough altitude to begin the maneuver. He put the nose down to build airspeed, hauled the stick back, and said "Now!" He let go at just past vertical, stuck the first LAW in the hole, and fired. He tossed the empty tube to the side and positioned the next LAW into the hole, feeling the airplane begin its inverted, rearward slide, the prop clawing the air and its blast over the wing and tail surfaces holding them straight for another split second.

Just as the airplane began shuddering into the stall, Dwight pulled the trigger, and the second round fired away in a white-orange flash.

Dwight grabbed the stick just as the world began its whirl in the windscreen, not needing to tell Rich that he had the airplane. The airplane had entered the stall and, because of the drag of the space where the door had been, twisted to the right and entered a tight spin to that side.

Dwight kicked hard left rudder as the ground became a spinning blur in front of them, only the center in focus. Because of the interrupted aerodynamics of the missing door, it took four full turns for the airplane to recover. Of more importance, they had lost well over a thousand feet and were now in range of the enemy's heavy machine guns. Three green tracers passed through the airplane—the first just in front of Rich, another through the right wing, and the third through the fuselage behind Dwight. He knew that that meant that probably another fifteen rounds had hit the airplane. The insistent pinging on the fuselage sounded more like fifty had hit them!

Dwight perceived the enemy's rage and fighting spirit returning. The spinning airplane had caused them to believe that they may have a chance again.

"You OK, Rich?"

"I'm OK; you?"

"Yeah, but we're not out of the woods yet!" Dwight said as a line of tracers passed them just outside the cockpit on the left, shearing away a four-foot-square piece of the leading edge of the left wing! The strong little airplane shuddered but held together.

Dwight picked up the remaining LAW and said, "I'm going to fire the remaining LAW out the top of the airplane! When I say so, pull the airplane up into a sharp climb; then, just before it stalls, nose over so I can get the angle to fire; OK?" They were again out of range of the enemy machine guns, headed away from the action.

"Roger; I understand."

Dwight unbuckled his harness and seat belt and said, "OK … now!"

Rich pulled up to a nose-up position, and Dwight stood on his seat with his right leg and braced himself on Rich's seat-back with the other, placing his body halfway out of the roof, facing backward. Holding the weapon on his shoulder, as it was designed to be held, he felt the airplane start its shudder to the stall as Rich pointed the nose down, giving Dwight first a little more altitude and then the angle to fire the LAW. He pulled the trigger. He felt the airplane shudder as he looked back, realizing his mistake. He had hit the propeller with the LAW's backblast! Pieces of it whizzed by him as it came apart like an old windmill in a Texas blue-norther.

"Way to go, ace!" Rich said, as he turned off the magneto switch before the engine blew up as it over-revved and vibrated in front of him.

There was now no sound but the wind pouring through the many holes in the fuselage, whistling like the Transylvania wind and changing pitch as Dwight dropped back into the seat and set up a glide to the field where the enemy tanks had been abandoned.

"I planned it that way; it reduces drag!"

"Eli Whitney thinks you're full of shit!"

He glanced behind him and saw the enemy column restarting its advance as the leading edge of First Battalion's column appeared from the tree line five hundred yards ahead of him. He dropped full flaps and pushed right rudder and left aileron, nose down, slipping the airplane to lose the remaining five hundred feet of altitude. Heading straight into the wind, the wheels were soon whispering their arrival in the calf-high grass. As they lurched to a stop, an enemy tank stood motionless not twenty yards to his right, looking as if it had been there for weeks in the knee-high grass.

Dwight jumped the three feet to the ground with Rich behind him. The day was bright and hot with a fifteen-knot breeze. The high overcast had dissipated, and the tank's sun-heated iron skin burned their hands as they clambered up, right foot on a tracked wheel, left on the deck below the turret, hands on the hot turret edge and into the cramped hold; their weapons clattered off their backs against the tank's silent hull.

Rich climbed past Dwight into the bottom deck and said, "This is a Russian T-54. Good tank. They told us about them, and we had flash cards of them in Advanced Infantry Training, so we could identify them. See if you can figure out the cannon and machine gun out; I'll try to get it started."

Dwight said, "Right, Captain," and pointed the big .50-caliber machine gun at a tree about fifty yards away and pushed the firing mechanism behind the double handles at its rear. The tank shuddered as it fired ten rounds at about the same rate as a Browning .50. He saw the tree shudder and leaves fall from it as it absorbed the big supersonic rounds. He saw that the ammo box, attached to the side of the gun, was full and that there were four more .50-caliber ammo boxes clipped to the top rear of the turret.

"Hey, LT," Rich said. "There's a gun mounted right beside me. It's got a short barrel. The ammo looks like seven-six-two."

"Do you think you can shoot it?"

"Are you kidding me? I can shoot the crates they come in!"

Dwight heard the forward firing machine gun rip off a quick ten rounds with such rapidity that it sounded like perforated cardboard being torn to open up a box of cereal and saw ten green tracers leap toward the tree line a half mile ahead, finally fading into the rocky ground and ricocheting up and to the right and left.

Rich said, "Man, I've never seen a gun fire so fast! This thing must have a rate of fire of over a thousand rounds a minute!"

"You got plenty of ammo down there?"

"Yeah … tons of it! Ammo boxes clipped all over the place!"

"Do you think you can start it and drive it?"

"Are you kidding me? I can drive the crates they come in!"

"OK, hotshot, let's roll."

Rich considered that the driver's layout looked pretty simple and conventional. The driver sat on the left and looked through a swiveled up open hatch in front of him. He could tell that the tank would be almost impossible to see out of with the hatch closed, as there was only a small slit covered with bulletproof glass, centered in the hatch cover.

There were traditional clutch, brake, and gas pedals on the floor in front of the driver's seat but placed high on the bulkhead. There were long levers on each side for steering and a shorter shift lever on the floor on the right side, beside him. He put in the clutch and pulled a large, round lever on the left side of the sparse panel. The starter motor turned the big diesel motor, and it roared to life. He let the clutch out while applying throttle and almost stalled it.

Damn! The driver left it in top gear in his hurry to get out, he thought. He began trying different shift lever positions, grinding gears; he was unable to get it into any gear now.

"Hey, Mario!" Dwight said. "Put it in neutral, let the clutch out, and rev it before you try to put it in gear!"

"I know how to double-clutch, asshole!"

It worked! Rich found a gear, and the tank lurched forward; the tach redlined at about five miles an hour. He grabbed another gear, double-clutching in neutral. Sure enough, it was a traditional "H" pattern, he realized as the big tank majestically emerged from its black cloud of overrich diesel exhaust smoke. Before either of them had time to think about it; they were barreling along in fifth gear at thirty miles an hour.

Dwight looked back and saw another tank starting to roll, also leaving a thundercloud-looking blob of black smoke. It was about five hundred yards behind him, and American airborne infantry was advancing on either side of it as it overtook them. He could see that they were tiring as they tried to double-time and could only manage a fast walk. They had been attacking for over two miles, and it was telling on them.

Ahead, the enemy troops were beginning to engage his platoon and had stopped their advance to organize their attack.

Dwight had loaded the cannon while Rich was starting the tank, so, noting that the barrel was only slightly elevated, he waited for the tank to be on a relatively level plane and jerked the lanyard, firing for effect. He couldn't use his sixth sense yet to shoot because the enemy troops weren't sending any signals. They didn't yet know that someone was coming after them with one of their own tanks.

He was glad that he'd thought to stand to the side as the big gun recoiled and automatically ejected the shell casing, which clattered around the turret for a few seconds and then fell into the hold. Five hundred yards ahead, he saw the round hit at the rear of the enemy column in a bright orange flash and a large puff of gray-black smoke.

"Great shot, LT!" Rich shouted, his voice barely audible above the clanking and rattling.

The tank was at least twice as noisy as American tanks, Dwight noted. OK; he saw how it worked and he had the range. It was time to go to work. He loaded another round and closed the breach. There were four large metal buttons arranged in a triangle on a panel to the right of the cannon's breach. He pushed the top one, and the barrel elevated. The bottom one caused the barrel to lower. The right and left ones turned the turret.

He raised the barrel, and, rather than look through the sight just under the hatch in the turret, he waited for the feeling that he'd come to depend on. Just then, he felt the enemy troops begin to realize that their own tanks had been commandeered and were being used against them. There! He had them! He jerked the lanyard and watched the round explode on the front edge of the column and heard a whoop from Rich. *Perfect!*

He quickly loaded another round, turned the turret a hair to the right, waited for the tank's motion to give him the right elevation, and fired. This time, the round exploded in the right front of the column, and they were now close enough to see that the round had hit in the middle of a group of enemy troops, probably officers gathered to coordinate the attack on his platoon, and several bodies had been thrown into the air. Another perfect shot stopped the enemy's firing and attack as they turned toward the rapidly advancing tanks.

It was over! The enemy was giving up! Hands were being raised in the air in surrender, and undershirts were being ripped off to use as white flags.

Watching his platoon jump from their firing positions in elation, Dwight hadn't been paying enough attention to the enemy machine guns. He didn't have time to duck the green tracers, especially the one headed for his head. There was barely enough time to think, *Oh, shit!* before his fast fade to black. There hadn't been enough time to see that a few of the enemy troops were not standing up and raising their arms in surrender. There hadn't been enough time to revel in his greatest conquest.

-CHAPTER NINETEEN-

THE HOSPITAL

THE NINETY-THIRD EVAC HOSPITAL sits in an area called Long Binh, where the road from Bien Hoa meets the highway to Saigon at a right angle.

Each section of the hospital is a separate corrugated metal building in the shape of an *X* with the nurse's station in the middle.

Dwight was in a semiconscious state, viewing and hearing the world as if he was at the bottom of a fifteen-foot-deep pool, the sights and sounds sometimes distortedly finding their way down to him.

Occasionally he would come near the surface and could see and hear more clearly. He even heard his own voice now and then; he knew that he'd been talking a lot but couldn't remember what he'd been saying.

Sometimes it was peaceful and dark. Other times he was struggling frantically to break the surface, to communicate with the people on the other side of the surface. He hadn't wanted to get to the other side for a long time. He'd been safe here. Why try if he was safe here?

Strangely he felt no pain, although he had felt close to death on many occasions, under here. Peacefully he had welcomed it. But now he knew he was going to live, and now he *wanted* to live again. He just had to break the surface of this once sheltering pool! What had been his sanctuary was now his prison.

As he rested on the bottom this day, he began recalling the night of his first action. It was finally coming back to him! He had known the sapper was coming to his tent with his satchel bomb. He remembered it now. He had raised the mosquito netting, taken two or three steps toward the entrance of the tent, and caught the satchel charge in the air. He saw the enemy soldier, dressed in black pajamas, his eyes wide in surprise. They had both stood there for a second, motionless. Dwight was aware of a fuse burning, hissing, and sparking, like a cartoon bomb in a Saturday morning kids' cartoon.

Fear gripped him, and he could hardly breathe. The enemy soldier finally reacted first after what seemed a long time but what must have been only a second. He ran past Dwight toward battalion headquarters. In slow motion Dwight had reacted; he remembered it now! He recalled diving to safety behind the wall of sandbags, safe from the coming blast that was meant to end his life.

He was safe from the blinding flash of white light and the pieces of metal tearing at the sandbags protecting him from certain death. He was safe, and he began to cry, thankful again for the protected seclusion here the bottom of the pool.

He began rising toward the surface again, as the memory kept revealing itself. At first, he could see the action as if he were looking through opaque glass or a shower curtain. *No!* He realized that the reason he couldn't see well was because of blood in his eyes. He wiped it away, blinked, and wiped again. The shower curtain slowly opened, and he could see clearly now.

Finally, the realization of the events of that night flooded into his memory. His eyes saw clearly now, and the terror of the unfolding scene slammed him back to the bottom of the pool as the blessed blackness of the depths enveloped him again.

Another day would come for him to see more. Now, he needed rest. He needed to sleep. He needed rejuvenation, to recover his strength. Maybe tomorrow he would see more. He was too weak right now. Rest—he needed more rest.

The next day was better. He was stronger. He felt for the big black crucifix around his neck. It was there, and he felt stronger still, reassured. He was near the top again. He could hear voices through the water. There's Rich! Rich is here! Thank God! He had hoped that Rich had survived the blast, but he hadn't been sure. The others were dead—all of them. He knew that. He'd heard their screams and moans and gurgles; he had seen their bodies.

The tremendous fear gripped him again, and he went back to the bottom. *No!* I shouldn't go there! I want to see Rich! I need to talk to him! "Rich!" he called out, and Rich reached for him with a bandaged arm but lost his grip.

Dwight saw Dr. Baxter's gentle smile before he went back to the bottom and away from the terror and into the blessed sleep. He'd try again tomorrow. He was so tired, so exhausted from his effort. He had almost made it, but now he didn't want to anymore. He only wanted to sleep—eternal rest and sleep. Maybe they would just let him go home.

He dreamed of going to college at the University of Texas in Austin. He wanted to go there and study to be a doctor, a surgeon, or maybe a veterinarian. Dogs—he loved dogs. Horses and cattle too. And bees. He remembered how they had needed water; they had needed water, like him now. Thank God for water.

He imagined that he was in a honky-tonk bar in Austin. He imagined loud country music and dancing all around him; people were shooting pool and laughing. He saw good-natured shoving and backslapping and pretty girls who wanted boyfriends and lovers.

He would be in a fraternity! He'd always wanted to be in a fraternity. He would buy a little sports car with the money he'd made while he was in Vietnam! There would be a lot of money waiting for him when he got home and got well. He could pay cash for the car, an Austin Healy 3000—that's what he would buy!

No one would know him. No one would know that he had been to Vietnam. No one would know how he was different from them—that he would never again be like them, never again. He would hide it from them. They'd never know! He would tell them that he'd been in a car wreck.

Peace. He would have peace. He would never think of war again. He simply wouldn't think about it. He could do that. He could just put it out of his mind when it came up. Just think of something else—baseball, sex, doctoring, anything. It would be easy, just like now. He could go back to the bottom of the pool where it was soft and dark and nice and where there was no more death and suffering and fear—especially no more fear. He couldn't stand any more fear. He went thankfully back to the bottom. He could cry down here, and no one could see. No one would know. And he could be the man he was supposed to be.

Would he ever not know war again? He had to try. He didn't want to live knowing life was like this. Maybe he could put a better face on it; he hadn't meant to kill all those people! He had never meant to see so many people die so violently, so painfully. It was just where he was at the time. Fate had caused it. He'd wanted to be a medic; he hadn't wanted to kill people. He'd wanted to save them! He settled back on the bottom. *Maybe tomorrow—maybe tomorrow I can talk to Rich.*

Dwight came to the surface easier today. He could even feel a smile on his face! He knew he would break out today. Dr. Baxter was there, beckoning to him. She put another needle in his arm. There had been so many needles, but they didn't hurt much; he welcomed them. They always made him feel better. He would break the surface today. The needle would help him do it. He sobbed as he broke out, and the kind doctor held his head to her chest.

"I didn't mean to! I didn't understand what I was doing! I swear! I didn't have enough time to think! I'm sorry. I'm sorry! I didn't want to die!"

"I know. I know. It's OK. It's OK, Dwight. You're going to be OK, now. You're going to be OK."

He struggled to dive back to the bottom. He tried to squirm away and go back down. He needed to go back to the peace. He needed peace!

A battery of 155-millimeter howitzers opened up in a fire support mission, a mile away, and the rounds began their whooshing roar over the hospital.

Dwight screamed, "No! Nooooo! Noooooooooooooo!"

Dr. Baxter said, "Goddamn those idiots! What in the hell are they thinking!" Mercifully, she put another needle in Dwight's shoulder and he dived back for the bottom.

Sleep. Merciful sleep would cure it all, if he could just sleep forever. *No!* He wanted to go to college! And have fun! And be a successful man, like he'd always known he would be, someday. A new day was coming and he would be home and the war would be over for him, never to be thought about again. He smiled at the thought. He'd be a good student and study hard and have lots of fun and be happy and be in a fraternity. And have a sports car. He'd think about it all another day.

Please, no more war noises. He had to get away from the war noises. Even jackhammers—he would stay away from them when he got back to the world. And big, open places like grocery stores and Kmarts. He wouldn't go to places like that. Who would watch his back? There wouldn't be anyone there to watch his back! He wouldn't sit in big classrooms, either—just little ones and he could sit at the back, and everything would be OK.

Dr. Baxter was waiting for him at the surface again. She was so patient with him. He knew he could trust her. *Men are bad; all of us are dangerous killers. Murderers. I don't want to be around any of us anymore. We can't be trusted. Men are capable of just about anything horrible.* He would tell them all, "You are all a bunch of no good sons of bitches, and so am I!" No, he couldn't say that, but it was a fact. He would know this the rest of his life. Women were different. They had the ability to produce people. They were mothers. They wouldn't have wars if they were in charge, he bet. He could never be comfortable around men again. Only women would be his friends. That was OK. He liked women more anyway. They were usually gentle and could hold him and make him feel safe. He could never be safe with men again. That's OK, but who would watch his back?

Coming to Dr. Baxter was easier this time.

"How are you feeling, Dwight?"

"Better ... much better. Is Rich OK?"

"Yes. You've talked to him a lot. Do you remember any of it?"

"No. I remember talking, though. Was he there?"

"Some of the times, he was. You talked a lot. Do remember what you talked about?"

"No."

She called to the nurse and told her to go get Corporal Richardson from trauma ward three.

"Do you know where you are?"

"Yes, I'm in a hospital."

"Where is the hospital?"

"Vietnam."

"Yes. Do you know how long you've been here?"

"A few weeks? A month? More?"

"You've been here three days."

"Three days! But it was nighttime so often! I slept so often!"

"It just seemed that way to you."

"But my injuries ... my wounds! They're healed!"

"Do you remember what happened?"

"I know about everything but the first attack, when I killed the sappers and saved the general's life, but I started remembering that a few days ago."

"What do you remember about it?"

"I knew the sapper was coming, and I jumped out of bed and caught the bomb in midair!"

"Yes, and then what?"

"I can't!" he screamed. "I *can't*! I want to go back into the pool! I can't do it!"

"Stay here with me, Dwight. It's OK. You're safe now. It's OK."

"I want to go back!"

"I don't think you can, Dwight. I think it's time to stay here with me for a while."

"No! Give me another shot, Suzy."

"How did you know my first name? No one in the hospital ever uses it."

"I talked to you at the awards ceremony, when I got the Medal of Honor!"

"There was no awards ceremony, Dwight. Your mind has suffered a tremendous trauma. You did something that your psyche couldn't accept, and your mind has been making up stories to compensate for what it can't accept that you did."

"What did I do?"

"You're going to have to do it, Dwight. You're going to have to recall it yourself so you can start healing, to get better."

"I dropped the bomb in the tent and dived over the sandbags to save myself, and I killed them all! Oh my God! I remember! They were screaming and moaning and dying, and I didn't try to save them! Arms and legs were blown off, and I was safe! I didn't do *that*! I couldn't have done *that*!

He was sobbing uncontrollably now, as Doctor Baxter held him to her chest and encouraged him to let it out.

He remembered it all now. The whole squad had died except for Rich, who'd suffered only minor shrapnel wounds. Rich had stood with him after they had all died and told him that he'd seen the whole thing, and then he'd asked Dwight how he could have done it. Why hadn't he thrown the charge outside the tent, on the other side of the sandbags? And Dwight had started firing

GG into the air until he burned his finger again reloading, and Rich had held him down on the ground and that had been the end of it.

Rich walked into the room and looked at Dwight, who was seated next to Dr. Baxter; he was no longer clutching her.

Dwight cried, "I'm sorry, Rich! Please forgive me! I didn't know what to do! I couldn't think! I just dropped the charge and tried to get away from it!" His tears flowed so hard that he couldn't see anything but a blurred image as Rich walked to him and put his arm around him.

Sobbing, he thankfully let Rich gently guide his head to Rich's chest as the big crucifix dug into Dwight's chest and Rich's leg.

"I'm so sorry. Oh my God, I'm *so* sorry," he sobbed.

"It don't mean nothin', Dwight; you're an FNG."

"I just wish I could have been braver, Rich!"

"We all do, man; we all do."

-THE END-

Glossary

AFRS—*Armed Forces Radio Service.* The only American radio station we had in Vietnam in 1965. It played almost all jazz. I heard that it played more rock and roll in later years.

AGL—*Above ground level.* Altitude is measured as MSL (above sea level) or AGL. AGL is used by parachutists and aerobatic pilots because their proximity to the earth is important to them.

AIT—*Advanced infantry training.* Basic training is primary infantry training.

AK—Short for *AK-47,* the basic communist assault rifle.

APC—*Armored personnel carrier.* Actually made of aluminum, so an AP round would go right through it. It held eleven troops (we'd often put in thirteen) and a crew of two. Armament was a .50 machine gun. They were death traps. We hated them. APC was also the primary pain reliever, consisting of aspirin, phenacetin, and caffeine.

Artty—Slang for *artillery.*

ARVN—*Army of the Republic of Vietnam;* the South Vietnamese Army.

Buck sergeant—Basic and first sergeant rank (E-5). Three stripes.

BN—*Battalion.*

BOQ—*Bachelor Officer Quarters.*

C rations—*Canned rations.* A box was issued for each meal. The box contained the main meal (beans and franks, beef stew, etc.), dessert (pudding, fruit cocktail, etc.), a pack of six cigarettes, matches, and a can of crackers and cheese or cookies and a slab of rubberized chocolate.

CIA—*Central Intelligence Agency;* our spies.

CIB—*Combat Infantry Badge.* Awarded to infantry soldiers who have served in combat. Medics get the Combat Medic Badge. They are worn on the left breast, along with ribbons (medals) and pilot and airborne wings.

CO—*Commanding officer.* Also *co* is the Vietnamese word for *woman.*

Concertina—Coiled barbed wire for use as an obstacle.

CP—*Command post.*

DET—Short for *detonation,* as in det-cord, which is essentially a long, flexible blasting cap, used to set off C-4 (plastic explosive) or as an explosive itself (three wraps around a tree will fell it). Daisy-chain claymore mines together with it.

Dust-off—Code name for helicopter medical evacuation.

DZ—*Drop zone.* Area where paratroopers land and equipment is dropped via parachute.

EM—*Enlisted men.*

EMQ—*Enlisted men's quarters* (as opposed to BOQ).

FNG—Slang name for replacement troops; *Fucking New Guy.*

Freq—Short for *radio frequency.*

FUBAR—*Fucked up beyond all recognition.*

GG—Dwight's name for his weapon, a .45-caliber submachine gun; called a grease gun because of its shape.

HALO—*High altitude, low opening.* Specialized military parachuting where the paratrooper exits the airplane at high altitude to avoid detection and free-falls to low altitude before opening his canopy, also to avoid detection.

Hewey—The primary troop-carrying (slick) and gun platform (gunship) helicopter used in the early days of the war.

HQ—*Headquarters.*

Intel—*Intelligence.*

Lambretta—Made by Lambretta (Innocenti) motor scooters, it was the most common group transport in Vietnam. It was composed of a motor scooter front with a covered, open seating arrangement in back. The passengers sat three on each side, facing each other. Used as taxicabs.

LAW—M72 light antitank weapon. A 66 mm shoulder-fired rocket with a telescoping fiberglass tube. Lots of bang for the buck at five pounds and with a length of two feet closed and three feet extended. Round can be lobbed over a half mile. Straight-aim range is about 150 yards. Round is armor piercing.

Lock and load—The term used to tell troops to chamber a round and set their safety. A slang term for "Get ready to fight."

LRRP—*Long-range reconnaissance patrol.* Pronounced "Lurp." The troops were called Lurps and were highly trained and respected paratroopers; usually Vietnamese Airborne qualified.

LT—Short for *lieutenant.*

LZ—*Landing zone,* a place for helicopters to land.

MACV—*Military Assistance Command, Vietnam.* All U.S. Army troops were under MACV command, before the 173d Airborne Brigade arrived on May 11, 1965.

MOS—*Military occupational specialty,* designated by numbers; e.g., infantry is 111 (one-eleven), and medic is 911.

NAS—*Naval Air Station.*

NCO—*Noncommissioned officer.* Technically corporal (E-4) and above but more commonly thought of among the troops as sergeant (E-5) and above.

NCOIC—*Noncommissioned officer in charge.*

O-Club—*Officers' club.*

OJT—*On-the-job training* (supervised practical experience).

OD—*Olive drab.* The green color of most army equipment.

PFC—*Private First Class* (E-3). Rank is designated on the sleeve as one stripe.

PIR—*Parachute Infantry Regiment.*

PLFs—*Parachute landing fall.* PLFs are taught and practiced for several days in Airborne School. Knees should be bent, feet together, toes pointed down, to absorb impact. Points of contact *must* be toes, calf, thigh, buttocks, and lat (side, back muscle).

PSP—*Perforated steel planking.* Made to make runways, it was the most ubiquitous building material in Vietnam, used to make everything from sidewalks to houses.

PX—*Post Exchange,* where military people buy everything from food to appliances and uniforms.

QCs—South Vietnamese military police. Rather than MP on their helmets and sleeves, they had QC.

R & R—*Rest and recuperation.* A leave from combat to a safe area. Usually two weeks or less.

Recon—*Reconnaissance.*

ROKs—Republic of Korea troops.

RPG—*Rocket-propelled grenade.* Seen often on TV news broadcasts being carried by insurgents and Taliban troops. It looks like a pointed bomb on the end of a stick. The operator fires it from the shoulder. The round is launched by a charge, and then a rocket motor ignites and carries it to the target. Those used against us in Vietnam had a range of about 300 yards and were usually armor piercing. Deadly when used against our APCs.

RTO—*Radio telephone operator,* also known as a radioman.

Ruck—Short for *rucksack.* A backpack. Usually has an aluminum frame for rigidity and carrying comfort and an even load distribution.

Special Ops—*Special operations;* Special Forces, Air Force Special Ops, Navy Seals, etc.

Spec-4—The first specialist rank (noncommand) NCO rank (E-4). Equal to corporal.

Squeet—Short for "Let's go eat."

S/Sgt—*Staff sergeant* (E-6). Three stripes up with one rocker stripe underneath.

SFC—*Sergeant First Class* (E-7). Three stripes up with two rocker stripes underneath.

SNAFU—*Situation normal, all fucked up.*

Spider hole—A small-diameter tunnel used by the VC to pop up from for ambush or to disappear into to hide. Usually covered with vegetation for camouflage.

T-10—The standard army paratrooper parachute. Was not steerable.

TO&E—*Table of organization and equipment.* Military units are organized via this document, which designated the personnel, equipment, and specific makeup of each operating unit.

V device—A gold "V" on a ribbon or medal denoting valor in combat.

VC—*Vietcong.* Communist guerrilla units/soldiers operating in South Vietnam.

Vne—Velocity, never exceed. A specific aircraft's limitation of airspeed that will harm the aircraft if exceeded. All aircraft have operating manuals where the V numbers are published (e.g., Vbg is best glide speed, Vfe is max flaps extended speed).

Web belt—Equipment belt, worn over fatigues. Brass grommets (holes) are spaced to hold canteens, ammo pouches, bayonets, etc.

XO—*Executive officer,* usually the assistant to the commanding officer.

JOHN HEINZ, a combat disabled veteran, served in Vietnam as an Army field medic in 1965-66. As a flying enthusiast he flew competition aerobatics in his Citabria and of late owned a Kitfox light sport aircraft. In addition to flying, his pastimes include motorcycles and golf. He is a blues (harp) musician and also plays the Navaho double flute. He's a member of the Society of the 173d Airborne Brigade, Inc.; the Dustoff Association, Wright Flyers, and the Aircraft Owners and Pilots Association. He lives in the Tucson, Arizona area with his dog, Buckshot.